Crystal Falls

Christine Wissner

Crystal Falls
Copyright © 2017 by Christine Wissner
Cover by Lyn Taylor
Formatted by Jacob Hammer
Published by Christine Wissner

Digital Edition ISBN: 978-0-9989673-0-1
Print Edition ISBN: 978-0-9989673-1-8

First Digital Publication: June 2017
First Print Publication: June 2017

CRYSTAL FALLS

Christine Wissner

Wissnerchristine@yahoo.com

Dedications

For **Kim & Melanie**… *my beloved daughters. You are my light, and I love you both with all my heart.*

For **Kandace, Kerra and Mason**…*my wonderful grandchildren. Every day you make me proud. The future lies with you.*

For **Janette Pricket**…*the 'editing' mortar between my bricks. Thank you for your eagle eye, my dear friend.*

For my gal-pals, **Bobbi, Nancy, Dorris, Betty, and Patty**…*thank you for the laughter (and tears) we've shared together these many years. Friendships make the world go 'round, and I've been so blessed with yours.*

And for **Cindy Nord**, *best selling historical romance author… my inspiration and mentor, as well as my cherished friend. Thank you so much for your cowriting and critiquing. You've transformed me from a journalist into a novelist. 'Twas one hell of a journey, for sure.*

Prologue

July 19, 1884

Lexington, Kentucky

Jason Jackson pressed his shoulder against a massive Corinthian column, a satisfied smile tugging at his lips. He skimmed his gaze from the veranda of his manor home, and further out across the pastureland of Crystal Falls. Beautiful. Peaceful. Serene. His beloved wife laughed and he returned his attention to her. A breeze rippled her tresses, and once again, he ached to burrow his fingers inside the luxurious chestnut locks. She had transformed from a carefree lass of yesteryear into this courageous "pillar of strength" sitting before him now. Each deepened line that carved her face spoke of the horror of their journey to reach this moment.

His gaze dropped to the sleeping infant in her arms.

Little Kate... a gift to us both.

He lowered his chin and swirled the bourbon in the bottom of his glass. His thumb brushed the condensation on the side of the crystal. With a sigh, he upended the tumbler and downed the remaining liquor.

A gratifying hiss escaped between clenched teeth.

He glanced to his mother seated nearby in her favorite rocker. A guiding light if ever there was one...and forevermore their corner stone. He inhaled, then scanned the empty chair beside her.

Father. A dominant force even in memory.

With a sigh, Jason pushed from the column and settled his glass on the side table. Six steps later, he descended to the flagstone walk.

"Where you going?" his mother asked.

"Checking on Infinity."

"Don't dawdle," Debbie added. "Supper will be ready soon."

"Just want to have a look at the animal's ankle, is all," Jason hollered over his shoulder.

He meandered along the ribbon of white fencing and delivered a sharp whistle that brought the muscular bay thoroughbred out of the shadows of the pecan grove. The stallion's brown coat glistened in the late afternoon sun, and a spray of dirt lifted from beneath the thundering hooves as he galloped toward Jason. With a snort, the animal lowered his muzzle and offered a nudge.

"Good boy," Jason said patting Infinity's forehead. "You're lookin' mighty chipper today." He draped his arms over the railing and leaned inward. "We never did get in that race down in New Orleans, did we, pal?" The beast's sharp snort underscored the words as Jason's thoughts tumbled backward...

Chapter One

Ten miles west of Lexington, Kentucky
Late spring, 1883

Over the course of the past eighteen years dramatic changes had reshaped a war-torn America. Bicycles and horse-drawn carriages filled the bricked streets. Electric lights replaced dangerous candles, and whispers of running water in every household echoed through the land. No longer a divided country, the nation stood on the threshold of hope for a strong and promising future. Now every man, no matter his skin color or religion, could work to fulfill his dream.

Taylor Jackson was no exception. He had created an empire, a legacy for his family. Pride, fortitude, and a love for life stoked the raging fires that had burned within him. Many obstacles had confronted him over the years, but nothing challenged him greater than the loss of his legs. A man who once stood well over six feet tall now faced life as an invalid. Mauled by a mother bear protecting her cub, Taylor lost the use of his legs. An inability to perform even the simplest tasks belittled his masculinity, and yet, time and determination only fueled his drive to remain independent.

Clenching his hands around the wheels of his invalid chair, Taylor pushed onto the graveled road that fronted his home. The chair bumped and jerked as he angled toward the stable that loomed at the end of the long drive. He cursed the obstacles beneath him as he struggled to control the chair's direction.

"Damn these rocks," he growled, sucking in a ragged breath. Heat flooded his cheeks as grit and jagged rocks dug deep into his callused palms.

With a thunderous blow, he slammed his fist into the side of the oak chair. "Move, you son of a bitch."

The horses in the pastures on his right raised their heads, several beasts snorting. Their gusty blows lent him much-needed encouragement. With renewed commitment, Taylor forced himself forward, the challenge of success weighing heavy across his shoulders. By all that he held dear, he *would* reach the stables without surrendering to the blasted pain.

The iron gates loomed before him, welcoming him back. He drew in another fortifying breath. On his left, attached to a stone pedestal, the sign that welcomed visitors to Crystal Falls needed repair. The large white stable beyond beckoned once more, and nearby, his farrier, Packey, drew water from a well. Taylor's gaze moved further to the lush Kentucky hillside. Mares with new foals nibbled at the long blades of bluegrass and yearlings frolicked beneath a grove of white-barked river birch.

Taylor flexed his shoulder and adjusted his weight in the wheelchair. Knots of tension pulled at his neck. Moving his head side-to-side brought him momentary relief. The downhill slope would present a clear problem. Deep ruts, cut by heavy wagon wheels, creased the quarter-mile dirt lane before him. He must keep his speed and balance under control, or he would tip.

He tightened his biceps and edged forward, ready to begin his descent toward the stable. He rolled past the gate. The wheels dipped, tossing him against the arm of the chair. Clumps of dirt gathered between the creases of his fingers. His palms burned as the wheels slipped through his grip.

Stay upright.

And focused.

Ten sweat-drenched moments later, he finally rolled into the stable yard. Shaken, yet triumphant, he whispered, "Thank God. I made it."

A gentle breeze soothed his burning cheeks. For now, his personal battle was over.

Large wooden doors, balancing on rollers, lay open before him. Entering the corridor, he inhaled and the sweet scent of fresh-cut hay filled his nostrils. Banging buckets drew his attention and he swerved his gaze to the sleek-coated thoroughbreds pushing their muzzles deep into steel pails to retrieve the last of their morning feed.

Taylor rolled forward and wrapped his arm around the outstretched neck of the closest mare enclosed in her birthing stall. "Hey there, Bess," he whispered. "Good to see you again." He pushed her head aside and grabbed the halter to get a better view of her protruding belly and her nipples were heavy with milk beads. "Anytime now, I see." The chair arm pressed into his ribs, forcing him to straighten. The mare jerked her head back, spilling a clump of saliva-filled hay into his lap. With an open palm he swept the mixture off his pant leg and chuckled as the muck hit the ground. "I've told you before not to share your meal."

A heavy thump from within the tack room echoed down the corridor. "Who's there?" he called, his deep voice radiating along the walls.

A youngster of near twelve stepped into view and walked toward him.

"Hi," the urchin said, shoving the ragged end of his oversized shirt into his denims.

Taylor's brow arched as a slight grin tugged at his lips. "And who are you?"

"I'm James, the stable boy."

Taylor's lips bowed upward. "So you're the new lad Jason spoke of." His gaze scanned the ruffian from the top of his unruly locks to the tips of his dusty boots. "Nice to meet you, James. Where's Jason?"

"He's got Infinity on the lunge line," he replied, leaning sideways to drape a lead rope on a nearby hook. "He'll be in shortly."

Taylor pushed back in his chair and nodded. The lad's grubby hands proved his work's worth. "So, how's the colt doin'?"

"He's comin' along real good," James proclaimed, shoving his fingers deep into his pockets. "I reckon they'll introduce him to a saddle and rider 'fore too long. Be nice to ride 'im one day. But, right now, I got too many chores that need doin'." Pride lifted his slender shoulders.

Taylor quirked his lips sideways. "I know how you feel."

I've often dreamed of riding him, too. My legs pressed against his sides. His mane whipping my cheeks as we race across the turf...oh yes, I've dreamed, too.

"He sure is the best lookin' colt I've ever seen," the boy added, pushing damp strands of hair off his forehead. "It's a real shame 'bout his mother. She could've had some great foals."

Memories whirled through Taylor's mind. "Yes, she was a special mare, though." *And not a day goes by I don't think of her.* "He peered over the boy's shoulder just as Jason entered the stable. Sunlight illuminated around his son's broad shoulders as the man's long legs moved, stride for stride, with his beloved Infinity. He coiled work-stained fingers around the young bay's halter, drawing the colt to an abrupt stop.

Taylor wheeled his chair around to get a closer look at the young horse. With trembling hands, he reached out and stroked the muzzle. Smooth and soft. Velvety. A smile flashed his lips. "He's beautiful, Jason."

His son loomed over him, dwarfing Taylor.

"Glad you finally came to the stable, Father. We can sure use your help."

Taylor snickered. "Don't know how much help I can be. I just want to be a part of this guy's life," he said, sliding his palm across Infinity's lathered neck. "I expect great things from him."

"You got that right," echoed the little urchin standing behind the invalid chair.

Jason pointed to an empty bucket. "Grab that pail and some rags, James. Let's wash Infinity down, and then you can put him back in his stall."

"Sure thing, boss." James led the horse away.

"Nice kid," Taylor said.

"Packey said the kid's folks are having a tough time, so I made a point of paying him double for his help around the place. He's a good worker." Jason stepped sideways and grabbed the handles of the wheel chair. "I was about to come get you, anyway. We've got company." "Company?" he growled, as his son pushed him down the corridor. "This is the first I've heard of it."

"Don't fret, father. You'll be pleased to see who has come to visit you."

Taylor's jaw tightened as he forced his words. "But...I'm not sure I'm ready to see anyone, just yet."

"We're done with allowing you to hide," Jason quipped. " It's time you get back to what you know best."

They advanced to the door, and Taylor pinched his eyes tight as sunlight splashed his face. For a fleeting moment, the stench of manure buried deep into his nostrils. He released a gravelly cough. Shuffling footfalls echoed around him and his eyelids again flew open.

Good God... John Butterfield.

As usual, his neighbor and closest friend stood before him all decked out in an expensive hound's-tooth business suit and bolo hat, expressing wealth and prosperity. Long, wiry sideburns skirted a chubby face and the Cuban cigar that dangled from the man's tightly clenched lips cost more than any finely crafted bridle from Crystal Fall's inventory.

Promptly, Butterfield stepped in front of him.

"Taylor," he yelped, their palms sliding together. He pumped his hand. "You old rascal. Damn good to see you. About time you got back to work. This place has gone to hell without you at the helm."

Taylor laughed. "I doubt that," he said, adjusting to a more comfortable position. "What brings you here? Trying to steal my prize horse?"

"Wish I could," quipped the competitive horseman. With an exaggerated movement, he removed the cigar from his mouth. "Your place is getting quite a reputation. As you know my friend, my stable once held that prominence. Why I had the finest thoroughbreds in the country 'til you came along."

Taylor offered back a mocking smirk. *You bastard. Always eager to belittle my achievement's.* "You taught me everything I know."

"So true. However, losing that mare to you in a poker game was the biggest damn mistake of my life."

Taylor snickered. "Yep, I'd agree with that." He stared at Butterfield through thick lashes.

The man glanced away, puffed out his thick barreled chest and grasped the lapels of his jacket, rocking on the balls of his feet. "Jason and I've been discussing our horses. Maybe it's time we combine our bloodlines. I'll let you breed a couple of your mares to my stud, King's Gold. In turn, you let me stud Infinity."

Taylor narrowed his eyes, a frown tugged just off the corner of his brow. "Infinity's not ready to mount any mare, and you damn well know it."

"Yes, I know," Butterfield dropped the half-finished cigar into the dirt and then crushed the expensive tobacco with the heel of his fine leather boot. He leaned forward. "And I'm willing to wait. You just promise me I can be first on the list."

Taylor straightened in his chair. "You know that without even asking, you dang scallywag."

"I want that in writing," he said, chuckling. Beads of perspiration trickled down Butterfield's temples and soaked into the steel grey of his hair. Chubby fingers fumbled at his coat pocket to retrieve a handkerchief. He blew his nose into the cloth before shoving the silk wedge back into place. "It isn't I don't trust you, Jackson...'cause I do. I just want something documented."

Like hell you do!

Taylor's gaze grew deeper as he scoured his good friend's face. "One way or the other, you're determined to own a piece of that colt, aren't you?"

"You're damn right." The man lifted his hat to scratch his balding head. "I've lost more sleep over that animal than anything else in my entire miserable life."

Taylor grunted. "Take it easy, John, or your anger will get the best of you and you won't live to see another day."

"That's why we'll need things in writing." Butterfield pressed forward, narrowed his eyes and jammed a finger into Taylor's lapel collar. "I'll even let you have the service of my stud twice a year until your colt is ready to mount." His voice sank deeper on the tail end of another chuckle. "That's my guaranteed promise, and I suggest you take it. You won't find a better offer."

Jason stepped between them, lifting his hands. "That's enough you two. I'm sure we can figure something out to satisfy two ol' codgers who've spent years of enjoyment digging at each other."

Taylor chuckled. "Son, you have to know this man." His gaze locked with Butterfield's. "When he wants something, he goes after it, no matter what."

"I can see that." Jason flashed a smile, placing his foot on the wooden step of the platform.

"Then it's a deal?" Butterfield reared back, cocked his head to the side, and grinned.

Taylor's breath slid out in a slow exhale. "It's a deal." Their hands interlocked on a robust shake. "I'll have Jason draw up the papers. Come by one day next week and we'll get everything signed."

"Great, now I can sleep." Butterfield chuckled. "Gentlemen, you just made my day."

John politely excused himself and walked to his carriage.

As the rig disappeared from sight, Jason said, "Well, that was unexpected."

Rifle fire split the air. Another bullet cracked, followed by another. Taylor pointed westward and his son swirled around and bound for the gate. With a jerk, Jason released the weathered lock, then cornered the building, disappearing from sight. Taylor pushed hard, struggling to cross the arena. His hands fought at the wheels as he surged forward, demanding more speed.

He rolled around the corner in time to see Packey lower his rifle. "What's wrong?" Taylor shouted, gasping for air to sooth his burning lungs.

"Wild dogs," Jason snapped. "James saw the pack last week and warned me about them."

"When I was at da supply store I heard two men talkin' 'bout seein' a bunch of dogs eatin' a dead buck." Packey sucked in a gulp of air. "At da time, I didn't give it much thought. Dogs feed on dead animals."

Taylor's heart pumped against his ribs. "Sounds like we've got a serious problem," he yelled. "I think we should bring all the horses in. It's too dangerous to leave the herd out in the pasture."

"I'll bring them up by the barn. Someone needs to be here 'round the clock, though." Jason drew in a sharp breath. "No tellin' when those dogs will come back. We need to be ready."

Packey reached into his rear pocket and drew out a scrap of muslin to wipe his brow. "James can bring in the horses," he said, sweeping over his ebony face with the rag. "I'll ride out and see if I can find them dogs."

"I'll go with you," Jason added, grabbing the wheelchair. "Saddle the roan for me while I take Father up to the house."

Taylor motioned him away. "Leave me here. I'll stay since the mare's about to foal anyway. James can help me."

Jason nodded in agreement.

"We'll return as soon as possible."

"Be careful, both of you," Taylor warned.

"Don't worry, Father. I'll take care of everything."

And thank God you can...as I used to do.

Back in the stable, Taylor pulled a hackamore off the wooden peg. The stiff leather, spilled a comforting aroma over him. Mellow. Strong. Dependable. He thrust the bridle toward his son and watched Jason slide the leather into place. Bitless now, the gelding's mouth remained shut, which meant no pain for the animal and complete control for Jason.

He draped the multi-colored wool and saddle onto the gelding's back, then pulled the girth tight, locking the strap into place. He gathered his saddlebags, placed them behind the cantle, and then shoved the Winchester into the sheath.

A split-second later, he pulled himself up into the saddle. An audible creak fell between them as he settled into the leather seat. He turned to Packey and gave a nod, then with a swift nudge of their heels, the two riders galloped from the stable.

Taylor watched the dust settle on the horizon.

He curled his fingers inward on an ache to feel the leather in his grip once more. He clenched his jaw and held his breath for several seconds. On a slow exhale, he released his pain, the longing, the desire to be whole once more.

A soft nicker pulled him back to the present and he rolled his chair to the stall. Infinity pushed a soft muzzle against Taylor's face.

He buried his hand into the colt's coarse, black mane. "Hey there, fella, we've shared a lot in your young life, haven't we?" His throat tightened, tears welling in his eyes. The contrite taste of worthlessness bit back. "Grow strong," he whispered, his angst entwining with the colt's warm chuffs. "Become my legs, Infinity. You are now my life."

Chapter Two

Jason halted his mount and scanned the surrounding area for any sign of rogue dogs. Nothing. He turned to Packey. "Hear anything?" he inquired, tugging on Blue's reins to settle the spirited horse.

"No sir. Them dogs ain't nowhere around."

Grabbing a handful of mane, Jason clamped his legs tight against the gelding's sides. "Yep. Let's ride on up by the river. If we don't see tracks there, we'll turn back."

Packey spurred forward, leading the way.

Jason evaluated the shadows traversing the valley floor. He inhaled, filling his nostrils with the sweet scent of honeysuckle and wild lavender flowers. Dogwood trees of various sizes and colors dotted the landscape. The path narrowed into arching shrubs and twining berry bushes that clawed at his denim pants. Reaching the shallow riverbank, he dismounted, his boot heels sinking into the muddy shoreline. He kneeled and cupped his fingers, drawing creek water into his hand. Cool droplets trickled down his wrist to soak his shirt cuff. He drank his fill, then swiped his hand on his pant leg.

Packey joined him. "There are no dogs here. Let's head home."

"Sounds good to me."

Jason regrouped the reins, then placed his boot into the stirrup. As he grasped the saddle horn a shrill scream reverberated off the towering pines around him. He whirled and scanned the area. *Give me a direction!* A flock of birds erupted with a noisy chatter, vacating the white river birch behind them.

Another desperate cry echoed through the valley.

"I heard it, too," Packey said, pointing eastward. "That way."

Jason pulled into the saddle yelling, "Let's go." The horse reared and lunged forward. The men galloped along the river bank, up a small ravine and between groups of evergreens. When Jason crested the ridge line, a stunning waterfall panorama filled his view. He jerked hard on the reins.

Oh no, not Crystal Falls!

"There," Packey yelled. "Beneath the falls."

Jason narrowed his eyes. The river's mist swirled around the frantic form of a woman. She stood thigh deep in water, her arms flailing to retain her balance. He recognized the flaxen hair and slight figure. His heart pounded beneath his ribs. "Oh, my God," he gasped. "Mother."

He slapped the rump of his horse and surged forward. The turf beneath them flashed past, changing from grassy soil to shale and sandstone. Metal horseshoes scraped the rocks and released an unnerving intonation of a grinding ax. Thick foam of lather coated the horse's neck as Jason lashed the reins from side to side across the roan's withers.

Finally, he reached the boulders clustered beneath the falls and lunged from the saddle into the cold water. "Mother," he shouted once more, fighting his way through the swirling current. His boots slipped, throwing him into the foaming water. Tiny pockets of air erupted before him and bubbled upward as he struggled to regain his balance. Breaking the surface, Jason stood and wrapped his arms around her. An easy lift brought her into his embrace. "Good God, Mother, why are you here?" He headed for the shoreline.

With ragged words she wailed. "Oh, Jason! Mason's gone."

The image of his young brother emerged in Jason's mind. "Gone?" he rasped. "What the hell happened? Gone where?"

He settled her onto the ground, but she pushed aside, her lips quivering. "He wanted to feed the fish while I went to get our picnic basket. I turned around, he was gone." Her fingers clamped his arm and she crumpled to her knees.

"What was he wearing?"

"His little blue outfit."

Jason turned to Packey. "Get the quilt from the buckboard. She's freezing."

Packey grabbed the patchwork blanket and tossed it to him. Jason wrapped her shoulders. "We'll find him, Mother. I promise."

"I'll check dis way," Packey said, mounting his horse. A moment later, he dropped from view.

Jason vaulted into the saddle and headed in the direction Mason was last seen. *He can't be far.* Jason searched the creek bed and along the path, all the while praying the toddler had not gone into the water. "Mason!" he yelled. Only the rushing current answered back. He spurred Blue around and headed to the meadow beyond. Beads of perspiration trickled down his temples and he raised his arm, wiping his forehead on his wet shirt sleeve. *Come on, Mason. Where the hell are you?* And then a childish giggle touched his ears, the sound emerging from a cluster of wild winter wheat before him. Then he caught sight of a blue cap. The youngster sat near an animal burrow, holding a baby rabbit. Jason dismounted and dashed over, scooping his brother into his arms.

"Mason, you scared me and mommy."

"Bunny," the towheaded toddler said, giggling as he held up the rabbit.

Jason took the animal from the boy's chubby hand, and dropped it near the hole. "Yes, it sure is," he chuckled. "But, we must give him back to his mommy. Now, let's get you back to ours. She's worried about you."

Moments later, reaching the buckboard, Jason stopped before his ever-so-grateful mother and placed the child into her outstretched arms. She wept as she drew the boy tight against her. Tears welled in Jason's eyes as he watched their reunion. He glanced over just as his farrier joined them.

Packey creased a smile. "Where'd ya find him?" he asked.

Jason laughed. "In the meadow, playing in a rabbit hole." He slapped his friend's leg with the back of his hand. "Now, we can go home."

Tying the roan to the back of the wagon, Jason slid onto the seat beside them and gave the mare a cluck. The group moved onto the main road.

"You all right, Mother?"

Her gaze met his. With a slight drop of her chin, she gave an affirmative nod. "Thanks, darling," she whispered. "I'm so sorry this happened."

"It's all right. Just promise me you won't come here for awhile. There are wild dogs in the area. It's too dangerous for you both to be out here alone."

Jason's thoughts drifted back to earlier. "By the way, did you know that father came to the stable today?"

"Yes," she replied, exhaling as she shaded the boy's face from the afternoon sun. "He spoke of going. I'm glad he did. His depression has been as crippling as his injury."

Wood creaked as Jason shifted on the seat. "I hope he comes more often. I'll find something for him to do."

Jason weighed his thoughts. Perhaps now might be a good time to speak of college. Besides, his mother always stood behind his decisions. Nervous fingers grew taut, working the leather straps in his hands. His throat tightened, yet his words refused to be contained. "I want to go back to school." he bluntly announced. The statement sounded shallow and selfish, even to him. "Now, don't get me wrong," he added, trying to lighten the truth. "I love working with the horses, but I really do want to become a lawyer."

"I know, darling, I know," she said, adjusting Mason in her arms. "Just be patient. Your time will come. And when it does, you'll be a fine lawyer. But your father needs you now." She placed her hand on his upper arm and tightened her fingers. "You know, we couldn't have survived this without your help."

Jason leaned back and sucked in a deep breath. "This is all bullshit. We both know father will never be able to run this place alone."

"But, there's no one else. Your brother is too young and I certainly can't do it. What else would you have us do?

Crushed with the truth of her words, reality cut him to the core. *I'm never going to get away from this damn place.* He glanced at his sleeping brother. "Do you want to lay him in the back?"

"No, we're fine," she said, pushing aside tresses of sodden hair.

The buggy jostled sideways as the metal rims of the wagon wheel scraped the protruding rocks in the road. Each revolution of the wheel further scraped away his dreams.

His mother turned to face him. "Have you seen Debbie, lately?"

The mere mention of his adopted sister's name sent Jason's heartbeat into double time. He jammed the buggy whip back into the metal bracket. "Nope." He refused to let his gaze touch hers. "Why, have you?"

"No," she replied. "Now that she's moved in to town, I rarely see her." She drew a soft breath. "She likes working at the hospital, doesn't she?"

He nodded. "Yes, but I think she could do a lot better."

"Doing what?" She folded the edge of the blanket across his brother's chubby legs.

"She's also a very talented singer who needs to go to New York and study opera. They've got a great Opera House there and it's a shame for her not to use her gift."

Her soft sigh reached his ears. "Have you discussed this with her?"

He agonized against the weight of her words. "Yes," he growled, "but she won't hear of it."

"How are things between you two, anyway?" Her hand touched his, and he swept it away.

His gaze held fast on the trail before them. "Mother, I'm not discussing this with you."

Not now, not ever.

She leaned forward, peering into his face. "So, how do you feel about her?"

He lowered his brow. "She's fine," he replied through clenched teeth.

"Let's just leave it at that."

"Are you in love with her?"

He glared at her. "Damn it, mother, quit drilling me."

"Fine," she said, dropping her gaze. "All I know is, since you took her to Louisville, the two of you are avoiding one another."

True, that trip changed his life. His desire for Debbie charged through his body like a raging wildfire.

"She should make a career out of music. But she won't." He bit his lip. The thought of her sent heated waves pulsing through his veins. "What the hell can I do? She's like a sister...uh...stepsister. Hell, I don't know what she is!" The blood pounded in his ears as his confusion deepened.

Why does everything have to be so complicated?

His mother pushed closer and placed the palm of her hand on his shoulder, then gently rubbed his back. "Jason, she's your father's adopted daughter. Nothing more. True, she's part of our family, but she is not blood. It is all right to be in love with her."

"I'm done talking about this."

The remainder of their journey was cloaked in silence.

Once home, Jason brushed down the pinto, put away the buckboard and changed clothes, before returning to the stable. A light rain began to fall as he rolled shut the heavy door.

Turning around, he spotted his father.

"What's the problem?" Jason asked, pulling the saddle from Blue's back. He settled the heavy leather onto the rack and then stepped across the corridor to join his father.

"Packey told me what happened." Taylor's gaze met his. "Your mother never thinks of danger at those falls."

"I'm just thankful we were nearby and heard her call for help." Jason pressed his shoulder against the large wooden post and folded his arms. "By the way, what do you think about the falls? You know the legend and all."

"I never gave it much thought. All I know is a tribe of Indians lived there and it's considered their sacred ground." His father cleared his throat. "Why? Is there more?"

"Well, folklore has it, drink the water on the night of a full moon, the spirits will protect you. Mother always told me the water droplets in the moonlight are actually crystals."

"So she named it Crystal Falls?" Taylor asked.

"Right." Jason paused to take in a shallow breath. "It's strange, you could feel something weird during a full moon. She even asked me to go with her one night."

"She never mentioned it." Taylor said.

Jason straightened. "I didn't want her to go alone, so I tagged along." He placed his foot on a bale of straw and lowered his elbow to rest on his knee. "Mother sat near the falls, just staring into the mist. Then, she took a sip of the water. I could hear her speaking, but the words weren't clear. I never asked what she said. Just figured it was private."

"You know, your mother and I met over twenty years ago and even though I was gone most of those years, I knew her pretty well. She's always been a dreamer."

Jason smiled. "Yes, I know."

"So, what became of the Indians?" Taylor quizzed, folding his hands across his lap.

"No one knows." Jason shrugged. "They were long gone before we got here. Once in a while, you can find arrowheads and such, but nothin' else."

Rustling of straw and a sharp crack of wood reverberated down the hallway. The anxious words of young James reached his ears.

"Mare's down," the lad yelled, waving his hand for them to join him.

Jason straightened, stepped behind the invalid chair, then pushed his father to the birthing stall. He peered through wooden rails. The chestnut mare positioned herself in the straw and rolled onto her side. Her nostrils flared, sucking in ragged gulps of air, and she released agonizing grunts as her sides surged and contracted. The rust-colored tail whipped about and blood-filled fluid announced the onset of birth. She lifted her head and thrashed her hindquarters to expel this new life. A dusting of chaff drifted upward as her labor continued. The mare's eyes widened with anxiety and she kicked with great force. Finally, a small head appeared atop two tiny hooves and the foal emerged. Within moments the torso escaped its mother's womb and dropped into a thick clump of straw. Wet and partially encased in afterbirth, the foal rose up and took his first breath.

"James," Jason said, draping his arm across the boy's lean shoulders. "You've just witnessed the miracle of life."

The urchin's blue eyes widened. "Is Bess all right?"

Taylor chuckled. "She's fine, lad. It's all part of nature."

Jason unlocked the gate and stepped into the stall just as the mare struggled to stand. "Nice job, girl." Holding her halter, he stroked Bess's neck and pulled wisps of straw from her mane. The mare nickered, lowering her head to clean her new foal. "We have a boy," he announced.

"What shall we call him?" Taylor asked, glancing over at James. The youngster's face, frozen in amazement, refused to respond. "Well, speak up, boy."

"I think Coal, 'cause he's black like coal," the lad offered, rubbing his nose against his shirt sleeve.

Jason glanced over at his father. He would leave the decision with him. *I'm so glad you want to be part of things, again.*

"We can add a little something to that later," Taylor replied. "For now, Coal it is."

Jason peered at his father between the wooden planks of the stall. The elderly man leaned forward; his aging lips creased a smile as the new colt wobbled toward Bess for a first taste of milk. Jason drew in a deep breath. *A new life begins as another nears the end. Life rotates like an endless clock I can't rewind. Oh, how I missed those beginning years of my life with you. Mother's right. He does need me and I need to make the most of the time we have left.*

Releasing a long sigh, Taylor said, "I think I've had enough excitement for today." He then rolled his chair around and started toward the door.

Jason pushed through the deep straw bed, his feet kicking up dust. "Wait," he said, exiting behind his father. "I'll take you home. You'll need help getting up the road."

A wedge of exhaustion appeared on Taylor's forehead. "Damnit, I forgot about the hill."

Jason laughed as he edged the chair to the loading ramp and up into a stock wagon. He grabbed a nearby rope, then laced the twine through the metal wheels and tethered each end to the side rails. "There," he said, stepping back. "Now, you hang on and I'll have you home real soon."

Taylor released a soft chuckle. "Thanks, son," he said. His hands clutched the arm rests as he awaited their departure. "I'm so glad you're here," he proclaimed. "I feel alive again."

Chapter Three

Kathryn placed Mason in his bed and covered his bare legs. His young skin reminded her of velvet. Soft. Smooth. So delicate. She touched his forehead, her fingers sifting through fine strands of platinum hair.

How beautiful you are. Just like your brother was as a child.

His long lashes fluttered. And Kathryn smiled. "Pleasant dreams, little man," she whispered. "Momma loves you."

You're so precious. I would die if anything happened to you. Perhaps the legend is true and the spirits do protect us.

She pressed her fingertips to her lips and then touched his cheek, transferring the kiss. Then she tiptoed across the braided rug and into the hallway, leaving the door ajar.

The rattling sounds of an approaching carriage followed by the front door slamming shut drew Kathryn to the head of the stairs. Her stepdaughter, Debbie, stood peering upward. Her chestnut hair, swept back on one side and held by a beaded comb, hung in tendrils over her shoulders.

Oh my, Debbie. What's wrong?

Kathryn grabbed the handrail and scurried down the steps. She cringed at the thought of Debbie's anguish.

"What is it, darling?"

Debbie stared at her. Lines of tension creased her forehead and her hazel eyes welled with tears.

Kathryn draped her arm across shuddering shoulders. "Come sit with me," she said, guiding her over to the leather wingback chair in the parlor. Kathryn drifted down onto the ottoman in front of Debbie. "Now, tell me what's wrong," she said, clasping hands.

"Well," Debbie began, taking a deep breath. "This little boy, about five years old, has been very sick." She bit her lip and lowered her head.

Kathryn whispered, "It's fine. Go on." She waited while Debbie regained her composure. Their gazes reconnected. A wisp of sable as fine as angel hair draped near her brow. Kathryn brushed it aside. "He died, is that what you are trying to say, sweetheart?"

"Y… yes," Debbie whispered.

Kathryn leaned forward and placed a hand on the girl's cheek. "I'm so sorry you witnessed that."

"Y…you don't understand, though." Debbie's voice cracked. "He begged me to help him and I couldn't. God, it was awful. Little children shouldn't die."

"You knew things like this would happen when you took the job. You said you could handle it."

"I know, and I have until now." She paused, wiping aside tears before continuing, "but this little boy was different. He had no family. I gave him special attention. Then he started calling me mommy. I didn't want to hurt him, so I went along with his affection. This was wrong, but I couldn't help falling in love with the little guy. He was so adorable."

"Darling, you were just trying to help him cope by showing him the love he so desperately needed. Women do that, you know. It's the motherly instinct in us."

Kathryn drew a hankie from her skirt pocket. With a flick of her fingers, the linen unfolded. Debbie's dark lashes lay heavy as crescents upon her face. With a gentleness honed from years of mothering, Kathryn dabbed the tears away. "Let's go upstairs," she whispered.

Debbie pressed her fingers against trembling lips and nodded.

Rising, Kathryn said, "I'll have Millie bring you a cup of hot tea. Perhaps you should take something. I'll fetch the tin of nerve powder from my room."

They climbed the staircase in silence, then made their way to the room Debbie used to occupy. She turned back the satin coverlet. Her gaze met Kathryn's. "Why weren't you my mother?"

Kathryn smiled, and then took the young woman's hands in hers. "There's a reason for everything, Deb. Besides, you had a lovely mother."

"You didn't know my mother."

"No, but Taylor often spoke of her."

"I didn't really know either of them. My father died before I was born." She paused, and then said, "My mother died when I was just a baby." Debbie slid down on the edge of the feather mattress.

Kathryn patted her hand. "Since the moment I met you, I cherished you. Love comes from the heart. When you came to us, we gave you our name and you became family." She cupped Debbie's chin. "And you met Jason. He is so lucky to have you."

"Is it that obvious I love him?"

Kathryn nodded, lowering her hand. "A mother can sense these things. All I need to do is look into your eyes when you two are together. You can't hide love."

Debbie sighed. "I think I've loved Jason from the first moment I saw him."

Kathryn's soft giggle filled the space between them. "I felt the same when I opened the door and saw Taylor. I love him more than life itself." Kathryn kissed Debbie's forehead and said, "But enough talk now. You need some rest."

Nodding in agreement, the young woman slipped her feet from her work shoes and slid between the covers.

* * *

The case clock, made from the walnut trees near Crystal Falls, struck seven as Kathryn took her seat next to her husband. A kaleidoscope of color cascaded across the dining room table from the crystal chandelier suspended above. Taylor met her gaze and his mouth bowed upward in a smile.

Jason entered the room and slipped into the seat across from her. He extended a cordial greeting, then tipped his head toward the extra setting of China. "Who's coming to dinner, Mother?"

Her gaze met his. "Debbie," she replied.

"I didn't know she was here." A smile tugged at the corner of his mouth. "When did she come home?"

"This afternoon. There was an incident at the hospital. She's very upset."

"That's the first I've heard of it," Taylor grumbled.

She placed her hand atop his. "Everything is fine, dear. Debbie's a strong woman. She just needs time to sort things out."

Throughout dinner, Kathryn glanced at Jason as he kept his gaze locked upon the entryway. Without finishing his meal, Jason finally shoved away from the table.

"I think I'll step outside," he said, tossing his napkin beside his plate.

"Are you all right, dear?"

"I'm fine, Mother," he snapped. "It's just a little warm in here."

A knowing smile crossed her lips. The warmth in the room had little to do with her son's frustration.

Jason ambled onto the veranda. He pressed a shoulder against the closest Corinthian column and stared into the night sky. His eyelids slipped shut. Visions of Debbie, standing on the outdoor stage in Louisville, filled his mind.

How beautiful you looked, in your red dress, there in the spotlight. And the next morning. You came to my room. We made love.

An abrupt slamming of the screen door brought him back to reality. His eyes sprang open, followed by a flood of fresh air sucking into his lungs. He pivoted, hoping to see Debbie, only to find his parents joining him on the veranda.

He fought to smile as his heart pounded hard against his ribs. His gaze met theirs as his cheeks flushed hot.

Did they read my mind?

Jason cleared his throat and straightened. "Beautiful night, isn't it?"

"Yes…yes, it is." His mother's words were soft and cordial.

Taylor rolled to Jason's side. A glow from the light in the hallway fell across his features. "Your mother and I think it's time you get back to your schooling." Concern etched deep in the old man's face. His voice grew heavy in tone. "But I've one request."

Oh God, what's he wanting now? I've already taken too much time away from my studies.

His neck muscles tightened as he clenched his teeth. "What's that, Father?"

"I want you to get Infinity ready to race before you go. Deal?"

Relief washed over him. "Deal," Jason agreed. *Finally, I can become a lawyer.* "I'll get our best rider, Billy, to come Monday and start the training."

"I want to be there," Taylor said, resting his hands in his lap.

"I'll make sure you're there every day we work with Infinity. I know how important that colt is to you." He placed his hand on his father's shoulder, and leaned forward. "Infinity will be the greatest runner ever."

Taylor's lips curled upward and he gave a nod of agreement.

Jason glanced at his mother. "I think I'm going to take a walk now. You two enjoy this beautiful evening."

Kathryn nodded and smiled.

* * *

Debbie held the oil lamp tight as she tiptoed along the upper hall and descended the stairs, hoping not to wake anyone. It was late, but her gnawing stomach demanded food.

As she stepped into the kitchen, the lantern light reflected off the copper pots and pans hanging above a wooden chopping block. Shadows danced about the walls as Debbie glided by glass-fronted cabinets and shelves filled with jars of scarlet red beets and pickled cucumbers. A tantalizing aroma of roast beef lingered in the air from the evening meal.

Debbie peered through an open window into the moonlight.

Silhouettes of roses swayed in rhythm as a gentle breeze touched their petals. And nearby, silver moon dust illuminated the delicate buds of morning glories awaiting the rising sun.

She inhaled, appreciating their precious fragrance. The redolence carried away her earlier sorrow. On a sigh, she closed the window and secured the latch, then refocused on fixing herself a midnight meal.

The oversized kitchen offered little in the way of an easy treat. While feeding her soul, it did nothing to fill her belly. Her gaze settled on a block of cheddar and a carving knife at the end of the counter.

She smiled. *A perfect snack.* Placing the lamp next to the cheese wheel, she sliced an adequate piece, then turned to get a cracker from the pantry. A large figure loomed in the doorway. She gasped, releasing the wedge onto the floor.

"I'm sorry," Jason said, stepping forward. "I didn't mean to scare you."

Debbie's face grew hot as the blood rushed up her spine. She locked her fingers around the front of her robe, pulling it tight against her breast. *Jason!* "What are you doing up so late?"

He stepped closer. "I was about to ask you the same question." He pressed his hip against the counter to face her. His muscular shoulders leveled before her. The moonlight washed a mesmerizing glow against his oh so handsome features. Debbie swallowed hard.

"I'm hungry," she said, trembling as she retrieved the slice of cheese from the floor.

His bronzed hand touched hers. "Don't eat that," he whispered, his breath rushing past her cheeks. He took the wedge from her fingertips and dropped it aside. "Let me fix you something good. What would you like?"

His nearness. His scent. Everything that made him her life rushed over her. Words locked in her throat and fought to come forward.

"Steak." A tremulous smile lifted her lips. "Millie said we got in a fresh shipment of beef."

Fresh shipment of beef? That's all I could conjure up?

"You got me," he said, releasing a snippet of laughter. "I can't cook that well. Would you like another slice of cheese?"

She giggled. "That'll be fine," Picking up the knife she placed it in his open palm. "Slice away."

Plucking the cracker jar from the pantry she added, "And why are you up so late, anyway?" Her heartbeat quickened as he stepped closer, drawing his Bay Rum scent nearer, yet.

"I've been out walking." He placed the wedge on the cracker before him. "I'll be going back to school soon."

"Good, I know that's what you really want to do."

"It is, and you? What are you going to do? Mother told me what happened today. Are you returning to nursing or are you going to New York to study music?"

Her gaze touched his and a chill welled beneath her skin. "That's not fair. Not today, anyway. I love my job most of the time."

"You love music, too." He retrieved a crystal glass from the hutch, and his hand clutched the pitcher. Pouring her water, light from the nearby lantern entwined with the stream of liquid as it filled the stemmed vessel. Her fingers brushed his as she took the goblet into her hand. She glanced up. Dark hair edged the neck of his shirt and she turned away, gulping the water in an attempt to quell the burning need for this man. Debbie glanced into the mirrored hutch. The reflection outlined his masculine frame. Her body refused to move. She placed the glass on the counter as he stepped near her. The warmth of his body pressed against her back. Her eyelids dropped shut and he placed his hands on her arms. Jason's touch sent a wicked shiver racing through her. Another sigh escaped her lips. Stubbles of his evening beard brushed against her cheek while his breath rushed across her ear. She did not fight him. Her legs grew weak beneath her. His moist lips crossed her neck and settled near her shoulder.

"I can't help myself," he groaned. "You smell like the roses in our garden." His hands drew up to her shoulders. He turned, engulfing her in his embrace. Her head tilted back and she gazed at him. His eyes drifted shut as his lips covered hers.

A wave of undeniable bliss rushed through Debbie's body. Her hands lifted and she wrapped her arms around his neck. She wanted to lock him in her embrace forever. His kiss deepened and she responded, allowing him complete access to her passion. When his lips finally lifted, he moaned against her mouth, "I've wanted forever to do that again."

"Me, too," she confessed. "But… what can we do? Everyone thinks we're siblings. It's shameful. We're family" Her fingers tunneled through the locks of hair that met his collar. "I love you so much," she sobbed. Tiptoeing, she tasted his lips once more. He was in her arms and she yearned for him. She wanted him to touch, taste and caress every inch of her body, again.

An upstairs door slammed shut. She pushed back. "We can't do this here Not in the kitchen. Someone may walk in. Stop…stop!"

He stood back and held her at arm's length, offering a bitter smile.

"If you want me to wait, I will. But know that I want you more than anything in this world."

She drew a breath and lowered her head. "Yes…Yes. We must stop."

His face drew tight as lines deepened across his forehead. He edged closer. "I'll take care of it… and soon. I promise."

A repulsive void sucked the bliss away from her. With all her heart she wanted to scream, *please God, don't make me wait.*

Finally accepting her fate, she nodded in agreement.

Jason's lips touched hers…this time gentle, yet full of promise. Then he stepped away, disappearing into the darkness.

Chapter Four

Debbie slipped out of bed and stepped to the window. Pulling aside the tapestry she squinted against the full force of the morning sunlight. Her eyelids dropped and she tried to focus. Fresh air filled her lungs as she pushed the partially opened window to full width, allowing a warm breeze to fill the room. Even the weather concurred that this would be a special day. The corners of her mouth rose as she whirled around, then advanced to the wardrobe. *Now, to pick a nice dress for such an occasion.* Thoughts of the previous night in the kitchen with Jason brought a flutter into her heart. *Jason still wants me.* A tingle sparked her spine. She wanted to sing at the top of her lungs. Her fingers wrapped the brass knobs and she swung open the wardrobe doors, releasing an instant aroma of cedar. A small selection of dresses gathered at one end. Perhaps, she should not have taken so many belongings when she moved to town. She touched the pink dress with its white lace neckline. Yes, that would do nicely. She plucked the garment from the wooden hanger and headed for the bathing room.

Now for a good soaking bath.

Stepping into the hallway, she heard the maid in the next room. "Millie," Debbie called.

A spry little woman dressed in black appeared at the doorway. A sheer dust cap crowned her graying hair and a white ruffled apron gathered about her waist. "Yes ma'am," her high-pitched voice reverberated down the hall.

"Could you fetch me some hot water. I'd like to bathe soon."

"Yes, ma'am, I'll get right on it." The woman closed the door and hurried down the back stairs.

Three hours later, now fully dressed and pacing the parlor floor, Debbie glanced at the clock on the fireplace mantle. Encased in white porcelain, the two brass hands pointed directly at the three. Jason should be finished working with the colt, by now. She tightened her hand around the handle of the picnic basket. The aroma of fried chicken radiated from beneath a checkered cloth. Her steps seemed nonexistent. Thoughts of the hospital vanished from her mind. Her heart thundered beneath her breast, knowing she would be alone with the man she loved. Ashamed? No. She felt no shame in her desire for him. Most women her age would not allow themselves such pleasure. She smiled. During her bath this morning she decided she would not wait for a wedding ring. She giggled beneath her breath. *How wicked of me.* After all, she went to him that morning in Louisville. His deep kisses and passionate embraces confirmed his desire for her. Their remembered coupling danced through her mind, reminding her all over again how much she loved Jason Dillon.

Impatience sent her out the front door and down the flagstone walk to the gravel road. The clang of heavy chains drew her gaze. Glancing over her shoulder she saw an approaching wagon. She shuffled to the side, allowing the mule drawn vehicle to pass. An elderly man, in a plaid shirt, raised his hand and waved. Debbie flashed a smile then continued toward the stable.

Several steps later, she arrived to find Jason standing by the stone-covered well. He drew up a cup of water. Small streams of the liquid etched their way down his chin and dripped onto his bare chest. The droplets glistened in the sunlight and disappeared into the cluster of thick hair that gathered in a wedge, tracking to his waist. Wiping away the moisture with the back of his hand he returned the dipper into the metal bucket. With the swipe of a cloth, he removed the wetness from his chest and picked up the white shirt that draped the lip of the well. Golden skin held tight to his ribs outlined a strong chest which tapered down to an oh-so-perfect waist. Debbie sucked in a ragged breath. Jason put on the shirt, adjusted the collar and racked his fingers through his shoulder length dusky hair. He strolled toward her, closing the pearl buttons that fronted the white muslin.

"There you are," he said, with a grin. His nostrils flared. "Mmmmm, fried chicken. That Millie sure knows how to cook."

Debbie flashed him a smile. Gliding up next to him, she snaked her hand across his arm and peered into his hazel eyes. "Where are we going?

"Do you feel like walking?"

"Sure." She would go anywhere with him, including the moon, if he asked.

"Let's go to the lake behind Packey's place," he suggested, adding a wink. "There's lots of weeping willows along the shore and it's very private."

"That sounds wonderful." She skimmed her hand down his arm allowing their fingers to entwine. The pleasure sent a warm rush through her.

Safe. Protected. Secure.

The late afternoon sun splashed across her face as they pivoted toward the western horizon.

"When are you going back to work?" he questioned.

She lowered her head and scuffed at the rocks beneath her feet. "Probably tomorrow." A pause broke her words. "I'm not sure I want to go back, though."

"I know you've always wanted to become a doctor, but maybe medicine isn't for you."

She looked up. "And music is?"

"Well, you could always give it a try." His gaze caught hers. "How will you ever know, if you don't?"

They rounded a corner and a charming two-story bungalow came into view. The slam of a screen door halted their steps. Packey's wife, Pearl, appeared with a basket of wet laundry propped on her hip. She descended the porch and headed toward the wire lines on the side of the house. Her two-year-old son,

Packard Jr., toddled close behind, his tiny hand clutching a half-eaten biscuit. Debbie smiled as the Negro woman waved.

Jason cupped his hands around his mouth and yelled, "Mother's looking forward to watching little Pack, tonight. I hear you have a special dinner planned."

"Yes sir." The hem of her checkered black-and-white work dress ruffled in the breeze as she stepped closer. "We's havin' roast pork 'n' apples, 'n' a blueberry pie fer after. I gots the pig on the pit right now. It's gonna be a real special supper when Packey gets home from town."

"Three year anniversary. Time passes fast," Jason hollered. "Well, you folks have a good evening."

Debbie laughed. "Enjoy your celebration."

With an agreeable nod, Pearl turned and began hanging her laundry.

"Being alone with the one you love is so wonderful." Debbie glanced over her shoulder. "She's such a nice lady." She slipped her hand against Jason's and they headed over the hill. Their footsteps muffled as they crossed the bone dry dirt path.

"Yes, Packey is a lucky man." Jason released her hand and placed his arm about her shoulders. Debbie quivered. "Are you all right?" he asked.

"Just a chill from the breeze." The words barely escaped her lips. *A valid excuse.* His touch created such an evocative quake. He drew her closer. The top of her head met the tip of his chin and she rested against him. She could hear his heart beating beneath her ear faster and faster. Passion welled within her. Would she pass out or merely die in his arms? *God, no! Let me live to enjoy this man.* She drug in a deep breath. Her eyes closed and she submitted to his lead.

Cresting the hill, Jason pulled her to an abrupt stop. Her eyes flew open.

"Look..there...on the hillside." He pointed. "Wild turkeys."

She shielded her eyes and gasped. "They're so big."

Jason chuckled. "And did you know the large one out front is called the cock? See how he fans out his tail. He's strutting for his women."

The heat in Debbie's cheeks fanned out too, wider than the cock's tail. Her laughter joined Jason's.

"I don't think I've ever seen so many."

"That's because you stay inside too much, darlin'," he said.

She turned and before her a beautiful lake glistened as tiny waves danced across the water. The long wispy branches of the willow trees moved with the motion of ballet dancers pirouetting across a stage. Debbie's mouth curved upward in delight. "This is so beautiful, Jason."

"See all the wild flowers and tall cane near the water?" He pointed at a cluster of orange Daylilies, Cattails and strange looking bamboo near the shoreline. "We have a lot of it near our lakes and streams. There are only two kinds of bamboo in the world and this type mostly grows near here. In fact, there is so much of it in our area that many wanted to name our state Canetuckee."

"Really? I had no idea. I don't think I've ever seen it before," she confessed. "How interesting."

They descended along the narrow path, then Jason stopped abruptly. He cut back and stood silent.

"What is it?" she asked, turning around, too.

"I thought I heard something." His gaze locked on the horizon. "Oh, no!" he screamed. "The wild dogs are back!"

Chapter Five

"They're headed for the horses." Jason grabbed her hand and propelled forward. "We gotta get back. My gun's in the barn."

Debbie fought to keep up. The muscles in her legs refused to carry her at such a wicked pace. "Go on," she pleaded. He released her hand and the distance between them continued to increase. Gasping for air, she slowed to catch her breath. Suddenly, Jason cut from the path and raced across the lawn up toward Packey's house. "Oh, no," the words tumbled from her lips. She forced her legs to move faster. The blood pounded in her ears. Each breath became harder to find. She dropped the picnic basket. Her fingers folded into the front of her dress clutching the crinolines beneath. *These damn garments.* Without warning her shoe caught on an exposed tree root and sent her sprawling into the dirt. Drawing a ragged breath, she fought to get back up on her feet. Her palms burned. In a glance, she could see the blood etching through the dirt onto her fingers. There was no time for concern with minor scrapes. Her thighs ached, yet she willed her legs to ignore the torture and press on. Jason needed her help.

As she drew near the white frame house the shrill barking of dogs pierced her ears.

Pearl swung a broom trying to ward off the animals as they edged nearer. Jason grabbed the ax from a wood pile. Six. Eight. A dozen or more dogs circled the pair, pinning them inside an arena of death.

"Help," Debbie screamed. Her voice barely audible above the fierce barking. "Someone help!"

James came running from the stable.

"Get a gun," she demanded, flailing her hand toward the stable door.

The boy pivoted and raced back into the barn. Moments later he appeared with a rifle and a pistol. Her hand locked around the barrel of the Winchester. In one sweeping motion she spun and headed toward the assault.

James followed, gripping tightly to the wooden grip of his Colt revolver.

Every breath Debbie drew burned her lungs. Her mouth went dry. Fear engulfed her, her head pounding.

Each step brought her closer and closer to the horror that sprawled across the front lawn. She narrowed her gaze on Pearl, crumpled in a heap beneath the clothesline.

A blood curdling scream erupted from the woman's throat as she hovered over her little Packey, protecting her son from the snapping jaws of the pack of wild beasts.

Sunlight drenched the gruesome scene, and Debbie gasped for air as she hurtled herself toward Pearl. Streaks of grey darted before her, the wild dogs ripping at the woman as she covered her child. His cries entwined with hers.

Ten feet from the carnage, Debbie stopped and raised the rifle.

Jason turned, swinging his ax wide to knock aside the beasts. He missed one, then connected with the second bone thin animal. Another dog surged around him and tore into his flesh.

Pain radiated up Jason's side and he stumbled, dropping the ax.

On a gasp, he tumbled to the ground.

Debbie aimed the gun and pulled the trigger, only to have the bullet sink into the dirt near the closest dog.

Her heart sunk to her gut, fear exploding in a calliope of torment.

This can't be happening!

Two additional mangy-haired dogs rounded the house dragging the half-cooked carcass of the roasted pig with them. An iron rod still protruded from the swine's belly, torn meat dangling from one end of the spit to glisten in the summer sun.

A deafening rifle shot passed her ear, and Debbie turned to see Pearl's husband lunge from the wagon. He stumbled up the grassy slope, firing without aiming.

Three of the dogs turned to face him.

Debbie's screamed, hoping the man would hear her warning call.

Tears blurred her eyes as the image of big Packey loomed closer. Her hands shook as she tried to steady the Winchester. Again she peered through the rifle sight and pulled the trigger.

Her fire coincided with the others to fill the air with a cacophony of sounds.

She hit her mark.

One dog dropped, his blood staining the ground in a wash of scarlet.

Packey fought his way to his wife and child. He dropped to the ground in front of them and fired his Remington as several of the animals lunged forward. He draped himself over his loved ones, using his body as a shield to protect them.

Jason continued to swing the ax, inching closer and closer to their bloodied, mangled forms.

A yelp, and his ax met the mark.

Another dog died.

Debbie stood frozen as one animal leaped at Packey's neck.

Another pulled at his boot.

His Remington discharged sending a bullet deep into the closest beast. A moment later, however, Packey released a blood curdling scream as the other two dogs jumped upward and ripped at his throat. Blood sprayed across his shoulder and down his arm. He dropped the gun and grasped his neck falling forward. Debbie took aim at the dog over him and fired. The bullet hit the animal's hindquarters. It yelped and careened away.

Debbie's gaze lanced to Jason.

He struggled to rise as his wolf-like attacker backed off. The animal lowered on his haunches, blood-filled saliva dripping from jagged fangs.

Then the dog lunged, ripping at Jason's side once more. A scream tore his lips. He locked his hand around the creature's neck and squeezed. The dog pulled back, released its grip and Jason flung the animal aside. In a spiraling motion he clasped the ax in his hand and crashed the blunt end of the mallet into the dogs head, killing it instantly. Packey's attacker lay nearby growling. Jason took two steps forward and with one mighty blow severed the dog's neck. James kept shooting until he emptied the pistol. A mind-staggering moment later, the remaining animals ran off into the field. Everywhere she looked carnage surrounded Debbie.

The child's cry still emerged from beneath his mother's now limp body. The ax dropped to the ground as Jason slumped to his knees. Debbie, shaken from her daze, rushed to his side. Loose flesh, mixed with blood-filled muslin, hung from what remained of his shredded shirt. Quickly surveying the wounds, she placed her hand on his shoulder and ordered him to lay down.

"James," she yelled. "Help me."

The young man ran to her side and fell on his knees beside her.

She lifted her dress and tore away the cotton under slip. "Do you have a pocket knife?"

"Yes, ma'am."

She handed him the slip. "Cut this into large strips."

Her fingers fumbled at Jason's shirt. Blood, flesh and crimson material gathered in her hand. "Hold this." She placed his swollen hand atop the wound to stop the bleeding. "I'm going to check on Pearl and Packey."

She stumbled to her feet and rushed to their side. The man's ebony face drew silent and Pearl made no attempt to move. Gently, Debbie rolled her over onto her back. The child sat up from beneath her skirt. Streaks of blood covered his clothing and his little hand raised to wipe his weeping eyes. Debbie placed her fingers on the woman's neck. The heartbeat was faint. Multiple wounds appeared beneath the ragged openings of her dress.

"Here," James said, handing her the long cotton strips.

With trembling hands she folded one. "Give this to Jason. He needs to replace the one beneath his hand. Then take this one and wrap his leg. I'll check it in a minute. They have lost a lot of blood. I need to get them all to the hospital. When you finish, get the wagon so we can get them in to town?"

"I can drive the wagon." The boy said, wiping his mouth on the shoulder of his shirt. Tears rimmed his widened eyes.

"You run up and tell Mr. and Mrs. Jackson what happened. Tell 'em we need help. And hurry."

"Oh, God," Jason moaned, his voice garbled. He raised his arm and placed his wrist across his forehead. "Sonofabitch!"

"Take it easy," she yelled over her shoulder. Unable to attend everyone at once, she knew Pearl was unconscious and fading fast. And Packey? She swallowed back her vomit. Well, he was already gone. The dog had severed the main artery in his neck. He had bled out before she could reach him.

Her professional training kicked in keeping her strong and focused. She doubled one of the strips of cloth, raked aside the torn dress and pulled the material tight around the woman's thigh. Debbie's vision blurred. Tears rushed from her eyes as she fought to save Pearl's life. The child stood and held up little grubby arms. And an undeniable sob burst from Debbie's lips. Her hands shook as she removed the bandana from Pearl's head and wiped the smear of blood that clotted across the woman's cheeks. Debbie staggered to her feet and swept the youngster into her arms. "Oh, Pack, I'm so sorry." She squeezed the boy tight against her breast and buried her face next to his.

The clang of chains on an approaching wagon summoned her to face the road. James thrashed the leather reins across the backs of the stocky horses urging the team up the hill. He slammed the break-stick forward, wrapped the reins, and leaped to the ground.

"Mrs. Jackson's on her way." The words toppled from his young lips. "Mr. Jackson is over at Butterfield's. They're doing business and he won't be back 'til late."

" James!" Debbie yelped as she sat the child on the lawn. "Help me get Jason into the wagon. We gotta get him and Pearl to the hospital." She knew her words were minced and hard to understand. Three short steps took her to Jason. With James's help, she brought Jason to his feet and they guided him to the wagon. A loud groan escaped his lips as he pulled up onto the stacks of horse feed. "Try to lie back," she encouraged.

Debbie dashed back to Pearl. Kneeling down she checked the woman's pulse once more. She felt nothing. "Oh, God, no." Her voice shrieked with pain.

Jason rose onto his elbow and yelled to her. "What is it?"

"They're both dead." She said as the words tumbled from her quivering lips."

"What," he hollered as he struggled to rise. "Noooo…No!"

Debbie swept up the child and ran for the wagon. "James, you stay here. Get a blanket from the barn and cover them until we get back. You get your pistol loaded and sit on the porch. Shoot anything that comes near them."

She placed the child on the seat and climbed into the wagon. Turning to Jason, she said with biting words, "Lay down, before you fall down." Her shaking hands unfolded the reins from the brake stick. With a loud, "Heeyaa," she urged the horses forward. Pulling hard on the left rein she made a sharp turn. The wagon lumbered forward and ascended the hill. Pounding hooves and iron-covered wheels grating against the shallow rock riveted against her ears. Her eyes tightened as they neared the gate. She could see Kathryn racing toward them. Debbie pulled against the reins, and the horses drew back on their haunches, sliding to a halt.

"Jason," Kathryn screamed, gulping air as she came to a stop. She peered into the wagon. Her face drew into a mask of horror and her fingers flashed upward to cross her lips. "Oh, my God," she shrieked, clutching the wooden planks separating her from her son.

"I'm taking him to the hospital. We must hurry," Debbie said.

"I'll go, too." Kathryn began to climb into the seat next to the child.

"No, you take the boy. Packey and Pearl are dead."

"Oh, God, no!" Kathryn's foot slipped and she staggered backwards. A flood of tears rained from her eyes as she doubled over clutching her fists between her breasts.

Jason reached out to comfort his mother, but weakness pushed him back to the stained burlap bags of grain.

Debbie stood and picked up the child. "Take him; I can't tend to both of them."

Wiping her tears on her shoulder Kathryn nodded, then lifted her arms to receive the weeping child. She cradled him close as they both wept.

Debbie chanced a quick glance to affirm Jason's position, and then slapped the reins against the horses' rumps. Their hooves dug deep into the gravel, transporting the wagon forward at a wicked pace. Nightfall would be upon them soon. Traveling then could be dangerous. But, delay of any kind would be unacceptable. She must get him to the hospital.

"Heeyah," she screamed, snapping the reins to propel them toward help.

Chapter Six

Kathryn waited while the servant assisted Taylor into nightclothes and settled him into bed. "Thank you, Jeremiah. We so appreciate your assistance. I know this is a difficult time for you and your family."

Through trembling lips, he whispered, "Yes'm, Pearl was da baby. We's sho gonna miss her." With tear-filled eyes, he exited the room, closing the door behind him.

Golden reflections rippled up the wall as Kathryn settled the oil lamp on the night table. She cupped her dress, then eased down onto the quilt-covered bed.

Taylor stroked her arm. Their gazes met.

"I'm worried about Jason," she whispered. "They've been gone so long."

"I know." He shifted to his side. "I'm worried, too."

"And Packey and Pearl. I can't believe they're dead." She bit her bottom lip as she recalled their friend's wedding several years before. The sweet embrace of blooming roses wafting over the garden. Their joy when lil' Pack was born. Such wonderful memories flooded Kathryn's thoughts. The bond between the couple mirrored the love she and Taylor enjoyed. She pulled in a steadying breath, before releasing a heavy-hearted sigh.

"He was a good man and I'm going to miss him." Taylor said.

Their fingers interlocked. "We would've never met if it weren't for him." Tears emerged, cooling a path down her face.

He squeezed her hand. "And thank God for it, too."

Her eyes slipped closed around a twenty-year-old memory of a bitter January morning. A handsome stranger stood in her doorway holding young Packey in his arms.

"Found this slave boy on the road," he said. "Was told he belongs to you."

Snow swirled around the man's boots as he drew the child against his chest, to shield the lad from the biting wind.

"Please come in," Kathryn said, stepping back to allow this mountain of a man to enter the foyer. His rich voice unleashed an awareness she had not felt for some time. "Thank you for bringing him home. Where are his parents?"

"They're dead."

"Dead?" she gasped. "Oh, no! What happened?"

"I found their wagon overturned just east of Lexington. They'd been shot."

An ember from the parlor's fireplace popped and she swirled. Her eyes widened. Smoke bellowed upward as flames streaked across the rug. Within moments, an inferno engulfed the parlor.

A clap of thunder broke into Kathryn's pensive musings'.

So many twists of fate had structured the foundation of their love. She released Taylor's hand, slid off the bed, then ambled to the window. An eerie tingle crept beneath her skin as she peered into the darkness. Had the grim reaper framed everything surrounding them with doom and damnation? She jerked the curtains together and turned away from hell's door.

This horror must stop.

She glanced at Taylor. His eyes were closed.

If not for you, my darling, I would've perished in that fire.

She'd lost all her worldly goods that day and was forced to secure safekeeping with an elderly aunt in St. Louis. And this stellar man agreed to take them there. But, his action required caution. He had been a Union deserter forced from the army to settle an old score. Execution was a given if he'd been caught. Traveling with a Negro child was difficult and people didn't understand, so the misfits avoided civilization on their westward journey. Yet, traveling together meant all three of them sleeping in close quarters. Her desire for Taylor grew. One evening as rain pelted them with driving force, they sought shelter in an abandoned homestead. And that night while the heavens rattled the world beyond their haven, Taylor gave her the greatest gift of all… their precious son, Jason. Upon reaching St. Louis, and unaware she even carried his child, she sobbed as Taylor Jackson rode from her life.

Tapping raindrops against the window pane drew Kathryn's reflections to her husband. She gazed down at the rhythmic rise and fall of his chest. Weeks had passed since his last tremor episode, but that series brought greater awareness to his ever weakening condition.

Memories captured her thoughts, strengthening her growing concerns. Her eyelids drifted closed. As clear as the water droplets of Crystal Falls, she again visualized that remarkable day four year ago. Chalk white clouds dappled an azure sky as a vibrant young man, Packey, helped her into the carriage to sit beside her handsome son. The clatter of an approaching horse brought her gaze to a rider atop a striking Arabian stallion. Summer sun splashed across the man's broad shoulders. Her heartbeat quickened and her breath trapped in her throat. Only one man had ever moved her soul to such depths. Taylor Jackson.

Oh, my God, he's home!

Taylor stirred, bringing Kathryn back to the present. Their gazes met. His hand opened, palm up, beckoning her closer. "Come, darling, lay beside me." She nodded and he drew her down, pressing her body against his gallant form. His touch sent soothing waves of completion over her.

"We've been through so much together, haven't we?" he whispered, his lips caressing her ear. A tantalizing ripple vibrated down her spine. "You know how much I love you. I need you. I'm sorry I'm no longer the man you married."

"Shhh"… She pressed her fingertips against his lips. "Nothing has changed," she said, opening her palm to cup his masculine face, adoring each weathered crease of her beloved husband's features. "You are why I exist and I will love you until my dying breath." Her lips slipped over his with the full weight of her devotion.

A knock broke apart the passion and Kathryn whispered, "I'll be back." She rose and traversed the room, pulling open the door. Debbie stood before her, eyes red-rimmed with tears.

"They sewed up his wounds as best they could, but Jason's lost a lot of blood." Despair cascaded down her cheeks. "He'll need to stay a few more days to recover."

Kathryn gripped her step-daughter's slender shaking shoulders. Her fingers dug deep into her upper arms. "But he'll live, won't he?"

"They say he will." Their moist palm's met. Kathryn interlocked their fingers, her knuckles popping. She captured her lower lip with chattering teeth. Every muscle in her body contracted in uncontrollable quakes. She released their grip and turned to pace the floor. Nausea, like a creeping serpent, slithered up her throat. She swallowed hard. The thought of losing her precious son loomed over her like a guillotine.

"I must go to the hospital now!" She wrung her hands. "What if they're wrong and something happens to him? I should be there."

"You're not going anywhere," Taylor bellowed from across the room. "And certainly not out on the road this late."

"Father's right." Debbie said. "We'll go together in the morning. I promise."

Kathryn pulled her chin high. "Fine. But come daybreak, I'm going not a minute later."

"And we will," Debbie assured her. "Jeremiah let me in as he was leaving. What about Packey and Pearl?"

"James took their bodies and lil' Pack to Pearl's family," Taylor said.

Kathryn lowered onto a nearby rocker, a throat-clogging helplessness enveloping her.

Jason must survive. I know he will. We have been through so much today.
She captured her breath and slowly exhaled her burden of fear.

* * *

By mid-morning, the two women arrived at the hospital. Debbie waited while Kathryn stepped from the carriage.

"Wait for me inside. I'll be right there," Debbie said, then guided the sure footed Morgan to a nearby stable and slipped the necessary funds into the groomsman's hand. Rushed footfalls pummeled the wooden walkway carrying her to the entrance of the medical building. A cool breeze tugged at her shawl, mirroring the uncertainty that frayed her nerves. Deep inside, the truth hallowed away at her confidence in Jason's recovery. His life now hung from a thread as thin as the spun fiber of a black widow's web. The dream of happily-ever-after with him tumbled to the ground as if it were yesterday's fried chicken spilling from her picnic basket. She straightened to contain her discouragement, raising her chin and thrusting back her shoulders.

We're going to get through this, no matter the outcome.

After a quick update from the nurse on Jason's stable condition, Debbie met Kathryn in the hallway. They peeked into her beloved's room. He was dozing, so Debbie closed the door. Taking her stepmother by the wrist, she guided a still distraught Kathryn down the corridor to the closest spindle-backed bench.

"He's running a low grade fever, but that's normal," Debbie said, her voice soft and reassuring.

Kathryn's brow lifted. "As long as he's not in pain."

"The morphine will help with that." Her hands interlocked with Kathryn's. "His ribs are bruised and sore and the doctor had a terrible time stitching his calf above his boot. Everything else is punctures or scrapes."

"But… they expect him to recover. Right?"

"We don't know. They'll need to keep him a few days. Of course, our biggest concern is dog madness disease. We'll be watching for a change in his behavior, or any excitability. What we don't want is paralysis. If that happens…"

She pinched her eyes tight to drive away the unthinkable.

Stay focused. Stay strong. I must have faith.

"This has all been so devastating," Kathryn whispered, glancing at the closed door. "I just keep thinking of Pearl and Packey." She slid her hand into her purse and withdrew a handkerchief. The linen swatch captured her falling tears. "Pearl saved her son, though. Lil' Pack didn't even have a mark on him." Another wave of tears dampened her cheeks.

"A mother will give her life for her child; you know this to be true." Debbie paused to gather a strengthening breath. "Did you know Pearl was pregnant again?"

Kathryn's head whipped up. "What?" She covered her lips with a shaking hand, the words muffling beneath the hankie. "No. I had no idea."

"I'm not sure Packey knew either." Debbie nodded at a co-worker as he walked past. "I saw her last week here at the hospital. She came to visit Dr. Brown due to her morning sickness. She was going to surprise Packey with the news at their celebration dinner last night." Debbie bit back a sob. "It's all too much to believe."

Kathryn twisted the hankie. "T-They didn't deserve any of this."

Debbie rose. Kathryn followed. "Come, let's go see if Jason is awake." She grasped her arm and they headed for the door.

* * *

The Southern Baptist church stood a mile and a half from Crystal Falls. A carved cross hung above the weathered door and a modest bell tower straddled the roof.

Inside, the close knit community gathered for the double wake of Packey and Pearl. Arms waved as they sang their songs about glory and salvation. An elderly woman screamed, "Jesus, Jesus…Praise the Lord." Heavy hearts were lifted by their love for this young couple.

Ominous clouds rolled overhead, releasing a mighty rumble as the hammer-wielding gods pounded their grief across the heavens. Mourners filed out of the white-framed building that Packey, Jeremiah and Taylor had helped build years before. Two wooden caskets were carried to the grave site. The aged pastor, his ebony face gaunt from years of lamentation, spoke comforting words to those present. A hollow clang cut through Kathryn's heart like a dagger, each doleful toll from the steeple's bell tower reminding her of their loss. Her gaze lifted to Jeremiah.

"We're indebted to you," she murmured, her hand pressing against his back. The grieving man creased a smile, yet never released his grip on Taylor's wheel chair.

His quivering lips parted. "You folks is my family, too."

She patted his hand. "And your loyalty and assistance means so much to us."

"I couldn't get along without you," Taylor added.

Kathryn tightened her fingers on the back of Jeremiah's hand. "We must all remember the good times we've shared."

The servant lowered his gaze and she stepped away.

The sharp-edged crepe ribbon on Kathryn's black, unadorned bonnet insisted on cutting a swath beneath her chin. A tug from her finger brought immediate relief. She had not worn her mourning ensemble for some time and the heavy capelet smothered her under the weight. Just like the weight of her sorrow, the weight of her broken heart, and the weight of an everlasting emptiness. She tightened her grip on her parasol to stifle the grief. The blood-sucking demon of death rode hard on her tenacity this day.

Packey, you have earned respect and you are one of my children, too. With God as my witness, no one shall say otherwise.

Her heart pumped with pride. Lifting the folds of her dress, tight-reined and composed, she rejoined her husband. His gaze trailed up to hers. She flashed him a reassuring smile, then with the flick of her wrist, she dropped open the slats of her mourning fan and waved the sandalwood slats before her cheeks. A flash of lightening beyond the treetops wrenched apart her sadness.

Kathryn glanced at the towering pines as the ever-darkening sky enveloped the graveyard. The heavens ripped open. Large droplets stung with the velocity of a bee swarm. "Let's go inside," she insisted, expanding her parasol to block the driving rain.

"Yes'm." Jeremiah said, pivoting the wheel chair around to follow after her.

The crowd scrambled to escape the torrent, shoving Kathryn sideways into Rachel. A strong arm wrapped her waist as the young woman scooped lil' Pack up and scurried under the white-washed eaves. Kathryn shuffled across the threshold of the church, stepping to the closest window. She pressed her hand against the distorted pane. Her heart thumped beneath her breast as she dug her fingertips down the cool glass. The storm pushed the coffins deeper into the saturated ground. She swallowed hard as thunder vibrated the building. Another bolt of lightning released its fiery branches, clawing the earth and paralleling Kathryn's grief. She turned from the window, her gaze falling upon Rachel, who rocked the boy in her arms.

Their gaze met and the younger woman nodded. "Miz Jackson?"

"I'm fine." Kathryn slowly shook her head. *I would challenge Satan himself for the souls of this young family.* "Even the heavens are weeping, my darling."

"Yes'm," the woman replied. "Daddy said your boy got hurt by dem dogs, too." Rachel carried many features of her beloved cousin.

"He's getting better." Kathryn placed her hand on lil' Pack's back and patted. "Jason will be coming home today. There's no dog madness, thank

God. He'll need to rest awhile, but he should be fine."

The woman smiled, then slipped to the far side of the room. The distancing rumble of thunder told Kathryn the storm moved onward. She peered out the window once more. The rain, now reduced to a sprinkle, allowed many of the Negro men, dressed in their Sunday best, to slip away and gather their wagons. She'd known these people most of her life. Her gaze gravitated once more to Packey's coffin. Pearl and the unborn child lay in the wooden box beside him. Kathryn's legs grew weak and her body began to quiver. She took a deep breath and exhaled with a distraught sigh.

"Are you ready to go?" Taylor inquired.

"Yes, I suppose."

He drew his watch from his vest pocket, the gold chain kicking a sad glint her way. "It's getting late. I have to make sure James fed the horses."

"You and Jeremiah go on to the buggy. I'll be along in a minute."

Exiting the church, Kathryn separated herself from the crowd and stepped across the puddles that dotted the lawn. Nearby the grave digger stood with his shovel, head bowed, sadness tugging at his features. Kathryn nodded and offered a tender smile.

She placed her trembling hand on top of the pine box. "Goodbye, Packey." The gentle words pushed through her lips. "I'll watch over your son, and he'll be a fine man like you one day. I promise."

Upon rising, Kathryn turned her knee, releasing a pain that spread down her leg. *My arthritis shows no mercy.* A wind gust whipped the hem of her dress. She lowered her hand to restrain the garment. As she favored her leg, fewer than a dozen footfalls brought her to the carriage. Jeremiah extended his hand and helped her into the black lacquered rig. She settled against the tufted cushion and watched the grave digger toss on dirt. The silent journey home engulfed them all in their grief.

Chapter Seven

"Well, good morning," Debbie said. She placed the breakfast tray on the side table beside Jason. "Just look at you sitting here in the rocker." She tracked across the braided rug and slid back the drapes, pushing open the window to bring in the scent of roses from the garden.

Sunlight spilled across Jason's face and he squeezed his eyes shut.

She laughed, retraced her steps, then placed a kiss upon his brow. "How do you feel this morning?"

His eyes sprang open and a playful grin tugged his lips. "Much better, now. But I'm starving near to death."

She chuckled and handed him a mug filled with steaming coffee. A delightful aroma spiraled upward from the imported brew. "Your favorite, my dear," she said.

Debbie maneuvered the breakfast tray onto his lap and smiled as he inhaled, expanding his chest.

"Mmmm…just the way I like it," he said. Appreciation radiated across his handsome face, the three day old stubble only adding to his swarthy good looks. He touched her cheek and she drew his hand to her lips, brushing his fingertips with a kiss.

"Well, you certainly look better than you did two weeks ago." Debbie swept the wrinkles from her dress and slid onto the bed beside him. "When you've finished eating, I'll need to change your bandages."

He pointed to a swath of gauze on his left side, then mumbled around a mouthful of scrambled eggs, "This right here keeps itching."

She handed him a cloth napkin. "That's because it hasn't healed."

He glided his fingers across his ribs. "Well, it still hurts here, too. And when the hell is this spot going to stop hurting?"

She laughed. "When you quit being so cantankerous, that's when."

"I can't keep lying here, Punkin. I've gotta get back to work."

Debbie straightened. "Good idea. I think I'll return to work myself come Monday."

"What? Y…You can't leave me," he sputtered, dropping his fork into the half-eaten meal. "I can't get well without your help."

Giggling, she rose to her feet. "Of course you can. Besides, your mother will see you're well-cared for."

"But, it's not the same." He slid his palm over hers, capturing her fingers between his. "I need you."

Debbie gazed into his long-lashed eyes embedded with flakes of green and gold. Haunting in their beauty, they shimmered before her. Electrified by the moment, her gaze deepened and euphoria swept through her, tugging at her heart strings. God, she loved this man. He and all his masculinity held her soul captive. She drew his hand back to her lips and brushed another kiss across his fingertips.

"You'll be fine, darling," she whispered, struggling to control her burning desire.

She released her grip and turned away to conceal her emotions.

He grimaced. "Well, as long as I have you, I can handle anything. By the way, did you hear that father has hired a new farrier?"

Debbie straightened the bed covers while gathering her composure. Then she glanced over her shoulder, forcing a smile.

"Is he the young man from Butterfield's staff?"

"Yes, Tom Bradley. And he's filling Packey's position. He's got four year's experience working thoroughbreds. He'll start Friday."

"Wonderful. I'm eager to meet him."

"By the way, did I tell you I'm returning to New York?"

She pivoted, bumping into the tray. A trembling hand clasped the rim, settling the dishes.

"So… you're going back to school?"

"Yep. I hope to start classes in the fall."

Her heart sank. How could she survive without him? Quivering fingers pushed back the hair from her brow. "Well, good, sweetheart. I…I'm happy for you."

"Come with me, Punkin. I'll find us a place and take you to meet the finest voice teachers in the country. Whatever you want."

Her heartbeat quickened. "Are you crazy? I can't just up and leave my job."

"Sure you can. If things don't work out, you can always work in a hospital."

She lowered her face, refusing to share her concerns. "I…I don't know."

Jostling the tray, Jason leaned forward and captured her chin in his hand. "Look at me," he whispered, lifting her face to meet his. Their gazes connected. "Can't we at least try this?"

Tears filled her eyes and slipped down her face. "Why are you pressing me?" she snapped, pulling free her chin. She pivoted and stalked to the door. Her fingers wrapped around the knob, yet she hesitated. Remembering his lips touching her shoulder that magical moment in the kitchen brought soothing warmth over her. Her gaze once again enveloped his features. There would be no happiness without him. Her deepest desire was to be his wife. Yet, she had discouraged marriage in order to establish a career. Could this confusion be her own fault? She loved this man more than life itself. Drawing a breath she exhaled her doubts. "I need to get fresh bandages."

"Don't leave,' he pleaded.

She stepped aside, slumping against the door frame. "How can I ever say no to you?" His tousled sable curls against the pillowcase and his bewitching eyes all claimed possession to her deepest desire.

He smiled. "Please stay!"

"I...I need to go get the supplies," she muttered, fighting to settle her nerves. Rotating on her heels, she took awkward steps into the hallway and closed the door behind her.

Life with Jason would fulfill her dreams. But, could she face a new career so soon? A troubled sigh slipped from her lips.

Why am I so afraid? Maybe I'm not ready for New York. My whole life will change. But, I love Jason and I trust him. God, I don't know what to do.

She straightened, focusing down the long corridor before her. Narrow and straight. The exact opposite of her jagged dreams.

"I must go with him," she whispered, then raised her chin and shuffled off to gather the medical supplies.

* * *

Taylor drew his hand to his brow, shading his eyes from the mid-day sun. He peered across the sweeping oval track covered by a medley of clay and sand. A white wood railing framed the turf and inside the center fence a soybean crop waved in the breeze.

The familiar chirp from a pesky mockingbird sang out from a nearby post. Taylor glanced up, "Good morning, my friend," he said with a smile. The bird was a familiar sight around the stable.

James guided Infinity onto the track. The young stud pranced, arching his neck as he fought the new bit. Wide eyed, his ears twitched and he jerked his head as James pulled him to a halt. He continued to dance in place, kicking up the sandy turf.

The jockey he'd hired last week stepped to the animal's side and adjusted the stirrups on the saddle. Billy's small frame, no bigger than a nine-year-old child, was weathered and gaunt. Like most riders, broken bones and unhealthy eating habits had plagued him over the years. He ran his boney fingers into his pants securing his shirttail, then clutched the reins in preparation to climb atop Infinity.

The farrier joined them and held the lathered horse steady. "Here, Billy, let me give you a leg up," Tom said. He lifted the jockey into the saddle, then shuffled over beside Taylor and rested his hip against the rail.

James scurried over and climbed up on a wooden box to get a better view.

"Well, he's lookin' good," Tom said, glancing at Taylor.

"You never know."

"He'll do fine," Tom assured him.

"I gave him an extra scoop of oats this morning," James said. "He always runs faster when I feed him more grain."

The two men looked at each other and chuckled.

Wide-eyed, Infinity edged inside the track. His hindquarters tightened as he bounced along swishing his tail from side to side. He jerked about, lifting on his haunches, and kicked clumps of clay into the air. Billy held a tight rein on the horse and ducked just as Infinity tossed his head trying to spit the bit.

Taylor tightened his lips. His palms filled with sweat as he watched the chess match between horse and rider unfold. He could feel the perspiration tracking down his temples. His eyes narrowed as he followed every step. Any minute he expected the young stallion to buck the rider and bolt.

Once Infinity settled his stride, Billy slacked the reins and encouraged the colt into a moderate walk...then a gentle trot. A tense moment later, Infinity's long legs reached out into a loping canter. A whip tap on his gleaming withers and the prized steed opened into a full gallop.

Taylor brushed his temples with his shirt sleeve and released a sigh.

So far... so good.

Cupping his hands around his mouth, he yelled, "Let's not work him too hard his first time out."

Billy waved his hand in acknowledgment. Finishing the second lap over the track, the jockey pulled hard on the reins. Infinity dug front hooves into the dirt and slid to a halt. Lathered and breathing hard, the colt pranced in a circle. Billy lifted his leg from the saddle and eased down to the ground, then tossed the reins to the youngster.

"Walk him good, James, and let him cool down." A dozen footfalls later, Billy stopped before Taylor. "By God, Mr. Jackson, he is one magnificent animal."

"You're damn right." Taylor boasted, puffing his chest out with pride.

"Great stride and smooth under the saddle, too. He's every rider's dream." The jockey added with a smile. "I'll be back tomorrow to work him again."

"Thanks, Billy."

Nodding, the rider stepped away.

Taylor's gaze settled on Infinity. The colt's wet coat glistened in the sunlight. His muscles, still tight from the intense workout, rippled across his withers. James released the saddle and cradled it under his left arm, then led the young stud away.

By God, this colt is everything I imagined.

His hands grasped the wheels on his chair and he followed James into the stable.

An unexpected visitor popped around the corner. Taylor choked back a snicker when he spotted Fred Jones wobbling down the path toward him, bowed legs reflecting the old boy's life. Western style shirt, pearl buttons and faded jeans was all he ever wore.

"Howdy," he said tipping his Stetson. "Remember me? I run the Silver Star Stables in eastern Kentucky. I saw you last year at the horse auction in Nashville."

"Sure do. You sold that grey stallion to John Butterfield."

He shook his head and chuckled, "That Butterfield is some character, isn't he?"

"Yes, he and I are real good friends." Taylor leaned back and gazed up into the man's face. "What can I do for you?"

"Well, I know you have the finest breeding stock this side of the Mississippi and

I'm lookin' for a couple of good mares. Perhaps one in foal. That is, if I can give a fair price," he said, adjusting his wide-brimmed hat. "I lost a good mare to colic a few weeks ago and I need to replace her."

"Sorry to hear that," Taylor said, pushing his chair through the sandy soil. "Why don't we step inside the barn out of this heat. I have a mare that might be just what you're looking for."

The horseman opened the stable door and Taylor rolled into the cool enclosure. His farrier nodded as the two men approached. He lifted his hammer and brought the steel mounting down hard against the iron shoe lodged on the anvil. A resounding charge filled the stable and sent a pulsating shock into Taylor's ears. A second later, the smithy thrust the hot metal into a water-filled barrel and steaming vapor hissed, spiraling upward.

"Doing a good job there, Tom," Taylor said, then reached for a rope hanging from a nearby hook. Rolling to the last stall, he reached inside and clipped the ring onto the horse's halter. "Now here's a nice mare that might interest you," he said, offering the man the coiled rope. "Bring her out so you can take a closer look."

Jones took the rope and Taylor opened the gate. He rolled his chair aside, and the bay mare ambled out into the corridor.

"How old is she?" the visitor questioned. He leaned over and lifted the animal's top lip to check her teeth.

"She's six."

"The cups are comin' out of the center and I can see a dovetail notch already formed in the upper corner. She looks more like seven or eight to me. But, I guess you have papers to verify her age."

"Sure do."

"Has she raced any?" He brushed his hand across the mare's withers and down her front leg.

"Half-a-dozen times," Taylor said, tipping his head to watch the man track the mare's back and flank. "She never finished less than third, though."

"Well, that sounds good. Whoa, what happened here?' Jones inquired, pointing a weathered hand at the curve of her hip. "Looks like a bad scar."

"She was kicked by another mare about a year ago. We sold that horse." Taylor pushed back in his chair and drew a shallow breath. "Can't stand a horse with an attitude."

The man scanned both sides of the mare, then examined each hoof lifting one hock at a time. "Well, she looks sound enough to me. What about foals? She appears to have been suckled."

"We still have her first foal. She's a yearling now. A nice little filly." Taylor held open the stall door as the man guided the mare back in and released her.

"I'm not interested in any yearlings."

A shuffling sound brought their attention to James leading Infinity through the open door.

Jones issued a high-pitched whistle "And, what do we have here?" He stepped around the wheel chair and stopped as James placed Infinity in his stall, latched the door, and skipped out of view.

"Now that's one fine animal," he exclaimed, leaning over the stall door to run his hand over Infinity's still glistening coat.

Taylor inhaled, puffing up with pride. His voice deepened. "This one's not for sale."

No amount of money you can offer will change my mind.

"Too bad, I could use a horse like that. He's sure a beauty."

Taylor huffed. "I have another mare in the north pasture with a three-week-old foal. If you'd like to see them, I'll have my stable boy fetch 'em."

"Damn shame," the man mumbled, his gaze still locked on Infinity. "You got a winner in this one."

"James." Taylor's voice echoed down the corridor.

The lad stuck his head out from the tack room. "Yes, sir." he said, clutching a saddle brush in his hand.

"Bring in Bess and the foal."

"You mean Coal?" His eyes widened as he pitched the brush aside.

"Yes, Coal. Now move it, boy."

James slumped, shuffling to the nearest rack of ropes. He tugged a lead off the peg and trudged out the door.

"How'd you come across that fine colt," Jones asked, pointing at Infinity.

"I won his mother in a poker game."

Jones shook his head. "Wow! That musta been one hell of a pot."

"Yes, and Butterfield is still upset."

He laughed out loud. "Butterfield! Oh, my God. Of all people. That's funny. That greedy son of a bitch, I'm surprised he didn't shoot you."

"Me, too," Taylor said, then turned as James stomped in the stable with the chestnut mare in tow. He passed the rope to Taylor and then wrapped his hand around the oversized halter on the frisky colt to stop the prancing. The foal fought to get free. "Hold still, Coal," James ordered. The young horse reared, lifting the lad off his feet before depositing him on the brick floor.

"Let him go," Taylor stated. "He'll stay with his mother."

James struggled to his feet, and brushed dust from the front of his denims with the palm of his hands. A frown creased the lad's forehead as his gaze met Taylor's.

"Are you alright?"

"Uh-huh," he muttered, lowering his head. "You ain't gonna sell Coal, are ya?"

"Yes, if Mr. Jones is interested," Taylor replied.

James swung around and ran down the corridor.

Mr. Jones examined both thoroughbreds and swept the chestnut's neck with his hand. "I like both mares, but I'm not sure I want a stud colt. Wish he was a filly."

"Not much I can do 'bout that," Taylor said. "Buy the mare, you get the foal. Besides, you can always sell him after he's weaned." The horseman offered him the lead rope. "If you don't mind, just put Bess and Coal into the birthing stall. I'll have Tom take them back out as soon as he finishes his chores."

The gentleman did as requested, placed the lead rope on a nearby hook, and then faced Taylor. "I'd like to make you an offer then," he said, tucking his hands into his pockets.

Taylor set a price, only to have the man shake his head in disagreement. "Naw, can't go that high."

After a half-hour of dickering, they settled on a price. Mr. Jones reached into his wallet, pulled out a printed draft and handed the note to Taylor. "Here's the information you'll need to draw up the bill of sales. I'll give you a deposit today and finish the deal next week when I come to pick them all up."

With the transaction complete, he slid his palm against Taylor's. "It's a pleasure doing business with ya, Mr. Jackson." His fingers touched the tip of his hat brim and he strolled out the stable door.

Taylor rolled his chair up to the birthing stall and gazed through the rails. Little Coal was nursing as the mare dipped her muzzle into a stack of hay. "Bess, you're a great mare," he said, his throat tightening. "I'm gonna miss you."

A bang of the tack room door and light footfalls brought James to his side.

Taylor glanced over his shoulder.

"Ya didn't sell them, did ya?" James asked his voice pitching.

"Yes, I did."

James pulled up on the stall rail. For a long moment he balanced in place, staring at the mare and colt. Snuffles followed as he turned to Taylor. "Jason wouldn't have sold none of them," he yelled, dropped from the railing, then ran away.

Chapter Eight

Four weeks later, Taylor rolled his chair alongside the training track and stopped before the finish line. He pulled out a silver timepiece and rubbed his thumb across the crystal facing. A smile creased his lips. This new gadget measured intervals of time in increments. Now, he could accurately measure Infinity's pace from start to finish in exact seconds.

What'll they think of next?

He narrowed his eyes as the young stallion pranced onto the track with Billy atop. A chill ran up Taylor's spine. Every nerve in his body tingled. This horse signified renewal, rebirth and a passion for life. Infinity poured strength into his soul. He lived and breathed this magnificent stallion.

The morning sun glistened on the colt's sleek coat. Ears forward and head held high, the animal advanced to the starting post. A month of practice had brought true confidence to the thoroughbred. Taylor lifted the field glasses and focused on the horse and rider. Approaching footfalls forced a glance over his shoulder.

"May I join you?" Jason asked.

"Sure," Taylor said, directing his gaze back to the track. "Glad to have you. How you been feelin'?"

"A little stiff and sore, but I'm fine," he replied, resting his foot on the split fence and bracing his elbows on the railing. "So you're going to put Infinity on the clock?"

"Yes. He's been doin' real good," Taylor boasted. "But he's still drifting on the turns."

Billy steadied the colt and gave the signal to go. Infinity dipped his haunches and surged ahead. Taylor clicked the stem on the time piece.

His heartbeat pounded in tune with thundering hooves. He pressed the field glasses tight against his eyes.

Billy tucked snug against the colt, becoming one entity. Infinity's muscles rippled as he hugged near the railing.

Taylor's body grew rigid.

Clumps of dirt kicked high as the horse and rider made the second turn. Long strides propelled them past the quarter pole and down the back stretch.

Taylor pressed forward in his chair and tried to steady his shaking hands.

Infinity rounded the final turn. They headed down the stretch. Tense seconds ticked away until the stallion blazed across the finish line.

"Magnificent," Taylor bellowed, rising high in his seat as Jason cheered. A chill rushed beneath his skin, confident the colt had finished in record time. He glanced down at his palm. "Damn it," he growled. "I forgot to stop the watch."

"I think you're starting to show your age," Jason snickered, patting his father's shoulder. "You can time him again tomorrow."

Taylor's lips drew tight and he shoved the silver time piece back into his shirt pocket.

Billy trotted the horse up before them and reined to a stop. "Well, how did we do?"

"We had a slight problem," Jason intervened, flashing a smile. "Infinity is finished for the day, Billy. Have Tom walk him out." He lowered his foot and stepped away from the rail. "Come on, Father, You're lunch is waiting." Jason fell in beside him as they headed for the stable.

Taylor glanced up at his son. "I'm getting around pretty damn good. Jeremiah brings me over every morning and James and Tom help me while I'm here. So, I'll be alright when you go back to school."

"That's great, 'cause I don't want to worry about you while I'm away." Jason opened the stable door and they entered the misty grey shadows. The uneven setting of the bricks beneath Taylor created an audible squeak from his chair. The strong scent of liniment circled around them.

"Your mother said Debbie's going to New York with you."

"I believe so."

Taylor turned the chair to face his son. "Are you thinking of getting married?"

"She doesn't want to marry, yet." Jason picked up a rake and leaned the worn handle against a nearby wall. "I have an education to think about and she wants to establish a career, be it music or medicine. She isn't like most women."

"She never has been," Taylor chuckled. "Even as a little girl, she'd pretend our dog had a broken leg, then she'd hold him in her lap and sing to him. I never dreamed that'd become a professional choice."

Jason chuckled, shaking his head.

An approaching rider drew their attention to the stable entrance. A heavy set man wearing thick spectacles stepped into view.

"Gentlemen," he spoke, offering his palm.

"Morning, Bob," Jason answered, shaking hands with their nearest neighbor.

"My condolences on your loss. Heard 'bout the wild dogs and Packey and Pearl's death a month or so ago. Terrible thing."

"Yes, sir," Jason nodded, releasing the man's hand. "I'm still recovering from my injuries."

"Well, you don't need to worry 'bout those sonsofbitches no more. They came to my place after my cattle, and we shot 'em all. Just thought I'd stop by and let you know."

"Obliged to hear that," Taylor said. "Sure don't want anybody else getting hurt by those bastards."

The neighbor glanced around the stable. "Nice place you got here, since the renovation," he said, raising his bushy brows. "Are all your horses thoroughbreds, now?"

"We have a few others; Morgan's and such," Taylor spoke, clearing his throat.

"Never knew much about race horses, but I can say for sure, you have some fine lookin' animals."

"Thanks," Jason said, walking Bob to the door. "I appreciate your stopping by." He shook the man's hand and watched him ride away. Stepping back to his father, he said, "I'm riding in to town, anything you need?' He drew a shallow breath and continued, "I want to file the papers on Bess and the colt. Oh, by the way, where is James? I haven't seen him this morning."

"He's probably up in the loft. I saw him going up the ladder earlier. He doesn't come around me much. I think he's mad because I sold the colt."

A frown creased Jason's forehead as blood rushed to his head. "Well, he needs to get over that," he shouted. "This is a business, and he can't get attached to these animals." He pivoted and heavy footfalls carried him to Blue. Jerking the halter from the horse's head he replaced it with a hackamore. Grimacing, he lifted the saddle from the rack and slung it up on the roan's back. He tightened the girth, then dropped the stirrup into place.

"I should be back in time for dinner. If not, have Millie save me a plate." He rose into the saddle, gathered the reins and tugged his hat brim low. Giving his father a nod, he rode away.

* * *

Late afternoon, Jason headed to the hospital to pick up Debbie. He found her in a back room gathering up her personal belongings.

"Hey, Punkin," he said slipping up behind her, folding her into his embrace.

A glance over her shoulder brought a smile to her lips.

He inhaled the lavender essence of her long locks and whispered, "How 'bout you and I get out of here. We've got the whole evening ahead of us."

She giggled, slipped her hand into his, and led him down the hallway and out the rear door. Several footfalls later, she pulled him into a copse of trees. Shade enveloped them, embracing them in coolness. "My roommate's home so let's stop here. I want to be alone. There's something I need to tell you."

"There is something I need to tell you, too," he chuckled.

They settled onto a wooden bench.

"I told Dr. Madison I would be leaving soon," she said.

Jason flashed a smile. "I know it was difficult for you to make that decision. But," he paused, pushed out his leg, and thrust his hand deep into his front pocket. He pulled out an envelope and slid out two tickets, presenting them to her. "I bought our vouchers for the train to New York. We leave three weeks from tomorrow?"

Her face went pale. "I wasn't expecting to leave quite so soon."

He tugged at her hand. "Now don't start having second thoughts."

"I guess I'm just afraid."

"I'll be with you every step of the way, Punkin. You'll see. You're gonna love New York."

She leaned into him and rested her forehead against his. "Thank you. I couldn't do any of this without your help."

He cupped her face. "Are you sure your roommate's home."

She smiled and lowered her gaze. "Yes, I'm sure."

Chapter Nine

Twilight settled across the landscape as Jason lowered the latch on the stable door and began his trek home. Above his head, puffy clouds faded into a grey mist across the sky and dirt devils swirled like miniature cyclones around his boots. Another damn day waiting for Debbie to make a decision. How had things become so complicated? His heels dug into the dry surface as he trudged along the lane toward the house. A good summer rain would help settle the dust and give his tobacco crop some much needed moisture. He locked the iron gates, then turned westward. Several footfalls later, he met John Butterfield astride a Morgan.

John pulled the sleek steed to a halt. "Good evening," he said.

"Evenin'," Jason replied, wrapping his hand around the horse's reins to steady the beast. "You been visiting Father?"

"Just spoke with him, but I came to see you, too. As I told him, I'm setting up a race at the county fair next week to run my two-year-olds. Thought you might want to try Infinity against other horses."

Jason squinted, focusing on the man's moonlit face.

Butterfield adjusted his weight in the saddle. John's physical health may have faltered over the years, but his mind remained impeccable. No one knew thoroughbreds better than Butterfield. And by God, Jason would always respect his opinion. "Sounds like a good idea to me."

"That's what your father said, too."

"We both believe Infinity is ready for some competition."

"Good. Then I'll see you next Friday around noon."

He nodded and watched as Butterfield disappeared into the night.

Brisk footsteps carried Jason up the flagstone walk toward the house and the sound of his mother humming reached his ears. She and father sat in rockers on the veranda, as they did most every summer evening, the oil lamp burning between them, illuminating their features. His mother waved a fan before her cheeks to stir the stifling heat, while father sat dozing in a favorite chair.

"Hello, darling," she said, as Jason stopped in front of them.

He smiled. "Bought tickets for Debbie and me to go to New York. She's already notified the hospital. We leave in three weeks."

"Can you leave that soon?" Kathryn asked, collapsing her sandalwood fan and placing it on the side table.

"It'll be fine. We just need to get a place to live. We'll have our belongings shipped later." His father stirred, drawing Jason's attention. "By the way, I just talked to Butterfield. If Infinity does well at the fair, then he should be ready to enter a major race."

"Do you think he's ready?" Taylor questioned.

"Yes. But, if you need any more help, Butterfield would be glad to assist."

A muffled laugh fell from his father's lips. "He'll assist all right. That conniving son of a bitch'll try to get Infinity any way he can."

Jason snickered. "Now, don't be so hard on John. You know you are best friends and he loves that colt as much as you do."

"Sure he does," Taylor grumbled. "That's why he wants him back."

With another chuckle, Jason pulled a letter from his pocket, then dropped the note onto the table between them. .

"This is the other thing I wanted to say." His gaze darted to his mother as a lump the size of Texas rested in his throat. "I went to the court house today and filed papers to have my surname changed to Jackson."

She released a small gasp.

Taylor raised the paper toward the lamplight and squinted.

Escalating anxiety bit at Jason's nerves as he awaited their reaction. "I grew up believing Sam Dillon was my father." The calmness in his voice concealed the twisting turmoil in his gut. The roots of this family were such a mess. He blinked, holding back the mounting tears. "You're my father and I know it. It's time I acknowledged my heritage."

Damn, even his palms were sweating.

His mother rose from the chair, as a soft snuffle escaped her lips. She stepped over and embraced him. "This means everything to me."

"It means a lot to all of us."

She leaned back. "I didn't want to burden you with my shame. We'd only been married a few months when he was called off to war. When he was killed, I had no choice but to declare Sam as your father. I had to protect you. That just seemed like the right thing to do."

He kissed her forehead. "Well, now it's time I did the right thing."

"I don't know what to say," Taylor mumbled. "I never expected this."

Jason slipped from his mother's arms and leaned over, hugging his father. "The Dillon name is put to rest. From now on, this is the Jackson Estates. There will be no doubt in anyone's mind that I belong to you both."

Taylor grasped Jason's hand, then whispered, "Thank you, son."

His mother drew a handkerchief from her pocket and dabbed her lashes just as Millie arrived at the front door to announce dinner.

"Let's eat," Jason said, "I'm starvin'."

* * *

Two weeks was too damn long not to see his love. Jason hitched the carriage and headed into town.

He pulled the mare to a stop before Debbie's apartment. As he jumped to the ground, he held rein on the smoldering desire that billowed inside. Taking the front steps two at a time, he bounded to the door. He swept his Stetson from his head, then raked his fingers through his hair, sucking in a deep breath. His heartbeat thundered as images of her naked in the moonlight swam to the surface of his thoughts. The passion she had displayed equaled any woman twice her age. Lovemaking for Debbie was as natural as breathing. He kept them apart for months while he sorted things out in his mind and heart. But no more. Every fantasy, every dream, screamed for him to take this goddess, again and again.

No damn pack of dogs or anything else will stop me now.

He rapped his knuckles on the door, clamping his hand into a ball. His palm grew moist as he waited. Blood rushed into the swell of his jeans, begging for relief. A flurry of curtains from the nearby window revealed his angel peeping at him through the glass. Her smile, once again, sent a driving need straight to the core of his groin.

A second later, the door wrenched open.

"Oh, Jason, I'm so glad you're here." She stood on tiptoes and kissed his lips. "What brings you into town?"

"I came to take you home for the weekend. Thought you'd wanna see the family before we leave."

"Let me get my things." She closed the door and brushed past him. The fragrance of roses wafted around him. Tresses as bronze as burnished chestnuts garnished her shoulders and caught in the play of the afternoon sun. She sashayed across the room. His gaze dipped to the curve of her buttock. Beneath his ribs, his heart pounded. He'd never been so captivated by any other woman. And whores he frequented in the past were a dime a dozen and meant little in his scheme of things. However, the sun rose and set in Debbie, stirring a need within him that engulfed his soul. Pure and genuine, yet provocative. His body tightened again.

She vanished into the bedroom and he drew a breath to calm his nerves.

The pendulum on the mantel clock grew more intense with each tick, teasing him as he waited for her return.

Moments later, she stepped into view, the bounce of her breasts catching his gaze. Lush. Full. Again, he longed to cup their softness. His breath trapped in his throat as the need for her ripened inside.

She dropped the bag in a nearby chair and pivoted to face him. He stroked her arm, then trailed his fingers across her shoulder and beneath her chin.

"Kiss me, Punkin," he muttered, and then without waiting for permission, he bent and captured her mouth. Slowly, his hand lowered, palming her curves. The warmth of her skin branded his fingertips and he gazed into her eyes. Dark flakes of gold surrounded by hazel taunted as radiant and pure as the moon glow on the evening of their first kiss.

He nibbled down her neck, tasting the richness there until he nestled his face in her tresses. Her scent, once more, enveloped him as she released a groan against his mouth.

"You're a Goddess," he rasped. "An angel from heaven. God, how I need you! "

She smiled, then whispered, "Wait… Come with me." She clasped her palm against his and led him down the hallway. The click of the bedroom lock closed out the rest of the world.

"Will your roommate be back?" he asked, peering into her bewitching eyes.

"No, she's gone for the evening."

"Nice." He smiled and drew her closer. His lips pressed against her collarbone as his fingers unhooked each tiny button down her back. The gingham waist unfolded and the material drifted from her shoulders. His gaze caressed every curve still covered before meeting hers again.

Her mouth bowed upward. "Do you like what you see?"

"Oh, yes!"

"Need help?" she asked, giggling

"You're a devil," he chuckled. "How many layers have you got on?"

"Enough to make it interesting."

He slid his hands down her camisole, delighting in the texture of the spun silk. With a flick of his wrist, the piece went up and over her head. A moment later, he dropped the pastel garment to the floor.

She touched his cheeks, then kissed him full on the mouth as she glided her hands down his torso. His muscles tightened and he moaned as her roaming fingers swept beneath his shirt and across his bare chest. His erection strained against his denims.

He pushed aside her petticoat. Each layer revealing more flesh. His gaze absorbed all of her beauty. Breathtaking. Incredible. She radiated like Venus.

"I want every part of you," he murmured.

In the distance, the mantel clock chimed. Jason smiled.

Time has no boundaries when I'm with you, my darling.

He drew her to him. Slower this time, he cherished her, kissing her lips. His hands tightened around her waist, and then down over her full hips. With a surge of power, he lifted her up against him. Rigid muscles pulsated with a torment to bury deep inside this angel.

Her hands slipped beneath his jeans and he sucked in a jagged breath. He reached to unbutton his shirt.

"Wait… let me do that." She nudged aside his hands. "How dare you deny me the pleasure!" Trembling fingers unlocked each pearl button as she made her way to his leather belt. She settled her hands on the initialed silver buckle and he engulfed her hands with his.

"I'll take care of that, my dear," he insisted. With one jerk he freed the belt from the loops.

"Well, Mr. Jackson, what a dynamic beast you are," she giggled.

He chuckled, then unfastened the metal buttons. The denims hit the wall and fell, as a smile creased his lips. His gaze enveloped her. "So, do you like what you see?" he asked, his lips shifting to a lopsided grin.

"I certainly do. I must say, you have a lot to offer a woman."

"You're the only woman I want. Now…or ever."

He swept her into his arms and placed her on the bed. An audible creak emerged from the bedsprings as he lowered her onto the mattress. She snuggled near him. His manhood surged to life beneath her skillful caress. He covered her breast with his mouth, relishing the exquisite perfection of her nub. The sweet nipple puckered beneath his tongue. Her body arched as he tasted every delicious morsel of her flesh.

"Oh, God, Jason," she panted. "I need you so."

He slipped his hand to the heat of her soul. Slowly, he caressed her until she offered him his reward. He eased over her, his weight forcing her deeper into the mattress. Her fingers tightened on his shoulders and she panted his name in his ear.

"Easy, Punkin," he whispered, locking her warmth against his bare skin. He wanted to savor every glorious moment. He drove into her with all the force of his love. They melted into one perfect harmony, rising and falling in a rhythmic wave. Each time reaching a new plateau. She cried out. He drove deeper, euphoria growing until she quivered and released her love. Moments later, he reached the summit and escaped into a haze of ecstasy. He groaned and clamped her in his arms.

"I love you," he rasped, kissing her soft lips.

"And I love you, too." She lifted her hands and stroked his cheeks.

For a long moment, he remained locked in her love. Rising on his palms, he gazed at her breasts, as the setting sun flickered across her skin.

"You're so beautiful," he said. "And I'm the luckiest man in the world."

She opened her eyes and smiled.

Finally, he fell exhausted onto the pillow. She pressed against him and he slipped his arm around her.

No more than a heartbeat later, voices radiated in the parlor followed by footsteps and a knock upon the door.

Jason raised and whispered, "Is that your roommate?"

She drew a finger to her lips to silence him."

A woman's voice etched beneath the door. "Debbie, are you in there?"

"I thought she was out for the evening?" Jason whispered, laughing.

She angled onto an elbow and said, "Shhh! I need to say something or she'll try to come in."

He nodded.

"Yes," she hollered.

From the opposite side of the door came a muffled question. "Have you seen my medicine?"

A frown creased Debbie's forehead. "I put the bottle in the cabinet where you usually keep it."

"Thanks," the voice reverberated through the keyhole, followed by footsteps trailing down the hallway.

Jason slid beneath the sheet as she rolled away. Her gaze met his. "Sorry," she whispered.

He snickered. "I'm just glad she didn't come ten minutes earlier."

She leaned over, her finger tracing his brow. "You have gorgeous eyes."

He caressed her lips and she captured his fingers between her teeth, holding them, gentle, yet firm. With a light touch she glided her tongue across the tips. The tingle exploded in every nerve of his body and he cupped her face.

"You little minx…that tickles," he said, rubbing his thumb against her soft jaw.

She giggled, then sat up covering her breasts with the pillow. "I wish every day could be like this."

Jason folded his arms behind his head. "They could be, if you'd marry me."

She swerved to face him. "You're serious? Marry you?" She scooted to the edge of the bed. "What about law school? And…and my voice training?"

"We can go to New York. Get married… and both attend school. It's not like we don't have the money."

He eased up behind her, pushing her long locks aside. His lips found her shoulder. "Marry me."

She glanced back and her lips met his, deep, passionate, reaffirming their love. As their kiss broke apart, she whispered, "Of course, I'll marry you."

An hour later and fully dressed, Jason placed Debbie's bag in the surrey. He helped her onto the rig and she settled onto the tufted cushion seats.

Jason climbed up beside her, lifting the leather reins. A sharp whistle later, the Morgan pulled forward, her sleek coat glistening in the moonlight. Prancing hooves clicked along the stone-covered street and onto the gravel road westward. A silver glow illuminated the hillside and brought a sigh to his lips. Shadows dappled the landscapes as clouds chased after the moonbeams. Debbie rested her head on his shoulder. Her gentle breathing told him she slept. Jason leaned over and kissed her forehead. The soft puffs of her breath echoed in every beat of his heart.

All is perfect.

Nothing could come between them now.

Chapter Ten

Pounding hooves echoed through the night. Three riders, blanketed in shadows approached the carriage. Jason straightened and glanced over his shoulder. His heartbeat quickened. Drinking and carousing on a summer's eve was common this time of year and their raucous laughter spilled into the night.

He stared at their silhouettes. One broad-shouldered and husky, the other two were much leaner. And all three were shabbily dressed. Their mounts were underfed, their coats unkempt and the tack old and worn. They drew closer and closer. He tightened his grip on the reins, slapping them against the Morgan's rump to double her gait.

"Wake up, Punkin," he said, touching her arm.

Debbie roused, pushing to sit up. "What's wrong?"

"We've got company." He lowered his hand beneath the seat, locking his fingers around the rifle's wooden stock. He gave a tug, but the Remington lodged between his boots and the bench. His muscles knotted as he fought to untangle the weapon from a rope he carried for emergencies.

The lead rider thundered past and grabbed the Morgan's bridle, forcing the mare to stop. A shaggy horse settled next to their carriage, as the bandit astride the saddle pointed his pistol at Jason. The other two men flanked the buggy. Debbie gasped as the ruffians drew their guns.

"I wouldn't try anything if I were you," the scar-faced bastard said, spitting a wad of tobacco to the ground. His gravelly voice swept from beneath a full beard, sending a chill down Jason's spine.

Glancing at Debbie, Jason saw tears gather beneath her lashes. His heart thundered at the thought of her being harmed.

His gaze darted back to the gunman. "What do you want?" he snapped, glaring into the hooligan's drunken face.

The bushy-faced, swollen-eyed sonofabitch refused to answer, instead wiping his lips across his shirt sleeve. "Pete," he snapped to the rider on his left. "Why don't you hop in the back there and make sure these folks don't try somethin' stupid."

The taller of the two men looped the reins around the metal railing, then swung aboard the surrey. The stench of whiskey gagged Jason as the man settled next to Debbie's traveling bag.

Debbie buried her face in his shoulder.

The bandit sunk filthy fingers into a fistful of her hair and jerked her head backward, forcing a scream past her lips. He placed his revolver near her temple, laughing. "Don't make me blow your head off these pretty shoulders, missy. You sit real still now."

Jason surged toward the bandit only to feel the blow of the third man's rifle butt against his head. Pain exploded above his cheek. The throbbing knot expanded, obstructing his vision. Rough hands shoved him back into his seat and metallic-tasting blood filled his mouth. He darted his tongue sideways to locate a chipped tooth.

Pete yanked Debbie's hair and she screamed, again.

Clamping his jaw tight, Jason straightened.

I'll kill every one of you bastards.

The bearded man growled, "Hand over that rifle you're hidin' before I blow a hole in your gut. And bring it up nice and slow."

Jason swiped away the blood, his gaze narrowing. He wrapped his hand around the rifle's cold metal and untangled the rope.

A quick pull brought the weapon up between them. The barrel slid through his palm, his knuckles cracked against the steel as he extended the Remington to the rider.

The gunman balanced the rifle across his lap. "Now." He pointed southward. "Turn this fancy buggy down that lane right over there."

The man swiveled in the saddle and Jason lunged toward him. The third rider's rifle butt again met Jason's head. The jolt whipped his neck around. A spray of blinding lights flashed before him as a numbing force swept through his body. He swayed, falling back to the buggy's seat.

Debbie cried out. "Please...please don't hurt him." She stretched sideways to shield him, but Pete yanked her back once more. Her sobs echoed around Jason as she pleaded for his life. He raised a limp hand toward her, only to falter. Lost in a daze, he dropped back against the seat.

Blood etched in a chilling path down his face and across his lips. He coughed, spraying a shower of crimson onto his sleeve. Tipping his head back, he fought against a hovering black void.

The leader waved his pistol in front of Jason. "Now, let's try this again, asshole. Move the damn rig, now," he grumbled.

"Go to hell," Jason sneered.

The rider leaned forward, sending forth a waft of rancid breath. "Wrong answer."

The hammer on his Colt clicked. The sound radiated through Jason and a sharp order brought the third rider forward.

A jangle of spurs and the slim man edged up beside the mare, then leaned down, grasping the bridle.

Jason's blurred vision tracked back to the leader. "Let her go and I'll do whatever you want."

The bearded man spit more tobacco and released a wicked laugh. He wiped his chin, then spit again. "I'm sure you will."

Debbie whimpered and Jason's heart wrenched. He could not protect her from these demons. Guilt spread through him with the raging fury of a wild fire.

The surrey rolled beneath Slim's urging. Fighting back the frustration, Jason stared into the darkness as the mare moved off the main road onto the lane. His muscles tightened. With every scuffle of the horse's hooves, Jason's blood pumped faster. He clinched his teeth. Outnumbered and overpowered, he pulled in a tattered breath trying to capture his last ounce of strength to battle these monsters.

I'll never rest until you're all dead.

The group led them into the forest under a stifling bower of hardwoods.

"What the hell do you want?" he snapped. "Just let her go. I'll give you anything you ask."

"Oh, you'll give us what we want all right." The rider pivoted to the man in the back seat. "Pete, shut this bastard up."

"Sure thing, boss," he responded.

Jason lunged for Debbie just as the butt of Pete's pistol flashed toward him. A crashing blow to his skull and a numbing pain exploded inside as everything went black.

* * *

Rustling sounds echoed in Jason's ears. He blinked, trying to focus on the swaying canopy of leaves overhead. A chalk white moon glared between tangled branches and a frown tugged at his brow. The throbbing pulse of his heartbeat pounded in his head. Pushing his fingers through blood-crusted hair, he flinched as he touched the lump on his skull. Dark shadows whispered mysterious calls in the night, bringing him forward.

Fear for Debbie's safety crushed him with the strength of a python, squeezing his tortured soul. His eyes narrowed. A haunting mist blanketed the forest floor. She was gone. He fell back and starred at the shredded remnants of a cloud as it passed the moon. Tears seeped from the corners of his eyes. Fallen pecan shells pushed at his back. He tightened his muscles to escape their punishment. His heart screamed for her return, but the night swept her away.

He rolled onto his side and angled upward. His elbows ground against spongy moss as he shifted onto his hip. The stench of a rotting animal carcass demanded a glance into tangled briars. Surrounded by unfamiliar terrain he pushed against the mossy turf and groped to his feet. The drumming inside his head shattered his thoughts as he weaved along the lane.

I should've protected you, Punkin... Good God, how I've failed you.

An owl screeched from high above. Jason stopped, swirling in place; he strained to hear a movement. Narrowing his eyes, he shouted her name. The darkness delivered back only silence. He tightened to stop the swaying of his aching legs. In the distance, he saw the outline of the surrey shrouded in a misty haze. He drew a deep breath and stumbled forward.

Several footfalls later, he arrived at the overturned rig. She, her luggage, and the horse were gone. His heart sank. He slid to the ground beside the buggy's wheel.

That wooly faced son of a bitch took her.

His stomach knotted. Vomit gathered in his throat. He swallowed hard.

They'll rape her or kill her.

Jason shoved to his feet, pain rolling through him.

I've got to find her, now.

He stumbled to the main thoroughfare. Noticing familiar landmarks he glanced in both directions. *Halfway between home and Lexington.*

Swerving toward town, he swiped at the fresh blood oozing from a gash across his nose. With each step, the lump on his cheekbone throbbed. A moan escaped his lips. His boot heels ground into the gravel, each stride reminding him of the stabbing pain he felt for Debbie's safety.

The distant sound of a lone rider approaching jerked him from his torment. He pivoted and narrowed his eyes, gazing down the dark corridor.

Have the bandits returned?

He stiffened, waiting for a glimpse of the horseman. Moments later, a young man aboard a stocky draft horse rode into view. Jason raised his hands flagging down the rider.

"What ya doin' out here this time of night?" the lad asked.

"I...I need help," Jason stammered, grabbing the boy's leg. "I gotta get the sheriff."

"What happened?"

"I was robbed." Jason's voice quivered as he choked out each word. "They beat me. Took my woman and my horse. I'll kill those sons of bitches when I catch up to 'em."

"Well, I'm headed into town. Hop on and I'll give ya a ride."

* * *

Two hours later, an orange sky washed the horizon as they finally rode into Lexington. Every minute away from Debbie was too damn long.

God only knows where she is now.

Jason slid off the horse as the rider continued his journey southward. A quick glance around and Jason spotted the jailhouse. Long strides carried him up the steps onto the wooden walkway. He tightened his hand and pounded on the door.

"Yah, come in," a muffled voice replied.

Slipping into the building, Jason scanned the dim room. An unfamiliar face glared back at him from beneath bushy eyebrows. Jason slammed the door behind him. In no mood to mince words, he slung aside a spindle-backed chair before the man. "Where's the sheriff?" he growled.

"Not here," he stated, flexing his jaw. He took a sip of coffee from a chipped mug, then lowered the cup onto the edge of a paper-cluttered desk.

"I'm the deputy. Somethin' I can do fer ya?"

"I've been robbed." Jason angled his head, peering at the man above his swollen cheek.

The deputy frowned. "You look like hell. Want me to fetch the doctor?"

"No! We've gotta find these bastards." He lunged forward, his words caught in his throat. "They kidnapped my woman."

The man shuffled through some papers, then opened a side drawer and pulled out a form. "Fill this out," he mumbled from beneath a thick mustache.

Jason drew a breath and leaned forward, his brows slamming together. "I don't have time for this shit. We've gotta go, now."

The man rolled his eyes. He sat back in his chair, crossing his arms. A forced sigh and he locked his stare with Jason's. "You need to fill the papers out first."

The blood surged through Jason's veins. "God damn it, you're not listening to me."

"Can't help you without it, son."

Clinching his teeth, Jason slammed his fist upon the desk. The chipped coffee cup rattled upon the pine. Droplets of thick black brew splashed across the paper. "Don't give a rat's ass about your form."

"You'd better settle down right now, mister," the deputy snapped, holding up the long draft.

Jason glared at the man, then snatched the paper from his hand. He grabbed a pencil and scribbled in the blanks. With a huff, he threw the form to the table and the draft slid across the desk to stop in front of the deputy. "Now, can we go?"

The man peered over the paper. "So, you're the one who owns Crystal Falls. I've heard of that place."

Jason felt the blood flush his cheeks. "Damn it, man, we need to move."

The deputy grasped the chair arms and his knuckles grew pale. He drew a ragged breath. "Let me get a couple of my men and we'll ride out and take a look."

I've had enough of this arrogant jackass.

Jason edged closer and glared into the man's eyes. "Where's the sheriff?"

"He's out of town for the week." The deputy nosed forward. "Get your horse and meet me out front so we can get started."

Anger ignited a demon inside Jason and he straightened. "I told you they stole my horse," he sneered.

"Head to the livery. I'm sure George will loan you a gelding."

"Fine. I'll be right back."

"Meet us out front." The deputy pushed away from his desk, stood and then folded the complaint form, stuffing it into a shirt pocket.

Jason tromped out of the jailhouse, slamming the door as he exited. He weaved his way toward the stable, squinting against the glare of the rising sun. Every muscle in his body tightened with the tension of an archer's bow. A bitter emptiness gnawed at his stomach. Each minute, each precious second, mattered. Debbie's life teetered on his success.

He widened his stride.

Rounding the corner, the stable filled his view. The owner, and good friend, George Parker, stepped from the shadows. "I need a favor."

Pivoting, the balding man creased a smile. "Sure. What do you need?"

"I need your fastest horse." He gave a brief explanation as he followed George into the stable. Horses munched on their morning feed as he scanned the dusty shadows. Rotting manure lay piled in haphazard mounds near the stalls. The stench stung Jason's throat and brought forth a bone-rattling cough.

"You all right, Jason?"

A quick nod was all the answer he allowed.

George pointed toward the last stall. "The bay with the blaze face is probably the best I have."

"He'll do fine," Jason mumbled.

The stableman brought the gelding out and tied him to a post. "I was at the fairground last week and watched your colt race," he said, placing the blanket on the bay's back. "That horse can really run. Why, he left the others in a cloud of dust."

"Yes, yes, I'm in a hurry. We can talk about that later," Jason said, as he handed George a bridle, then he pulled up into the saddle. "Thanks for the horse. I'll get him back to you." He jerked the reins to the side and cantered off into the street.

Meeting the deputy and his two companions, he speared the officer a wicked glance. "Ready?"

"Lead the way," the man said.

Jason dug his heels into the gelding's sides and galloped northward.

An hour later, he slid from the saddle before the over-turned surrey. "They came at us from over there," he said, pointing southward. "Then, they brought us here."

"Take a look around, boys," the deputy ordered.

The posse ambled along, bobbing from side to side. Heads lowered, the elderly rider pointed at a rut in the road and his companion shook his head.

Jason tightened his jaw.

The deputy rode ahead a quarter of a mile or so and then galloped back to join the others.

A frown tugged at Jason's brow.

Get off your horses, you jackasses. Take a closer look.

Minutes later, the men gathered at the road's edge. Jason strained to hear the conversation, then the deputy rode up before him and reined to a halt. "We don't see nothin'. I'll let you know if I hear anything."

"What?" Jason bellowed. "That's it? Can't you follow tracks or something?"

"Nope, ground's too hard; besides, I couldn't tell robbers' tracks from any others. Sorry. I'll tell the sheriff when he gets back. We'll keep your complaint on file."

Jason clinched his fist and turned away. His heart thumped as he tightened his jaw. The blood surged to his head and he wheeled around. "You stupid bastards. I knew you were worthless when I first saw you."

Squinting one eye, the deputy growled, "I could arrest you for talkin' to me like that!"

"Get the hell out of here, before I shoot your sorry ass."

The deputy jerked the reins and whirled around. Moments later the three men galloped away.

"Damn it," Jason ranted, kicking a clump of dirt from the lane. "All that time wasted." He dropped back against the surrey as tears gathered in his eyes.

Oh, God, Debbie. I'm so sorry.

His shoulders quivered as grief swept through him. The weight of her disappearance smacked him in the gut.

If I'd only stayed home, she wouldn't be missing.

The ache in his heart exploded and he sank to his knees sobbing.

Chapter Eleven

Debbie lowered onto a rickety crate inside an equally rickety woodshed. She waved her hand before her face as flies and mosquitoes swarmed around her. In a far corner, dangling from the rafters, a wasp nest buzzed with activity. Even a bumble bee had found his way in through a nearby knothole to join her.

Near the back wall, a pile of rotting logs rested beside a barrel and a half dozen or so empty feed bags. The only light, a campfire flickering outside the shack, weaved its light between weathered boards.

Trembling, she drew up her knees. The fear of a snake slithering from beneath the rubble caused her to pull her legs in tight. A moldy stench engulfed her lungs and a dry cough erupted.

Shaking, Debbie drew herself up into an even tighter ball, hovering between the good and evil of the past few hours. She bowed her head and sobbed.

Oh, Jason. Less than twenty four hours ago you made me the happiest person alive. Now, I just want to die.

A rustling beyond her prison caught her attention. Her gaze settled on the plank door. Male voices minced together as they drew near the shack.

She straightened, lowering her feet to the ground. Her eyes widened. Her palms grew moist.

The metal chain on the door rattled.

She sucked in a sharp breath.

Oh, God, no!

The panel creaked wide, allowing her mumbled prayers to escape. A piercing light spilled into the void and she narrowed her eyes onto grubby fingers holding high a lantern.

"Where's Jason?" she snapped, bolting to her feet. "Did you just leave him laying there?"

Her fractured words went ignored as Pete hung the lamp on the center post and stepped aside as his accomplice entered. The metal handle scraped across the rusty nail, underscoring the terror pummeling through her. Shadows flickered across their menacing features.

A broken smile loomed closer. "Tie her up," Slim demanded, releasing a guttural laugh. Debbie stiffened and turned away when Pete grabbed her wrist.

"Come here, sweetie," he rasped. "Tonight you're mine." He pulled a thick rope from his back pocket, then wove the raspy hemp around her wrists.

Weakening legs shook and her body stiffened as she braced to challenge their advance. "No, no." she whimpered. "Please. No…Go away." The devilish faces of the two men closed in. She screamed, backing up against the rough timber. "Leave me alone."

"Not on your life, sweetheart. I haven't had a poke in months and I'm gonna get one tonight, for sure."

The door rattled open and the bushy-bearded leader stuck his head inside. "I'm goin' after the wagon. She's a fine beauty, so don't rough her up too much."

"Sure thing, boss," Pete sneered. The door banged shut and he turned to his partner. "Help me get her down, then wait outside. After I have mine, then you'll have your turn."

"Why do you get her first?"

"'Cause I said so. Now get to movin'."

Debbie's eyes widened as the two edged nearer. The blood rushed to her head and she blinked to focus. The filthy bastards crept closer. She backed further into the corner. "No," she cried. "Please...no!"

Pete seized her arm and she buckled. Slim's greasy hold tightened around her waist.

Screaming, she kicked and flailed, trying to jerk free. The heathens held her in a vice-like grip and pushed her to the floor.

Pete looped the dangling rope end around a center pole while Slim struggled to restrain her thrashing legs. The sound of her pounding pulse merged with their devilish laughter ringing in her ears. Pete pressed forward, ripping aside her camisole. His callused hands dug into her breasts, then pushed beneath her drawers.

"Noooo!" she screamed, barely recognizing her own voice.

Slim leaned in.

"Get the hell outta here," Pete raged, shoving Slim toward the door. The hellion who bashed in Jason's head glared at her, then turned and stalked out.

A crooked smile crossed Pete's lips as he loomed over her. The cloying stench of whiskey and soured perspiration filled the air around her. Greasy hair slapped across her face as he forced a slimy tongue into her ear. She retched. A sharp breath lodged in her throat as he penetrated her, ripping her tender flesh with the same vicious brutality as the pack of wild dogs that ripped apart Pearl.

His sweat splattered onto her face, rolling into the creases of her lips. She spit, yet the vulgar taste remained. His body pounded hers and with each violent lunge upward, he crushed the air from her lungs. His mouth covered hers.

Clamping her teeth together, she jerked away.

Filthy hands squeezed her breasts, twisting them until they burned with pain.

She cried out.

Prickly whiskers braised her flesh as he ground his chin into her shoulder. Nausea swept over her and she swallowed back the bile, fearing she would strangle on her own vomit. She twisted her hips, struggling to deny him deeper penetration, but failed.

With all her strength, she spiked her heels into his legs, pushing hard to pry him away. He pelted her knees with his fists and then slapped her hard across the face. The numbing blow sent her mind reeling.

For an instant, she pulled free and scooted away.

He grabbed her leg and rolled her over, climbing back on top of her. Every rigid muscle in her neck denied her breath. With another heavy lunge and a rutty groan, he released his seed.

Panting, he rolled off her. Rough hands pushed against her shoulders as he shoved to his feet. A smirk pulled his lips askew as he hiked up his pants. For a moment he stood over her, but said nothing.

She returned his glare. *Rot in hell, you bastard.*

The vicious violation had stripped away her pride. Her life, now shattered, she could never return to Jason. Tears gathered in the corners of her eyes and rolled down.

Finally, he staggered from the building.

Her clothes lay torn and tossed aside, much like any future she had ever hoped to have with Jason. Trembling hands tugged at the bondage, but the rope cut deeper into her skin. Blood seeped onto the twine and she bit her lip to contain her screams.

Less than a heartbeat later, Slim rushed in and the terror of the night continued. As his body drove deep, she willed her thoughts into another time. Visions of happier moments with Jason in the kitchen that evening. On the way up the hill for a picnic. Wrapped in the splendor of his arms.

The less she fought the monster on top of her, the sooner the nightmare would end.

With a final grunt he finished his assault and she whimpered when he cut the rope from her burning wrists.

Debbie squeezed her eyes tight until she heard the slamming door. A broken sigh escape her lips and she settled her gaze onto the hornets' nest.

Their stings wouldn't have hurt nearly as much. Slowly, she angled onto her elbow. Chilled, she pulled on her tattered dress and pressed back, staring at the ceiling.

The lantern's light infused in the delicately woven spider webs swaying overhead. Harmless in appearance, each waited to capture unsuspecting prey, just as she was caught in an inescapable trap. She let her eyes drift closed and forced her pain to the far corners of her mind. Exhausted and sore, she slipped into an uneasy sleep, hoping the agony would somehow disappear.

The comfort of her dreams was shattered by voices outside the shed. Pete swung open the door and pulled her to her feet. A well dressed man leaning on a black lacquered walking stick stepped into view.

"This is the one," Pete growled, ripping the torn garments from her hands. She gasped. Her cheeks grew hot, and she shrugged, turning away. Pete grabbed her arm and whirled her back around. "Damn it, wench," he raged. "Stand still."

Debbie lowered her head, refusing to make eye contact with the white-haired man. He loomed closer, grasping her chin and twisting her face back to look at him. His gaze traced her body. He pointed the walking stick. "Nice breasts," he mumbled, peering through his spectacles. His free hand massaged the tip of a well-groomed beard. Aging lips creased a crooked smile and he said, "Turn around."

She glared at the man, then dropped to her knees. "No!" She gasped.

The man smirked.

Pete jerked her up. "Shut up and do as you're told." His palm landed a powerful blow across her face and she rocked backward. Regaining her balance, she drew a choppy breath and straightened. Tears welled in her eyes as she turned slightly before them. Her tongue touched the corner of her mouth and a bitter droplet of blood oozed from her lip. She lowered her gaze, slipping her eyelids shut. Tears rolled down her cheeks.

Oh, Jason, where are you? Please help me.

"Feisty little bitch, isn't she?" the visitor chirped.

Debbie opened her eyes and drilled her gaze into his.

"She'll do," he said. "Have her at the dock before dawn, day after tomorrow. I'll pay you half now. The rest when she is delivered. Alive."

Pete nodded and smiled as his guest picked four coins from a pouch and dropped them into his grime-stained hand.

The elderly man turned and swung the door wide. Flames from the campfire danced beyond his image, reminding Debbie of the hell she had just endured. She wanted no part of this repulsive mans plans.

"Pay?" she hissed. "I'm no slave. How dare you?"

He pivoted to face her and the door banged shut. His eyes sparked with anger. "Shut her up," he barked, thumping his cane in the dirt floor. His glare cut through the shadows. "I want her bound and gagged," he said, ramming his hand into his pocket and pulling out a small bottle.

"And use this if you have to. We can't have her raising a commotion on the boat."

She lunged at him and yelled, "Boat, what boat? Where are you taking me?"

Pete grabbed her shoulders and heaved her back against the wall. She heard the weathered boards crack and the impact shot a wicked pain across her already bruised ribs.

Everything whirled.

Her gaze drew upward in time to see the knuckles of a clinched fist sweeping toward her face. A numbing blow to her chin sent everything black.

Chapter Twelve

Jason's heart ached as he glanced across the forest floor. A woodpecker tapped on a nearby oak tree, mocking the throbbing in his head. A breeze rustled through the branches and a chill washed his body. Alone, exhausted and bewildered, he gazed up through fluttering leaves.

Where on God's earth are you, Punkin? It's my fault you're gone. I'm so sorry.

He struggled to his feet, then squinted, scanning the area once more. Even in this remote part of the forest, there was still no sign of her. Darkness settled fast across the clearing. He gathered the bay and grabbed a handful of mane pulling up into the saddle. Nudging the gelding forward, he followed the scattered hoof prints along the lane until night took away even the faintest marks of the captors or other horses and vehicle tracks. Reaching the main road he reined to a stop. Guilt echoed through every bone in his body. He released a heavy sigh, then spurred the horse toward home.

His thoughts settled on his parents.

They'll be devastated. Everyone loves Debbie.

Her smile flashed across his mind and then a choking sob of sorrow wrenched him apart.

An hour later, he stabled the horse behind the house, leaving a note for James to return the borrowed gelding in the morning. Heavy-laden footfalls carried him up the stone walk. A shaking hand settled onto the front door knob. He paused and drew a ragged breath. His palms sweat as he imagined the response from his parents.

I hate this...Oh, God, but I must tell them.

Everything blurred as his shattered dreams melted into the reality of this nightmare.

He steadied his shaking legs and his hand turned the knob. A slight hesitation and he stepped across the threshold. The dark hallway gathered around him, reminding him of a thief's cloak. Then his mother's soothing voice touched his ears and a favorite lullaby placed a lump in his throat. Stepping into the parlor, he stopped before her and she pushed back in the rocker and her gaze met his.

Her song fell silent.

A sleeping Mason snuggled closer as an audible gasp reached Jason's ears.

"My God, son, what happened? Were you in a fight?"

"Where's father?"

"In his room."

Jason leaned closer. "Put Mason to bed," he whispered, heading toward the sidebar. "Then you both come back in here."

"I'll be right back," she said and scurried past him.

Jason poured a shot of whiskey, gulped it down then poured another. He glanced at the clock. So many precious minutes, lost. Somewhere, someone must've seen those bastards. Moments later his mother returned, pushing Taylor into the room. The squeak of the wheelchair ricocheted across Jason's nerves.

"What's wrong?" she asked again, her eyes widening.

"It's... Debbie. S-She's missing."

"Missing?" his father bellowed, straightening in his chair.

His mother gasped, covering her mouth with her fingertips. "Oh, my God, Jason, what happened?"

His gaze shifted to his father. "We were on our way home. It was late. Three bastards rode up and pulled guns on us. One got in the buggy and put a pistol to Debbie's head. I had to do what they said. The next thing I knew,

I was on the ground. Debbie, the horse and her baggage…all gone." Jason's body quaked.

"She'll be raped," his father raged, lurching sideways. "They may even kill her."

Jason's cheeks burned as the blood surged through his veins. "Don't you think I know that?"

"Oh, my, this is terrible. I can't believe it," his mother cried out.

Jason's throat tightened as he barked out the words. "I've got to find her."

She stepped over and draped her arms about his waist. Their sobs entwined.

Taylor reared back in his chair. His features tightened. "Damn that bear for taking my legs," he ranted. "I need to help find my daughter."

Jason released his mother and stepped before him. Leaning down, he clutched his father's shoulder. "I'll take care of it," he said, his mouth dry and parched. "I'm gonna find her."

The leaders in his neck grew taut as their gazes locked. "I will find her, father," he grumbled. "I promise."

He stared at them. "Debbie agreed to marry me. We were on our way to tell you when this happened. No matter how long it takes, I'll never give up. I promise you both."

His father lowered his head and wept.

Jason stared at his mother. "I need a picture of her. I have to get some food and wash up, then I'm headin' back out to search for her."

She nodded and he headed for the kitchen.

Less than a half-hour later, with Blue decked out for travel, Jason filled his saddle bags with supplies and draped them behind the cantle. He checked his ammunition and buckled on his holster. Grabbing his Winchester, he jammed the repeating rifle into the sheath.

He refused to ever be commandeered again.

A quick glance around and he lifted into the saddle and spurred

Blue forward. Afternoon shadows followed him onto the main road and accompanied him on his quest to find his sweetheart.

* * *

The morning of the second day, Debbie raised shaking fingers and touched the lump on her chin. She flinched. Swollen and throbbing, she wondered if her entire face was one big bruise. *When will this misery end?* Resting against the center post, she sucked a deep breath. Frayed nerves challenged her strength. She bit her bottom lip as tears rolled from her eyes.

Oh, my love, are you alive or dead?

Without Jason, she no longer wanted to live.

Her eyes squeezed tight. Memories emerged, masking her misery. The tenderness of Jason's warm lips caressing her neck, the scent of his body, masculine, the smell of leather and the biting trace of the outdoors, all coupled around her to soothe her fears. She remembered his flesh pressing against hers, forcing her heart to thunder against her ribs. The magic of their love- making danced in her dreams like an enchanting fairytale. So unlike the horror that recently ripped apart her world.

She blinked, scattering the memories into the abyss of her mind. Shifting, she sighed and straightened.

Kill me and get this over with.

Tears slid down her cheeks. Trembling fingers brushed aside the streams of agony.

Pulling in a ragged breath, she stepped to the door and peeped through a splintered crack. The sound of water lapping against a creek bank touched her ears. She pushed against the weathered wood, bringing the stream into view. Sunlight danced across the rippling surface.

Shifting, she scanned the tall cottonwoods. A thicket covered with blackberries skirted the tree line. Butterflies fluttered among the clover and the larkspur that blanketed an open meadow. A narrow path weaved between the blossoms, disappearing into the landscape. The charred remains of a burnt cabin, flanked by a crumbling stone well, rested nearby.

Her gaze shot to a campsite in the rutted yard. Hunkered over the river's edge, Pete gutted a fish; while behind him, his partner placed a skillet over a fire. The crackling flames licked at the bottom of the battered iron pan. Moments later, Pete dropped the fresh catch into the frying pan. The sputtering carried on the afternoon breeze to her ears. The aroma of cooking fish followed.

Debbie closed her eyes and inhaled. Her mouth watered. The gnawing in her stomach reminded her she had not eaten in two days.

One bite, one morsel, anything.

Light-headed, she braced her hip against the door.

I've got to get out of here.

Her gaze shifted to the line-tied horses a few yards away.

If I could only get to them.

Damn it! There has to be a way!

She swerved and scanned the stack of crates lining the far wall.

"There's no way out of here," she mumbled.

Squinting, she spotted weathered leather peeking at her from beyond the shadows. Stepping closer, she gasped. *"My valise."*

Three steps took her to the one-of-a-kind Brussels carpet bag that Jason shipped from Europe to her last spring for her birthday. The gold snaps along the edge allowed the satchel to open as a blanket, but the luggage which kept people warm on a train would in no way help her in her escape. Debbie grasped the woolen garment bag and the valise pulled free from between the rickety crates. Embracing the reminder of Jason's love, she buried her face in the floral satchel and sobbed.

Aching moments passed before she lifted her chin and drew in a sustaining breath. Running her fingertips along the rich side leather and decorative tapestry, she returned to the day she received the gift. So beautiful. So unique and so much a part of Jason's love.

A quick tug and the leather handles parted, then a flick of her finger opened the latch. She peered inside, then dumped the contents onto the ground.

Two dresses, a corset, gown and slippers, tangled with her bloomers and stockings. Sorting through the contents she hesitated when her toiletries tumbled out across the dirt.

The fresh scent of lavender soap wafted around her. Her fingers folded around the small bar. Lifting the wedge, she inhaled. If only she could bathe and wash away the stench of her violation. A shudder and she dropped the soap.

Fumbling through the garments, she shook open the closest piece. Her favorite, the blue gingham lawn dress she had purchased for the trip to New York. Crisp, clean and inviting.

Draping the dress across the nearby crate she gathered fresh undergarments. She drew the cotton bloomers to her cheek and embellished the soft texture, so unlike the putrid stench that covered her most private parts. Straightening, she ripped off the soiled undergarments, then stepped into the fresh pair of bloomers. How satisfying to escape the vile odor of her captors.

For the first time since her capture, a glimmer of hope flickered through her mind, yet she remained locked in her dungeon of doom.

I must find a way out!

She shoved the old rags into the carpet bag, and her fingers snagged on something long and thin.

Pushing aside the articles, she fumbled across the bottom. Again, the cool piece brushed the back of her hand. Finally, she locked the strand between her fingers and gave a tug. The metal end caught on the lining. A swift jerk released the hold and Debbie withdrew the treasure. Dangling the keepsake before her, she recognized the elk's tooth necklace she'd misplaced months before. "There you are," she said.

The gold rope chain folded into her palm and she closed her fingers tightly around the jewelry as memories of Christmas morning emerged. She brought her fist up between her breasts and remembered Jason beaming as he spoke of the hunting trip which resulted in the elk's tooth and how he missed having her with him. He had the tooth engraved with her initials. She opened her palm and kissed the precious gift, then draped the chain around her neck. No matter what had befallen her, Jason would always be with her. One last glance and she tucked the keepsake beneath her dress collar. She shoved the contents back into the valise, then tossed the baggage aside.

A ray of light, no wider than a pencil, spilled onto a box beside her. She narrowed her eyes, following the beam to a break in the weathered boards. Scrambling, she knocked away spider webs and cast aside dirt-covered crates, making her way to the small opening.

So this is what cracked.

Dropping to her knees, she flattened her palms against the rotten board. An audible creak echoed around the enclosure. She gasped, then glanced toward the door. Surging to her feet, she scuffled over and peeped out.

Slim looked up from his frying pan and glanced over his shoulder.. "What was that?" he shouted. "Hey, Pete, I heard somethin'."

"You're always hearing somethin'," Pete jeered. "Shut the hell up. You're ruinin' my grub."

She held her breath as Slim shook his head, then continued eating. Her heartbeat pounded in her ears as she released a heavy sigh.

Turning, she rushed back to the splintered opening. She squeezed her fingers between the broken planks, and yanked. Nails near the bottom creaked. She tugged again. With a low groan the aging wood split free. Tossing the board aside, she grasped the next slat and yanked hard.

The hole in the wall expanded.

She drew a breath as freedom edged nearer. Turning, she stepped into the narrow passage. *Too damn small.* She slid back into her prison. One powerful kick and the jagged boards cracked, separating the wood. She cast the board aside. Sunlight spilled into the room. Once again, she wiggled into the opening. Splintered wood clawed her hair and scrapped her forehead as she forced her way through the narrow passage. The hem of her dress caught on a protruding nail. She grabbed the skirt-tail and jerked. The material gave way, setting her free.

She clamored to her feet.

Her heart thundered as she stepped into a thorn-filled briar patch. Picking up a strip of wood from the escape hole, she lashed at the thicket. The tortuous briars separated. She stomped down the prickly branches, then stumbled into an open field. Buzzing bees circled her head as they scattered from the broken thicket. Hiking up her skirt, she worked her way up the hillside. As she neared the top, a loud clang of metal on stone shattered the calm.

She whipped around.

Oh, God.

"Hell's fire, she got out!" Pete screamed. "Hey!"

The sound of his voice crested above the rush of blood pounding in her ears.

Slim jumped to his feet, tossing his plate into the dirt. "That little bitch broke free."

Pete bolted ahead. "We gotta catch her."

Panic clogged in her throat and she fought back nausea as she scrambled toward the trees. Thorns from the berry bushes clawed at her skin. Whelps surfaced on her hands and wrists. She jerked away and the vicious branches ripped across her arms. Streaks of blood smeared her gingham.

Her eyes widened in a frantic search for a place to hide. Leg muscles bunched beneath feverish steps.

She gasped as burning lungs squeezed beneath her chest. Perspiration poured from her, soaking the hair at her temples. She pushed on, stifling the whimpers that escaped her lips.

Each footfall carried her deeper and deeper into the forest.

She chanced a glanced back once again.

The heathens closed in on her.

Pete came plowing through the branches flailing his arms. His cursing rose above every gasp she made; long strides bringing his vile odor closer and closer still.

She wanted to vomit.

Please, God, don't let them catch me.

Fallen branches cracked beneath her traveling boots. Each step drug slower and slower.

Her strength spent and fighting for each breath, Debbie staggered.

A root caught her toe and she stumbled.

The ground rose up before her. Dirt and twigs raked her chin as she slammed into the turf.

Every bone in her body rattled and debris scraped her cheek like the rasping file of a blacksmith. The sudden jolt sent pain racing down her spine. A frightening numbness washed over her.

She drew her fists to her eyes.

God, just let me die.

Breathing hard, the two jackals towered over her and she rolled over to glare into their flushed faces.

Pete bent forward, clutching his palms to his knee tops. "Where do you think you're goin', sweetie?" he puffed. "I want another poke before you leave."

"You little bitch," Slim sneered. "We oughta kill you."

"Shut up. She's worth too much alive."

Slim drug his grimy shirt sleeve across his forehead, sopping up the sweat. "Well, I'm tired of messin' with her."

"Stop blabbing and help me get her up." Pete grumbled.

The hoof beats of approaching horses echoed between the pines. Lifting his gaze, he pointed to the dirt lane. "Here comes Tater with the wagon."

Slim wrapped his hand on Debbie's arm and gave her a jerk. She struggled, then moaned and went limp.

"Tater," Pete called, motioning for him to join them, "Over here."

Debbie peered through swollen eyelids as the creaking wagon crushed the clover and larkspurs beneath its wheels.

"What the hell's going on?" the bearded man asked, pulling the team to a stop.

Her gaze blurred as Pete raked back greasy strands of hair draping his eyes. "Damn bitch slipped out the back of the shed."

"But we got her," Slim chirped, puffing his chest.

Tater jumped from the wagon and clamored toward them. "Bring her back and tie her up," he demanded, his gaze narrowing on hers. "It'll be dark soon and we need to travel."

Slim kicked her shoulder with the toe of his boot. The pain exploded and Debbie bit back a scream.

"But she won't get up," he said.

"Then pick her up and get to movin'. If we miss the exchange, I'm gonna shoot both you jackasses."

Pete jerked her up and hauled her over to the wagon, then threw her into the back. Debbie gasped as the collar of her dress ripped open and her gold chain tumbled forward. The elk's tooth dangled against her breast.

"What's this," he asked, sliding his palm beneath the piece. The tooth gleamed in the afternoon sun. This was all she had left of her beloved. They'd taken everything she treasured. Life offered nothing.

Her future was now cast into a vile pit of inescapable horror.

Anger surged through her like a raging fire, burning away her weakness. A void ripped at her gut. She leaped forward grabbing his hand, her fingernails digging into his palm.

Pete jerked away, snapping the chain. "Hey, Tater, look at this," he yelled, dangling the object from his hand.

Debbie grabbed out for the necklace again. "Give me that," she begged.

"What is it?" Tater questioned, leaning against the sideboard to get a better look. Pete tossed the necklace to his boss.

Debbie fought to reach the heirloom, pleading. "No! Please don't take it."

Tater rolled the tooth about his palm, then held it up to the light. "Looks like some kind of stone." He turned the piece over. "There's letters on the back. It must be somethin' real important."

"It's not a stone," she said, scooting back in the wagon. "It's a tooth."

"A tooth? I never seen one that looks like that. It's no bear tooth 'cause it ain't shaped right."

She drew a ragged breath. "It's an elk's tooth."

"Why would a lady wear an elk's tooth?" He tossed the heirloom back to her. "Keep it. I don't need the damn thing." He turned to his partners and ordered, "Give her some grub, then tie her up. And this time make sure she don't get away. It'll be dark soon. We need to get goin'."

Chapter Thirteen

A rumbling thunder brought Kathryn's gaze up from her handiwork. The stifling heat that preceded the oncoming storm only added to her misery. She laid aside her knitting and reached for a hanky, wiping perspiration from her brow.

Her gaze settled on her sleeping husband.

A book lay open in his lap, yet the scowl that creased his features accentuated his aging face. She pulled in a deep breath and returned her attention to the half-finished shawl in her lap.

The room darkened, blanketing the parlor beneath a cloak of despair. Unraveling nerves skimmed along her forearms as she contemplated the weight of their recent upheaval. Debbie's absence created an aching void that echoed throughout the family.

Kathryn slowly straightened, nestling the ivory needles into the yarn basket at her feet. Again, she glanced at Taylor.

His somber gaze locked on hers.

"Are you all right," she asked, leaning forward.

"I'm scared for Debbie. She must be terrified."

Kathryn nodded. "It's hard to imagine what she's going through."

"I wish there was something we could do."

"Surely to God this will all end soon."

A gust of wind slammed the main door against the foyer wall. She gasped and whirled to face the front of the parlor. Dried leaves and debris scattered across the entryway.

Kathryn rose from the chair and rushed across the floor, pushing the wooden panel shut. A flick of her wrist secured the latch. She brushed aside the curtain and peered through a side window. Ominous clouds rolled in from the west, as jagged lightening jabbed the hillside.

"Storm's nearly here," she whispered, wretchedness thickening each word. "This waiting is torment." Tears gathered behind her lashes. "Why can't anyone find her?"

"It's been days since Jason left. He may never find her."

"Don't say that," she said, slipping beside him. She rested her head in his lap. "We mustn't give up hope."

Taylor slid his fingers through her hair. "But we can't shut our minds to the truth, my love."

The shrill clamor of the doorbell caught them both by surprise.

Kathryn surged to her feet as the bell summoned again, followed by someone's frantic knock upon the glass. She swept across the parlor and into the hallway, then pulled aside the curtain. In the waning light, James stood with his nose pressed against the windowpane, peering inside and his hands cupping his temples. Chestnut hair ruffled around his head.

Her mouth bowed upward, as she swung wide the door. "Hurry, sweetie. Come inside before you're blown away."

Nodding, he stepped over the threshold.

She drew him onto the rug to prevent his drenched clothing from dripping on the floor. Her smile faded as the lad struggled to catch his breath. "What is it, James?"

"Infinity. He's loose." The words tumbled from quivering lips. "Tom went after him."

"What?" Taylor's voice boomed down the hallway. Seconds later, he rolled up to join them.

The boy's eyes widened. "Yes, sir. I was bringin' him in 'cause of the storm. Lightning hit the weathervane. He reared up and threw me to the ground."

"Damn it!" Taylor raged, jerking back in his wheelchair. "I can't trust you to do anything right."

"I…I didn't mean to let him go," the boy stammered, tears building in his eyes.

"Get outta here and go help Tom find him or you'll never work another day in my stable."

James' face washed as pale as bleached cotton. "Yes…yes, sir," he mumbled, then spun and raced from the house.

Kathryn closed the door upon his exit, then faced her husband. "That was a bit harsh, don't you think? After all, he didn't lose your horse on purpose."

"Purpose or not, Infinity's gone." Taylor's face grew red as he fidgeted in his chair. "As if things weren't bad enough," he ranted, gesturing in frustration, "now my prize horse is gone." Mumbled curses followed and a moment later, he pushed away. Kathryn stared as he rolled from room to room, checking the view out each window.

With a heavy sigh, she dropped into the rocker. "You're fretting isn't going to help," she snapped. "Be patient. They'll find the horse."

"Patient?" He rolled back into the parlor, glaring. "Damn it, woman, I don't have time for patience. That horse may die... and…and Debbie…" he paused, then sucked in a deep breath, turning anxious eyes upon her. "I'm so damn useless now. Don't you understand? I should be out there helping Jason, helping Tom and James. But instead, I'm stuck in this damned chair."

Like a bolt of lightning, clarity arrived. She ached for this proud man and his increasing helplessness.

The tick of the hall clock grew louder with every pendulum swing. She stepped to the sideboard, her hands sliding around a cut-crystal decanter. "Darling, I completely understand your frustration." She sloshed a generous shot of whiskey into a matching tumbler. "I feel helpless, too. But, they're all working to do what we can't."

He inhaled and leaned forward, sliding his palms together. "I'd give my life to have Debbie home."

"And so would I," she whispered, handing him the half-filled glass.

Taylor tightened shaking fingers around her offering, his knuckles straining white. His deep guzzle followed.

"Sip slowly, darling," she cautioned. "Getting drunk won't solve a thing."

The rhythmic sound of galloping hooves caught Taylor's attention. Another gulp finished his whiskey. He settled the glass on the sidetable, then backed around and wheeled into the foyer.

Kathryn followed, and pulled open the door.

Beyond the veranda, a windswept deluge fell in a silvery curtain. She glimpsed a shimmering figure from just beyond the reach of lamplight. Her gaze narrowed upon their farrier sliding from the saddle.

He emerged from out of the rain to stand before them. "We've found Infinity. Down the road about a mile. He's in the swamp near Eagle Creek, tangled in wire."

Taylor drew a heavy breath. "Barbed wire?" The words raked from his throat.

"No, but it's rusty. He's fighting hard." The man swiped his forehead with the back of his hand. "James is there with him, tryin' to keep him calm 'til I can get back with some snips. Can't really tell if the colt's injured or not, but he's a foot deep in mud."

"There's a wire cutter in the stable out back. Should be hanging on the wall by the tack room. Take a lantern with you."

Kathryn edged up behind Taylor and placed her hand on his shoulder. "Is there anything I can do," she asked.

"No, ma'am. Just gotta get Infinity out of there." Tom's gaze darted back to Taylor. "…just wanted to bring you both up-to-date." He whirled on his heels and raced down the steps. Within an instant, he faded into the rain-soaked night.

Taylor met Kathryn's gaze. "Tell Jeremiah to come in here. He's taking me down to the stable. I'm going to be there when they bring Infinity."

Chapter Fourteen

Debbie flinched when Pete shoved a bowl of beans into her lap. She stared down at the watery mess. Insects darted around the slop and she swatted them away with an agitated hand. Her gaze shot to her captor who now slouched against the closest tree. The lopsided smile he sent her way only compounded her frustrations.

With a drawn pistol, he motioned for her to eat. "This ain't no fancy eatery, Missy," he sneered. "That's all you're gonna get."

Debbie clasped the spoon and filled her lungs with air, then slipped the foul concoction into her mouth. Her tongue pressed against the soupy mixture, the beans crunching between her teeth like aged peanuts. Staring at Pete, she swallowed the murky mess.

Surprisingly, her stomach accepted the meal. Famished, she consumed every morsel. Within minutes, she set aside the bowl, and asked, "May I please have a drink of water?"

"Pitch me your canteen," Pete hollered as he glanced over his shoulder toward Slim. "The princess wants a drink."

His partner tossed the metal bulls-eye in their direction and Pete seized the canteen in mid-air.

The filthy cloth strap smacked Debbie across the cheek.

Pete laughed as he dropped the vessel into her lap.

She uncorked the canteen and pressed the metal to her lips. Only three gulps of the tepid liquid had passed her tongue before he yanked the container away.

Water splattered her face.

"That's enough," he growled, rejamming the cork. He slung the canteen back to Slim.

With her dress sleeve, Debbie wiped the droplets from her chin. *I hope you burn in hell for all eternity.*

From the opposite side of the wagon, Tater hollered, "Come on, boys, let's get movin'."

Her gaze narrowed on Pete. "Where are you taking me?" she snapped, her muscles tightening.

He jerked her to her feet. "You don't even want to know."

With a hard thrust, he forced her hands behind her back and bound her wrists. The supper she'd consumed in such a rush now churned inside her stomach. And before she could even catch her breath, Pete jammed a rag between her teeth.

She fought to turn away.

"Damn it woman...stop fighting me." Her glare met his just before he slammed his hand against the back of her neck, rocking her head forward.

Tears emerged as did a muffled cough. Debbie trembled against the unfolding wretchedness. *Oh, Jason...where are you?*

Pete pulled her to the wagon and shoved her into the back of the vehicle. With a smirk on his lips, Slim brought out a length of hemp and bound her ankles. A moment later, he rolled her onto the weathered boards.

Sunlight disappeared when burlap sacks covered her from head to toe, smothering her. Dust filled her nostrils and Debbie nearly gagged. Struggling for each breath, she fought against her bindings. Finally, a satisfying lungful of air burrowed into her lungs.

Her eyelids slid shut, forcing out her misery.

Oh, God, I can't bear this.

With a jerk, the wagon lurched forward. Screams for help tumbled into the abyss of her mind. Life had been so beautiful inside Jason's arms. But, today, with no Jason, she lived a hell that went beyond her darkest nightmare. Every minute, her thoughts spiraled deeper into a pit of damnation she could not escape.

Hour after hour, the sounds of plodding horses, the ache of the rutted trail, and the creak of the damnable wagon rattled her soul. Exhaustion claimed Debbie and she fitfully dozed off and on in an attempt to flee her torment.

At last, the wagon lurched to a stop.

Her body stiffened when muffled voices reached her ears. And then, the tapping sounds of a cane against wood forced her eyes to widen.

The old man who bought me?

Moments later, the vehicle rocked and footsteps scuffled onto the wood beside her. Several hands slipped beneath her body and lifted her up and over the side of the wagon.

Disoriented, she strained to identify her surroundings: lapping water, shuffling feet, and men shouting directions to others to load cargo onto a ship.

A dock!

But which one? Debbie squirmed in their arms, even now struggling in a futile attempt to break free.

Heavy footfalls tromped across wooden flooring. Door hinges creaked. With heaving growls, they tossed her onto some kind of soft surface. Rattling springs identified a bed. She twisted to get away from her captors.

"Take the sacks off her," Pete ordered.

A hard tug separated the burlap from Debbie. Rolling sideways, she blinked several times to remove the dust and chaff from her eyes.

Pete loomed into view and removed her gag. With a smile, he freed her hands as, near her feet, Slim cut the ankle ropes. The hours of darkness had temporally blinded her and she coughed, raising a palm to shade her eyes.

She blinked hard to regain her vision.

"You can get up now," Pete sneered. "You're locked on the *"Sally Mae"*, so scream all you want. There's nobody on this cargo tub that cares."

Debbie sat up, massaging the rope burns on her wrists.

"Come on, Slim," he said, smacking his partner on the shoulder, "let's get out of here and get our money." He looped the ropes into a knot and stuffed them into his back pocket.

Debbie glared up. "Where are you taking me?"

"We ain't going along, but you'll find out where soon enough." He pushed his friend toward the door. "And good luck. You're gonna need it." At the doorway, he paused and looked back, a smirk lifting his grimy face. "Oh, and thanks for the poke, Missy."

She threw the pillow, but he ducked and slammed the door closed. The bolster slid to the floor as the lock clicked into place, trapping her inside.

A well-placed fist pummeled the mattress and she flopped backward across the berth. *How can I get off this damn boat?* Tears welled in her eyes as she stared at the ceiling. Her body tightened. Little by little, sorrow squeezed passed her lashes and rolled to her temples, soaking strands of her knotted hair.

She swiped a clenched fist across her swollen eyes and drew in a fortifying breath. Rubbing her cheek against the shoulder of her dress, she banished the tears and sat up. A quick lift of hips brought her to the edge of the bed.

Debbie scanned her newest prison.

Bleak walls blackened from years of oil lamps and coal tar lent little warmth to her surroundings. A small, round window beside the bed boasted murky panes that eked in little light. Her gaze settled on a pitcher, a wash bowl, and a bedside chamber pot...a luxury she'd not enjoyed these past few days.

She drew a breath and reached for the blanket folded on the foot of the bed. The faded, light-weight wool riddled with moth holes opened in a heap across her lap. Her hand slid across the thread-bare linens that covered the mattress.

Filthy... but no signs of vermin.

Another sigh escaped her lips. At least she was no longer ruled by the demons that had captured her. For that, she was thankful. On bent legs, she scrambled across the mattress and pressed her nose against the window.

The deck of the *Sally Mae* filled her view.

Myriad workers loaded crates and boxes onto the vessel, if this rundown, floating heap of rubbish could be called such. She waved in frantic desperation, but no one paid her any mind.

Anxiety swelled inside.

She scanned the dock beyond the freighter. A couple of dilapidated shacks, a stable, and a ramshackle house dotted the hillside where rutted roads led out of the shantytown to parts unknown.

Several taverns loomed along the pier, and a one-legged begger still wearing Confederate gray teetered on his gnarled crutch near the entrance of the closest one. He extended a battered tin cup in hopes of donations from any passersby. Beside him, several others sprawled across outside benches lost in their own drunken stupors. A rising sun crested the hillock and spilled morning brightness across her window.

Debbie blinked and refocused. And then, a glint caught her attention. She scraped her gaze sideways toward an approaching rider on horseback.

Her eyes narrowed.

Blue? She surged to her knees and pressed closer to the dirty glass, her breath fogging the pane. With a frantic swipe, she palmed away the moisture and refocused on the rider.

With his back to her, he dismounted and headed toward the crippled veteran.

Her ribs squeezed her chest, vaulting her heart into her throat. She would recognize that strong gait anywhere.

Jason?

Oh, my God. Yes!

"Jason," she screamed, her hands fisting. She pounded on the window.

"Jason. I'm here. I'm here."

Her gaze narrowed upon a tintype he pulled from his pocket. He angled the picture toward the old man who shook his head.

"Oh, my God," she gasped. "Jason, I'm here!" Pushing forward, she drew her hands into fists and repeatedly pounded the window pane. "Jason," she screamed. "Over here, Jason. I'm over here!"

She dashed to the door and jerked on the handle. No success. She banged the weathered wood and begged for someone to help her. Silence. A strangled sob fell from her lips as she raced back to the window.

With picture in hand, Jason had moved to confront several of the dockworkers.

Again, heads shook.

He disappeared into the taverns and moments later, stepped out, a frown creasing his handsome face.

Frantic, she screamed, "Jason, I'm over here."

Shoulders slumped; he turned in a full circle and scanned the shanties. As he turned back toward the boat, a disillusioned look darkened his face. He gathered the reins and swung into the saddle.

Her heart nearly ripped from her chest. "Noooooo," she begged, her hands battering the windowpane. "Please don't leave me."

His chin lowered and he touched the brim of his hat toward the old soldier. A second later, he flipped a coin into the old man's cup.

With a nudge to Blue's flanks, Jason turned in the opposite direction and cantered up the hillside.

"No. No. No," she cried, her words barely a whisper now. "Please don't go." Her gaze blurred as the love of her life disappeared over the ridgeline. "No, no…Please…no" With a trembling voice, Debbie collapsed onto the bed.

Chapter Fifteen

A howling wind raced across the countryside, ushering in a late fall. Trees bowed beneath nature's fury, twisting their branches asunder. Like blackbirds gleaning a harvest field, autumn leaves swirled. Jason jerked back on Blue's hackamore when a deafening crack split the air. On his left, a huge limb plummeted to the ground.

The horse reared. "Easy, boy." He patted the roan's neck as leather-clad hands reined the gelding into a meadow. Dead tired and drenched to the bone, Jason eased the horse along the mud-slicked hillside fronting Crystal Falls.

*Home, at last...*yet grief swelled inside. *Debbie.* Helplessness shredded his heartstrings.

He inhaled and faced the wind, dipping his chin. A tug brought his hat brim lower. With a slap of leather and a nip of spurs, he forced Blue into a canter through the iron gates.

Moonlight wedged between the clouds and spilled an ivory glow across the stable on his right. Thunder rumbled across the heavens and Jason cut his glance upward.

Haven't seen a storm build like this since the day they buried Packey.

He released a ragged breath. The parched earth needed a soaking just as much as he needed sleep. A new day, a fresh start, and a different plan would offer hope to his crumbling confidence. For now, he could only pray for Debbie's safety until he could hold her in his arms once more.

Nearing the barn, his gaze settled on the main door. A light flickered from inside, sparking an edginess over him. He reined Blue to a stop and slipped from the saddle. A cautious glance through a window and he released a sigh.

Why is the old man here this time of night sleeping in his wheelchair?

With a hefty shove Jason rolled open the stable door and guided the roan into the corridor.

"Father," he said, tying the horse to an iron ring on the closest post.

Taylor stirred and glanced up. "Oh, my God, son, I'm so glad you're back." A frown creased his brow. "Where's Debbie?"

"I couldn't find her," Jason said, unbuckling his gun belt. He shoved the weapon into a metal cabinet, then faced his father. "I showed her picture to every person I met, but no one has seen her. It's like she's just disappeared off the face of the earth."

"You can't give up," Taylor rasped, settling his hands into his lap.

Jason propped his foot on a tool box and stared into his father's eyes. "I'll never give up. She's my life."

"Every damn thing is going wrong at once," his father grumbled. "But, right now, I need your help with other matters." Their gazes deepened. "Infinity ran away during the storm. Tom and James found him wrapped in wire down by Eagle Creek."

Jason shook his head. "I knew that damned wire was gonna be trouble when they strung it."

"Go help them," his father pleaded. "Infinity may die."

Lowering his foot, Jason straightened. *Sonofabitch. I want a hot meal and a soft bed. I don't want to chase after horses in this god-awful weather.* "All right," he sighed. "I'll take care of it." He yanked the reins from the ring.

Frustration twisted his gut as he shoved his boot into the stirrup. On a groan, he swung back into the saddle.

The creases around his father's eyes deepened. "Tom came back for light and some cutters a while ago. Infinity's just off the road to Eagle Creek. Hurry, son."

Jason nodded, reined the roan around, then galloped from the stable.

* * *

A short time later, he pulled Blue to a stop alongside the creek as James' eyes widened.

"Boss!" the lad yelled, jerking back on a strand of wire.

The farrier glanced up and bellowed above the thunder. "Good God, Jason. I'm glad you're here. Come help me raise Infinity so I can cut this strand across his back."

Jason slid from the saddle, and plunged into the water beside them, startling Infinity. Shrieking, nostrils flaring, the stallion thrashed his forelegs near Tom's head. A flash of lightening streaked above them, brightening the wire that coiled ever tighter, slicing the metal deeper into the colt's bunched muscles. Shod hooves slammed back into the water and sent a muddy wave over them.

"If he slides beneath the water, we'll lose him," Jason screamed as he grabbed Infinity's halter. With a heaving grunt, he tugged upward. Again the horse yanked, slamming back into the quagmire.

Waving his hand, Jason shouted, "Cut free the wire across his withers, Tom. He's losing too much blood."

"Can't see shit," Tom grumbled, hanging onto the horse's mane. "I busted the lantern earlier."

Stretching out his arm, palm up, Jason demanded, "Give me the cutters, I'm at a better angle over here! And James, you hold Infinity's halter."

Tom tossed him the tool and leaned back, just as thunder boomed overhead. The ground vibrated the water, sending ripples against Jason's hip. A blinding flash followed, and the deluge falling from the sky intensified.

"Another storm," James cried out, grasping the halter. "They just keep comin'."

"Forget the weather," Jason yelled. "Let's get Infinity loose and get the hell outta here."

Heavy puffs from flared nostrils spewed swamp water over Jason, momentarily blinding him. Squealing, the frightened horse fought to pull away.

"Stop fighting me, damnit!" Jason screamed. The stallion blew hard and plunged back into the muck once more.

"Tom, brace against Infinity's side," Jason yelled. "Hold him upright so I can cut the damn wire near his shoulder. He's gonna fight, so be ready."

The farrier gave a nod. "I'm ready."

A bolt of lightning branched across the sky, illuminating the horse in a brilliant wash of white. Every muscle in his body knotted as Jason squeezed the blades together.

The wire sprang loose, whipping off into the marsh with a violent twist.

Infinity snorted, drawing Jason's attention. Eyes widened, the colt thrust back his ears and released a shrill squeal. Again, he fought to rise upon his feet, his front legs flailing to gain a foothold in the swamp-filled muck. An instant later, his haunches tightened, and the animal rose from the water, fighting hard against the swamp's sucking hold. The glint in his widened eyes spoke of a hellish fear as the colt sucked in gulps of air.

Jason rubbed the sleek neck in a strong and downward stroke reassuring the horse of their presence. "Easy, big fella...we're just trying to help you."

The animal trembled.

"We'll have you out real soon," Tom added. The farrier grabbed the halter and Infinity again struggled to his feet. Jason angled the cutter upward through the rusty wire. "Come on, you sonofabitch. Turn loose." The tool cut wire and he felt the tension lessen. "Thank God." Jason threw the rusty section aside.

James staggered to regain his footing as Infinity clambered his front hooves up onto the bank.

Jason shoved the cutters toward Tom. "Hold these for a second," he ordered, adjusting his position. "I need to check the back hocks for any other strands."

Lightning forked in streaks above them and a glowing bolt struck a nearby tree, splitting the trunk and sending sparks into the air. Fire erupted, but the fierce wind and rain doused the blaze.

"We need to get out of this lightening before we get hit, too," Jason wailed, raising his arm to wipe his eyes.

He reached for the final stretch of metal that wrapped Infinity's hind leg. Clinging moss hid the section of wire that stopped any freedom. Jason rammed his shoulder against the horse's side to anchor himself. "Hand me the cutters now," he bellowed, an open palm outstretched. Broken flesh bloodied the long strand of filament around the hock. The horse screamed at his touch. "Easy boy," he muttered as he tugged on the cable to gain purchase.

The storm buffeted him, challenging his strength. Teeth gritted, Jason fought to maintain balance. A heartbeat later, the sky lit up and he set the cutter blades across the wire. On his next breath, he squeezed his hand shut and the cord snapped in two.

Infinity reared.

James grabbed the lead rope. Tom held a firm grip on the halter.

Both of them struggled to hang on as the stallion lifted them off their feet, tossing his head violently.

Jason's biceps burned as he yanked the strand free. "Get him outta here," he yelled, slapping the animal on the rump.

Tom pulled the horse to safety. James followed, slogging through knee-deep water and up onto the road beside Infinity.

Blinding curtains of rain pelted Jason. He raised his arm to shield his face and stumbled through the marsh to retrieve Blue. On a sigh, he vaulted into the saddle. Every muscle in his body throbbed. He blinked hard, then fixed his gaze on the injured stallion.

Thank God, he's safe now.

"I'll take Infinity," Jason shouted, holding out his hand. Tom slapped over the lead. "I'll see you both back home."

"Sure thing, boss," Tom replied, swiping aside long strands of dipping hair from his forehead.

"And good job, boys," Jason yelled, turning toward Crystal Falls.

He chanced a quick glance across his shoulder. The two young men had climbed aboard their horses. Soon, their silhouettes faded into the night.

* * *

Jason lowered the stallion's leg, a frown creasing his brow at the swollen hock that now forced Infinity to limp. Oozing blood covered the deep gashes that encircled the bloodied ankle.

This will probably end his racing days before they've even begun. He settled back into the saddle and slowed their pace home.

A cock crowed announcing the promise of sunrise. Jason's gaze lifted to the hillside where the retreating storm brightened the far horizon. The dying winds brushed at his damp clothing. He pulled in a deep breath and shivered. An hour later, he arrived at the stable.

"Damn," his father muttered, rolling his chair over to accept Infinity's lead rope from Jason's hand. "I was afraid of this."

Jason eased out of his saddle and dropped the reins of the gelding to the floor, ground-tying the roan. "The vet needs to take a look at him. That deep cut on his chest needs stitches."

"Ah, hell," his father raged. The horse dipped his head and sniffed the old man's hand. His father stroked Infinity's forehead, then tunneled his finger through the coarse mane. "I'm so sorry, fella," he whispered. Tears welled in his eyes. His gaze lifted, locking with Jason's. "Will he be all right?"

"I think so," Jason said. He turned back to his roan. "But he won't be racing any time soon." He tossed the clipped words over his shoulder. His hands shook as he slid the saddle from Blue's back. Another grimace and Jason removed the bridle. His muscles bunched as he guided the horse into an empty stall. After a quick check of the water bucket, he latched the gate.

Boot heels scraping the floor, Jason rejoined his father. "Let me have a closer look now." He focused on Infinity. The rain had washed away most of the grime from the horse's coat. "This is bad," he said, sweeping aside the blood that seeped from the neck wound. "I gotta clean this out. Don't want it to get worse. I'll send for the vet."

Jason gathered supplies, secured Infinity in a chute, and then washed the wounds, applying iodine to the injuries.

"That'll have to do for now," he stated, stepping back. He grasped the halter. "It's been a rough night, hasn't it, fella? Let's get you to bed." He pushed aside the gate and led his father's prized stallion to his stall. "I'll stay home for a few more days and get Infinity back on his feet, but then I'm heading out again to search for Debbie.

Chapter Sixteen

The sun burned overhead when Jason trudged down the lane toward the stable, his mind reeling from the previous night's battle to free Infinity. The colt could take months to heal, if not longer.

He shook his head at the unrelenting disruption of his life.

Kicking mud from his boots, he stepped into the shadowy stable. The comforting aromas of liniment, hay and oats swirled around him. A screeching from above drew his gaze. The resident barn owl flew from the rafters and Jason ducked as flapping wings grazed his head. The pesky creature circled above the stalls, then swooped out the open door.

"Damned bird," he grumbled, raking his fingers through his hair. "I'm gonna kill that feathered bastard some day."

He narrowed his eyes and headed for the stallion.

An earsplitting crash halted his steps in mid-stride. His gaze cut sideways and settled on his farrier. Horse implements and other gear littered the ground around Tom's feet as the man lifted a cabinet back into position.

"Mornin'," Tom muttered over his shoulder. A sheepish grin lifted his lips."Sorry to spook you."

Jason quirked a smile as his heart thumped back to normal. "Didn't expect anyone in here."

"Came in to check on the Infinity."

"Felt the same way." Jason chuckled. He helped Tom straighten the metal sideboard.

The farrier grabbed a small package of horseshoe nails resting near his boots, then slid the box onto the cabinet's upper shelf. "Damned thing tipped when I went to fetch a hammer. Gonna have to bolt this into place, I guess."

Jason nodded, heading toward Infinity. The colt had kicked off the bandage from last night. The hock had swollen twice its size and streaks of blood still oozed from the wicked gash. *I'll be amazed if this animal ever races again.* He shook his head, then heaved a sigh. "Tom."

"Yes sir," the farrier replied, stepping to the stall door.

"Go fetch the veterinarian."

"Already done. Sent James for him 'bout twenty minutes ago."

"Good. How's that boy working out for you now?"

"He's doing fine. Listens well and does his job as told. He's an old man in a young lad's body."

"My father can sure spot a horseman." Nodding, Jason latched the door and meandered over to the farrier, leaning forward on the table near Tom. "He found you. And I can't even imagine what we'd do around here without your skills."

Jason stared out the window at the stone well. Visions of Debbie carrying her picnic basket tumbled into his mind. What a wonderful day they had planned. Who could've predicted the horror that followed? His thoughts surged forward to the night of the ambush.

I should've done more to protect her.

A heavy pressure dug into his chest and sucked the air from his lungs. Guilt's torment ripped at his heart.

His gaze snapped to Infinity. *And now this mess.* His jaw clinched tight. *I don't want this... a lame horse. Responsibility.* Agitation spiked his nerves. *I want Debbie.* He bit back his rage and shoved against the table, straightening to face his farrier. "I'm headin' back to the house for lunch. Let me know when the vet gets here."

Jason stepped into the sunlight and surveyed the horizon. Last night's squall had cleared the air. Yet, scattered limbs and standing water gave testimony to the storm's fury.

Frustration bubbled through his veins as he lengthened his stride. A gnawing pain bit at his thighs and he grimaced. The long days spent in the saddle had taken a toll, yet the throbbing in his legs seemed minor compared to the ache swelling inside his heart.

Where are you, my love?

Nearing the house, he caught sight of his mother knitting in her favorite front porch rocker. His father rested close by, smoking his daily cigar.

Routines controlled their worlds.

Jason sighed.

"Come join us, son." His mother patted the arm of a nearby rocker as Jason shuffled up the steps.

He settled onto the cushioned seat beside her. "I'm glad to catch you both here. There're some things I need to discuss."

She nestled her knitting into the yarn basket. "Your father said you couldn't find Debbie."

Jason's gaze met hers and his throat tightened. "No, not yet. Nobody has seen her."

"Did you follow the tracks from where she was abducted?" his father asked leaning forward.

"There were some wagon ruts but I lost them on the main road." He paused to take a breath, then continued, "I'm going to town later to see if the sheriff has any news. I still have a lot of ground to cover. I'm not gonna give up."

"You'll find her soon, sweetheart," she said, tears collecting. "We all need her home."

Jason sighed and leaned back, staring at the stable in the far distance. "I'll stay for a few days to make sure Infinity's all right, but then I'm heading out to search for her again." He swiped his hands over his face. "I've decided against going back to school right now. Not while she's missing." The catch in his throat tightened. He could barely draw his next breath. "I-I can't go anywhere without her, mother."

"I know, darling," she whispered, laying her hand atop his. "This is all such a nightmare."

Jason nodded, tamping back his emotions. Moments passed in silence, broken only by the creak of his mother's rocker, the swirl of cigar smoke wafting across the porch. His thoughts shifted to James. "What about Packey's house?" He finally asked, glancing toward his father. "You know James' family is having a tough time, right now. What if we allowed them to move into that place? I mean, Tom could use Perkins' help at the stable, and his Mrs. could help with the house chores. They could sure use the money and we could use the help."

"Hmm, I never gave it a thought. Might work." His father exhaled another stream of smoke. "I didn't like that house sitting empty, anyway."

The encompassing scent of cherry-flavored tobacco penetrated Jason's nostrils, reminding him of stability and happier times. He inhaled, his shaky mood eased into one of more control.

"I think this is a wonderful idea." His mother smiled at him. "Millie's getting up in years. She'd appreciate the help."

"Fine," Jason said, straightening. "I'll speak with them tonight. And one more thing…Tuesday is James' birthday. I've been thinkin' about giving him Duke. The boy's been comin' to work on his dad's old crippled mule and Packey's buckskin is too good a mount to just be stabled."

"Another good idea, son," Taylor said, reaching over and clasping Kathryn's hand.

Smacking the top of his knees, Jason stood. "Think I'll go have some lunch, now. Then, I'll head back to the stable. The veterinarian should be there soon."

"I'll join you," his father said.

* * *

That afternoon, they waited impatiently while the vet examined Infinity. Jason admired the doctor; had known him for years and valued his opinion.

"Thanks for coming, Peter," Jason said. Their palms slid together into a firm hand shake. As youngsters, they'd attended school together and even courted the same girl. Years later, that same young lady had become Peter's wife. Jason smiled, remembering the day they'd asked him to be Godfather to their only child.

"I hear Infinity has had quite a night," Peter said, pushing his glasses further up the bridge of his nose. "James said he tangled with some wire."

Jason stroked Infinity's muzzle, then slipped his fingers beneath the halter to steady the animal. "His chest and left hock are the most damaged."

His friend straightened, removing the blood-soaked bandage from beneath the horse's neck. "Mmmm, this is pretty nasty. Was the wire barbed or rusty?" He pressed his fingertips beside the jagged cut. Infinity flinched. "Easy boy."

Taylor wheeled over for a closer look.

"It wasn't barbed," Jason replied, holding the halter tighter. "But I'm sure there was rust."

"I'll clean and stitch this up." Peter kneeled beside the horse, smoothing his hand down Infinity's leg. "He'll be fine."

Jason nodded.

His father's eyes misted.

Peter stepped past them. "Now, let me take a look at that hock. There's a lot of swelling...all right, let's put him in a chute where I can manage him and then I'll get to work. He glanced over at Jason and winked. "Think we should give him a shot of whiskey."

Both men chuckled.

"Or maybe let's all have one," Jason said, his gaze sliding sideways to settle on his father's still-concerned face.

"Will he be able to race?" Taylor snapped, the aged lines deepening across his forehead.

"Not sure," Peter admitted. "All according to how well the ankle heals. He may never be more than a child's saddle horse. Only time'll tell."

Ten minutes later, Jason followed Peter to the outside corral where the veterinarian's own mount waited. "How's the wife?"

"Betty Jo's fine. Pregnant again."

"Damn, Pete." Jason laughed, elbowing his friend. "You must be keeping her happy."

They both laughed as his friend shoved his foot into the stirrup and prepared to mount.

Just then, the side door of the stable crashed open, drawing their attention.

James ran from the dwelling, screaming. "Jason, come quick. There's something wrong with Mr. Jackson."

Chapter Seventeen

After hours spent below deck, Debbie welcomed the freedom of the open air. She leaned against the boat's railing and inhaled, burrowing a cool September afternoon into her lungs. The rocking motion of the boat upon the waves unsettled her and she widened her stance for balance. Pressing forward, hands tightly gripping the weathered wood, she peered into the river.

Her gaze chased the swirling splotches of foam churned up by the fast-moving vessel. Free from her stifling quarters, Debbie released a sigh of liberation heavenward as she scanned the steep banks at the water's edge.

A splash against her cheek brought a sharp gasp.

Reality swept in.

I'm so far from home... Jason will never find me.

She glanced to her left, surveying the upcoming shoreline. *Too far to swim.*

Her gaze drifted along the railing. Two men sat on the deck nearby cleaning their catch. The stench channeled across the stern, filling her lungs with the offensive odor. As they worked, she could hear them speaking, but their words were unfamiliar. She raised her brows. Everyone aboard spoke this strange language.

Her thoughts dissolved with the slamming of a door. She turned to find her owner.

"Are you enjoying your trip?" Laffoone asked, stepping beside her.

Anger festered inside and she glared into his eyes.

How dare you make casual conversation with me, you bastard?

Laffoone braced his weight on the ebony cane. "I thought you'd be happy to move about the boat."

She tightened her jaw, refusing to respond.

"We'll dock in New Orleans tomorrow," he said, resting his arm across the railing. His gaze crept over her like green slime on a stagnate pond.

"I'll see that you get new clothes once you're settled into your room. As long as you behave, you'll be treated well. If not, you will be disciplined." He paused and his stare locked with hers. "Do you understand?"

Her eyes narrowed. "Never," she hissed.

"Defiance becomes you, my dear," he said, smiling. "You are quite beautiful now that I see you in the sunlight. Perhaps I shall keep you for myself. It's been some time since I've met a woman as lovely as you." His gaze lowered to her breasts. "Yes, you do have a lot to offer."

Debbie turned away.

He smoothed his hand over her shoulder. She flinched, then jerked forward.

"Don't touch me," she sneered through clinched teeth. "You may own me, but you'll never have me."

"We'll see about that," he quipped, steeping back. "Enjoy the remainder of the journey. I'll see you tomorrow." He swung around and stepped to the door. "Oh, yes...and one other thing. My name is John Laffoone. You will address me at all times as Mr. Laffoone." He scanned her body from head to toe, then disappeared inside the vessel.

She bit her lip. "Lucifer would be more appropriate." Her words lashed at the vacant doorway.

Tears filled Debbie's eyes as she stared at a fast-approaching paddle wheeler rumbling toward her. The bright paint and colorful flags offered little cheer to her grief, and the mass of passengers waving at her were too far away to hear her cries for help. A shrill whistle pierced her ears and she dropped her gaze to the rippling wake that rolled across the water.

I should jump in and end my misery.

Her shoulders shuddered. She began to sob.

No! I'll never give up. Some way… Somehow…I'll take back my life. I swear it.

Debbie straightened and sucked in a ragged breath. Lifting her chin, she returned to her cabin. An image of Jason, bronzed from the sun and smiling as he'd prepared their picnic, brightened her sorrow. She swiped away her tears. Oh, how she yearned to touch him.

From this day forward, I will be one day closer to returning to you. Please wait for me, my darling. With God's help, I'll be home soon.

Chapter Eighteen

Breath catching deep in her throat, Debbie turned toward the rattling doorknob. *Please don't be Laffoone.*

Relief engulfed her as a robust servant, head swathed in a red-and-white checked turban, waddled into the room. The large-framed woman barked out her orders. "I's been told ta clean ya up fer dinner."

Debbie raked her glare over the messenger of grief. "Dinner? I'm not one bit hungry."

Cheeks as round as croquet balls underscored the Amazon's timeworn features. Her garment, though clean, had faded from years of wear. Worn leather slippers slapped against the floorboards with each step the servant scuffed toward Debbie. She stopped just short of knocking her over.

With a muffled grunt, she anchored her plump fists atop well-rounded hips. "Don't matter what you want. Da boss says I's to give ya a bath, and dats what I intends to do."

Debbie crossed her arms. "Have you lost your mind? I'm being held against my will. Dinner with that jackal is the last thing I want to do."

The servant leaned forward and waggled a taunting finger before Debbie's face. "Ya'll do what da boss says. And he wants you clean when you visit him in his room."

Her words cut through Debbie like a straight razor. "He's not my boss."

"Listen here, missy, I ain't losin' my job over no stubborn woman. I's got youngins' ta feed 'n I makes good pay. So, you just hop right on up here 'n let's get ya washed." Perspiration skimmed down the servant's temples and gathered in the thick folds of her ebony neck. "Stand up, child," she snapped, motioning her hands toward Debbie. "We's gotta get busy."

Debbie cocked her chin. "I know what he wants and it isn't dinner."

"What's the matter with you, girl? Yo's ain't here to entertain no preacher." The woman sunk her fingers in the soft flesh of Debbie's upper arm. "If yo's don't obey, it'll be off ta da Adams House, fer you. And ya sure don't wanna go there. I's worked da Adams many times and the lowest of life wallows in dat filthy place."

"I'm a prisoner no matter where I am," Debbie sneered.

A frown creasing the servant's forehead, she pressed closer. "Don't make me call fer help." She pulled in a deep breath and then softened her tone, her hold releasing. "Come on, child, don't ya realize you's special. I's worked fer Laffoone for a long time now, 'n' no woman he's ever bought had the privilege of dining with him."

"Privilege?" she scoffed. "He can rot in hell, for all I care." Her glare burned into widened ebony eyes.

"What's wrong, child?" The servant released her grip and eased back. "Most women begs him ta be his mistress, but he don't pay 'em no mind. He says they just wants his money."

Debbie lowered her chin, fighting back tears. "I don't want his money or anything else. Don't you understand? I just want to go home." Her hand trembled as she covered her mouth, choking back the misery.

"Lord, have mercy. Ya done got yo'self in a real mess, haven't ya?"

"P-Please help me?" Debbie pleaded, her heartbeat quickening at the possibility of escape. "I-I beg you. I don't have money now, but when I get home I'll send you whatever you ask."

The servant took a cloth from her pocket and swiped her brow. On a sigh, she shook her head. "No…I can't do dat," she mumbled, "I'd get shot fer sure. I's seen da boss kill a feller fer just talkin' 'bout helpin' one of his whores get free. No... no, I ain't doin' dat."

Debbie's stomach knotted and she wrenched at the fading hope of freedom. Her chin lowered, forcing back a wave of tears.

A blink later, a warm hand touched her arm.

"Just do as da boss says 'n' he'll treat ya good," the servant insisted, all harshness in her voice fading. She flashed a comforting smile. "Let's get ya cleaned up 'n pick ya out somthin' nice ta wear. After dat if'n ya still don't wanta go, I'll tell da boss ya ain't feelin' good. "

"Y-You'd do that?" Debbie tightened her lips and drew a broken breath. The woman nodded.

Finally, someone I can talk to without fearing for my life.

"What's your name?" Debbie whispered.

"Folk calls me Cotton, 'cause I use to work da cotton fields up north."

Debbie shoved the tattered blanket aside. "So you've been here awhile, then?"

"Yes, 'em. I's been here ten years. I lives on a boat in da Bayou, but I works in Naw-lens."

"You have children?"

"Sho' do." Cotton's eyes twinkled. "I has four youngins' and dey's da reason I do dis. Dey ain't gonna waste away in no cotton fields. Un-uh." She clutched Debbie's hand. "Now, enough talkin', let's get ya ta da washroom and outta dese rags."

Cotton led the way down the hall past Laffoone's personal quarters. Bile rose in Debbie's throat as she scurried past. The boat shifted on a wave beneath her feet and she fought to maintain her balance. She slammed her hands against the door frame. "I-I can't do this," she stuttered.

"Yo's gonna be just fine," Cotton said, as she shuffled over the threshold of the empty room and headed toward a copper claw-foot tub. Curlicues of steam rose from the water. "Get outta dose nasty clothes, child. Once ya get freshened up ya's gonna feel much betta."

The odor of fish seeped through the partially-opened window, gnawing at her queasy stomach. Debbie staggered into the wash room. Her gaze swept the darkened interior. Shelves hugged the far wall and all manner of supplies filled the space. Obviously, some sort of storage area. She stepped from her slippers, her hands trembling as she fumbled to untie the knotted belt around her waistband. With a shrug of her shoulders, she sent the garment to the floor.

A racket outside drew her attention. "Ugh," she uttered, forcing back another bitter rush up her throat. *Why can't they throw the fish guts off the boat?*

Cotton placed two towels on the stool next to the tub. After sprinkling lilac petals across the water's surface, she laid a wash cloth and soap on the seat of a nearby chair.

A sensation of helplessness coiled around Debbie as she stepped into the tub. Warmth caressing her aching body, she slid into the water. A mellow glow enveloped her and she closed her eyes.

"I needed this, Cotton. Thank you." The words fell from her lips in a mumbled whisper.

"I's be back in a moment," the servant replied, the door clicking shut behind her exit.

Debbie eased back against the smooth metal edge. The haunting darkness of the past few days began to fade. Her breathing slowed, easing the tension that held her in bondage.

A moment later, the door creaked and she straightened with a splash.

Cotton smiled. "It's only me."

Debbie watched as the energetic woman gathered the soiled clothing and tossed them into a wicker basket.

"Ya take yo' time, missy. I's gonna clean yo's bedding, then I'll be back with ya somethin' to wear." The servant plucked fresh sheets from a nearby shelf before exiting the room.

Debbie drew a deep breath, then once more lowered into the water.

* * *

The setting sun streaked through the window reminding Debbie that nightfall would soon cover the land. Dressed in a blue brocade evening gown, the hem of the bustled garment whispered over the floor as she crossed to the filthy panes and peered out. The wooded shoreline beckoned her. If only she could swim such a distance. Perhaps happiness loomed just beyond the trees. Or, better yet, Jason would be there astride Blue, waiting to take her home.

She sighed, pressing her forehead against the window.

If only that were true.

A rustle at the door drew her attention and she whipped around.

Laffoone stepped into the room.

Her chest tightened, capturing her breath.

She glared at the monster.

He pretends to be a gentleman, but I'm wise to his charade.

"You're quite beautiful," he said. He raked his gaze over her body, pausing at the generous swell of her breasts above the low-cut décolletage.

Her cheeks flushed and she glanced away, a sickening desolation flooding over her.

He stalked closer. "Come, my dear, we're dining on the deck this evening."

"D-Didn't Cotton tell you, I'm not feeling well?"

His fingers tapped the handle of his cane. "Perhaps you just need a good meal." His gaze locked with hers and he leaned forward.

Debbie stumbled back.

Dark shadows streaked the walls and threatened to close around her, their cloistering grip emphasizing this menacing monster and his evil game. He blocked her path to freedom.

Another rush of blackness loomed before her.

Vomit slid up her throat, burning, igniting her fear. She squeezed her eyes shut. "I...I really do feel sick," she stammered.

He raised his cane, and brushed the black-lacquered tip against her hair. "You do look a bit pale."

She slapped the stick away.

He smirked, then reached into his pants pocket and withdrew a metal container.

Her lips pulled tight, capturing her breath. "What are you doing?"

"Here, I'll give you something that will make you feel better."

"I doubt that," she growled, turning away.

"Perhaps a glass of wine would ease your stomach. I have a nice selection in my room."

She shook her head.

I'm not going into that chamber of horror.

A deafening silence seared her nerves. He turned away and with each step he took, the cane tapped the weathered floor.

Debbie winched. The door creaked open and he spoke to a man in the hallway. When the barrier clicked shut, she pivoted. The obnoxious beast stood before her.

She shuddered, driving her chin upward. *Go away you bastard.* "Good night, Mr. Laffoone."

He laughed and stepped closer. "You amuse me, my dear."

Debbie thrust her fists into his chest and kicked his leg. He staggered backward dropping his walking stick. His face washed scarlet with anger and her breath locked in her throat. The fire in his eyes sent a bolt of terror through her. She pivoted and he grasped her upper arm. Her body tightened and she closed her eyes. A painful jerk brought her to face him. She gasped. He pulled her tight against him. His vile breath, rancid with tobacco and whisky, rushed up her nostrils. His mouth crashed upon hers, pushing apart her lips. His tongue darted toward hers, igniting a craving for revenge. She bit down hard.

He forced her aside and grasped at his throbbing flesh. "Damn it, woman," he yelped. A quick glance at the blood on his fingertips and a fire raged in his eyes.

"You little bitch," he growled, advancing toward her. "You don't know what hell you've created for yourself."

He shoved her to the bed and fell across her, the weight of his body entrapping her. Desperation pulled at her chest as she fought to breathe.

Blood forced to her head, pounding with every heartbeat. Frantic, she curled her fingers into a fist and struck his face.

Fumbling hands groped at her dress and jerked.

A rush of cool air crossed her shoulder. She sucked in a gulp of air, then twisted to the side. His lips found her neck and she pushed at his jaw to escape.

"No," she screamed.

His tongue trailed a path of saliva across her chin and tracked to her nipple. She wrenched and drove her knee into the monster's groin.

A high-pitched yelp followed as Laffoone rolled to his side.

She leapt from the bed. "I'm not your whore," she yelled. "I'll never surrender to you. I'll fight you with every ounce of strength I have, you disgusting son of a bitch."

He staggered to his feet. "You just made the biggest mistake of your life."

Gasping for air she stumbled backward. "I doubt that." She glared at the swine, refusing to yield.

Laffoone wiped the blood from his lip and strode to the door. "Bruce. Get in here."

The servant stepped into view.

"Have a carriage at the dock in the morning. We're taking this bitch to the Adams House." He settled his gaze on Debbie once more. "She needs to learn a thing or two about how to please a man."

* * *

A loud commotion shook Debbie from a sound sleep. Sliding to the edge of her bed, she rubbed her eyes, then peered outside. Dawn's light glanced off white sails gliding past the small opening. She staggered across the room and pressed her nose against the glass. Orange streaks cast an eerie glow through a thick grey fog that hovered above a busy harbor. Four-masted ocean-going rigs and rickety shrimp boats vied for positions along the dock.

She tightened her lips.

New Orleans!

The *Sally Mae* bumped against a hard surface and the floor beneath her shuddered. The impact against the pier pitched her sideways to the bed. She scurried across the mattress, sprang to her feet, and returned to the window. Two men shuffled into view. The morning sunlight glistened off the worker's biceps as they wrapped thick mooring ropes around wooden posts.

She pressed her nose against the glass and strained to peer out across the waters. Dozens of majestic vessels, filled with cargo she could only imagine, loomed on the horizon like frigates readying for battle. Another loud thump drew her attention.

Stout, bare-chested workmen, their dungarees soiled and tattered, extended a wooden plank from the *Sally Mae* to the dock.

Blindsided by the click of the lock behind her, Debbie gasped. She whirled to face the door. The barrier swung open and Laffoone entered, followed by a short, broad shouldered companion.

"Get dressed," Laffoone snapped. "We'll be waiting outside." He scanned her bare shoulders, settling his cold blue gaze on her breasts. Her heart vaulted to her throat. The gleam in his eye bit at her soul.

Laffoone massaged the walking stick's silver knob as a wicked smirk twitched his mouth. He lifted his cane and prodded her trembling hand. "Will you come along civil, or do I need to give you something? Matter's little to me. Either way, I would like this to be a peaceful transition."

Debbie glared at him. "I...I won't make a fuss," she mumbled. Blood rushed through her vein and every nerve spiked like jagged glass. She swallowed back her words.

If I had a gun, I'd blow your head off.

"Good," he growled, vacating the room.

Debbie climbed from the bed and swept up her soiled dress. Cotton had earlier stitched the torn garment and memories of the previous night flooded Debbie's thoughts. *By the grace of God, I won that battle. A small victory in a sea of defeats.*

She fumbled with the tiny buttons, securing each loop along the seam. She smoothed along her waist and across her hips, dashing away the wrinkles. A quick twist of her locks, a pin placed here and there, and her tresses rested in a chignon on the nap of her neck.

Her mind whirling, she stared into the broken mirror.

The Adams House.

Can it be as terrible as Cotton described? She squeezed her eyes shut. *I don't know how to be a whore. How can women do such unthinkable things and survive? Maybe they don't. Maybe they end up dead.* She pulled in a ragged breath and glanced at the door.

There's no escape. Not now. Not ever.

Tears filled her lashes as she stepped into the hallway.

Laffoone jerked her closer to him and led her down the ramp to a waiting carriage.

As they traveled into the city, the streets became narrow and less congested. The horses' hooves pounded against the pavement. Her thumping heartbeat matched the rhythm of the carriage wheels and mirrored the terror locked beneath her corset. Her jangled nerves pricked her skin like a thousand bee stings. Each drawn breath became more difficult than the previous.

Debbie swallowed hard and forced her gaze across well-groomed lawns and wrought-iron fences. The colossal brick mansions with white columned verandas reminded her of home.

Memories of the Jackson Estates beckoned her away from the fear and anguish that ripped at her heart.

She yearned to be wrapped in the safety of Jason's arms.

A glance at Laffoone washed away the comfort of her musings. His fingers tapping against the silver-knob pricked her anxiety once more. She choked back the torment and glanced away.

Strange moss dangled from the trees. The wispy grey strands sent another chill through her. What unthinkable creatures lurked inside?

The carriage wheels clattered on the bricks as the rig rounded the corner. They traveled down Canal Street, then turned onto Royal St.

Moments later, the carriage stopped before a run-down brick building that captured her breath.

The Adams House.

"Your new residence," Laffoone snarled, pointing his cane toward the entrance. His glare chilled her soul. He narrowed his eyes and she yelped as he yanked her from the carriage. Several footsteps later, he shoved her across the threshold.

A large-framed woman, wrapped in a scarlet satin dress and black silk stockings met them inside the dimly lit entry. Debbie gagged as the smell of soiled furniture and body odor rushed up her nostrils. She blinked to clear away the stale cigar smoke that burned her eyes.

This vile pit of filth was all that Cotton had warned…and more.

"Here, take this whore," he ranted, shoving Debbie forward. She jerked around and bolted for the door.

He cracked his cane across her shoulders and she crumbled to the floor. Her cheek scraped the aged wood. Her palms pressed against the grit beneath her and she staggered to her feet.

Glaring at Laffoone, her unleashed anger spilled in revenge. "Y-You monster. Someday…someway, you'll pay for what you've done."

He laughed, "I doubt that." Turning toward the Madame, he snarled, "Get her out of my sight before I kill her."

Chapter Nineteen

"Mr. Jackson fell straight to the ground. You gotta hurry," James screamed, his hands flailing.

Jason slammed the chute closed and drove home the lock. With the vet on his heels, he dashed outside.

His father lay crumpled beside the overturned wheelchair. "Get the wagon," he shouted over his shoulder to the stable boy. "We've got to get him back to the house."

Peter leaned forward. "I'll help you roll him over."

The vet grabbed Taylor's leg as Jason grasped his father's shoulders. With a controlling push, they rolled him onto his back. Jason checked his father's breathing before staggering to his feet. "He's still alive," he declared.

Crunching stones preceded the wagon hurtling around the corner. James pulled back on the reins. The Belgian draft horse slid to its thick muscular haunches, hooves digging deep into the loose gravel.

Peter swung into the wagon's bed and tossed aside feed bags to clear a spot for the old man. They lifted Jackson into the back.

Jason ordered, "You drive. And James, you go fetch the doctor."

The lad pitched Peter the lines and dashed away.

Bracing his feet against the seat, Jason wrapped his arms around his father to hold him still. The wagon jerked and then rumbled forward across the hill.

Within moments, they arrived at the front walk. An abrupt stop tossed Jason sideways. With a grimace, he jumped from the wagon.

His mother bolted down the steps and rushed to their side. Her face washed pale and her eyes widened. "My God," she rasped, reaching for his father's hand. "What happened?"

"Don't know," Jason puffed, pushing past her as he balanced the old man's limp body. "He just collapsed."

"Jeremiah," she yelled to the towering servant hovering in the hallway. "Come quick. We need help."

With a determined nod, the servant rushed to their aid, slipped his massive arms beneath Taylor and lifted.

They clamored into the house into the downstairs bedroom and rolled Taylor onto the mattress.

Jason glanced at his friend. "Thanks for your help."

"Hope he's alright," Peter rasped. "I'll go back and take care of Infinity." He exited the room.

Kathryn lowered onto the edge of the mattress. Leaning forward, she again reached for Taylor's hand. "I love you so much," she whispered. "Please don't leave me." Tear-filled eyes met Jason's and he offered a nod of support.

She pressed her cheek against his father's chest, biting back her whimpers.

Swallowing hard, Jason pivoted on a boot heal and left the room. Heavy footfalls carried him to the veranda. Slumping against the closest Corinthian column, he stared at the black void above him.

One disaster follows another. There's no time to resolve anything.

"Damn it," he snarled, slamming his fist against the railing. "What the hell's happening?"

Grief gnawed at his soul and every muscle in his body begged for the torment to end. A meadowlark called from a nearby fence post and Jason glanced across the lawn. Grazing horses and golden fields eased back the tension. His eyes squeezed shut. Unbidden tears seeped out, rolling down his burning cheeks. He shifted his head. A shadowy reflection skimmed beneath his eyelids. A long exhale preceded the frown that tugged at his lips. The image of Debbie with heathens, who neither knew, nor cared for her, tore at his soul.

He dropped into the nearest chair. Frustration bit at every nerve. He leaned forward, shoving his fingers through his hair. *Damn it, Punkin, where are you?*

Scuffing steps brought him around and he settled his gaze upon his mother in the doorway.

"Son, your father's stirring. Come back now."

Jason captured his bottom lip with his teeth. Duty had summoned once more. He straightened and tightened his jaw. Pulling his shoulders back, he followed her to the bedroom and Taylor rested his gaze on them. "Kathryn," he mumbled.

"Yes, darling," she said, her voice quivering. She rested her hand atop his grizzled cheek. "You must stay quiet. The doctor's on his way."

She glanced up at Jason and he nodded, confirming he, too, saw his father's inability to move his left arm. He'd heard about the paralyzing effect of such an event. Confident the doctor would identify the cause, he settled into a nearby chair to wait.

An unbearable hour passed before riders galloped down the lane to break his vigil. He stepped to the window and shoved aside the covering.

"Doc's here," he declared.

The front door slammed and a moment later a silver-haired man, clutching a medical bag, swept into the room.

After a thorough examination, the doctor removed his glasses and faced Jason. "His heart's weak. You must keep him quiet. Only time will tell the severity of his condition."

Jason embraced his mother. With a quiver, she turned and buried her face against his chest.

"The next few days are critical," the doctor continued. "Someone should stay with him."

Jason inhaled, accepting the responsibility. "We'll keep him comfortable."

The doctor removed the wire rimmed spectacles and shoved them into his coat pocket. "I'll be by tomorrow to check on him."

On a sigh, he patted Jason's upper arm, then vacated the room.

Hours later, the hall clock chimed midnight.

Jason leaned forward in the chair and rubbed his eyes. *I must've dozed off.* Taylor did not stir as Jason approached and adjusted the lightweight blanket across his father's shoulders.

Pivoting, he peered out the window. Dawn's glow fell mellow across the fields. A breeze rustled nearby branches. He loved this time of year. The remembered stroll with Debbie through the forest last fall warmed his heart. A kiss beneath the oak tree with their carved initials reinforced their love. Yet, strands of her long chestnut hair, tossed by the wind, replicated the turmoil in his life. Even the fallen leaves crunching beneath their feet like empty pecan shells chewed at his uneasiness. And the echo of her laughter surrounded him, driving the grief deep into his soul.

Heavy footsteps scattered his thoughts and his gaze darted to the doorway.

"Good morning, sir," Jeremiah said, stepping into the room. "I'd be pleased to stay with Mr. Jackson 'til the Mrs. comes down." His smile reflected the gentleness of this husky man. "Also, Millie has your breakfast ready, Sir."

Jason nodded and left the room.

* * *

Late morning found him checking on Infinity. As he leaned forward to examine the injured hock, Jason's attention was drawn to an approaching wagon. With a frown, he faced the stable door.

"Howdy," the stranger said, stepping closer. He offered Jason a handshake. "Fred Jones, with the Silver Star Stables. Bought a couple of mares and a foal from you last spring."

"Yes, I remember." Jason shook the man's hand. "You made that deal with my father. I'm his son, Jason. What can I do for you?"

"I could use another mare if you've got one to sell. I've been pleased with the last two I purchased."

"Don't have any available right now." Stroking his chin, Jason continued, "However, I do have a nice two-year-old filly that'll make a good broodmare one day. She's got strong bloodlines. Thought I'd race her for a year or two and then breed her."

Jones contemplated the offer, then replied, "I need one that's already been bred."

"Nope," Jason replied, resting his shoulder against the stall door. "I've got nothin' in foal right now."

James raced down the corridor and slid to a stop before them, swallowing hard. "S-Sorry," he said, gasping. "But there's a colt out front that looks just like Coal."

Jason faced back at the visitor. "You have Bess's colt with you?"

"Yes, I'm taking him to auction. He's the meanest son of a bitch I've ever ran across. He should've been named Black Devil instead of Coal. Don't know how his mother could be so gentle and he could be such a jackass."

Jason winked at James, then returned his gaze to Mr. Jones. "So, you're going to sell him?"

"You're damn right," the man assured him. "He's kicked me twice and bit me, God only knows how many times. I just wanta be rid of him."

"What do ya want for him?"

"Anything I can get," the man said, adjusting his Stetson. "It'd save me a trip into to the auction."

James gawked. "Y-You mean we're gonna get him back?"

"Sure," Jason said, a smile lifting his lips.

"Great." James dashed from the stable.

Squinting one eye and tipping his head, the man asked, "You sure you need that wild heathen?"

"Who?" Jason laughed. "The boy or the colt?" He shot a gaze toward his stable hand and winked. "Yes, I'm sure. Sides, Coal's got good bloodlines. Maybe he'll outgrow his orneriness one day. You come back in a couple of years," he added, with another chuckle. "You may want to buy him back, then."

"Not on your life." Mr. Jones snarled.

Chapter Twenty

Early December and still no word on Debbie's whereabouts.

A cold rain pelted Jason, drenching his hair and sluicing past the collar of his black slicker. He pushed open the heavy stable door, then kicked the mud caked on the soles of his boots. Long strides carried him across the threshold of the new addition. He turned and headed toward the corridor that housed Infinity's stall.

"Infinity," he acknowledged when the stallion bobbed its massive head. Jason clutched the leather halter and leaned forward to view the horse's hock. The ankle had healed, but scars were a constant reminder of that horrible night. His gaze lifted to the chest wound. *No sign of infection.* He caressed the jagged flesh and the colt flinched. "Still tender, isn't it, fella?"

Releasing the leather, Jason petted the animal's silky neck, then headed down the corridor toward his office. A mountain of paperwork awaited him. The rattle of a carriage halted him in stride and he tilted to get a clearer view.

With a hand atop his derby, John Butterfield dropped from the rig.

Smiling, Jason held open the stable door. "What brings you out on this nasty day?"

"Headin' up to visit Taylor." He swiped the raindrops from the shoulder of his dark brown Chesterfield frock. "Thought I'd come by to aggravate him. Heard he's been a might depressed since the accident."

Jason rested his shoulder against a nearby post. "We can't get him to do anything. Hardly talks. Just sits and stares out the window."

"Hell, everybody gets depressed this time of year," Butterfield mumbled, removing his hat. "I know I hate to see winter comin'. Damn cold makes my knees hurt." He glanced at Infinity. "How's our prize stallion doin'? Think he'll be able to run come spring?"

"Worked him a bit yesterday, but he's still stiff."

"It's a damn shame." The man shook his head. "That horse was destined to be a champion."

"Still could be," Jason assured him. "He may not look good, but if he keeps improving, he can run a hell of a race."

"He's got the bloodlines. That's for sure." Butterfield spun around to peer into the stall next to him. The black colt lowered his ears and nipped at Butterfield's arm. "What the hell?" He jerked away.

Jason leaned over and pushed Coal back into the stall. "This is Bess's last foal."

"He's a mean little bastard."

Jason laughed. "We can thank that stud of yours for his temper."

The man's pudgy features twisted, mocking Jason.

"Once we get past the feisty temper though, he'll make a damn good sprinter."

Butterfield faced the window. "Someone livin' there now?" he asked, pointing a gloved finger at Packey's house. "I see a light over yonder."

Jason glanced at the familiar two-story framed cottage that hugged the hillside near the well. "Our stable boy, James, and his family moved in this past Thanksgiving. They're working for me now."

"Your place's sure growin'. Guess you can use the extra help."

"Sometimes I wonder if it isn't getting too big."

Butterfield met Jason's gaze. "You can never be too big, son." He winked, pulling a gold watch from his vest pocket. "Well, guess I'd better get to see the ol' man and stir him up a bit," he chuckled. "When I mention Infinity, he'll have plenty to say." He started for the door.

"Thanks, John. You're a good friend." The two clasped hands and Butterfield stepped out into the morning mist.

* * *

Noon brought a clearing sky. Jason finished his lunch, then headed for town.

An hour in the saddle and he arrived at the jail. A short note tacked to the door explained the sheriff was gone on a short errand. Jason drew a breath, then released the air on a ragged sigh. *Damn.* He needed to know if there was any news on Debbie's disappearance. He slammed his fist against the nearest post. *More wasted time.* Scanning the street he settled his gaze on the general store. *He'd pick up some peppermints for Mason while he waited for the lazy bastard to return.*

Entering the shop, Jason nodded to the salesman stocking shelves, then angled past a rotund lady examining a bold of blue gingham fabric. She'd need more material than that to cover her girth. He stifled a chuckle as he strolled to the glass container filled with sweets. Rotating the clear jar, he sorted through the treats.

The door behind him creaked open, drawing his attention.

His gaze cut to the figure lumbering toward him. Jason's eyes narrowed. His heart hammered against his ribs as the wrangler passed.

"Give me a twist of tobacco," the ruffian demanded, slapping a silver coin onto the countertop.

The clerk plucked the item from a box on the shelf behind the register.

Jason's breath held tight in his throat as he glared at the hooligan.

This bastard took Debbie.

A fire ignited in Jason's veins and his hand shook as he grabbed the man by the arm.

Fury fractured Jason's words, "Y-you're the one that held me up and kidnapped my woman."

The ruffian's features tightened and he jerked away. "Leave me alone. Don't know what you're talkin' about."

Jason's brows slammed together and he stepped in front of the vile smelling coward. "Oh, I think you do." He clinched his teeth as his fingers dug into the heathen's flesh. "What did you do with her? Where're your partners?"

A deep ridge of panic creased the man's weathered face. "Get away from me," he yelled struggling to free his arm.

Jason shoved him against a wooden post. A grunt fell from the bastard's mouth. Jason wrapped his hand around the man's unshaven throat. "Where are they?" he growled. "Where are those bastards you run with?"

Behind them, a lady shopper screamed and raced out the door.

"They're dead," the bandit gasped, tobacco-filled saliva dripping from the corner of his mouth.

"You're lying," Jason raged, blood pounding in his head. A flash of the attack bolted through his mind. Debbie's cry for mercy screamed around him. How dare this filthy animal touch her? Jason's nostrils flared, sucking enough air to empty the room. He loomed closer, hissing. His words dripped with enough venom to rival a rattle snake. "Where are they?"

The heathen struggled to escape Jason's death grip.

"I tell ya, t...they're dead. They got gunned down a month ago," he wheezed, spit spraying from his sun-blistered lips.

"Where's my woman?" Jason ranted, grabbing a handful of greasy hair and slamming the villain's head against the post. "Where is she?"

Jason caught a glimpse of the sales clerk lifting a shotgun from beneath the counter.

"I-I don't know," the wrangler muttered, his bloodshot eyes bulging. "We t-took her to the dock at Pigeon Point. Someone else took her from there."

"I went there," Jason sneered, slamming the man's head again. " No one saw her."

"'c-cause we delivered her at night. She was covered with feed sacks."

Jason drove his fist into the man's jaw. Blood spurted from the busted mouth as the bandit ricocheted off a nearby table, slamming onto the floor.

A heart-pounding moment later, Jason nudged the limp body with the toe of his boot. "You sonofabitch, I oughta kill you," he muttered.

Glancing at the clerk, he shouted, "Give me the gun and get the sheriff."

The shopkeeper tossed him the shotgun and rushed from the store.

Jason rolled his prisoner over and pressed the gun barrel against the bastard's temple. Shaking, Jason braced the sole of his boot on the man's boney chest.

The ruffian moaned and slid his eyes open.

"Your ass is gonna hang from the highest tree," Jason growled. "Then you can burn in hell with your partners."

Chapter Twenty-One

Christmas Day

Dinner with all the trimmings still did not fill the emptiness inside Jason. He settled into the parlor chair near the fireplace, sinking against the leather. The glowing embers sent back a shimmer of Debbie's eyes, flickering in the fire to beckon him. Desire swept through his veins. He craved to wrap her nakedness against him and slide his fingers through her silken tresses.

The mere scent of her lingered in his memory and hardened his aching groin.

These past weeks searching for her, wore him and his horse down. He wanted Debbie between his legs, not the damn gelding.

A log collapsed onto the grate. He straightened. His fingers tightened on the cool brass tacks that formed along the leather. He shoved to his feet and headed for the sidebar.

Pine scent wafted from the nearby Balsam tree and mingled with the fire's smoldering ash.

A giggle drew his attention to Mason playing beside their father. The toddler's infectious laughter reverberated with happiness and hope for the future.

I could use your optimism, little brother.

He lifted the decanter and poured a hefty shot of bourbon into the cut crystal glass. Bringing the cool tumbler to his lips, he downed a generous gulp. The smooth liquor swished across his tongue, then burned a trail to the pit of his stomach. He tightened his lips. A hiss escaped between clinched teeth. Another gulp of his favorite drink and he ambled to the fireplace.

He reached for the iron rod and jammed the piece into the logs to break them apart. The charred wood ignited, sending orange and gold flames spiraling upward.

Heat radiated against his chest to remind him all over again of Debbie's gentle warmth. He eased back. Shadows danced along the walls with haunting implications. Frustration amplified inside him with each tick of the mantle clock. Blood pounded in his head and his ears rang like a hundred church bells.

He tightened his fingers around the glass, his thumb sweeping away the cool condensation. Five months was too long to be without her. How could he spend any holiday, or any other damn day, without his beloved? He churned up more precious memories. He loved teasing her with short puffs of air across her ear. She'd giggle, squirm, then tighten against him, begging for more. Again he traced his tongue along the soft curve, pulling the lobe between his teeth.

Every moment, every touch, every smell, completed him.

Another laugh from his brother punctured Jason's escape.

Perspiration beaded his forehead and he swallowed back his heartbreak. Misery swept in and gnawed at his gut, once more. Infinity's injuries, his father's illness, everything held him hostage. He lowered his chin and brushed aside the anguish.

A rustling nearby forced him to cut his gaze to his mother. She strolled over to join him. "Here, darling, I brought you a slice of fruit cake."

Jason slipped his hand beneath the dish and snorted. "This was Debbie's favorite."

"I remember," she whispered, reaching toward the fire's warmth. "There's a real chill in the house tonight."

"A chill?" He jammed the fork into the desert. "I feel like I'm in a damned oven."

"I know." She rubbed her hand across his back. "She's gone. That's so wrong."

"Everything's wrong. She should be here, mother. This was her favorite time of year."

"We all miss her."

Frustrated, he poked the fork tines at the crumbs, scraping across the bitter truth of his loss.

"I'd hoped by finding the kidnapper we'd learn more. Instead the bastard hung himself in the jail cell. All I know is they put her on a boat."

"One day, there'll be a break in the case."

"Better be soon. 'cause I'm not waitin' much longer." He slammed the empty dish on the mantel and the fork rattled onto the wood.

"Please, for me, set aside your misery. Tonight, let's just enjoy being together."

Jason exhaled, glancing toward the ailing, aging father. "Is there anything more we can do for him?"

"No." The word caught on the end of her sigh. "There's little chance for improvement."

He felt his father's hopelessness. Without Debbie, he too had no future.

"Mommy," Mason interrupted, tugging at her skirt.

The toddler raised his arms, whimpering. A heartbeat later, she lifted the child against her. His younger brother rubbed his eyes. Yawning, he rested his head against her shoulder.

"It's too early for bed, little man," Jason said, opening his palms to the toddler. "Come with me and we'll rustle up some more Christmas cookies."

The boy smiled and fell forward into Jason's arms.

Two hours later, the house had silenced. Jason returned to the parlor to blow out the candles on the Christmas tree. Odor from melted candle wax wafted across the room.

Drawn by a shift in the logs, he faced the fireplace. Dying embers draped eerie shadows over the parlor floor. He crossed to the wood box and gathered logs to bank the fire. Three short strides and he shoved the pieces onto the simmering ash. A burst of flames brightened the hearth. He stepped back and lowered into the leather chair.

Sleeplessness had tortured him, but tonight he could not shake the haunting spell of the fire. An unexplainable urgency burned inside him along with a beseeching fear. He grasped the nearby crystal tumbler and downed the last of the whiskey.

I'll never stop searching for you, my love.

Never.

* * *

Church bells rang across New Orleans and families gathered for Christmas celebrations.

In the city's core, a brothel blazed a contradiction to the joy of the season. A flicker, then an orange glow, radiated from the house of ill repute. Flames lapped from a third floor window as the Adams House lit up the night sky.

Holiday visitors on nearby Bourbon Street quickly learned of the blaze. Panic spilled into the street.

A heavy pounding brought Debbie to her feet.

"Fire," the frantic voice yelled on the opposite side of the weathered panel.

She gathered her robe, dashed across the room and swung open the door. The backside of Madame Charlotte faded into the darkness.

Smoke churned in black waves down the passageway.

Debbie coughed, grabbing for the elk's tooth necklace sewn inside the hem of her nightgown. Needing to save nothing more, she sucked charred air into her lungs and bolted into the hallway.

Screams and thundering footfalls spiked her fear. Intense heat smacked her cheeks as she groped past fleeing residents. Flailing arms pounded her body, shoving her aside. Each staggering step took her down the staircase. Her throat burned as she heaved out choking fumes. Several people lay strewn before her and forced her to crawl across their limp bodies. Fumbling toward a distorted light, she fell through the opened front door and into the street.

With tears blurring her vision, fresh air assailed her lungs.

Hooves pounded and clangs from an approaching fire wagon ripped across the night burrowing into her ears.

A woman ran past her, shrieking, her gown on fire. Moments later the prostitute fell to the ground beside Debbie.

Lowering on one knee Debbie ripped away the burning material. Each layer encased with melted flesh that channeled into her nostrils.

Vomit edged up her throat.

The woman's hair dangled, singed and matted. Her features distorted. She gulped for air, then died in Debbie's arms.

Debbie gagged, then turned away. Her own mouth parched. The tip of her tongue brushed her lips. The taste of soot followed.

Burning flesh and flaming wood surrounded her.

Whaling pleas from trapped victims ripped through the night. She jammed her hands against her ears to muffle their dying cries.

A shudder sent helplessness over her.

Men with buckets shouted orders as they formed a brigade and splashed forward. Debbie pivoted, her bare feet chilled against the bricks.

A robust man and a frequent visitor to the brothel, lumbered in front of her in a confused daze. He grabbed her arm and she flashed him a wicked glare. Pulling away, she curled her lip. "Leave me alone, you son of a bitch." She shoved his shoulders, rocking him back on his heels. He stumbled to the ground.

Her eyes widened.

Oh, my God. This is my chance. I've got to get out of here. Her heart pounded as she scanned the crowd for a familiar face. *I need to go before they see me.*

Trembling, she darted into the night.

Weak leg muscles burned as she plowed forward, her arms thrashed, dispensing the smoke. She scrambled along the walkway faster…and faster still.

Oh God, Jason. I'm free.

Her feet raked across the swirling debris. Each breath clawed a path to her lungs.

Escape propelled through her veins and drove her forward.

She turned the corner, her robe swinging open. A broken railing on a wrought iron fence impaled the sheer peignoir. An immediate jerk scattered the buttons across her feet. On a deep-throated grunt, Debbie tumbled to the ground. Stones embedded her palms as she braced her fall. Dazed, she pressed upward onto her elbows. Rolling over, she slipped her hands across her belly.

Her throat clamped shut.

Precious seconds passed.

A flutter rippled beneath her palm.

The baby's alive.

With a sigh, Debbie surged to her feet and stripped away the flimsy robe. Her last connection with the Adams House fell to the ground. Picked up by a spirited wind, the garment fluttered away and faded into the darkness.

"Jason," she whispered. "I want to come home, but I can't." She touched her stomach once more. "I can't bring you a bastard child. I love you too much. Please forgive me."

A deafening explosion swept her back into the moment. Her gaze cut to the flames. She tensed as her prison crashed to the ground. Tears washed her cheeks.

Thank God, I'll never have to return to the Adams House, again.

A stampede of fleeing onlookers knocked her sideways. Her heart ramped to a feverish pace. She widened her stance and regained her balance. On a ragged breath, she melted into the crowd.

Exhaustion bit at her thighs and she ducked into the nearest alley. With a heavy pant, she doubled over, clutching her knees. Minutes passed like hours as she huddled in the dark.

The shrieks, the screams and the shouts of the firemen receded on the backside of her fear. A long sigh slivered from her lungs. With each broken breath, her pulse slowed.

Debbie stumbled forward into the flickering shadows and a half dozen steps later, she collided with a soft figure exiting a rear door. The glow of a nearby oil lamp spilled over the woman's shoulders as they stumbled backward.

Debbie peered into the woman's ebony face. "C-Cotton?" she sputtered. The sight of a friend, no matter how brief, warmed her heart. A smile tightened her lips. "Is that you?"

The woman smacked at Debbie's hand and reared back. "You gets away. Yah hear. I don't knows you."

Debbie swallowed hard. "It's Debbie. Remember? We met when Mr. Laffoone brought me to New Orleans."

Cotton stared at her. A moment of hesitation later, the servant's features softened "Yes, now I 'members you. But, why's ya here?"

"The building's on fire. I had to get away." She rubbed her fists against smoke- filled eyes. "You were right. The Adams House was pure hell," she mumbled.

"Yes 'em. Ya's lucky ya ain't sick from bein' dare."

Debbie shivered, then dropped her gaze. "I'm not sick. I'm going to have a baby."

"What? A baby? Lord have mercy...Ya poor child."

Chapter Twenty-Two

Debbie bit back her tears just as an ebony hand reached over to pat hers. "Where you gonna go?" Cotton asked, a frown creasing her forehead.

"I-I've no idea." Debbie quivered. A lump tightened her throat. "I have no place to go."

Cotton patted her trembling hand, tenderness filling her voice. "Come child, let's go inside. You's chilled to da bone. I'll get ya a cup of warm tea."

"Oh, Cotton, I- I'm frightened," she snuffled. Clutching onto the woman's hand, Debbie followed her into the kitchen.

"Don't you fret. We's gonna figure dis out."

The endearing words embraced Debbie. She exhaled a slow push of air and lowered onto a nearby rocker.

Cotton scurried off to the linen closet, then returned with a patchwork quilt and wrapped Debbie's shoulders.

A swish of the woman's huge hips and she plucked a kettle from the coal stove. A moment later, she placed a cup of steaming tea in Debbie's hands.

"You's lucky ta get outta dare alive," Cotton said, nestling on a wooden stool.

"I-I just kept running," Debbie sputtered, "I thought I was gonna die. People were screaming…their clothes were on fire. I-It was awful."

A twinge in Debbie's belly caught her breath and her eyes widened.

Cotton leaned closer. "How long has ya knowed 'bout da baby?"

"A few weeks." Debbie sighed and pressed the porcelain cup to her lip, sipping the tea. "When I realized I was with child, I wanted to die. You've no idea how bad my life's been. I was kidnapped, raped, sold like a slave and cast into that hellish Adam's House."

Cotton pinched her eyes tight. "When Laffoone built dat place, dat was da finest brothel in da Vieux Carre. Den a bunch of sailors brought da fever dat killed off most of da sugar lips, n 'ores. After dat, nobody wanted ta come dare no mo.'"

Debbie shifted in the rocker, "It should've burned down years ago." She paused, then slipped her hands beneath the blanket and unraveled her elk's tooth necklace from the gown. For a moment she stared at the piece. Her hand quivered. The mere touch sent

Jason's love pounding through her veins.

He's my life.

Her gaze met Cotton's. "This is all I have. No money, no home." *Nothing.*

Cotton narrowed her eyes. "Don't let me hear ya talk dat away. You's free now from all dat filth."

If it weren't for this necklace, I'd of given up months ago. When I hold this, I feel strong and hopeful. Don't you see, this is how I survived?"

"Then ya needs ta go back to yo family." Cotton pressed closer. "Ya's free, child. Go home."

Tears gathered between Debbie's lashes. "Even if I had a way to go back, I can't. Not now, with this child." Hesitating, she glanced away, then reconnected her gaze with Cotton's. "I need to get my life together, first."

"Well, ya gotta start. Ya got a new life in ya. Dat baby needs ya." She leaned closer. "Ya's comin' home wif me 'til ya get's on yo feet."

Debbie's heartbeat quickened. "I –I can't do that."

"Sho' ya can."

"B-But, I'll be a burden to you and your family."

Cotton reared back. "Life's a burden. What's one mo' person."

Debbie tightened and the blood drained from her head. "But, what about Laffoone? What if he comes after me?"

"Naw," Cotton spouted, waving her hand before her. "Laffoone's gone."

Debbie widened her eyes. "Gone?"

"Yes 'em. He went ta France on business and won't be back no time soon."

"Then you don't work for him anymore?"

Cotton shook her head. "I work's here at da hotel."

Debbie straightened. "Thank God."

"Now ya finish yo tea," Cotton said, wiggling off the stool. "I be right back."

She shuffled from the kitchen and returned moments later with a pink chenille housecoat draped across her arm. "Folk's is always leavin' their stuff behind. Here, put dis on. Ya needs somethin' warm fer da ride home."

Debbie dropped the blanket and slipped into the soft, new robe. Straightening, she looped the belt into a knot and drew a calming breath.

Cotton's lips bowed upward revealing the wide gap that separated her two front teeth.

Debbie eased back in the chair. She recognized the kindness in this woman. Love and compassion, once ripped away, now warmed her heart with hope from this beautiful soul.

A humming tune preceded a slight-built lady sauntering into the kitchen. Her arms were filled with tins of lard. She nodded and placed the containers on the counter. Cotton acknowledge the cook, then plucked the blanket from the floor. Leaning near Debbie's ear, she whispered "She burns everything she touches." A soft chuckle followed as she patted her knee. "Come on, child. We needs ta go now. Pappy's waitin' ta take us home."

* * *

Several weeks in the bayou swept Debbie into an unfamiliar world. Everything about her new life helped mend her fractured soul. Each morning she woke to the chatter of wild birds beyond her window.

The scent of the bayou, rich with decaying swamp grass and clumps of moss clinging from the Cypress trees, lifted her spirit. Even the water's ebb and flow with each new tide reminded her how precious life and freedom were to every creature on earth.

Brisk footsteps carried Debbie to the end of the wooden dock. She pitched the pan of dish water across the shallow waves, then pivoted. Ed, lovingly know as Pappy, rowed into view. The setting sun shimmered across his shoulders and long shadows followed him home.

She raised her hand and waved.

Moments later, he guided the boat alongside the dock. As he straightened, the craft shifted and he spread his feet for balance. Glancing up, the willowy-figured man flashed a toothy smile her way, then handed her the oars. With a hefty tug, she lifted the wet paddles onto the dock and secured them beneath a nearby bench. He tethered the boat, then gathered his catch and climbed onto the pier to join her.

"Looks like you had a good day," she said, pointing at the stringer of catfish and perch.

"Sho' did," he said, holding the fish out for her to examine. "Tomorrow I's gonna teach you how ta fish."

"I don't know about that, Ed."

Jason took her fishing once, but he did all the work. *I can't imagine touching those slimy creatures.*

With a long sigh, she turned and followed the old man.

Ed stowed away his gear and they meandered to the houseboat.

Blue-planked wood with white window frames brightened their modest home. Debbie smiled, remembering the tale Cotton told on their ride to the bayou. Blue was the color she wore when she first met her man. A soft chuckle returned to Debbie's lips. The first time she'd seen Jason she was wearing a celery green day dress.

The next morning, the sun had barely crested the eastern horizon when Ed approached her with an armload of fishing-tackle. She lowered her cup of coffee. Her heart sank.

"Time fer a lesson," he said with a smile.

Her brows tightened and she folded her arms across her chest, hoping her gesture of defiance would deter him.

"Finish yo drink 'n' come along girl. Times a wastin'," he snickered and swung around, scraping the wall with the end of the cane poles

They've been so kind, I can't say no.

She pushed her cup aside, her lips pulled tight and she eased out of the chair. The soles of her boots scraped the floor as she shuffled forward. Her nerve ends tingled in apprehension.

Damn it, I don't want to go.

She shoved open the door and stepped into the sunlight.

He lifted a crooked finger toward the western shoreline. "Let's go down by da point and try snagging a fish or two over yonder. Dat is if 'in da gators ain't ate 'em all." He chuckled.

Her eyes widened. "Are there really gators down there?"

His calloused hand wrapped her wrist. "Dem gators is everywhere. Ya just gotta be watchin' fer 'em. They can be sneaky."

Her mouth parched. "Maybe we shouldn't go." Biting back her fear, she scanned the water's edge. Her muscles knotted.

A slight tug and he pulled her forward through the tall, swamp grass. No damn fish was worth getting eaten alive by an alligator. She forced a deep breath and pressed close to his side.

Four miserable hours passed and they returned to the house with their catch. Debbie shoved her bucket of splashing critters in front of Cotton. "I actually caught something," she snickered.

Ed eased up behind them. "She did good. I's sendin' her back to get mo' while I gets us some crawfish."

"What?" She gasped. "Alone. I can't go alone."

"Sho ya can," Cotton spouted, giving her a nudge on the shoulder. "I be right here if in ya needs help."

"B-but I can't take those wiggly things off the hook," she stammered. "And what about the gators?"

Ed poured himself a cup of coffee and slipped onto a cushioned chair. "Ya gonna do fine. Just take 'em off da hook like I showed ya 'n' drop 'em in da bucket."

"B-but the gators?" She felt the blood drain from her head.

"Just stay in da clearin' and keep watchin'. Sides, most are nappin' on a log somewhere. They's waitin' for evenin' to eat white folks," he chuckled.

Beads of perspiration dotted Debbie's forehead. She drew a heavy breath. "I need to lie down. I don't feel well."

An hour passed before Debbie mustard up the nerve to return to fishing. With palms sweating and eyes as round as silver dollars, she cautiously eased back to their previous spot. Every rustle of a branch or splash in the water and her frayed nerves ratcheted up a notch.

An hour and two catches later, her tension eased. With shaking hands she baited the hook and tossed the line back in the water. Focusing on the twine, she settled onto an old tree stump.

Moments later, the string jerked.

She jumped to her feet, locking her hand around the bending pole. The line became rigid and she held tight.

The water agitated in a fury of splashes.

She backed up. Her eyes widened, then she screamed and dropped the pole. A hissing, mad-as-hell, alligator came charging toward her. She screamed again, then ran for the houseboat. Half-way there, her shoe stuck in the soft ground and she tumbled into the mud.

Panting, she glanced over her shoulder.

The gator hissed, then turned and slithered back into the water.

Debbie's heart slammed against her chest so hard she thought it would burst. For minutes she lay staring up into the sky. Each breath eased her fear. Tears streamed from the corners of her eyes.

No more. I can't do this anymore.

She rolled onto her side and covered her face with her arm and wept.

* * *

Cotton washed the fresh catch for dinner and dipped the fillets in seasoning, then arranged the strips in an iron skillet. The hot grease sizzled and popped as the fish fried.

Debbie leaned near her shoulder, "Can I help?"

"No, ya better rest. Ya had enough excitement fer one day." Cotton poked the strips with her fork. "You 'n' Pappy done caught a nice mess fer supper."

Debbie glanced at the children as they gathered at the table for dinner. Her gaze cut back to Cotton. "Can I go to the city with you tomorrow? I need to look for a job."

The woman turned to face her.

Debbie touched her shoulder. "I-I appreciate all you've done, but I must find work," she stammered.

A frown tightened Cotton's brows. "Ya know ya's welcome ta stay here 'til da baby comes."

Debbie drew a shallow breath. "I know, but I really must prepare a home for my child," she said, rubbing her hand on her ever-expanding stomach. "You've been so kind. I couldn't have survived without your help."

Brushing the corn meal from her palms, Cotton wiped her hand on a nearby towel. "Why don't ya go back ta da home ya left up north?"

Debbie lowered her gaze. "I think about that every day. But, I can't."

"Has ya ever thought of givin' up da baby?"

Debbie's eyes narrowed. "No. Even though I don't know who the father is, I could never give up my child. Besides, I was with Jason the night before I was raped. What if this baby is his? I would never forgive myself."

The woman gave a nod. "You's a good mother. Most women, especially the whores, wants ta get rid of their babies. I knew you's special."

"I just can't go back to my family. Not now."

She crossed to the window and peered at the sunset reflecting on the water. "It's so beautiful here. I'll never forget this place and how you gave me a new life. But, the time has come for me to prepare for the future." She turned to face Cotton. "I can do this. I know I can."

Chapter Twenty–Three

Camden, South Carolina
February 28, 1884

Race day arrived in glorious fashion. The Governor's Invitational brought together the finest thoroughbreds in the country. Thousands of people from all walks of life flocked to Carolina Downs. Shaded by towering oaks and a multitude of hemlocks, a three-tiered grandstand protected the crowd from the heat of the blazing sun.

Tents overflowing with all manner of folks nestled beneath a grove of pecan trees and radiated the aromas of hot buttered popcorn and frankfurters stuffed inside yeasty baked buns. Green painted benches lined a railing that hugged the race track and offered those who chose these seats an even closer view of the race.

Ladies wearing their best frocks, their bustled dresses made of watered-silk and brocade, rustled with every step as they strutted beside their handsome escorts. Mink stoles draped their shoulders and large hats, garnished with feathers and colorful flowers, were the rule of the day. Sunlight glinted off lavish jewelry as the ladies proudly twirled their ruffled parasols.

A smile and nod was readily offered to anyone who dared glance their way.

And off to the side, a man playing a calliope challenged for a space to be heard. Each piping note swirled around the backdrop of conversations and blended in the afternoon air.

Jason sighed as he scanned the crowd. *Time to get back to business.* He pitched the last handful of Caramel corn into his mouth, crumpled the bag and then tossed the paper into a nearby barrel. Pivoting, he headed for the stable.

After weeks of training Infinity and even though he was the last entry on the list, Jason deemed his stallion ready to face the seven fastest thoroughbreds in the country. Slick and solid, Infinity possessed the strength to make his mark in history. The silver cup and bountiful purse would also significantly increase Crystal Falls' value.

Besides, you're the only bright spot in my life.

Jason arched his eyebrow and leaned closer to the animal's ear.

"Hey, big guy, there's a lot of folks here to watch this race. Let's show 'em what a real champion can do." He patted the slick neck and the horse pushed his forehead against Jason's chest. Jason sucked in a ragged breath. *Let your strength be mine.* "We can win this, I know we can."

He snapped the lead rope on the halter and led the young stallion from the stall.

His gaze darted to a group of businessmen with their fine cigars dangling from their mouths. They flashed fists-full of dollars, eager for their moment to place their bets.

He snickered beneath his breath.

Wonder if they'll wager on Infinity?

With a sigh, he shook his head and headed toward the race track.

He scuffed his boot heels as he trudged past a pile of manure. The stench swept up his nostrils and burned the back of his throat. His brow lowered and he scrunched his nose. Waves of heat distorted his view. He squinted. Steaming wisps rose from the mound of aging fertilizer.

Something moved. He did a double take.

"What the hell?' Amid the odorous mound of muck, he recognized two jockeys buried up to their necks in the manure. "What're you doing in there?"

he yelled.

"Shedding some pounds," the younger man said. "It's hotter than hell in here."

Jason shook his head. "Good God. I've never heard of that before. You two are sick sonsofbitches to climb in there to lose a little weight."

One man laughed. "We'll do whatever we can to be lighter atop our horse."

Jason chuckled. "Well, good luck, gentlemen. Just don't sit beside me at dinnertime." He tugged on the rope, lengthening his stride behind the other horsemen. In a precise, orderly column they guided their thoroughbreds across the open field. A crescendo of clapping, cheers and chattering voices rippled in his ears. Jason tightened his grip on the lead. His slick palm worked against the leather as jangled nerves escaped through his sweating hand. Guests along the fence rail pressed closer to watch the horses parade past.

A bead of sweat rolled past Jason's temple and he brushed his forehead with the cuff of his shirtsleeve to soak up the moisture.

Taking a deep breath, he shifted his gaze to the viewing stand. On an elevated platform ,near the finish line, sat the Governor and his family. Toddlers ran between the adults, laughing as they clutched onto expensive wool trousers or bright silks.

For a moment, Jason's thoughts tumbled backward to the day he received the Governor's invitation. A smile lifted his lips as he pushed through the front door that morning, waving the paper like his pants were on fire.

"Father," he howled, rushing to the old man's side. "Look, we've an invitation from the Governor of South Carolina to race Infinity. This is the biggest event in the country." He spread open the official document and slipped the parchment into unsteady hands. His father merely stared at the elegant script, no light in his eyes.

Jason's enthusiasm waned. "Infinity will be famous," he muttered. "Even if he doesn't win, he'll be known by every horseman across the land."

"He'll win," his father whispered as a tear seeped from the corner of his eye.

A dagger shot through Jason's heart. The raw truth of Taylor Jackson's disability ate at his gut. He swallowed back his disappointment.

A shrill bugler call-to-post brought him back from his sorrow.

Sunbeams cut through the clouds forcing him to narrow his eyes. Streaks of light bounced off the metal roof to shift his thoughts. The ray's reflection warmed his heart as he recalled the brightness of Debbie's smile.

He lowered his gaze. *Everything reminds me of you.*

"She should be here, too," he whispered to Infinity.

The stallion nickered as if in reply.

"So, you miss her too, huh?" Jason said, releasing his sadness on a lingering sigh. He led the stallion into the paddock.

Skimming past owners, trainers and jockeys, Jason searched for a glimpse of Billy's red shirt. His gaze stopped by the watering trough. His rider waved at him, widened across the craggy face of the jockey. Jason nodded and guided the horse toward him.

"He's looking real good now, Mister Jackson.," Billy said, slipping Infinity's bridle over his ears. Braided mane entwined with red ribbon topped Infinity's long muscular neck. His tail had been brushed and groomed to perfection. The bay's rich brown coat glistened in the afternoon light. His ears perked forward and his eyes were as alert as a fox on the hunt.

Jason rubbed the stallion's soft muzzle. "That he does, Billy," he whispered. "That he does. Now, go get the win and make my empty life matter."

He pitched the reins to an attendant and slipped a white wool blanket with the number 5 on the stallions back.

"Give me the saddle," he called to the helper.

Billy held Infinity while Jason secured the girth, then barked out orders to the aid. "Walk him, so folk can get a better look"

Jason scanned Infinity's ankle for any sign of lingering distress.

Billy squinted an eye. "Horses have a way of knowing what's expected of 'em. He's so calm you'd think he's been racing for years."

"Just ride him like you always do. I think he can handle the distance."

"I'll keep him near the front, then make my move."

"Sounds good."

The walker returned and stopped in front of them.

Jason gathered the reins, then hoisted Billy into the saddle.

"See you at the finish line," the jockey proclaimed.

Jason flashed a grin and watched them maneuver into position down the line of readied thoroughbreds.

Sunlight glinted off the barrel of the starting gun gripped in the official's hand. The man beside him lifted a megaphone and called, "Number one is Sweet Sundance from the Donley Stables in Newport, Maine. Number two is Friday's Girl from Willington Stables, followed by number three, Sugar Sue from Dallas, Texas. Number four is a colt from right here in Camden… Red Dragon. Number five, Infinity, hails from Crystal Falls Stables in Lexington, Kentucky.

A wave of applause sent goose bumps rippling down his arms. Pride puffed at his chest. His cheeks grew warm. He remembered the day of the picnic when the Tom turkey strutted his colors before his woman. Jason choked back a tear.

His own woman was nowhere in his life now

"Next is number six, Cool Cat from New York, and at the final post is Black Bart's Bay," the announcer said. "There you have it, folks, the Governor's best picks for this year."

Cheers from the grandstand erupted.

Jason pressed against the railing and lifted his field glasses. His hands shook and the muscles in his shoulders tightened into stone-hard knots. His gaze honed in on his horse. Adjusting the lens on the field glasses, he noticed streaks of lather bubbling from beneath the reins on Infinity's neck.

"Easy boy," he whispered.

A hand settled on Jason's shoulder. He flinched.

"He'll do fine," a familiar voice echoed in his ear.

Jason swung to see Butterfield hovering nearby and a smile lifted his lips. "What the hell are you doing here?" he asked.

"Just delivered a mare in Charleston. Thought I'd drop in. You know I couldn't allow that horse to run his first big race without me here to cheer him on."

Jason chuckled.

The old man always seemed to appear at the right moment to fill the void left by his father's absence. "I guess you're right."

Butterfield adjusted his Derby. "I only wish Taylor could be here."

The ache severing Jason's heart widened even farther. "So do I."

A gun-shot cracked overhead and swerved back to face the horses.

Infinity reared.

Another horse bucked.

Jason held his breath.

Each hoof-beat brought the animals forward.

He lifted his field glasses as the thoroughbreds thundered past.

"Red Dragon's leading the pack," the announcer called. "Cool Cat's a neck behind, then comes Friday's Girl."

As the pack rounded the first turn, Jason lost sight of Infinity in a cloud of dust. Sweat rolled down his temples as he searched for his horse.

"He's third," Butterfield hollered. "There's the top of Billy's cap."

Jason pressed closer. "I see him."

The horses galloped down the back stretch, their hooves kicking up clumps of dirt into the air.

He shifted, widening his stance.

The crack of whips against leather hide entwined with the cheering crowd.

He sucked in a gulp of air.

"Infinity's blazing up the inside rail," the announcer yelled. "A half-length from the lead,"

Impatience bit at his nerves. He clenched his fingers against the cool metal pressing the implement harder against his face. His shoulders bunched.

Don't let that ankle give out now.

The cheering ratcheted up another notch, the noise reverberating off the metal roof.

"You can do it," Jason howled. His chest tightened, threatening to explode.

Butterfield pressed forward, thrusting against Jason, knocking his field glasses into the grass. Undeterred, Jason scooped them up and captured Infinity's image in the lens once more.

Rounding the far turn, Infinity moved up beside the leader.

Jason pounded his fist against the wooden railing. "He's gaining on 'em," he yelled. "Come on, boy. Show 'em what ya got."

Butterfield tossed his cigar into the dirt and shoved his arms into the air. "Break away," he shouted. "Beat them bastards."

"Here comes Infinity," the announcer yelled. "He's pushing into the lead. He's ahead by a length…two lengths. My God, this horse is winning by a good six lengths."

Infinity thundered over the finish line, ushered across by the deaf-defying roaring of the crowd.

Billy stood in the stirrups and waved his hand in victory.

Jason hugged Butterfield. "We did it," he yelled.

"Sonofabitch," Butterfield howled. "I love that horse." He pushed his hand into his vest pocket and pulled out a slip of paper. "Besides, I just won myself two hundred dollars."

Jason's smile vanished as their gaze locked. "Y- You bet on Infinity?"

"Hell, yes, I did," Butterfield bellowed. "That's what horse racing's all about. Didn't expect me to bet against him, did you?"

"No. I never considered betting at all."

The old man reared back and peered at Jason down his bulbous nose. "Are you sure you're Taylor's son? Cause he would've bet the farm on that animal."

Jason laughed, his momentary emptiness of earlier lifting. "I'm sure you're right."

He glanced up as Billy rode by the grandstand. A tingle rushed down Jason's spine.

He sighed and draped his arm across Butterfield's shoulders. "Come on, John, walk with me. This is your day, too."

"Don't mind if I do." Butterfield beamed, nudging Jason aside.

In the winner's circle, the Governor congratulated Jason, then presented him with the silver trophy. He clutched the treasured piece in his hands and thrust the cup high for all to see.

Damn, how he'd worked for this moment. He glanced at Butterfield and gave a wink.

He fronted Infinity and waved to the crowd. A deluge of cheers and applause thundered in his ears.

He swept the crowd as he patted Billy on the shoulder. "Good job, my friend. I couldn't have won without you atop him. Now, come on, let's get our big boy back to the barn and cool him down."

That evening, after dinner, Jason meandered to the stable. He stepped before his horse and grasped the halter. "Thanks, fella," he whispered, rubbing the champion's forehead. He pushed aside Infinity's head and glanced down.

Jason's stomach lurched.

The horse's ankle had swollen twice the regular size. "That sonofabitch is as big as a grapefruit," Jason's muttered. He unlatched the stall door and shoved inside. Easing his hand onto the horse's rump he slid his palm down the muscles to the injured hock.

Heat radiated across Jason's fingertips.

Infinity nickered and stepped aside.

I've gotta get the veterinarian over here.

* * *

Another sleepless night filled with nightmares of Debbie's capture and Infinity's battle with wire drove Jason from his bed. He huffed about the room as darkness of the predawn hours beckoned through his misery

Shit, I've ruined my horse.

Hands curling into fists, he stomped across the rug.

Sonofabitch…more delays.

With shaking hands he dressed, then stepped out into the silvery night. The joy of yesterday's win dissipated on the cool night breeze. Doubts loomed heavy on his mind as he trudged through the pre-dawn mist, yet a soft breeze whispered hope for the new day.

Exercise riders scurried about preparing their mounts for another round of racing. Questions riddled Jason's mind.

Would Infinity ever race again? What would this do to Crystal Falls? This horse was the lifeline to the stable's future.

Damn, I don't want to deal with all this right now.

His nostrils flared as he pulled in a heavy breath.

Brisk steps carried him to the rider's kitchen where he joined other owners and trainers in their morning gathering. Their chatter centered on hopes of winning, yet his hope was just to get his horse back to being a possible contender.

Frustration gnawed at his gut as his anxiety spiraled upward.

Even congratulations on yesterday's win proved no distraction.

Jason gulped down two bitter cups of coffee, then tossed aside the mug and pivoted on a boot-heel and out the door.

As he passed several stables, clanging buckets from within bit at his nerves. He focused on the distant stable that housed Infinity.

Stepping inside the final barn he spotted his horse. The swollen hock had not improved. "Damn it," he muttered, patting the horse's neck.

Wish to hell Peter was here. He'd know what to do.

A rustling from behind drew his attention. He pivoted, his gaze settling on a man wearing thick glasses. The stranger held out his hand. "Hello, I'm Dr. Jordan. Heard you have an injured horse."

"Yep, came up lame after the race," Jason stated, slipping his fingers beneath the leather strap to hold his horse steady. "Hoped you might take a look at him."

The man leaned over and pressed on the hock.

"He got tangled in wire a few months back," Jason explained, leaning over the man's shoulder. *Tell me he's gonna be all right. I can't stand anymore hell.*

The doctor said, "Looks like that cut went through a tendon. Can't do much to fix that. He'll probably have trouble with it all his life. Have ya considered retiring him?"

Drawing a heavy breath to center his frustration, Jason stared at the man. A sickening wave surged up inside him. He fought back the urge to vomit."I didn't want to retire him, yet. I wanted to race him another year or two. He's only five."

"You've gotta let that swelling go down. Might get a few more races out of him, but that's all. And if you do that, you're gonna cripple him." The man straightened and tugged on the hem of his vest. "Of course, the choice is always yours. You've just paid me for advice."

Jason shook his head. "Yesterday was his first win. And now this." His jaw tightened as his gaze locked on the man. "I was hopin' for better news."

"Sorry, Mister. I call' em like I see 'em."

Jason released the horse and they shuffled backward out of the stall.

"Ice down that ankle and soak it in salts," the man added, grasping Jason's shoulder. "Nice horse, by the way. Good luck to ya."

Jason shoved his hand in his pocket, the heat of his anger clashing against the cold coins that rolled into his palm. He dropped three silver dollars into the veterinarian's outstretched palm. "Much obliged for your trouble."

The man nodded and exited the stable.

Jason turned back to Infinity. "Damn it, why did you have to get tangled in that wire?"

He grabbed a nearby rake and slammed it against the wall.

I can't believe this is happening.

He slung the broken handle to the ground. With a heavy sigh, he lowered his chin

and slumped against the stall door.

If I had protected Debbie, none of this would have happened. This is all my fault. Not only did I fail my horse, I've failed my woman. My life is a goddamned mess.

That afternoon Jason loaded Infinity on the train and headed back to Crystal Falls.

Chapter Twenty-Four

Debbie closed the hospital door and stepped into the sunlight. A breeze tossed wisps of hair across her cheeks. She swept the strands back and gazed into the crisp blue sky. Clouds resembling pulled cotton drifted above her head. *What a beautiful day.* As she headed toward Canal St., she passed a playground, alive with children. Their laughter and comical antics tightened her smile. Her thoughts danced around her hope for the future. *Perhaps one day my child,* or Jason's child if her prayers were answered, *will play here, too.*

As she wandered down the wide street, she passed the Union Hotel, then the newly renovated Grand Opera House. Her thoughts flashed back to her days as a singer. *If I wasn't with child, I'd waltz right in and audition.*

Another block and she stopped before a haberdashery. An array of men's suits and accessories decorated the window. As she shifted forward, her eyes slipped closed. An image of Jason wearing the grey-vested suit brightened her mind, the gold chain she gave him for Christmas, glinting back at her from the watch pocket. *You are so handsome, my darling.*

With a sigh, Debbie fluttered open her eyes and continued on down the boardwalk. Windows skimmed past her gaze, lining the top floors of the brick and stone buildings across the way. Undoubtedly apartments for shopkeepers. She paused. *I must find a place to live.* Her brows tightened and she crinkled her nose. *No Job. No wages. No apartment.* She scanned both directions, then crossed the street and increased her steps.

Several blocks later, she glanced into the window of a jewelry store. She paused at a display of glistening pins and rings. As she pressed her nose against the cool glass showcase, her breath caught deep in her throat.

WE BUY GOLD AND FINE JEWELRY.

Her heartbeat quickened at the words.

My necklace!

Maybe I could sell the elk's tooth.

But, what would Jason say if she did?

Her gaze dropped to the swell of her stomach. *It doesn't matter now, my child needs a home.*

She narrowed her eyes and focused on the sign once more. *And Jason isn't here.*

A frown tugged her brow as she remembered leaving the jewelry back at the houseboat for safe keeping.

I've got to find Cotton!

She pivoted on the heel of her leather boot and headed for the Cornstalk Hotel.

Quick steps carried her down Canal to Royal. Several blocks later she fronted the beautiful building. Bustling with arriving and departing guest, the Cornstalk provided the finest establishment in New Orleans. Elaborate carriages lined the street as colorfully-attired attendants greeted each guest.

Debbie scurried past a trio of businessmen near the entrance to the garden piazza. Her mind tumbled backward to that crisp Christmas morning when Jason led her into their rose garden back home. A heavy frost covered twisted vines, void of their oh-so-beautiful red blooms. The chill of winter nipped at her skin and she pressed close to her beloved for warmth.

"Open your hand," he whispered.

Her heartbeat matched his passion-filled voice as he eased the beautiful elk's tooth necklace into her palm, then folded her fingers overtop.

"For you," he said, against the curve of her ear. "Wear this when we're apart so you'll always remember my love."

Debbie lifted her gaze to his. "It's beautiful." Tears blurred her vision and she caressed the piece with her fingertips.

Plucking the necklace from her palm, he clasped the chain around her neck.

"I will wear it always, my darling."

Laughter brought her musing back to the present. The three businessmen moved on as she bit back her tears. The thought of never seeing Jason or his beautiful gift again drove a dagger straight through her heart.

She gulped a calming breath and refocused.

Pushing past the sea of strange faces, she swung open the front doors and headed straight for the servant quarters.

As she neared the rear of the building, a strong scent of lye soap wafted through the air to burn her throat. She coughed, then slipped down the narrow hallway, void of embellishments. Several steps later brought her to an attached laundry room. Her eyes widened. Pale walls and bare windows magnified a stark contrast to the elegant décor she so admired throughout the hotel.

Heat from pots of boiling water radiated across her face, forcing her backward. An abrupt turn brought her face to face with Cotton.

Debbie gasped, the palm of her hand pressing against her chest.

A sharp snort from her left drew her attention.

She glanced across the room. Her muscles tensed as another servant burrowed a blistering stare into hers. She was not welcome here and she damn well knew it. A lump knotted her throat and her mouth parched as dry as a riverbed.

With a gulp, her gaze returned to Cotton.

A frown creased her friend's forehead as she tossed the wet towel into the metal washtub. "What are ya doin' here?" Cotton grumbled. "Ain't nobody 'pose ta be back here but us."

"I-I had to talk to you," Debbie muttered.

Her gaze cut sideways to the two servants still staring at her in a stone-like stance. Sweat-soaked turbans wrapped their braided hair and streams of perspiration tracked down their temples. Both were rail thin and the years of hard labor ravaged their features.

Debbie swallowed hard. Their distraught expression only added weight to the extreme temperature penetrating the dark and dismal room. She shifted her shoulder as perspiration rolled down her back to soak her waist.

"I need your help," she stated, watching the others from the corner of her eye.

Cotton rocked back on her heels. "Help? What kinda help? I thought ya was out lookin' fer a job?"

Debbie leaned closer. "I found a position at the hospital. I need to go home with you today and pick-up the rest of my belongings."

She peered over Cotton's shoulder at the woman beside the window. Her dark eyes narrowed and she slung a towel into the suds. With a grunt, she angled a hand on her hip. "Ya betta get outta here, now," she sneered.

Cotton pivoted and waggled a finger at the woman. "Pinky, ya just mind yo own business. Dis don't concern ya. Ya get on back ta work, right now."

Debbie drew her lips into a tight seam.

The oppression of these people burned in their souls. She could feel the fire of their resentment toward her and others more fortunate than this woman. Most were forced to believe their only job was to serve the white folks and keep them happy with good whiskey, elegant clothing and extra fine cigars.

Debbie's nerves tightened like a watch spring. Another glance at the servant and she felt the sting of the woman's glare. The last thing she wanted to do was to intimidate any of them by her presence.

With a huff, the woman thrust her hand into the washtub and shoved the linen onto the scrub board.

Cotton grabbed Debbie by the arm and led her to the doorway. "I ain't goin' home. Pappy's pickin' me up after work and we's goin' to his sister's fer supper."

"Oh, shoot." Debbie lowered her brows. "I need to go today."

Cotton brushed by the door frame and fronted her. "Do ya think ya could find yo' way ta our place?"

"Yes, but I don't have a way to get there."

"Pappy should be at da pier in 'bout an hour," Cotton said. "Go there 'n' tell him I said ta let ya use da boat. Be careful though, dem canals are dangerous. Watch fer gators. Don't want nutin' hurtin' ya and dat baby."

"Thanks, Cotton. You're the best friend I've ever had."

The woman's cheeks flushed. "Now get, girl, 'for I lose my job fer talkin' too much."

Debbie gave a nod and scurried out the door.

A brisk, forty-five-minute walk later brought Debbie to the local docks. Many of the swamp people used this strip of shoreline to dock their personal crafts while they worked in the city.

She scanned the pier for Ed and a moment later, his silhouette rowed into view. He slid the boat up alongside the weathered pier.

She waved to catch his attention.

"Miz Debbie," he shouted, wrapping a line around the post. He stepped onto the weathered wharf. "What cha doin' here?"

She touched his forearm. "I must return to your houseboat to gather the rest of my belongings." She settled up next to him. "Cotton said you wouldn't mind if I borrowed the boat. I'll not be gone long."

He lifted his straw hat and scratched the top of his balding head. "Da bayou can be pretty tricky, Missy. Don't want ya gettin' lost."

"I won't," she said, patting him on the shoulder. "I'll be back before sundown."

He pointed at a cluster of thunderheads that dotted the western horizon. "Ya may run in ta some weather. Stay at da houseboat 'til thing's clear. Don't want ya out in no storm."

"I will." She said with a smile.

He lowered her into the small dinghy, then unraveled the rope. A grunt later, he pushed the boat from the shoreline.

Debbie gathered the oars, her arm muscles straining as she splashed the paddles through the murky water. Like a duck with a broken wing, the craft circled just off shore. Debbie peered at Ed; a grimace tightening her face.

"Get over here," he called, motioning her back.

Embarrassment burned Debbie's cheeks at her inability to row the small vessel.

"Move over," Ed huffed, stepping into the hull. "I'll take you."

"But, what about Cotton … and dinner… and your sister?"

"If we hurry, maybe I won't be too late." He took the oars and skillfully turned the boat northward toward Lake Pontchartrain. With smooth strokes, he glided the boat through the water.

The sound of flapping wings brought Debbie around. A lone crane lifted and swept into the sky as they rowed past its vacated nest. A cry of disapproval erupted from the large bird as she flew away.

The hypnotic motion of the oars changed as the boat entered a narrow canal.

Debbie eyes widened and she scanned the undergrowth. "This isn't the way."

"Dat's 'cause we don't usually go dis way. Too narrow and 'dere's lots of gators."

"Oh, my!" she said with a gasp.

"We'll be all right, though," he said on a chuckle. " Ya just keep an eye out fer dem devils."

On a hard swallow, Debbie suppressed the shiver that rippled up her spine.

Low branches scraped and pulled against her sleeves as they passed fallen trees and bushes. Jagged nerves spiked with each splash she heard.

The canal widened and huge cypress trees rustled in the wind. Their overpowering presence enveloped her. Unseen ghosts taunted her from within the twisted branches, capturing her breath. Spanish moss reached out for her soul, sucking at her strength, reminding her of the cobwebs in the shack where she was raped. A chill etched beneath her skin.

Perhaps this wasn't a good idea.

She drew a shaky breath to stabilize her withering thoughts.

Sunlight broke through the clouds and spilled across Debbie. She raised her hand to shade her eyes from the harsh rays. Watching the choppy waves wash into infinity, images swam before her of the lake behind Packey's house where she and Jason planned their picnic that fateful day.

Rounding the next bend, she caught sight of the blue-painted houseboat. She sighed and let go her held breath.

"Here we are," Ed said. His warm chuckle eased back her foolish fears.

She grasped the side of the boat. "Whew, I'm glad that trip is over."

"Well, we still gotta go back," he chuckled.

Several neighborhood skip boats were tied along the bank and bobbed to the rhythm of the incoming tide. Children played nearby, their laughter soothing her jangled nerves.

Debbie raised her hand in a warm greeting and they ran away giggling.

Why would anyone want to raise a family in this God forsaken place?

She hurried down the dock and stepped inside the houseboat. Her eyes adjusted to the dim interior. With haste, she gathered her items and pinned the necklace inside her dress pocket, then rejoined Ed. A glance found him chatting with a strange man on the pier beside the boat. His dark eyes widened as she approached.

"Frank, this is Debbie Jackson," Ed said, nodding. "She's a friend of the family and new in the area."

A skeptical gaze darkened the man's features.

A chill rippled beneath her skin as he scanned her from head to toe.

Ed returned his gaze to Debbie. "I used to work for Mr. Grant."

"Nice to meet you," the man mumbled.

"Likewise," she replied. "Cotton and Ed were kind enough to allow me to stay with them until I could find a place of my own."

That should set the inquisitive man straight.

He smiled just as Ed pushed forward. "Frank raises horses north of here."

"Horses?" Her interest peaked. "What kind of horses?"

Ed smiled. "Thoroughbreds. You know, race horses?"

"Of course, my family has raised them for years."

Mr. Grant locked his gaze on hers. "Where's your stable?"

"Kentucky," she said, lifting her chin. "Lexington, to be precise."

He rocked back on his heels. "Great horse country," he said. "I'm sure your family has done well."

"Quite well, thank you."

He cleared his throat and turned back to Ed. "Well, how about it? Will you come work for me, again? I could sure use the help."

"Let me talk ta Cotton. I'll let ya know by da weekend."

The two men clasped hands. Frank flashed a smile toward Debbie, "Ma'am," he said, then trudged up the bank to his horse. Seconds later, he disappeared over the ridge as a wind gust brought the scent of rain into Debbie's nostrils.

"You worked with race horses?" She stared at Ed as the strengthening wind whipped her hair across her face.

"Sho' did." He released the rope and pushed the craft away from the dock. "I mucked da stalls and feed da horses. Whatever he asked, I'd do."

Another strong gust stirred the nearby Cypress trees. The wood popped and groaned as the branches twisted. Debbie grabbed the edge of the rig while the choppy waves pounded the side of their boat. "You never mentioned that…Why'd you quit?"

"There was a fire 'n' he lost lots of animals."

The houseboat faded from sight as the ghostly bayou grew closer. "So now he wants you back?"

"Yes ma'am."

Debbie placed the clothing on the seat, then glanced at the ever-darkening clouds. "What do you think Cotton will say?"

"She probably'll want me at home. She likes me cookin' 'n' watchin' da youngins. But, I sho could use da money. I wants 'em ta get a good education. Not workin' odd jobs like's I do. "

A clap of thunder interrupted their conversation. Ed jerked the oars from the water and peered up through the towering cypress. The trees swayed as another strong wind gale pushed the tangled branches overhead.

"Don't like da sound of dat," he said, lowering his brow. "We gotta move fast."

Debbie locked a glare on Ed. The muscles in his broad neck bulged as he steered the rickety boat through the swamp. Each oar stroke splashed droplets against her hands. The rocking motion of the vessel upon the choppy waves, sent a rush of nausea up her throat.

Fighting back the rise of morning sickness, she tightened her hands around the boat's edge until her fingertips grew numb.

She stared upward at the roiling clouds.

Her heart rammed against her ribs and she swallowed hard, choking back her fear. God, how she wanted to be home, locked in the safety of Jason's embrace.

Strong gusts of wind challenged the old man's ability to guide the craft.

Debbie grimaced as Ed's bulging neck muscles blurred beneath her tears. Then the unforgiving undergrowth raked across her arms, clawing at her like tendrils of despair.

A streak of lightening branched across the sky, followed by a deafening clap of thunder.

Debbie ducked and slapped her hands over her ears.

A half- muted cry escaped her lips.

Tears fell as she squinted and peered over Ed's shoulder at the lagoon ahead.

Was she mistaken?

Could that be?

Oh, my God, no...A huge alligator sprawled atop the ground, its leathery skin and stubby talons reminding her of a dragon stalking its prey. She sucked in a breath and held tight.

Every muscle in her body tensed as their rig pushed closer.

The reptile's mouth sprang open exposing long jagged teeth.

From even where she sat, she heard the hiss... Her eyes widened as more tears fell.

Her glare locked on the gator and a heart-stopping moment later, she yelped as the reptile slithered into the water. The boat scarped against... something.

The craft tipped to the side.

She screamed. "W-was that the gator?"

"Naw, just a stump," Ed said, pointing at the distorted image that shimmered back at her from just below the water.

Debbie gritted her teeth. How did such undeserving horror become her life?

I've fallen into a bottomless pit to hell.

She glanced skyward.

Rain pelted her face.

She closed her eyes and gulped a shallow breath as she fought against the unraveling urge to sob.

A nearby splash and her eyes sprang back open.

What was that?

She scanned the shoreline for another ghastly Laffoone waiting to overpower her and drag her into more misery. She lowered her gaze to her stomach.

All I have is my baby, now.

Long strands of hair wrapped her cheeks. Another clap of thunder boomed in her ears.

She stared at Ed's broad back. Her lifeline, he appeared undaunted as he continued to stroke the water.

The boat bobbled past the grassy mound then something brushed against her ankle.

She dropped her gaze to the hull of the craft.

A stick-like object slithered before her.

The creature twisted and coiled.

With a gasp, Debbie surged sideways, shrieking. "A…A…snake."

"Careful," Ed ordered, his voice calm, a beacon beckoning out to her in this horror-filled nightmare.

Debbie released a blood-curdling scream and lunged backward.

A heartbeat later, she snagged her heel on the wooden seat. Losing her balance she plunged head first into the slime-covered water.

She sealed her lips tight as the bitter rush of the water engulfed her. Twisting and thrashed, she franticly searched for direction.

The vile settlement of the swamp burned her eyes.

Debris and algae coated her arms and her legs. Smothering her beneath a crushing panic.

She wrenched as nausea swept up her throat.

Fear spiked. The crushing grip of death tightened her chest. Her hands flailed in desperation while she fought back the urge to inhale. The tightness in her lungs screamed for life-sustaining air.

The water enveloping her grew darker.

Each beating thump of her heart brought the thunder into her ears.

My poor baby. We're going to die.

As her mind shuffled between life and death she heard familiar words calling out to her. The distorted image and soothing voice of Jason enveloped her.

"Relax," he whispered. "Follow your breath." He nodded, then faded into the darkness.

Jason. Come back.

She unleashed the air trapped in her lungs and hundreds of tiny air bubbles scattered aloft.

Of course! The air will rise to the surface.

Narrowing her eyes, she followed her heart, her Jason, her fleeing breath upward.

Moments later, she burst through the surface and thrust her head above the water. With a gagging cough, she cleared the muck from her lungs.

Thank God.

Sucking a gulp of air, she grabbed for the boat.

The crack of a nearby limb brought her back to reality.

Wide-eyed, she jerked to the side scanning the rain-driven swamp.. *The gator.*

The beast had entered the water only minutes before and could be lurking anywhere.

She thrashed her legs and pulled against the vessel in a futile attempt to get aboard.

Ed sunk strong hands into her upper arms.

With a grunt he lifted. The boat rolled to the side and water surged into the hull. He moaned, then rocked back, releasing his grip.

She plummeted backward into the water once more.

Through tear-filled eyes, Debbie watched her dresses, pantaloons and her only camisole, floating to the shoreline. Just like her life, everything that brought her happiness was slithering away.

She glanced down. A ripple of crimson water washed next to her. She lifted her arm. Beneath the torn sleeve, blood bubbled out from a wound near her elbow.

"Oh, my God, I'm bleeding," she shrieked. "I've gotta get out of here. I will not surrender to this God-awful swamp."

Lightening branched downward, followed by an instant clap of thunder.

"Hurry, swim ta da island," Ed hollered, pointing toward the knoll.

Debbie swung around and gasped for breath, then headed for shore. Her loose fitting dress twisted as she thrashed in the water. The weight of her soggy boots threatening to pull her under.

Her arms ached with every stroke as she struggled for the surface.

Several frightening moments later, she spilled onto the shoreline.

Prune-like fingers wrapped a cluster of swamp grass. She hauled herself upward, but the moist soil released the tall weeds and once more she plunged into the water.

Her weight drug her downward.

Again, strange shadows twisted around her, sucking away her strength.

Seconds later, a strong hand grabbed her shoulder and plucked her from beneath the darkness.

A spray of heavy rain pelted her face. She gulped in life-sustaining air.

Ed sank into the mud and stumbled as he drug her up the grassy knoll. Finally, he released her onto the bed of swamp grass. Standing overhead, panting, he yelled, "Ya all right?"

She nodded, longing for home, the smell of hot apple pie, the laughter of another family dinner, the love all around her and the love she found in Jason's arms.

If only this was a terrible dream.

Tears seeped out as she lay on her back gasping for air.

Her weakness eased with each breath. A flutter of hope rippled inside her belly. This little life depended on her. She took a deep breath and rubbed her palm over her belly.

I'll always protect you, my little one.

Moments passed, then she heard movement. She rolled onto her side and peered through swollen eyes.

Ed tipped the rig onto the side and dumped out the remaining water. A bolt of lightning illuminated the muscles bunching his upper arms. She truly appreciated his strength in these harrowing moments. The thunderous blast that followed shook the ground with enough fury to make even the big man stumble. Debbie squeezed her eyelids tight.

Her heart pounded so hard she expected it to burst.

The driving rain stung her cheeks and her vision blurred. Ed stood mere feet away.

"Come on," he said. Stepping closer, he offered his hand. "We gotta go. That gator'll return any moment."

Taking a deep breath, she struggled to her feet.

The snake from the boat slithered up the bank nearby. She tightened her lips and kicked the reptile into the water. "Get the hell outta my life," she shrieked.

Inhaling, she turned to Ed. "Let's go home."

Again, the lightning split open the heavens.

Debbie grasped the man's boney hand and lowered into the boat. Her stomach churned and she tasted bile. By God, somehow she would escape the jaws of this unforgiving back swamp.

Ed pushed away from the bank and back out onto the murky lagoon.

He paddled over to the base of a cypress tree and retrieved two of her dresses. She plucked the garments from the tip of the oar. With a flick of her wrist she shook free the debris, then neatly folded the dresses and slipped them onto the seat beside her.

A quick skim of her hand proved the elk's tooth was still pinned in her pocket.

Drawing a deep breath, her spirit lifted to a new height

The past's gone. She lowered her gaze to her protruding stomach. *We have a new path now, little one.*

The rain eased and they continued up the canal.

A half-hour later, they emerged into the open waters of Lake Pontchartrain. The storm clouds dissipated and the night grew quiet.

The only sound Debbie heard was the creak of wood and a steady snap of the paddles as they cut through the water.

Only this time, her destination had changed.

A new life awaited her.

"There," Ed said. Lifting his hand, he pointed to the emerging city hugging the horizon in shades of purple and grey. "I see da lights. We ain't far, now."

"I'm so sorry to have put you through all this," she snuffled.

"Don't ya worry. We's all right, now."

Debbie nodded and offered back a tentative smile. "Yes, Ed…I do believe we are." Again, she clutched her stomach. "I hope Cotton isn't mad."

"Don't ya fret. Cotton's a good wife. She don't gets mad over little matters."

Debbie peered through the darkness at him. "Little? I'd hardly call any of this little." She touched her skirt pocket.

At least I have the necklace.

"And ya learned a thing or two back dare in dat swamp, didn't ya?

"That I did, Ed. I'm the master of my emotions."

She stared down at the gash on her arm. The bleeding had stopped. Tightening her lips she gathered her frustration and gazed heavenward.

A canopy of twinkling stars filled the sky.

On the horizon, silver moonbeams broke through the departing clouds and spilled out across the water.

Beautiful…like that night in the kitchen with Jason.

The glow of stardust enchanting the garden.

The magical scent of his body.

She closed her eyes. Thoughts of him touching her and the warmth of his lips engulfing hers, toying with her heart strings. She smiled. The brush of his breath across her ear tugged at the core of her passion. No one could take these memories away.

He would be pleased with my survival.

The boat bumped against the dock and her eyes sprang open. Ed stepped ashore and secured the rope to a weathered post.

"Careful," he said, offering her his hand. "It'll move on ya."

"Don't I know." She laughed, straightening her shoulders…ready for whatever else life might throw her way.

Draping the dresses across her arm, she stepped out onto the boardwalk. Several men approached carrying homemade signs and burning torches.

"I's gotta go, Missy." Ed spoke, urgency in his frightened voice. "You get on home now 'fore dey see's us together."

Why? Who were these white-hooded men, looming like ghostly specters before them.

Debbie nodded, looking back at Ed.

But, her friend had disappeared into the night.

Chapter Twenty-Five

With the dresses draped across her arm, Debbie headed toward the group of protestors. She'd heard of the growing struggle between the local politicians and the freed Negroes. Night after night, murder and arson raged throughout the city as the powerful droves of former soldiers fought to maintain their superiority over good people like Ed and Cotton. Post-war years left deep resentment in many people, yet freedom from slavery continued with a fragile acceptance in the south.

Debbie had grown up on a ranch in Oregon and had only read about the bitter differences back east. Now, she understood first-hand the constant fear Ed carried. Thrusting her chin high, she brushed past the first few men, then a stout- framed giant side-stepped her and blocked her path.

"Where're you headed?" he snapped, his hood pushed back to reveal beady-eyes.

She glanced over his shoulder. A slight-built man with a dark beard carried a sign praising radical reconstruction. She grimaced. The insistent local uprisings were far different than the unity Washington D.C. had promised the war-torn south, fighting against the hateful aggressiveness of these bloody butchers.

Her glare met his. "I'm going home," she replied.

He lowered his torch and a frown crossed his brow. "Didn't I just see you with a…"

Debbie coughed, interrupting his words. Her heartbeat quickened. "Yes, he stopped to ask directions."

"Was that all he wanted?" he grumbled, pushing closer.

"Yes, and he was very polite."

The group hovered closer. "How come you're all wet?" another asked.

She lowered her chin. "I got caught in the storm. Now, if you don't mind, I really would like to go home."

Lifting the torch, the robust man stepped aside. "Go on. We don't mean you no harm. Be careful. This is a dangerous area at night."

Yes, and people like you make it that way.

"Come on, men," another sang out. "We're wasting time. There's gotta be a mess of those bastards hunkered down by the railroad."

The group separated, allowing her to pass.

Debbie drew a deep breath and hurried off into the shadows. Tears blurred her vision as she made her way through the narrow streets. Rounding the corner, she confronted another group of protestors. She pivoted into the nearest doorway.

Breath held, she waited for them to pass.

A shuffle behind her broke her attention. "Ma'am, could I help you with the door?"

A broad-shouldered, well dressed man peered down at her. Shadows concealed his features, but his voice eased low and comforting over Debbie. She forced a smile and his hand brushed past her to grasp the metal knob. With an easy pull, the door swung wide.

A burst of loud music filled her ears. Stepping aside, he gestured for her to enter.

She nodded and eased into the smoke-filled room.

"Something wrong?" he asked.

Hesitant to continue, she swept her gaze over him. Flaxen hair, lying long on his collar, highlighted the man's tanned complexion. Her heartbeat slugged against her ribs as he flashed a perfect row of white teeth beneath his well-groomed mustache. And then something caught her attention. His too fashionable jabot, the ruffled cuffs of his shirt sleeves, as well. And the cologne that wrapped around her to underscore what this man might be. Was he...one that preferred men over women? She had heard of such men, but had never met the sort.

"No...no, I'm sorry, I don't belong here," she stammered.

"Did I offend you?" His blue eyes twinkled as he met her gaze.

She glanced down at her wet clothing."I'm a mess," she said. "I got caught in the storm on my way home."

"Of course, your husband is probably worried about you."

"I don't have a husband," she blurted out. *Why did I say that?*

"Then let me escort you home. A lady shouldn't be alone on these streets at night." He placed his hand on her upper arm and the scent of hair pomade again wafted over her. "Do you live nearby?"

She pulled away from his kindness and overwhelming presence. "Thank you. No, I'll see myself home, sir."

As she stepped back out to the street, she glanced both ways. The area cleared of the unruly crowd of moments before.

He tipped his hat in her direction.

She replied with the briefest flash of a smile.

* * *

White blossoms the size of dinner plates, bloomed on Magnolia tree sending their fragrance around Debbie. Inhaling the delightful scent, she made her way down Canal St. to Michelson & Bailey's Goldsmiths and Jewelers. Selling the elk's tooth was the right thing to do.

On a sustained breath, she shoved open the door and stepped inside. High ceilings and burgundy velvet drapes complimented the stylish wooden cases that hugged the sides of the elegant room.

She stepped past the clerk while he squeezed the atomizer of an expensive fragrance for a customer to inhale the sweet-scented vapor of violet. The middle-aged woman reared back and fluttered her hand before her face, inhaling the sweet smell. Debbie smiled as she brushed against the lady's stylish bustle. An image of a well dressed Kathryn emerged. She adored fine perfume.

Debbie meandered about the room surveying the wide variety of articles. She passed the black -lacquered gun case, and slid her palm across the sleek polished edge. A few steps forward and she stopped before a set of fine china on display near a sterling silver tea set. Picking up the dinner plate, she checked the maker's mark stamped on the bottom. Her family owned this same collection. Debbie smiled as her fingertips glided across the surface, caressing her past.

The voice of the store clerk pulled her away from her musing. "Good afternoon, ma'am," he said, closing the case of imported perfumes. "Is there something I can help you with today?"

Debbie glanced up as the previous customer shuffled out the front door. Her gaze cut back to the clerk. He had more hair on his mutton chopped face than he did on his entire head. She stifled a smile, then cleared her throat. "I saw the sign in your window. Could you look at my piece of jewelry and tell me what its worth?"

"Certainly," he said, peering at her through narrow spectacles.

The aroma of violets lingered on the man's sleeve and Debbie swallowed back her nausea.

"Well, uh," she stammered, pulling the handkerchief from her pocket. With a sigh, she slipped the cloth onto the highly-polished countertop between them. "The chain's broken, but can be easily repaired." The small-framed man plucked the piece from the hanky that had once belonged to Kathryn. With a wide smile, Debbie stroked her thumb across a frayed initial "K".

He held her precious necklace up to the light. "Hmmm," he uttered. "This is a tooth."

"Yes sir. An elk's tooth to be precise."

"Don't see many of them around here." He retrieved a magnifying glass. Sunlight bounced off the scrolled silver handle. Angling her treasure beneath the lens, he nodded. "I see a couple of letters engraved here."

She leaned closer. "They're my initials, I do believe."

"I suppose if someone didn't like that I could polish them away and place a stone of sort's there. What's your asking price?"

She drew back and tightened her lips. "What'll you give me?"

"I must say, it's very unique. I've only seen a couple of these in all my years in the business. They're mostly found up north. Of course, that's because the elk live up there."

Debbie puffed a childish snicker.

He glanced up, his gaze penetrating hers. "Tell ya what," he bartered. "I'll give you ten dollars for the bobble. You can keep the chain. I have plenty of these."

Her bottom lip puckered. "I was hoping for twice that much."

"Well, I, too, do have to make a profit," he said lowering the necklace onto the handkerchief. "Take it or leave it."

Frustration and loss coiled through her. She lifted her chin and fought for more. "I'll accept nothing less than twenty," she snapped.

He glanced at her protruding stomach, then stepped back and exhaled a heavy sigh. He plucked a twenty dollar Liberty gold piece from a side drawer and then slid the shimmering coin across the countertop. "Twenty. No more." His gaze lifted.

She glanced over his shoulder. Behind him, emblazoned with the words Dion & Roberts, stood a fire proof safe. Father owned one exactly like that in his study. Same black and gold trim. Same gold tumbler. Same impressive size. A wistful smile tugged at her lips.

Six turns left to 20

Three times right to 42

Two turns left to 58

How many times had she peered over his shoulder when he retrieved an important document from within?

Her gaze returned to the clerk's. She smiled. "Sold."

Thank you, Jason. You've always been there for me.

A few days later, Debbie found a room at a boarding house just a few blocks from the hospital. The tiny apartment consisted of an iron bed, a table and a dresser. A window facing east gave her sufficient light during the day and two lamps illuminated the tiny enclosure at night.

She stepped back to survey her new surroundings. Her heart surged. At least she had a home.

I'll buy a second-hand cradle and rocker, first.

A wave of confidence swept in to solidify her accomplishment. A soft sigh slipped out as Debbie ambled to the small, wavy-paned window. She streaked a fingertip through the soot and dirt that clouded the glass.

"Jason," she whispered. She scanned the northern horizon. Six hundred miles separated her from her beloved and Crystal Falls. "I send you my love. I may never see you again, but I will always love you." Tears escaped her eyes and trickled down her face. With shaking fingers, she closed the faded curtains placing miles between the memories and her beloved, as well.

Chapter Twenty-Six

A rustling to his left forced Jason to lower the newspaper he was reading. Settling opposite him, Butterfield swept off his derby and propped the beaver-felt hat on an uprising knee.

"All aboard," the conductor shouted.

Butterfield drew his watch from the vest pocket that strained his girth. "Right on time," he chirped.

Jason glanced at late arrivals scurrying to find an empty seat. "Looks like we have a full coach today," he said, adjusting on the seat.

"Don't know why they can't make comfortable benches on these damn trains,"

his traveling companion quipped. "I'd rather ride a swaybacked mule than sit on these hard sonsofbitches," he added with a chuckle.

"John, you're too damned spoiled."

Butterfield's bushy brows smacked together and his lips drew as tight as a bow string. After a glaring moment, he gave a grunt, then quickly changed the subject. "How's Infinity today?"

"Ankles still swollen," Jason admitted. "Got to rest him a week or two 'fore I can work him again."

"That's a damn shame. A fine thoroughbred like that; why this could end his career."

The train gave a jerk and began rolling along the tracks. Jason grasped the arm rest to steady himself. "That's what worries me," he stated, peering out the window at the landscape. "I wanted to race him for three or four years before I retired him to stud."

"Early retirement wouldn't be so bad where that stallion's concerned. I'll certainly be happy when he's ready to breed my mares."

"I'm sure you will." Jason said peering back as his friend fished inside his suit pocket.

Striking a match, John's whiskered cheeks cratered as he held the flame to the end of an expensive cigar and sucked in. With his exhale, long grey wisps of smoke weaved past Jason.

"Father'll be devastated when I tell him Infinity's racing days are about over," Jason said.

"Damn right he will and I can't blame him," Butterfield said. "I wouldn't want to be the one to tell him."

Jason exhaled a heavy sigh. "Maybe I won't tell him. At least, not yet."

The iron wheels of the train pierced through his dissatisfaction.

"My brother and his wife are coming in next week to visit," John said. "I'm having a few folks over for dinner. Why don't you join us?"

"I don't know. I'm not very good company these days."

"You should meet new people; get something else on your mind. My brother has a real gift for gab. You'll like him." John made an unsuccessful attempt to cross his legs. "He's a salesman. Travels near the whole southern territory. Sells all kind of shit." John squinted his eyes shut as he bellowed out a laugh. "Say's he ain't no peddler, but hell's fire, I don't know what else you'd call him." He leaned forward meeting Jason's gaze and whispered, "Say you'll come and keep me company."

"He sounds like a real character, but I'm not really interested in socializing right now."

"Just give it some thought. If you change your mind, my invitation stands."

* * *

A chill settled in Jason's bones as he drew his overcoat tight across his chest. Gloved hands clutched the stiff leather reins he held as his whistle urged Blue along the gravel road. *Butterfield had better appreciate me getting out on a night like this just to meet his brother.* Jason tugged at the brim of his Stetson, lowering the hat onto his brow. The harsh winter wind brushed his cheeks and with squinted eyes he glanced up at the darkening sky. Snow lurked among the swirling mass of clouds looming overhead. *I'd damned well rather be home by the fireplace.*

With a light tap of his heels, he nudged Blue into a slow lope.

Guests had already arrived when Jason rode onto the Butterfield estate. He reined to a halt and slid from the saddle. Music filled the air as he approached the door. He narrowed his eyes against the bright light that splashed across him from within. The butler gave a cordial greeting as he held open the heavy oak panel.

Jason stepped inside and swiped off his Stetson. A quick tug removed his overcoat. The butler draped the expensive wool piece across his arm as Jason meandered into the parlor.

Butterfield waved a hand, then shuffled over to greet him. "So glad you decided to come."

Jason nodded, his gaze skimming the room.

Horsemen collected at the sidebar, their hands clasping glasses full of the finest scotch and bourbon in the state of Kentucky. Off to their right, he saw their well-dressed wives gathered upon a blue velvet sofa and chairs in the parlor. Silk and brocade with lace and beaded trimmings splashed an array of color across the room.

Hens at roost, for sure.

He scrunched his forehead and expelled a shallow sigh.

I've nothing in common with these people.

"Let me introduce you to my family," John said, grasping Jason's arm.

His muscles tightened. As they approached, the couple turned to face him. The balding man had John's features; even the same steel grey hair and mutton chop sideburns. The woman's brows lifted. Her dove grey hair lay neatly stacked in a twist on the back of her neck; each lock held tight with a gold comb sprinkled with diamonds.

"I'd like you to meet my younger brother, Charles. His wife, Edna."

"Nice to meet you both" Jason said, clasping the man's palm. His gaze dropped to the piece of jewelry dangling around the woman's neck. A large ruby stone embedded in the center of the tooth. His gaze narrowed. "A beautiful necklace," he stated.

"Thank you," she said with a whispered giggle. She caressed the jeweled elk's tooth. "Charles bought this for me in New Orleans."

"I had the ruby added. Her birthstone," Charles said, pushing closer.

Jason's heartbeat quickened.

Debbie had her elk's tooth on the night of her kidnapping.

"My fiancée had one similar to that, only hers had initials carved on the back."

"This one had letters, too, but I had them buffed out and put in the stone," Charles said.

A bundle of nerves lassoed Jason's throat. "Do you remember the initials?"

"Naw…I've no idea," Charles said, downing a shot of whiskey. "Wasn't really interested."

Edna's gaze locked with Jason's. Tears blurred his vision. He excused himself and stepped away.

As they awaited the announcement for dinner, Jason kept looking at the jewelry around Edna's neck. A special piece. He'd never seen another like his. Was this even possible?"

Piano and violin music entwined with the laughter plucked at his nerves.

He scooped a glass of scotch from a servant's silver tray, then wandered through the crowd. *New Orleans.* He settled into a chair near the fireplace.

Damn, he wanted to examine that elk's tooth, again. A soft hand touched his arm. He turned to find Mrs. Butterfield peering down at him. A young lady stood by her side.

"Jason," she said. "This is my granddaughter, Elizabeth."

An oppressive rush of heat blazed up his spine. *Damnit, Butterfield is playing matchmaker.*

Jason surged to his feet. His cheeks grew warmer as he gazed into the young woman's face. Chestnut eyes matched dark auburn hair resting on her slender shoulders. Wearing an almond lace covered silk dress with a full bustle, she was too thin for his liking. His words struggled past the lump in his throat. "Nice to meet you, Elizabeth."

Damn, it'd been too long since he'd bedded a woman, or for that matter even cared to try.

Mrs. Butterfield pressed her hand upon the girl's shoulder. "Darling, this is Taylor Jackson's son. Your grandfather and Taylor have been friends for years. His family owns Crystal Falls Stables."

"I've heard grandfather speak of him. Doesn't he own a famous horse?"

Jason chuckled. "Well, he isn't famous, yet."

Mrs. Butterfield's gaze reconnected with his. "Liz will be staying with us for a few weeks. Her parents left for Europe last Tuesday. This is her first visit with us in a number of years. We usually go to their home in Texas. Her father runs a big oil company and they rarely get away. Perhaps while she's visiting you can teach her about the racing business. She loves thoroughbreds."

Jason's gaze slipped back to the young woman standing before him. She fluttered her fan before her cheeks. A pleasant smile radiated from her cherry-red lips. A chill crept beneath his skin. She wasn't Debbie. Hell, nobody was Debbie. He glanced away, his foolish mind playing devilish tricks on him. A crimped grin gathered at the corners of his mouth, then his thoughts were jolted by the call to dinner.

His tension eased on a lingering sigh.

A beautifully-set table beneath a crystal chandelier greeted him as he stepped into the dimly lit room. His own place sported the same crystal piece and he'd much rather be there with his family.

He bit back his unease.

First the elks tooth, now Miss Elizabeth. Sonofabitch.

As pleasant as the young lady may be, he wasn't a damned bit interested.

He stood to the side and waited for the ladies to be seated, then slipped onto a chair at the end of the table… away from Butterfield's granddaughter. A dangerous glint flickered in her eye as he glanced her way.

During the meal, Jason heard a commotion and cut his gaze to Charles. One cough, then another. A heartbeat later, he lurched away from the table, rising to his feet. A mask of fear swept the man's face and he grabbed his throat. Gasps filled the room as Charles fought to breath.

Jason threw down his napkin and bolted from the chair.

Guests scrambled from the table, while others remained frozen in their seats. Jason raced to the man's side.

Grabbing the younger Butterfield's shoulder, he pounded on the man's back.

Charles crumpled onto the heavy oak, sending plates and utensils awry, and expensive porcelain breaking. Jason angled against the table and pulled Charles up from behind. His eyes bulged. Flailing his arms the man swung around to face Jason. With a powerful thrust, Jason drove his fist into the man's gut.

Charles doubled over gagging and a mouthful of food expelled onto the tablecloth. A deep gasp followed by a cough and a thundering sneeze. His plum colored face lightened. He struggled to stand, and his body quivered while he sucked huge gulps of air.

Jason steadied his hand against the man's trembling shoulder. "You all right?" he asked, clutching the struggling gent.

Charles nodded, then spoke in a raspy whisper, "I believe so."

"Good." Jason lowered him into a nearby chair, then stepped away, allowing Butterfield's wife in closer.

Everyone deserted the table and scattered about the parlor, chattering like a flock of birds in a harvested cornfield.

An elderly guest stepped up to compliment Jason. He nodded and smiled, then picked up the chair he'd broken earlier.

John rushed over and clamped his arms around Jason. "I can't thank you enough," he said. Releasing Jason, he rocked back on his heels. "Your quick action saved my brother's life."

"I'm just glad I could help." Jason glanced sideways. "Sorry about the furniture."

"Forget that. We can buy more furniture. I can't replace Charles."

Jason smiled. "True."

* * *

After dinner, Jason hovered near the sidebar. His gaze drifted across the ladies in their fine dresses. They sipped imported coffee, and gossiped like a group of Cochin Bantams.

He choked back a snicker, then glanced into the den.

Several horsemen gathered to share their sleazy jokes or smoke John's Cuban cigars.

On a sigh, he downed another shot of whiskey, then stared into the crystal glass. Debbie's beautiful face reflected back at him. And around her neck she wore her elk's tooth necklace.

The potency of the strong drink shot to his brain. He scanned the room for Charles's wife, but she and the necklace had vanished.

Jason settled his gaze on the window, then crossed the room and peered out into the darkness. A blanket of white covered the lawn. "Damnit," he mumbled. *I need to get the hell out of here.*

He gathered his coat and hat, then stepped into the foyer. As he reached for the door, a hand grasped his arm. He pivoted. Edna smiled and held out her hand. "Here," she whispered. "Charles and I want you to have this."

He bit back his shock as she settled the necklace across his palm. "Perhaps this will ease your pain. It's the least we can do. You saved my Charles' life."

"B-but," he stammered.

"No buts." She smiled and closed his fingers across the piece. "Carry this with you in your search for Debbie. And start in New Orleans. That's where he bought this. I'll pray each night; God will help you find her." She tiptoed and kissed his cheek, then turned away.

He opened his hand. Tears blurred his vision as he stared at the necklace.

Oh, God, Debbie, I've another place to look.

He drew a ragged breath and stepped into the night.

Chapter Twenty-Seven

Kathryn shoved her hip against the door, then shuffled into the winter kitchen. With a grimace, she swung her wicker-basket full of day lilies and irises onto the sink. All morning spent in the blinding heat of the garden had brought a fine sheen of sweat to her brow. She patted the tail of her apron across her forehead. *I should've worn my straw hat.* Turning, she caught the flurry of a blue bird as her daily visitor flitted past the open window. She giggled and leaned forward, peering into the garden. The bird had perched onto a low-hanging branch of the pear tree.

A breeze fluttered the leaves, and she leaned further, the damp curls stuck to her forehead lifting. Even the red checked curtains stirred .

I love spring.

The aroma of baked bread cooling on a nearby countertop spiked her taste buds and drew her back inside. Her empty belly growled and she smiled, anticipating the delicious baked chicken she would have for supper.

She laid her gardening tools aside, then removed her gloves. Knots in her finger joints had swollen to the size of pecans. She rubbed each knuckle to ease back the pain. Exhaustion drove her against the counter. Her shoulders slumped as she pulled her basket closer.

Footfalls drew her attention. She cast her gaze sideways. The silhouette of her son filled the doorway.

In three strides he crossed the kitchen. "I'll take care of that."

"Thank you, darling." With a soft moan she pressed her hand to her lower spine and straightened. "My back isn't what it used to be. Just put the flowers in the parlor. I'll tend to them later."

"How's father today?" Jason asked, as he plucked the irises from the copper sink and traversed the room.

"He had another bad night, but he's sleeping now," she said.

"Is Jeremiah with him?"

"Yes. I'm going to finish up here and grab a bite to eat, then I'll go up and relieve

him. Would you like a plateful of roasted chicken?"

"Sounds good."

* * *

Twenty minutes later, with his hunger satisfied, Jason lowered the basket of flowers beside the grandfather clock in the parlor. He ambled to the sidebar and pulled a bottle of bourbon from the liquor case. A quick scan found a tumbler and he splashed in a generous serving of the brew. Swirling the glass, he glanced at his mother scurrying around in her daily tasks. He took a swig. "Mighty good stuff," he said as he sauntered back to her.

She stared at the bourbon, then at him, an expected scolding recrimination darkening her eyes. "A little early to be drinking, isn't it?"

Jason snorted, then downed another swallow before sliding the half-emptied tumbler onto the table. "Needed a good start to my day, so don't preach." He pushed up his sleeves and leaned over to pump the handle. Water splashed into the basin. "I'll clean these for you," he said, pushing the hand tools into the liquid.

A lengthy sigh fell from her lips. "Fine. We'll pretend like things are well with you." she snapped a clean towel in the air to unfold the linen. "And when you've finished, put them on the sideboard to dry." She crossed to the pantry, and emerged a moment later, her hands filled with dried rose petals. Jason narrowed his eyes as she bustled beside him, scattering her bundle atop the table. With a grimace, she crushed the faded petals with a rolling pin. A final smack and she straightened. "Has there been any word on Debbie?"

"Well, I have this," he said, slipping his hand into his denim pocket and withdrawing the necklace. A lopsided smile tugged at his mouth. Sunlight sparkled along the gold chain as he dangled the piece before his mother. "Butterfield's sister-in- law gave this to me and suggested I start my search in New Orleans."

His mother leaned closer. "That looks a lot like the one you gave Debbie, except for the stone."

"Yes, and her husband added the ruby."

She lifted her gaze. "Do you really think that's the same necklace?"

He slipped the delicate piece back into his pocket. "Don't know, but I'm sure as hell going to find out."

He watched as she poured the crushed rose petals into a jar, his throat tightening. "I hate to leave you alone with father in such poor health."

She blew aside a dangling strand of hair from her face, then glanced over her shoulder. "We'll be all right. You go find Debbie."

Jason pivoted, grabbing a nearby chair. Wood scraped poplar as he sank into the seat. Stretching his leg before him, he stuffed his hand into his pocket and once more withdrew the elk's tooth. A breeze from the open window swayed the chain, laying a glint across his glass. His eyes narrowed as he rotated the gold links between his fingertips.

Debbie.

He drew a settling breath, then closed his eyes. The scent of roses wafted over him. *Her favorite flower.* The sweet aroma plummeted him back to their first moments alone.

A cloudy evening in November and a sky heavy with the promise of snow. He picked her up just after work. Anticipation bubbled through him when she stepped into the surrey. She lowered a bouquet of roses onto the seat between them. "Thank you for the ride home."

Jason snapped the reins and the horse moved toward home. "Where'd you get the flowers?"

"The staff gave them to me," she said, straightening. "I sang at a gathering for our patients. Once a month we do something special for them. That helps ease their suffering."

"Sounds like something you'd suggest doing."

"Actually, I did." She laughed, tipping her palm upward. Snow settled onto her glove like feathers floating to earth. "I love the first flakes of winter. Even though it's cold, they're clean and bring a promise of the holidays. "

He turned, reaching backward to grasp the carriage blanket. A quick shake opened the red plaid wool. Leaning forward, he spread the warmth across her lap. "This'll help. I'll also drop the side curtains to block the wind."

As her gaze met his, a gentle smile gathered at the corners of her mouth. "You are ever the gentleman, Jason," she said, laughing. A warm pat to his upper thigh followed. "It's too bad you're my brother...or, rather my stepbrother."

The heat from her touch radiated up his leg. He stared at her, the snowflakes gathering in a veil across her chestnut hair. When had she changed from being the pest he remembered into this exquisite woman who sat beside him now? His heartbeat slugged his chest and expanded the lump in his throat. He tapped the horse's rump and they continued their journey home.

Jason squeezed his fingers around the leather reins, his palms clammy. His groin tightened. Her words danced in his ears as she shared her stories about life in the northwest. He blinked hard, but couldn't take his eyes off her. Her charm cast a spell over his soul. *She's enchanting.*

Cresting a hill, a herd of deer dashed across the road before them.

She gasped. "Aren't they beautiful?"

Jason chuckled. "And they taste good, too."

"Don't say that," she scolded. "I think they're magnificent. They remind me of the elk out west."

He glanced at her, arching a brow. "I'd imagine they're delicious, as well."

She tightened her lips and lowered her chin.

With a nudge of his elbow, he whispered, "I'm just teasing you."

Her gaze lifted and she smiled.

An hour later, Jason reined the mare to a stop in front of their home. His heart thumped against his ribs. "Debbie, will you see me again, alone?" His throat tightened and the blood pounded in his temples.

Her gaze pushed deep into his. "I would like that," she said, creasing a smile. She gathered the roses, then stepped from the surrey, her boots crunching onto the new fallen snow.

As she turned, she slipped.

"Be careful," he hollered even as she tumbled to the ground. He jumped from the carriage and rushed around the horse. She slid her palm across his and struggled to stand.

"You all right?" he asked, pulling her against him. The warmth of her curves ignited a fire within his groin. He swallowed, envisioning her body naked beneath him.

She stepped back and brushed away the icy flakes from the front of her frock. "Thank you," she murmured, her gaze touching his, then darting away. "I'll be fine, really."

His *sister* by no blood ties...his sister no more.

The back door banged shut to shatter the memory.

He upended his glass and downed the remaining whiskey in two gulps. Emptiness tore at his heart. He shoved out of the chair and stomped to the sink. Tight jawed, he slammed the glass against the copper sheeting. Slivers of fine crystal sprayed across the metal and caught the sunlight, glistening.

Just like Debbie's eyes.

His neck muscles tightened and he narrowed his gaze. The slivers merely reflected his agony, his wretched vulnerability, his loss of purpose without her. She completed him and the trip to go to New Orleans ripped at his soul.

He turned away and glared out the window.

I will never give up, Debbie. I need you more than life itself.

* * *

April showers washed away winter's despair and the sadness that had accompanied Jason. The earth burst into life around him. Trees budded, flowers bloomed, and new foals pranced in the nearby pastures.

The sharp trill of a mocking bird forced him to glance up from his ledger of past due bills. Bronzed shadows dancing from the single oil lamp on his desk draped each corner of the room. The thump of hooves against the closest stall reverberated through his open office door.

Laying aside his pencil, he closed the journal. "That's strange," he mumbled. "Birds are usually nesting by now and the horses are still stirring."

Three steps took him to the window.

A chalk-white moon hung low in the evening sky, a hazy halo cresting full. Streaks of wafer-thin, blue-grey clouds smeared the light that illuminated the country. Emerging stars twinkled, reminding him of water droplets he'd seen dancing in the mist at Crystal Falls.

Jason inhaled, sucking in great gulps of night air and embraced the warmth surging through his body.

Turning, he grabbed the wire-handled lantern and crossed the room. Stepping into the corridor of the stable, he strode to the tack room, then saddled Blue.

"Come on, boy," he said, tugging his horse toward the opening. He swept into the saddle, then tapped his heels against the flanks and headed into the twilight.

The screech of an owl filtered from the towering pines as he urged the gelding over the hill. With each strong stride, the scrape of Blue's horseshoes reverberated against shale rock.

Jason reined to a stop, the rumble of water crashing over the falls beckoning him closer.

He urged Blue along the rocky slope.

His heart rammed against his chest as the rapids plummeted to the boulders below. Mist rose from pools between rocks and created tiny rainbows that sparkled in the moonlight.

An eerie rumble drew him closer. Voices, muted and haunting...specters in the mist...beckoned him ever closer to the water's edge. His muscles tightened. Rippling wakes slapping against stone echoed in his ears.

Wide-eyed, he pivoted to locate the chanting thrum that reverberated across the night. Goosebumps rippled up his arms in prickling anticipation.

Within minutes, he reined Blue to a halt at the base of the waterfalls. Trembling, he slid from the saddle and strode to the riverbank. He lifted his chin as droplets showered his face, thrusting him into an inescapable spell.

With squinted eyes, he embraced the halo of colors while ghostly figures danced around him .

Debbie...Debbie...Debbie...

A swarm of bats surged from a nearby cave. Their fluttering wings, a black cape against the night sky. Jason pivoted and glanced upward. The creatures circled above with a flurry of chattering cries. With held breath, he stared until the cloak disappeared into the darkness.

He blinked. The night grew still.

Pebbles crunched beneath his boots as he stepped into shallow water. His pallet chalk dry, he kneeled and scooped the cool liquid into his palm. Two gulps washed away his anxiety. He straightened and peered heavenward. Not a cloud over head. The silvery moon scraped the treetops on the distant horizon.

With a tug of the reins, he led Blue across the gravel shore, then settled onto a cluster of crabgrass and fox tails. The bitter-sweet aroma rushed up his nostrils as the weeds crushed beneath his weight. He pressed aside the long stems that gouged his ribs, then lay back upon the cool ground.

Drawing a breath, his eyes slid shut. He drifted into a deep sleep, his beloved scurrying through his dreams.

"Debbie," he whispered, his voice laced with passion. She glanced over her shoulder, her face covered by a mask of fear. He lurched forward and she sped away. His heart thundered as he grabbed for her, only to draw back cool air. A heartbeat later, he turned a corner and she stood before him smiling, wearing her elk's tooth necklace. She touched the jewelry then the piece disappeared, just as she had vanished from his life. He thrust his hand out and her distorted figure faded into the darkness.

The cry of a lone wolf brought Jason upward. Startled, he skimmed the landscape. His heart rammed against his ribs, fighting to burst through. He blinked and glanced into a star-filled sky. The moon, directly overhead, stared back. He stumbled to his feet. "Damn," he said on a tight groan. "How long did I sleep?"

Only the falls heard his question.

With the sweep of his hand, he brushed the grass from his pants, then turned to locate Blue. The horse grazed in a nearby meadow. Jason glanced at Crystal Falls, then started toward the roan.

The crack of a stick brought him around.

He narrowed his eyes peering into the darkness. Nothing moved. Were the spirits taunting him again? On a huff, he pivoted and stepped beside Blue. His hand closed around the grip of his rifle. An easy tug eased the Henry repeater from the sheath. He cocked the rifle and peered over the horse's rump.

"Don't shoot," came a mumbled response.

A flurry of twigs snapped and then James staggered from the undergrowth. Jason lowered his weapon. "What in the hell are you doing here?"

"I...I followed you," his stable boy said, moving closer.

"Why?"

"I saw you ride out. Figured you was comin' here. Heard the stories 'bout this place and wanted to see fer myself."

"Well, you shouldn't be here." Jason shoved the rifle into the sheath. "Where's your horse."

The lad stuffed his hands in his pockets and lowered his chin. "I- I walked."

"Walked? That's a hell of a distance."

"Yes sir, but I didn't mind." He stared at Jason for a long moment, then sputter. "I...I'm afraid."

"Afraid? I'm not going to hurt you."

The boy frowned. "I'm not afraid of you."

"Then, what?" Jason placed his hand on the lad's shoulder.

"Well, I went down by the water, then I heard someone call my name. I looked on the other side and saw Packey standing there."

Jason kneeled, meeting the boy's gaze. "Are you sure you weren't dreaming?"

"No sir, I wasn't. It was Packey. He had on the same clothes he wore when he died. Told me you should look for Debbie near the big water. Then he pointed that way."

The urchin gestured southward.

Jason pivoted. "That way?"

"Yes, sir."

Jason lowered again and faced the boy. "Did he say anything else?"

"No, sir." Tears glistened in his eyes. "When I looked back he...he was gone."

Jason stared at him. Everything was coming together. The haunting dream. Mrs. Butterfield giving him the necklace, then telling him to look for Debbie in New Orleans.

And now, Packey pointing the way.

She must be there.

He grasped the boy's shoulders. "So you've heard about the legends told by the Indians of dead people appearing near the falls on a moon-lit nights?"

James nodded.

"Are you sure you didn't imagine this?"

"N-No sir, I saw him."

Jason straightened and drew a deep breath. "Spirits help us on our journey through life. Some are evil and make bad things happen. Promise me you'll never come here alone."

"I...I promise," James sputtered, then threw his arms around Jason's waist, sobbing.

"Come on, son," Jason said. "Let's go home, before your folks miss you."

Chapter Twenty-Eight

The following morning

Jason locked the office door and hustled down the corridor to the tack room. The rich smell of leather swept over him as he stepped inside. His gaze fell on the saddle with matching bridle, mounted on a free-standing mahogany frame.

Sunbeams cut through the nearby window and bounced off the silver trim before sending splashes of diamond-like reflections up the opposite wall. His lips shifted into a lopsided smile. Father's gear symbolized his importance and Jason drew a breath. *He'll always be a part of this stable.* Even the saddle underscored this truth.

A boot scrape severed his thoughts and he glanced sideways to settle his gaze upon James.

"What you got there?" Jason asked, stepping closer to his stable boy.

The lad stumbled to his feet, dropping a bridle to the floor. "Morning, Mr. Jackson. Just saddle-soapin' the leather."

Jason stepped closer as the haunting memory of the message from the falls sent a chilling reminder up his spine. He settled his palm upon the boy's shoulder. "Those spirits last night were mighty creepy, weren't they?"

"Sure were."

Jason squeezed, then dropped his hold. Turning, he grabbed his saddle. "I'm headed to Butterfield's. Take care of the place. Should be back around noon."

"I understand, Mr. Jackson."

"Let's just make it Jason…that'll do just fine. All right?"

The young man nodded, then scooped up the bridle and refocused on his work.

* * *

As Blue cantered along the country road, Jason skimmed the terrain. The vibrant greens of early spring washed the hillside. The bracing rebirth brought promise to his own bleak and tattered soul. He lifted his gaze heavenward. Turquoise enveloped him and set a perfect canvas for the billowing clouds. A smile tugged as he envisioned Debbie dancing in her exact blue-colored Easter dress last spring. The memory of her laughter rippled in the wind as the rustling leaves on nearby pecan trees whispered new hope for her return.

He surrendered a sigh built on months of suppressed yearnings.

The rattle of an approaching buggy cut through his musings. He shifted his attention to the bend in the road ahead.

A carriage pulled by a frisky chocolate brown mare rolled into view. He reined Blue to a halt beneath the shade of an oak tree. Beaming sunlight skipped across his roan's neck.

Jason sighed and pinched his brows together.

Another delay. At least he could admire the animal that pulled the rig. The filly demanded appreciation. He'd seen so few boasting that rare color blend.

Liz raised a hand and waved at him.

Jason tightened his grip on the reins. The very thought of her squeaky, high-pitched laughter dug into him like a swarm of bees.

He cringed, then nodded as she pulled up beside him. "Morning Liz."

"Oh, Jason, so good to see you. I've wanted to come by to visit."

"I'm gone a lot. Busy with the horses and such."

"Well, I'll try not to be a bother," she said, gesturing with a flip of her hand.

Jason flinched, as her mare turned and nipped at his knee.

Liz jerked the leather straps, then giggled her monstrous squeak. "Sorry," she quipped. "She's a wicked little thing. Anyway, I'm headed to town to do some shopping. I must have a new outfit for the trip to New Orleans."

He choked back a snicker. Butterfield must spend a fortune clothing her. *God help the fool that marries this woman.* He leaned forward. "Is your grandfather home? Infinity's ready to race again so I need to make arrangements to ride along with you all."

"That's wonderful news." The corners of her mouth tipped upward as her lashes fluttered.

Jason cleared the expanding lump in his throat.

The mare nipped at his knee again.

Liz jerked the reins once more. "I need to go. And, yes, Grandfather's at the stable." She leaned forward and winked. "Happy to hear you're going with us."

He tightened his jaw and surveyed her broomstick-like body. *Too scrawny...and annoying as hell.* Jason touched the brim of his hat. "Good day, Liz."

She nodded, then tapped the mare's rump with her buggy whip. The rig rattled, then rolled forward. A cloud of dust rose, grinding away her flirtation. A frown tugged at Jason's brow and he exhaled his frustration.

Just another damned hurdle in my life.

With a slap of the reins, he spurred Blue forward.

A half hour later, Jason topped the hill leading to the Butterfield estate. The strong silhouette of a roof line appeared, then seconds later, Copper Creek Stables filled his view. A row of blue and gold chevrons fluttered atop the building. A chill etched up his arms. The stable colors were chosen by his best pal, John's eldest son, Robert, who died at Shiloh.

His life cut short by a damned Reb's saber.

Jason's thoughts tumbled back to one of the days when the stable was being constructed. He and Robert were playing near the site.

"We're gonna buy some thoroughbreds," Robert bragged.

"Race horses?"

"Yep. They'll be the best in the country."

Jason leaned against a pile of new lumber. "You gonna have special riders, too?"

"Sure will. The colors they'll wear will let everyone know what's ours." He waved toward the half-finished stable. "Gonna put flags on the roof of this place, too."

"How come?"

"Father says it makes a statement." Robert said, scuffing the toe of his shoe in the dirt. "He even said I can pick his colors, so I'm thinkin' red and white."

"Everybody uses red," Jason said with a frown. "You need colors that mean somethin'."

Jason straightened and stuffed his hands into his denim pockets. "What about sky blue or green like the grass?"

"Blue sounds good, but not green. Yuk, frogs are green."

Jason squinted into the afternoon sky. "How 'bout yellow, then? The sun's bright and get's your attention."

"Mmmm...maybe." Robert lifted his hand to shade his eyes and scanned the wheat field. "Gold. That's it. Blue and Gold."

"I like that, too," Jason chirped.

"Come on," Robert said, tugging at Jason's arm. "Let's go tell father."

The cry of a hawk flying overhead brought Jason back to the present.

With a sigh, he released his sadness, then steered Blue through the iron gates and up the lane to the stable.

Sliding from the saddle, he tied his horse to the hitching post, then strode inside. He swept off his hat, boot heels thumping against the worn flagstone floor.

A stable hand approached him leading a feisty stallion.

Jason stepped aside.

The rambunctious five-year-old thoroughbred, slick-as-a-ribbon chestnut, had proven to be one of Butterfield's finest studs.

Jason chuckled. *Go shake your tail, big boy.*

Butterfield's voice bellowed down the hallway and bounced off the rafters.

Jason smiled and pushed toward the sound. A rustling commotion from a nearby stall grabbed his attention. He peered between the wood slats into a small, straw-filled area.

The robust frame of John Butterfield thrusting high his arms as he barked out orders filled Jason's view. Perspiration rolled down the closest stable hand's temples as the man trembled beneath John's fury. Panic creased his features while he struggled to contain the thrashing mare that reared onto her back haunches. Snorts flared the animal's nostrils.

John's face turned blood red. "Your grip on the lead is too tight. Ease off."

"I'm tryin'," the worker yelled.

John jerked the rope from the stable hand and edged to the entry. "Get the hell outta here and go unload the hay."

Nodding, the man surged toward the opening. "I'm sorry, sir." A second later, he and his buddy burst into the corridor and scurried from view.

Jason choked back a scoff, then stepped up behind Butterfield. "How's things goin'?" he asked, touching John's shoulder.

The old man pivoted, eyebrows rising. "Pretty damn bad. Just can't find good help these days." He slammed the barred gate shut. "Some days aren't worth gettin' outta bed for. Just bred this little gal to my best stud and she kicked the shit out of him."

"I saw him as I came in. Fine lookin' animal."

Butterfield yanked a handkerchief from his back pocket and swiped his forehead. "Damn, it's hot." He waved the cloth before his cheeks. "Speakin' of fine horses. When're you gonna let me breed my ladies to Infinity? I need that blood line back some way, boy."

"Soon," Jason chuckled. "I expect no later than next spring. He's ready now, but I want to get a few more races outta him before we take his mind off running."

"Yep, just like a man. Once they mount a woman, they can't think of anything else."

Jason laughed. "I'm here to see you about the New Orleans trip. Like to go along, if you don't mind. There's a chance Debbie's in the area. So, I can race Infinity and search for her, too."

"You heard somethin'?"

"A few leads. Nothin' definite. But, I need to go check things out."

"Walk with me," John said, motioning to the well-lit mahogany-filled office at the end of the grey stone path. I've got a sheet with all the information. Gonna take a couple of fillies down next week. They're calling the big doing's The World's Industrial and Cotton Centennial Exposition, or some such nonsense. Somethin' about praising the south's cotton industry. The newspapers are shortening thing's down a bit to the World's Fair."

Jason turned, spurs clinking as he shuffled alongside John. "But, the races are this spring, right?"

"Sure are. There'll be several events occurring."

Jason followed him across the threshold and toward the oversized desk. The leather top was cluttered with files, forms and a mound of loose papers.

Stepping behind his work space, John sorted through several documents. "I've actually got a system here," he mumbled.

Jason choked back his laughter. *Hell, he couldn't find his ass with both hands.*

"Here it is," Butterfield said, holding the notice up to the light.

"Everything you need to know is listed right here."

Jason scanned the paper. "Good to see there'll be quality horses there." *But, I'm more interested in finding Debbie.*

Butterfield nodded as he dropped onto the chair. "There'll be thoroughbreds from all over the world. Couldn't ask for any better. Why, I wouldn't waste my time if it were just a county fair. Hell, they're erecting a Horticultural Hall that will be the biggest greenhouse on earth. The racetrack is laid out beside this damned thing."

Jason folded the info and shoved the paper into his shirt pocket. "I'll make arrangements for someone to take care of the stable while I'm gone."

"What about Taylor? Is he capable of getting out, yet?"

"No. He's less interested as each day passes. Doesn't even ask about Infinity anymore."

"Hell's fire, I thought if anything would keep him going, it'd be that horse."

"Me, too," he shook his head. He just doesn't care anymore. Mother says he's getting sores from lying in bed. If he gets the fever, he won't last long."

"Damn, I hate to hear that. We've had our differences over the years, but I sure don't want anything more happening to that ol' coot."

"The incident at the stable when he collapsed pretty much did him in. Mother cries a lot at night, now. She's grieving over him, bad."

"How long've they been married?"

"Six years."

John nodded, then leaned over and flipped open a pine wood case. A dozen cigars nestled within. Each cylinder of fine Cuban tobacco was encircled by a gold paper band that bore the initials of the importer. John plucked one out, removed the band, then struck a match and raised it to the cigar. Three quick puffs and the end of the Principe de Gales glowed red. Clamping the stub between his teeth, he released a breath of smoke sideways. The aroma of sulfur and tobacco melded together in the room. "Shame it couldn't be longer."

"We both missed a lot of good years with him." Jason drew in a deep breath, appreciating the luxurious odor of the tobacco.

"About Infinity… why don't you start thinking which mare you want him to breed?"

"Oh, I've been thinkin' about that for some time, son." He inhaled, then released the smoke through the same crease. "I've at least five ladies in mind."

"Five?" Jason echoed. "You know the fee will be substantial?"

"The best always are," John chirped. "Besides, I've more money than my wife and granddaughter can ever spend. It's my turn, now."

Jason bellowed, the rumble erupting all the way from his gut. "All right, I'll give you an exact date sometime after Christmas."

"Christmas? Hell, I may be dead by then."

"You're too ornery to die."

John crushed the butt of the cigar on his boot heel. "Guess you're right, at that," he snipped. "I can be pretty rank when I wanta be."

Jason shoved his hands into his pockets. "Where you gonna stay in New Orleans?"

"I'll get us rooms at the Plaza. Liz wants us close to the shopping pavilion, God help me! How 'bout you?"

"Don't know. I'll get everything arranged to ship Infinity, then I'll let you know my plans."

"Sounds good. And you tell Taylor he'd better get out of that bed or I'm coming over and kick his ass clean into next week."

Jason smiled, left the stable and headed for home.

An hour later, he passed the gate at Crystal Falls. A sharp call brought him around and he jerked back on the reins. Peering over his shoulder, he spotted James astride a horse.

"There was a Mr. Jefferson here to see you," the lad said, riding up.

Alex Jefferson. The short, stout image of the agent he'd hired last fall to investigate Debbie's disappearance flooded his mind. "What did he want?"

"Asked when you'd be back. I said around noon."

Jason's eyes widened as he leaned closer. "Did he say anything about Debbie? Has he found her?"

"Nope, nothin. Just said he'd see you later."

"Damn it," Jason rasped. *I'm paying the sonofabitch a fortune and he doesn't even wait for me.*

Blood rushed to his head as his ire mounted.

With a jerk, he reined Blue around. "Tell Millie I won't be home for dinner. I'm goin' into town."

The boy nodded, then Jason slapped the roan's rump and galloped away.

* * *

Months without resolution wore heavy on Jason's patience. One problem at a time would be enough, but the weight of his misery came three-fold. With a shallow breath, he loosened the reins and tapped his spurs against Blue's flanks. The horse broke into a full gallop, spraying dirt and gravel behind them.

Jason compressed his lips as he steered the gelding into the town's livery stable. Sliding from the saddle, he straightened and stretched his back muscles.

With a flurry of instructions, he pitched the stable boy a silver coin, then exited through the side door. Lifting a hand, he shaded his eyes from the afternoon sun and scanned all the way down Lexington's main street. His gaze stopped on a black mare tied to the hitching post in front of Jefferson's office.

His horse. He's here.

His heartbeat quickened. Long strides carried him down the street toward the investigators office. A light flickered through the dusty window pane. Jason grimaced. *About damn time.*

He crossed the boardwalk, then halted before the door and drew a breath. Lips pulled tight, he centered his thoughts. Anxiety lanced his nerves as he raised his fist and rapped his knuckles against the weathered wood.

Within seconds, a gravelly voice responded. "Come in."

Jason entered with narrowed eyes. Sunlight streaked through the dirty front glass to lay a hazy sheen across the room. A strong smell of coffee swept over him. Swiping the hat from his head, he spotted Jefferson behind his desk.

Inhaling, Jason stepped toward his agent, the floor creaking as he traversed the sparsely-furnished office.

He scraped to a stop before Jefferson.

Their gaze met.

The man's elegant, expensive glass eye he'd special-ordered from Chicago drifted to the left side of his eye-socket.

Jason glanced away as he suppressed a chuckle.

Inhaling, he looked back.

Unruly muttonchops, too long for decent society folks, drug across the man's collar. Deep-cratered wrinkles and an overgrown mustache only added to the troll's ghoulish appearance.

With a grunt, Jefferson spiked his elbows on the cluttered desk. "Pull up a seat," he said. "Glad you stopped in."

Jason dropped onto the closest chair. "My stable boy said you stopped by."

"Yep." The ruddy-faced man surged to his feet and rounded the desk. His sagging belly draped over his belt and his worn, tattered pant cuffs brushed the floor as he shuffled to the stove. Lifting the coffee pot, he splashed the contents into his cup. "Care for any? Not fancy and tastes like hell, but better than nothin'."

"No, thanks," Jason said, placing his hat on the desk top.

The man raised the old, cracked, porcelain cup to his lips and gulped several swallows.

A grimace later, he lumbered back to his chair.

He scooped up several pamphlets and then dumped them onto a nearby table. "I have a lead on that lady friend of yours."

Jason's heart rammed against his chest. "Yes...What?" He glared into the man's good eye, but could not resist a quick glance at the black dot on the glass imposter. Torn between the euphoria of good news and the hilarity of this man's face as the fake eye waggled in all directions before him, Jason stifled another laugh.

"Well, I can't be sure this is the woman you're looking for, but she does have the same name."

"What have you found?" With a grunt, Jason leaned forward, his throat clamping tight. "Where is she?"

"She's working at a hospital in New Orleans."

"A hospital?" His pulse ratcheted up a notch. "Of course. She's gotta be there."

"But, hold on now," the man said, frowning. "This gal doesn't quite fit your description."

Jason tightened his shoulders as panic throbbed through his veins. *Vacant information... just like this man's damned eye.* "How?" he snapped, slamming his palms against the edge of the desk.

"This woman's married. But, that's about all I could find on her."

"Did you show them her picture?"

Alex shook his head. "Naw, I just found her by tracking the name."

Jason surged to his feet, then paced the room. He stopped before the filthy glass and peered out. Fingers bit deep into the wooden window-frame. "Debbie used to work here at the hospital. It makes sense that she would seek the same kind of employment." He swerved back to face Jefferson. "But why, if she's free, won't she come home?"

"Maybe she doesn't have the money."

"She could've wired me. I would've sent her the funds. She knows that."

"Never did understand women. Guess that's why I didn't get married."

The slurping sounds of him gulping his coffee slid over Jason in annoying waves. "Did they tell you what hospital?"

"Yah, I have it here somewhere," the man replied. "Place is run by a bunch of nuns. They built some big convent and church a few years back across the street. " He unfolded a crumpled paper. "Damn, I spilled coffee over this sonofabitch. Sorry. Anyway, them nuns are called Ursulines. But, I can't make out the name of the building on the corner of Rue Chartres and Rue Ursulines."

"I'll start there," Jason said, angling toward the door. "Much obliged. Send me the bill and we'll settle."

"I will," the man said, picking up the yellowed cup. With a nod he saluted. "Hope you find her."

* * *

Stepping outside, Jason glanced up the street, "I need a drink," he grumbled.

Frustration bit at his nerves as he trudged along the walkway to the nearest saloon. Piano music blasted over him and his ears rang like a swarm of hornets. He wedged up against a worn oak bar, pitted from the many brawls over the years. He propped his foot on the brass rail and the toe of his boot rocked the spittoon on the floor beside him. Splatters of chewing tobacco surrounded the disgusting container and Jason edged away. *Don't want no chaw on my boots.*

A short, stout barkeeper wiped the countertop, his gaze meeting Jason's. "What'll you have?"

"Whiskey," Jason growled.

The man turned and grabbed for a glass.

Jason slapped his hand on the bar. "No," he grumbled. "I want the whole damned bottle, my friend."

The bartender peered at him over wire-rimmed spectacles. "Bad day, huh?" Easing back, he plucked a full bottle of Old Forester off the shelf, then slid it toward Jason.

"You've no idea." Jason grasped the neck of the container. With an easy tip, the cool glass lip met his mouth and he gulped. Cheap alcohol slid across his tongue. He closed his eyes as the brew kindled a flame down his throat to churn the bonfire already inside his gut.

By slow degrees, the blaze spread through his veins, searing against his misery.

His eyes sprang open. He glared at the bartender. "Get outta my face."

The man rocked back on his heels, nodded, then, hands buried within a tattered apron, he shuffled out of view.

Jason drew out two silver coins. With a loud chink, he dropped them onto the bar. Grabbing the Old Forester, he headed for the exit.

An hour later, he reined Blue to a halt near a bridge less than a mile from home. Twisting, he tipped the now, near-empty bottle upward and gulped another swig of whiskey.

The liquid slid down his chin and onto his shirt, soaking the durable cotton. A belch rumbled from his throat and he swiped his shirtsleeve across his mouth.

With a frown, he stared at the small amount of liquid that still sloshed inside the bottle. "Blue...I think I'm drunk."

The horse flicked back his ears and nickered.

Jason chuckled. "You think so, too, do ya?"

Leather creaked as he slowly straightened, then upended the bottle and swallowed the remainder.

Another belch followed as he hurled the empty into the weeds. "There, I'm done. Not gonna feel sorry for myseeeelf no more," he slurred.

Weaving in the saddle, he tugged on his hat brim, then squinted skyward. Shades of yellow and tangerine fanned the horizon as the sun rested on the hillside. "Come on, fella," he ordered. "Damned near sundown. Let's get goin' before I fall off and you have to drag my sorry ass home."

He spurred the roan forward.

And a half-hour later, Jason bedded Blue down, then grabbed a lantern and wobbled for the house. Puny flickers of light matched the minimal news he'd received in regards to Debbie's whereabouts. All he knew was that Debbie was in New Orleans.

And I'm sure as hell gonna find her this time.

Chapter Twenty-Nine

Sunshine splashed across Debbie's cheeks warming her with great expectations for the day. She shuffled along Royal St. toward the hospital. Birds chattering in the trees forced her gaze upward. Budding leaves brought a new beginning. She smiled, inhaling deep the scent of blooming azaleas. She enjoyed the soft shades of pink and crimson that painted this multi-hued picture of spring.

The clang of church bells lanced her ears as she scurried through the entrance of the medical building. She nodded at a woman that swept the floor, then dashed past her.

A nun on duty shot Debbie a pointed glare as she approached her work station. With a puff of dissatisfaction, the Mother Superior straightened, then stuffed her fists beneath the creases in her black habit. "You're late," she snapped, lifting her chin. "And we admitted a new patient. Go check on him first. Third room on the right."

Debbie nodded and jotted the orders down on a tablet. From the corner of her eye, she swept her gaze down the long hallway. A moment later, she looked back to the self-ordained Saint. Debbie bit her lower lip as her dislike of the battle-ax deepened. *I refuse to lose my job over your attitude.* With a sigh, she dropped the pen onto the desk, folded the paper and strutted down the corridor toward her patient.

Easing the door open, she peered around the edge. "Mr. Baker?" she called, slipping into the dim lit room.

The patient faced the window away from her.

"William Baker?" she repeated.

With a rustle of blankets, the man rolled to face her.

Her eyebrows shot upward. Fair haired; skin tan as a doe. *He's the man who helped me the night of the storm.*

"What do you want?" he grumbled.

"I've been assigned to care for you tonight. And I do believe we've met somewhere before."

A deep crease cut across his forehead. His expression held firm as he scanned her from head to toe, then a smile softened his features. "Yes, I remember. You're the young lady at the tavern. The one who ran away."

"That's right," she replied. "I apologize for my rude behavior that night. I'd had a very rough day." She glanced down at his chart. "I see you've injured your ankle."

"Actually, my horse kicked at a dog and hit me instead."

Their gaze reconnected.

"Bad timing on my part," he said, with a chuckle.

Her cheeks flushed as she smiled. "Do you mind if I see?" She reached for the covers. His unruly blonde curls tossed as he shook his head. Forcing her gaze from his, she lifted the blanket and peered at the injury. "Mmm. That looks pretty nasty. Are you in pain?"

He crinkled his nose. "Yes, it hurts like hell."

"Well, your ankles quite swollen, I'm afraid." Aqua blue eyes met hers, once more. She cleared her throat and turned her focus back to the chart. "I'll get something to make you more comfortable."

The bed creaked as he tightened the covers and shifted onto his back. "Do they serve any food around here? I haven't had so much as a slice of bread."

She giggled. "I'll look into that."

Jason swept into her mind. Food was his priority when he was bedridden, too. *Are all men the same? Sex and food...their only concerns.*

She started for the door.

"Wait," William hollered. "You haven't told me your name."

She pivoted. "I'm so sorry. Debra." His charm was no match for Jason's, but she did want to count this man among her new-found friends. "But, everyone calls me Debbie."

"Debra," he repeated. "I like that. It fits you. May I call you by that?"

She smiled. "Sure. It just seems so formal."

"I believe there's more to you than you want anyone to see. Somewhere in there," He pointed to her chest. "I suspect dwells a very sophisticated young lady."

He's flirting with me. Debbie swallowed back the temptation of his charm. "Hardly," she stated. "I'm just a poor working girl."

A glance at him in the crumpled covers brought back memories of her beloved. Visions of Jason being in bed tumbled through her mind. He was her life, every minute of every day.

A shuffling sound brought her back to reality.

William cocked his head. "Are you all right?"

She brushed her sweaty palm across her skirt, then flashed a crooked smile. "Yes, I- I'm fine," she stammered. *I need to get out of here.* She started for the door. "Good day, Mr. Baker." With a nod, she slipped into the hall.

* * *

A cool morning breeze fluttered the curtains on the open window near Debbie's bed. The aroma of fresh baked bread from a nearby pastry shop drifted into her tiny rented apartment. As she inhaled the spicy scent, her gaze followed the streaks of sunlight that flickered across the ceiling. She smiled. *I remember Millie baking cinnamon rolls each Sunday for breakfast.*

Homesickness oozed through her.

A chatter of voices on the street below shattered her longing.

Time to rise and dress. Don't want to upset the old battle-ax of a supervisor.

She lowered her feet onto the braided rug and her gaze shifted to the carved oak cradle at the foot of the bed. Her lips pulled sideways as she settled her hand atop her swollen belly. The used baby bed, purchased at the outdoor market, would serve her soon-to-be-born babe. On a sigh, she slipped forward to gather her work clothes.

* * *

Two hours into her shift, Debbie gasped when Sister Anna grabbed her arm. The nun stepped before her in the hallway. "There's a patient on the second floor asking for you."

Debbie tightened her lips. "William?" she muttered, staring into the woman's eyes. "Is he all right?"

"Oh yes, he's doing quite well. He just keeps requesting you." She leaned closer. "Do you know this man?"

"We've met by chance one evening. I don't actually know him."

"Well, go see him right now to settle him down."

Debbie nodded.

The nun scowled, then gathered the folds of her habit between her fingertips and continued down the corridor.

Debbie turned and wiped her palms on her apron. She stiffened her lips and scurried up the stairs to the second floor. The lump in her throat expanded with every breath. *He seems nice enough. But why does he insist on seeing me?*

"Debra," he said, flashing her a grin when she stepped into the room. "Where have you been?"

She forced a smile. "I've been working." Three steps took her to his bedside. "There *are* other patients, you know."

"They're sending me home tomorrow," he stated. "And I needed to see you before I left." He leaned over to retrieve a small calling card from atop the side-table. "Here, take this. All the information of where you can find me is here."

She blinked, staring at him. "Why would I need to find you?"

He grasped her arm and shoved the paper into her hand. "Take this. You're alone. You need someone to contact, if you're in trouble."

"No... you don't know me." She attempted to break free from his hold. "I could be a hatchet killer or a...a voodoo woman."

"I doubt that," he snickered, then, again, pointed at the card. "I own that cotton mill. You can ask anyone in town. They'll tell you I'm an honest person."

"I'm sure you are. But, if you're well-off, what're you doing in a hospital for the poor?"

"I'm sick. I've hurt my ankle. Besides, I give them a lot of money to help the church." He paused, then asked, "Do you have any relatives here in the city?"

"No." Panic surged through her. "My family lives far away...and frankly, sir, that's none of your business."

She exhaled her dissatisfaction on a ragged sigh. Her lips seamed shut. She pivoted toward the door.

"Debra, please don't be upset. I just want to help you."

She whirled back around. "I-I appreciate your offer, but... no, thank you." She hurried from the room.

Rounding the corner near the stairwell, she paused and slumped against the wall. She gulped sharp panting breaths as she unfolded the crumpled paper. Her brows drew tight.

I'm so confused. He seems sincere.

Her hands trembled as she stared at the card. His home, business address and other contacts filled the sheet. *Perhaps I'm being too judgmental.*

She drew a breath and shoved the information into her pocket.

Swift steps carried her back to her station. Gathering blood-splattered instruments she dropped them into a pan of sudsy water and scrubbed away the filth, along with her doubts. The rape, Laffoone, the bayou, all ate at her misery; she did not need another troubling aspect in her life.

Time passed quickly as she shrouded her thoughts in her work.

Finishing the last piece, she spread the clean tools on a towel, brushed back a strand of fallen hair and glanced up.

Heavy shadows from a nearby window crossed the wall. Late afternoon. *Thank goodness, my day is nearly done.*

Her hand closed around her satchel and she headed for the door.

"Debra," a masculine voice shouted from behind her. She pivoted to face the man walking toward her. His dark hair and olive skin reminded her of a young doctor from India. "Hello, my name is Seth Rios," he said. "Will asked me to find you and see that you get home safely."

"Will?" she echoed, then paused. "Oh, you mean William, my patient." She stepped back, trembling. A shiver trickled down her spine. *Why don't they leave me alone?* "No," she said. "No, thank you; I can manage."

"The streets are very dangerous." A frown etched the young man's forehead. "Will doesn't think you should be out at night, alone."

Aggravation bit at Debbie's patience. "Tell Will I appreciate his concern." She stepped to the side. "Please excuse me, I must go."

He lowered his chin and brushed past her.

Debbie listened as his footfalls disappeared down the hallway. With a sigh, she closed her eyes. *I've had enough of this William fella.* A knot tightened in her stomach. She bit her lip. *I need to set him straight once and for all.*

She grabbed her sweater from a nearby hook, then headed for his room.

Refusing to be stopped by the closed door, she forced her way in.

Her eyes widened as she froze in her tracks.

She choked back a gasp. She squeezed shut her eyes and pivoted on her heels. *Please God, tell me I didn't just see Seth kiss William.* Embarrassment spilled over her.

She would gladly crawl beneath a rug and disappear had there been one under her feet. Her left eye peeped open, then her right.

Mortification shifted into panic.

She swept around and started for the door.

"Don't go." William's mellow voice soothed her pounding heart. "I know what you're thinking."

Her gaze lanced from him back to Seth as she struggled to control the bile that crept upward.

They both smiled at her, their hands interlocked.

"Debra," Seth said, lowering his companion's hand to rest atop the covers. "Will and I have been together for a long time."

"I'm sorry you had to find out this way," William added. "We try to keep our lives private, but there are no locks on hospital doors. So our secret is compromised when people do not knock to tell us they are entering."

"I-I'm so sorry," she stammered. "I shouldn't have just barged in."

"You're fine." William said with a grin. "I would've eventually told you. You just beat me to it."

Debbie fumbled with the buttons on her sweater. "I...I really should go," she stammered. "I don't feel well."

She lowered her gaze, then turned and left the room.

Her steps quickened. Tears streamed down her cheeks and her trembling hand dashed them away.

She swung open the hospital's main door, then hurried out into the fading sunlight.

Pulling a deep breath, she slowed her pace and fought to calm her pounding heart. As she turned the corner, she melted into the crowd along Bourbon Street.

Her eyes widened.

Jazz bands played in smoke-filled taverns and the music entwined with rowdy laughter.

A couple staggered past her just as a sharp pain cut through her stomach.

The young man grabbed her arm. "You alright?" he asked with a slur. His burly muscles bulged beneath his shirt as he steadied her against the vine-covered building.

Several gulps of air later, she straightened. "I'm all right. Thank you."

He released his grip, then shuffled back into the partying crowd. Another sharp pain had her doubling over.

Debbie's head swirled as her trembling legs forced one foot in front of the other.

Is the baby coming?

With blurred vision, she skimmed the area. Noise heightened her anxiety and she hastened her steps. A few blocks later another piercing pain cut through her side. She wrenched in pain, then dropped to her knees.

Everything whirled around her. She lowered her hip to the ground, then closed her eyes. A cloak of darkness swept in.

* * *

Debbie gazed through a milky blur and blinked to clear her sight. Sister Anna hovered over her with a comforting smile.

"Are you feeling better?" the nun asked, while her gentle hand touched Debbie's cheek.

"I...I think so." Debbie squeezed her eyes against the bright light. "How'd I get here?"

"You were rushed here by folks who thought you were about to have your baby."

Debbie rose onto her elbow. "Am I?"

"Not yet," the nun said with a chuckle. "You've worked too much. You were overcome with exhaustion."

"But I had sharp pains in my stomach."

"That often happens when delivery time is close. You've been putting in a lot of hours here at the hospital. What you need is rest. We'll keep you here overnight, then you go home and stay there for a few more days."

Debbie lowered her chin. "But we're so busy. I really need to be here."

The woman squeezed Debbie hand. "You do as I say. We'll be fine." Sister Anna pressed her lips to Debbie's forehead. "Now you get some sleep."

The nun shuffled from the room.

* * *

The following morning Debbie woke to a loud chatter of voices in the hallway.

She sat up and strained to hear the jumbled words.

Slipping from the bed, she grabbed her sweater and crossed to the door, peeking into the corridor.

William stood perched on one leg, his arm draped over a crutch. He argued with the head nurse.

"You need to go home," she stated.

"Let me stay one more day," he insisted. "I promise I'll leave tomorrow."

Debbie eased up behind him. "Why do you want to stay?"

"Oh, there you are," he said, turning to face her. He stared at her for a long moment. "Could you help me back to my room."

"I want you out of here in the next hour," the nurse grumbled.

"Bitch," he snorted, hopping on one foot beside Debbie. "That woman is as vile as a copperhead."

Together they waddled down the hallway. She helped him into his room. He lowered onto the mattress, casting the crutch aside.

"Evil, she's just plain evil," he growled.

"Why don't you want to go home?"

His tone softened. "I needed to see you again before I leave. After yesterday, I was afraid you'd never call on me for help."

"William, I'm the most confused person in New Orleans right now. I don't understand why you want to help me." She lowered onto the closest chair. "Yes, I was shocked by your relationship with Seth. But every person has a right to live their life without being judged by others. Me, I just want to be left alone. I'll be a mother soon; I must look out for my child. My life has already been destroyed. I don't need any help making it worse."

His gaze locked on hers, then, he held out his hand. "Please," he said. "You need a friend. I want to be that friend." He took her hand in his. "I don't know what happened in your life, but I do know you need someone to protect you until you're able to untangle the mess that has brought you to this point. Let me be your strength…at least for now."

No one but Jason is my strength.

She released his hand, lifted to her feet, then turned away.

He scooted from the bed and touched her shoulder. "Don't be angry with me."

"I'm not angry," she whispered.

The door swung wide and Sister Anna appeared.

Debbie lowered her chin and mumbled, "Excuse me, I need to go." She stepped past the nun and hurried down the hallway.

Chapter Thirty

Muffled pounding jarred Jason awake and burrowed into his misery. He tightened his muscles to stop the sensation of swirling. "Damnit," he grumbled, as the drumming on the bedroom door continued.

He tossed back the covers, his mind still murky from the whiskey. On another curse, he stumbled to his feet.

"Jason," his mother pleaded from the other side of the door. "I…I need your help."

"J-Just a moment."

"It's…It's your father…" her voice trailed off into a broken sob.

Three staggering steps took Jason to the robe that lay on the floor. He jammed his arms inside the sleeves as he headed toward the door. A quick loop of the cloth belt closed the robe. He flung wide the heavy panel. "W-What's wrong?" he stammered.

Shaky fingers tugged at his wrist. "I…I can't get your father to calm down." Jason's heart sank as his gaze fell upon her swollen, red-rimmed eyes.

"H-He's out of his mind. Raving about going off to war," she added.

He clinched his jaw. *Sonofabitch.* "I-I'll be right down," he muttered.

She nodded and rushed down the hallway.

A splitting headache gripped the back of his eyes as he turned around. He braced his hand against the wood, then closed the door. Moonlight washed an eerie glow into the room as silver and grey shadows streaked the floor. He grimaced against the cloak of despair that now shrouded hope for his father's recovery. A roiling churn centered in his gut as he tunneled his hands through his hair. "Ah, shit. I think I'm gonna puke."

He staggered toward the wardrobe. "Damned cheap whiskey," he grumbled. With a gulp, he forced down the bile. He didn't have time to wallow in self-pity. His mother needed him and he knew a hellish fury awaited downstairs.

He grabbed his trousers and shoved into them. His boots followed. Still buttoning his pants, he thumped down the stairs, two steps at a time.

At his father's door, he drew a breath to steady his rattled nerves. His hero was dying and he couldn't do a damned thing to prevent the outcome. Everything of importance to him was being ripped away.

He gulped back another rolling wave of misery.

Ragged voices from behind the barrier penetrated his despair. He jerked open the door and his gaze cut to the bed.

His mother laid spread across the thrashing form of his father.

Jason surged forward. "Let me have him," he yelled, grasping Taylor's flailing arms.

Kathryn stumbled to her feet, whimpering, "He's never slapped me before."

Jason clamped his jaw and shoved against his father's shoulders, pushing his enormous form against the mattress. He braced his full strength on the man's chest. Head pounding, vision blurred, he stared down into this monster's face.

Demons now glared back from the once loving gaze of the man who used to be his father. Disease had finally conquered Taylor Jackson. The massive weight of the truth centered Jason. "Calm down, I don't want to hurt you."

Taylor grunted and jerked his arm clear.

An uppercut met Jason's chin. Pain exploded in a cacophony of hellish streaks behind his eyes.

He heard his mother gasp. A moment later, her hand gripped his arm, fingers digging inward. "Jason, are you hurt?"

"Stay back, mother," he snapped. And she obeyed, shuffling aside several steps.

He sucked in a quart of air, then shook off the numbing ring that echoed in his ears. His mind ached beneath the oppressiveness of change that crashed down upon him.

Another wave of vomit climbed upward.

He staggered and grasped the iron bed to steady his balance.

"Let me go, you damned Reb," his father hissed at him. "I'll run you through with my sword, I swear I will…you sonsofbitches aren't gonna hurt my family." He slammed his fist down upon Jason's hand.

"Father," he yelled, snagging Taylor's wrists. "Stop fighting me."

Behind him, his mother sobbed, great gasps of sorrow that pierced through him. He glanced over his shoulder. Devastation had twisted her beloved features, lines etching deep into a searing landscape where his childhood had once thrived. Protecting her now poured through his veins.

His heart sank and he glanced down at Taylor slumping against the pillow. Red-rimmed eyes and a glassy stare cut into Jason like broken glass.

Acceptance lanced through him as the knowledge that he now filled this man's boots intensified. Panting, Jason straightened and again swallowed the burning bile in his throat.

He rocked back on his heels, then turned to his mother. Tears cascaded down her cheeks as her gaze met his. His lips tightened. In every way, her life mattered to him, as did Mason and Crystal Falls. Without his father's guidance, they would falter.

God help me, I'm now in charge…of everything.

He inhaled and pulled back his shoulders. "Do you have any medicine for him?"

"Not for the fever," she sniffed. "I gave him the last dose of morphine yesterday."

"I'll send Tom for the doctor in the morning."

She nodded and dabbed her swollen eyes.

Soft moans rumbled from his father as he rolled toward them and closed his eyes.

Jason grasped his mother's arm, guiding her toward the door. "How long has he been like this?" he asked, slipping his arm across her trembling shoulders

"During the day h-he's fine. But...at night he gets s-so violent," she muttered, her voice cracking. "You've had so much on your mind...I-I tried to shield you from his decline."

Taking a calming breath, Jason squeezed her to his side. "He's settled for now, mother. You need to rest. I don't want you getting sick, too."

She glanced up. With shaking hands, she touched his chin.

He flinched and gave a grimace.

"I'm so sorry he hit you," she said, pressing her head against Jason's shoulder. "H-He's never been so violent. Are you all right?"

"I'm fine." He kissed the top of her head and motioned toward the stairs. "He's resting now. Go on up to bed. I'll stay with him for awhile."

She brushed his cheek with a kiss, then headed for the door.

Jason forced back tears as her sagging shoulders confirmed her broken spirit.

His gaze shifted to the nearby chair. Two strides and he dropped into the rocker. He leaned forward and dimmed the lantern on the sidetable. Shadows spilled in uneven curtains along the wall of books.

Years before, the room had been a library. Childhood memories of playing at his mother's side in this special room tumbled into recall. He saw her sitting at the desk, writing her own stories to read to him before bed. Her constant presence, her joys, her strong and solid dependability, all defined this woman whom he cherished.

He smiled as a recollection of the scolding she gave him for climbing atop the rolling ladder returned.

How simple life seemed back then.

Inhaling, his gaze drifted to the leather-bound law books gathering dust. All were a haunting reminder of his lost dreams. How different would things be today had he just gone away to school?

With a sigh, he glanced at the prostrate form of his father. We missed so much, dear man. *Imagine the memories we could've shared during my childhood if only you'd been here.*

A rattle from the bed springs brought Jason upward.

His father rose onto his elbows and shouted for Kathryn.

The hair on Jason's neck bristled and he surged forward. *Not again.* The man's eyes were ablaze and his thinning grey hair disarrayed. He tugged at his clothing. Woven threads of cotton gave way beneath his strength and ripped apart... just as Jason's life had torn into shreds.

"No," Jason yelled, surging from the rocker. "Don't do that."

The old man cursed and slung the nightshirt onto the floor. "I'll do whatever the hell I wanta do," he jeered. "Where's my wife? She'll tell you. I'm the man of this house."

The lump in Jason's throat expanded. He again swallowed bile. "I know you are, father," he whispered. Retrieving the fallen garment, he tightened his hand around the cloth. The weight of his duties had shifted. He was no longer just someone's son. Now he was in charge and he damned well knew it. He shoved the shirt toward the man's withered hand. "Put this on to keep from getting chilled."

"Chilled? Hell, I'm sweatin' like a pig. I need a drink."

Jason clinched his jaw, and then picked up a glass of water from the nightstand. "Here," he offered.

His father grabbed the goblet and glared down inside. His wiry brows pinched together. On a curse, he slung the cut-crystal across the room, shattering the glass against the door. Water spewed into a thousand droplets and sent the fragments of fine crystal glistening atop polished wood.

Jason's pulse spiked. The bile climbed upward again. "Damnit," he yelled, as the pounding in his head intensified. "Stop it; you must settle down."

A creak of the door drew his glare.

His mother peered back.

"Wait," Jason shouted. "There's glass everywhere. He motioned for her to stop. "Let me handle this."

"I-I'll clean it up," she said, stooping to collect the jagged pieces.

"Mother…please. Don't. You'll cut yourself. Go get Jeremiah. He'll take care of that."

She nodded, and then backed away as fresh tears streamed down her face. On another sob, she closed the door.

"Where's my whiskey?" Taylor demanded, tossing aside the covers.

Jason pivoted to face the madman. With a tightened fist, he swung, driving his knuckles against his father's chin. The blow drove the old man to the mound of covers, knocking him unconscious.

Jason rubbed away the pain in his hand and then eased down onto the bed. He struggled to swallow back his tears. "I love you, father," he whispered, staring at the limp form. Sobbing heaves bent him forward over the pitiful form.

* * *

A creak of the bedroom door stirred Jason awake. He opened his eyes to find Jeremiah striding toward the window. A quick jerk and the servant separated the heavy brocade panels, allowing morning light to crash into the room.

"Son of a bitch," Jason snapped, shielding his eyes. "Pull those damned things closed,"

"No, suh," the servant retorted. "Miss Millie's got da coffee brewin' in da kitchen. You get up now and get yo' self a cup. I'll sit with Mr. Jackson fer a spell."

Pushing on the arm rails, Jason heaved himself upward. "Fine," he huffed. "I'll go. But, if you need anything, you holler."

He headed toward the back of the house. And a half-hour later, his mother joined him in the dining room. "Mornin'," he said, scooping up a fork full of eggs. "Did you get any rest?"

"Not much." She eased onto the chair across from him. Dark crescents draped beneath her eyes. The obvious torment of his father's condition had purloined her usual joyous nature. He missed the warmth of her smile. "Were there any more episodes last night?" she asked.

He swallowed, then mumbled, "Not really. He fussed a bit longer, then went to sleep." Pushing aside the empty plate, Jason met her gaze. "Why does he get so violent at night?"

She inhaled and leaned forward. "The doctor said he's suffering from dropsy, but he's not sure what causes the mania."

Jason didn't miss her shaking hand as she flipped open the napkin and settled the cloth onto her lap. He cleared his throat. "Well, I sure as hell don't like it."

Millie shuffled in with a pot of coffee. The aromatic bite of Columbian beans swept over Jason. He sighed and lifted his cup for a refill; eager for the strength the magic beans would bring.

Father's favorite morning start.

"May I have some, too, please" his mother whispered. Millie tipped the pot and sent a stream of dark liquid into the coffee cup before her. Kathryn nodded and selected a sugar cube from a nearby bowl.

My vulnerable mother...trying so hard to be strong.

Jason wiped his mouth with the cloth, dropped the swatch of linen to the tabletop and then pushed backward. "Tom's on his way to fetch the doctor for you. Should be here before noon."

"Thank you," she said, the words barely audible. She slowly lifted her dainty, rose-patterned coffee cup toward her lips. Jason once again noticed the tremble of her hand as the contents shimmied against the expensive porcelain. "Oh, son," she whispered, her lips almost on the rim. "Everything is falling apart at such a rapid pace. Y-Your father can't take care of the place any longer. And...and now you're going away, too."

The truth returned, pressing ten-fold upon his frustrations. "I'll make sure things are in order before I leave. And I won't be gone more than a week. Two at the very most. If I don't know anything about Debbie's whereabouts by then, I promise to return home." Their gazes met and her tear-swollen eyes narrowed. "My concern now is to take care of you."

"But...what about your father?" she asked, blowing a wispy breath across the coffee to cool the liquid.

"He must have constant care now, Mother. Far more than you can give. You know this, right?"

On a nod, she finally sipped her coffee. *Defeated? Yes, perhaps. But brave? Always. The bravest woman I've ever known.* "Yes, son, I see this. All too clearly now, I'm afraid." Her words confirmed his thoughts as a tear slipped free and rolled down her cheek.

"And you're exhausted," Jason added. "I can't have you breaking down, either. You understand this, too, don't you?"

"But, what am I to do?" she whispered as her gaze burrowed deep into his.

"We'll get him help, Mother. There are places that specialize in this exact kind of sickness."

He stood and offered her a guarded smile. "But, first, I just need two weeks to find Debbie. If I can't locate her in that time frame, I'll return. I'll never let her go, but I'll assume control of our family and Crystal Falls. I promise." Chest tightening, without waiting for her acknowledgment, Jason pivoted on a boot heel and vacated the room.

* * *

Coal galloped up to the fence, greeting Jason as he scuffed along the shortcut to the stable. Jason snickered. "Howdy, there, big boy," he said, brushing his palm against the colt's slick neck. The animal rubbed his head against Jason's chin. "Careful, there" he said, flinching. "Jaw's still tender from my old man's blow." He pushed the colt's head aside and stepped back. Coal pranced in a circle, his black coat shining in the sunlight. Admiration filled Jason. "James sure keeps you lookin' good, fella. Won't be long before you'll be racing alongside Infinity."

The colt kicked up his heels and galloped away.

Young and carefree. No responsibilities. I'd like that...

Three workers unloading a wagon filled with oats caught his attention. On a grumble, he stifled his selfish weakness and waved to them. He had no time for talking this morning, though. There was too much work to do before he left for New Orleans.

He pushed open the stable door and headed for his office.

The resident barn cat sat on the step, cleaning her paw. "Out of my way, Cleo," he said, easing her lazy highness aside with the tip of his boot. The feline hissed and swiped at him before slinking off to hide beneath a wooden crate.

Even the animals are in a foul mood this morning.

He scuffed to his office chair and then dropped onto the leather cushion. Plowing his fingers through his hair, he glared at the bills piled before him. His frustration ramped up another notch. "Jeezus! What else can go wrong?" He swiped at the papers, sending the pile scattering. As they fluttered to the floor, Jason grit his teeth, his fists balling on the tabletop. *We need help and we need it now.* On a shallow breath, he mumbled, "What the hell can I do right now?" He straightened. "Jeremiah," he muttered and chinked a lopsided smirk. "Yes, I'll hire him into full time service. That'll give mother extra help while I'm away. And Jeremiah will welcome the extra pay." He'd also hire another maid to help Millie with the cooking and cleaning.

He settled back in his chair and stared out the window. Movement along the hillside caught his attention. He leaned forward and centered on a rider nearing the stable.

James waved and reined Duke to a halt.

Pushing back from his desk, Jason inhaled a calming breath. Seconds later, a knock fell upon his door. "Come in," he stated.

James swung open the panel and the sound of buckets banging and horses nickering, overrode the voices of the other workers. The lad removed his worn hat and stepped inside, closing out the everyday resonance of a working stable.

Jason nodded toward James as the lad's smile brightened the room. *Always eager to please.* He appreciated, especially now, the youthful spirit of the boy. *As refreshing as Coal. Young. Hopeful. Blissfully living without responsibilities.*

All the things he no longer had the freedom to be.

"Tom's back with the doctor," James said. "Do you want me to get Infinity ready for his workout now?"

"In a minute," Jason replied, motioning toward the chair fronting his desk. "Sit down. We need to talk."

James' face grew somber as he stepped past the documents spread across the floor. "Somethin' wrong?"

"No," Jason said, frowning at the clutter.

James bent to scoop up the mess.

Again, Jason saw a reflection of himself in the boy's loyalty. He recalled the times he'd scrambled to please his own father.

Those days were gone forever.

A new purpose gave him direction as he sized up the lad stacking the papers on his desk. James was on the cusp of adulthood. Now would be a good time to teach him a thing or two about responsibility.

Leaning back, Jason folded his hands. "I'm taking Infinity to New Orleans for a race in a few days. I'm going to need you to run the stable while

I'm away. Do you think you can handle that?"

"Really?" The boy's eyes widened, his face brightening even more. A quick nod brought a smile to Jason's lips. "Y-Yes sir. I believe I can. I know I can."

"Well, this is a big task I'm asking, but I think you know enough about the operations around here that I can trust you with the job."

Jason remembered the first time his father left him in charge of Crystal Falls. It was a life-changing moment he would never forget.

"I'll take care of everything, sir. I promise." A twinkle brightened James' eyes as his mouth bowed upward.

Like father...and now like son.

"Jeremiah will handle things up at the house concerning father, but you must check on Mrs. Jackson. Every day. Several times a day. And if she needs anything, you do whatever she asks. Tom will be here to help you out at the stables. If things go bad, lock the place down. Understand? I'll be back in two weeks."

James nodded and fidgeted with the brim of his hat.

"You're a man now, son," Jason added. "I need you to act like one."

"Yes, sir. I will, sir. I'm more than ready."

Jason pushed his hand beneath the lad's overall suspender strap and tugged him closer. He peered straight down into James' blue eyes. "And, if you do a good job, you can consider Coal yours."

The blue eyes widened further. "W-What?"

"That's right. He's yours. But, I gotta be able to count on you. All right?"

"You got it." James' face beamed with excitement.

Jason released his hold and then pointed toward the door. "Run along now and get Infinity ready for his workout. I'll be out shortly."

The lad tugged his hat into place atop his tousled hair, then skipped from the office.

Jason stared at the door. He could not stop the changes in his own life, but he could damn well brighten James'. The lessons he'd learned from Taylor Jackson over the years had taught him how to move forward. He would draw on that courage and responsibility to face the final chapter of his transition. "I can do this," he whispered. "But only if Debbie's by my side."

* * *

Early afternoon, Jason headed to the house, hoping to get an update on his father. He strode into the foyer just as his mother stepped from the staircase.

She led him into the parlor. "Doc gave him laudanum and suggested I put him in the hospital for a few days, until we decide on a more permanent location. The sores on his back are quite large and putrefied."

Three strides took Jason to the sidebar. He poured a generous shot of bourbon into a tumbler and then tossed back the fiery liquid. A hiss ripped from him as the fire blistered down his throat. "That sounds like a good idea."

She stepped closer and took the empty glass from his hand. "Don't you think it's a bit early to start drinking?" He chuckled. *It's never too early.* She placed the glass on the sideboard and then turned to face him. Her features grew somber. "He's so frail, but the doctor believes this is the best treatment for him."

"Well, he'll just keep getting worse if he stays here, right?" His hand slid across her shoulders.

She nodded, and pressed her lips together into a seamless line.

"Let him go, Mother. He'll get the care he needs at St. John's."

He peered deep into her eyes. Grief stared back. He had never seen her spirit broken, and his heart ached as he shared in her anguish.

She inhaled, straightened, then lifted her chin. "Fine, he can go."

"Did the doctor say when we should take him?"

"He said right away," she muttered.

"Good. I'll get the carriage ready and we'll take him now."

An hour later, they carried Taylor into the Lexington hospital on 5th Street. Jason paced the corridor. "Damnit, when are they comin' out?" he mumbled. His mind whirled as thoughts of Debbie entwined with concerns for his parents.

The sound of footsteps brought his gaze around to his mother.

"He's finally resting," she whispered. She gestured toward a bench. "Let's sit here."

He lowered onto the pine bench, a frown tugging at his brow. "What if something happens while I'm away?"

"Jeremiah and I will be here with him. And you've got James watching the stable. Nothing will happen. And besides, these doctor's are skilled in knowing what to do in regards to Taylor." Love bloomed in her eyes as she squeezed his wrist. "Bring Debbie home. You two have your whole lives left to live. Every day without her is time you can never replace." She touched his cheek. "Go find her, darling."

"But I…"

She placed her fingertips across his lips. "Shh… Go. We'll be fine."

He hugged her, then grasped her shoulders. "I'll bring her home for all of us."

Chapter Thirty-One

Hazy afternoon sunlight filtered across New Orleans. The Gulf Stream breeze carried a tangy, salt smell off the ocean to settle onto nearby ports. Debbie pulled open the hospital door, eager to return to work after her three-day rest. A slender, silver-haired man brushed past her as she pushed through the entrance. Her gaze narrowed on the visitor leaving the hospital.

She stifled a gasp.

Yet another scalding reminder of the Adams House.

With a jerk, she turned her head, hoping he'd not recognized her. A lump gathered in her throat as she weaved down the crowded hallway. Several heartbeats later, she glanced back.

He left the building, proving that horrific part of her life had closed. Debby exhaled a relieved sigh. *I must concentrate on my future now..not the past.* A voice bellowed out her name and she stopped, glancing sideways.

Seth dashed toward her.

"Glad I found you," he puffed. He shoved his hand into his pocket and drew out a voucher. "Here, Will ask me to give you this. There's a dinner at the Plaza tonight. I can't go, so he wants you to accompany him. He'll meet you in the lobby at seven o'clock."

"But, I…I can't," she stammered.

"Sure you can. It's a wonderful event and the food is good, too."

"No…I-I'm exhausted. Besides, I've nothing to wear. I mean, look at me, Seth." She laid her palm across her swollen stomach. "I could have my baby at any moment."

"Don't worry. I'm here to escort you to the fancy dressmaker on Canal St. for a new dress. Will's gift. What time does your shift end?"

Shock thinned her voice. "At five. But, no. I can't possibly go."

He laughed. "Will told me you'd say that, too, but I'm not to listen." Seth grasped her wrist. "You'll have a good time. I promise."

She drew in a steadying breath. "I-I look a mess."

"You look fine. Besides, you need to get away from this miserable place for awhile. Have a glass of wine and relax."

She glanced over his shoulder. The head doctor trekked toward them. "I must go now," she whispered.

"I'll be waiting out front for you at 5:00 o'clock sharp," he said, smiling.

She lowered her head, swung around and ducked into the nearest room. A shallow breath later, the doctor poked his head in the doorway behind her. "You're needed in surgery," he snapped. "Not sure how long the procedure will take, but you need to go right away."

She lowered her chin. *Why is there always a road-block to my happiness?* Her shoulders drooped as she pivoted and headed to the open ward.

At five-thirty that evening, she signed out and hurried to the front entrance. Would Seth still be there? Her brows lifted at the sight of her newfound friend resting against a brick column.

He stood and smiled. "I just about gave up on you." He guided her down the stone steps. "Let's go."

Four blocks later, Seth escorted her into a charming boutique. He explained to the clerk what they wanted and assured the woman Will would cover the expenses.

Seth turned to Debbie. "I'll leave you with my cousin, here. Jenny will help you pick out something beautiful. Have a wonderful time tonight." He kissed her cheek and left through the side entrance.

Debbie wandered about the shop. She scanned the room and slid her fingers across the expensive fabrics. Her gaze settled on a collection of accessories sparkling in a glass case. An ivory cameo captured her attention. She remembered Kathryn wearing a similar piece to a friend's wedding.

Debbie pivoted and approached a selection of dresses made of figured Manchester cloth and an all-wool cheviot neatly trimmed with satin. Her heart fluttered with admiration. She ached to be presentable once more and envelope herself inside luxury. A sigh escaped her lips as she fingered the folds of Colton's serviceable garment that swathed her swollen body.

"Here's a lovely green suit that just matches the hazel color of your eyes," Jenny said. "We made one similar to this for the mayor's wife just before she had her second child." The clerk held up the two-piece item for her perusal. "Notice how the flowing style of the jacket conceals the expanded portion here? It's very elegant."

"I'm really not in condition to try anything on ," Debbie said, gesturing toward her soiled attire. "I just left work at the hospital."

"Do you want to take the suit with you?" A crease of concern crossed the dark- haired lady's' brow.

A prickling sensation rippled up Debbie's arms and she turned away. "Heavens no, what if something happened to the garment?"

"Ma'am," The clerk touched Debbie's shoulder. "I know Seth, and he wouldn't have asked me to help you if this wasn't important."

"But…I have only an hour before I'm to meet William. I can't go home, bathe and get to the hotel by seven o'clock."

The woman paused, and then turned Debbie to face her. "I have an idea. Come with me."

Chapter Thirty-Two

The store clerk clomped up the rickety stairs with Debbie in tow. Cobwebs draped the exposed beams in the small attic. Debbie stifled a cough from the dust that draped the unopened crates. A stack of boxes dangerously teetered near the railing as the musty overwhelming stench of age rasped her throat.

She settled her gaze on a rack of evening gowns peeping from beneath a sheet. Her thoughts recalled a past Easter…singing in concert for Mayor Brown. Her crimson and gold dress, *Jason's favorite*, caught the candlelight and shimmered as if aflame. Before her performance, Jason had latched the hooks of her gown all the way up, his breath pausing to rasp warm against her neck. The tingle raced down her spine. He brushed his lips beneath her ear and whispered, "Good luck, my darling."

If only I could return to that moment.

Jenny traversed the storage area, stepped past a crate of broken bottles and pushed open the window. A breeze rushed in wafting a strong aroma of perfume around her. The scent was the choice of the queen of England. *My favorite is Eau de Cologne.*

She tunneled through the maze of dresses suspended from a rope line and closer to the clerk.

"There's a place to wash up over there," Jenny said, waggling a finger toward the back wall. She plucked a garment free and dangled the pale pink evening gown before Debbie. "Clean up and come out. We'll try this on first."

"Thank you," Debbie said as she slipped into the curtained dressing alcove. A circle of glass, much like the porthole on the *Sally Mae* provided adequate light to the cramped area. She lifted a chipped pitcher and poured the water into the matching ceramic washbowl.

Leaning closer, she stared at her reflection in the mirror, her eyes glistening with unshed tears.

What are you doing? Jason would have a fit, knowing you're meeting another man. On a disheartened sigh, Debbie refocused her thoughts and with trembling fingers, slipped the first button free.

Ten minutes later, well scrubbed and decked out in appropriate maternity corset and pantaloons, she stepped from the alcove.

"Could you help me lace this corset?" She muttered fumbling with the strings. "I can't seem to make it lay properly."

"Of course," Jenny quipped with a giggle, she finished the job ending with a gentle tug. She turned and gathered a collapsed bustle in the crook of her arm, then pivoting scooped up the brocade outfit from a hook.

Debbie brushed the garment's sleeve. "This is so luxurious," she whispered.

"Try it on," Jenny urged.

Oh, to look like a lady again.

Bubbling warmth rushed over her skin. Surely she deserved one night of happiness. Jason would understand. Before she could change her mind, "All right, I will." She grasped the frock and slipped behind the row of dresses. Like a soft wind, she eased on the gown, then stepped from the alcove.

Jenny gasped as obvious pleasure etched her face. With a groan, she pulled a full length mirror into the center of the small room.

Debbie peered into the looking glass, her shoulders drooping. *Where is the lady I remember?* As disappointment tugged at her heart strings, she scanned her image. "I look terrible," she whispered, her words trailing off into a sigh.

"Now, don't get discouraged," Jenny said, patting her on the upper arm.

"I have another outfit that'll be just right for you" She scurried over to the rack and in a flash returned with a different dress in hand. "Burgundy's all the rage this year." She lifted the velvet overskirt and the material swirled into a swath of wine-colored brocade. "And just look at this matching train."

Debbie widened her eyes. The prickling sensation returned as hope bubbled through her veins. "Fabulous," she whispered.

"And have you ever seen such intricate passementerie around a bodice?" Jenny added. "Such delicate workmanship… with hand-sewed beading on the white lace."

Debbie nodded and touched the design. A glimpse of her past, of hours spent toiling over such handwork, returned. Wonderment underscored her excitement. "This one is so beautiful…the time invested…yes."

Jenny's voice softened as she flipped over the garment. "Also, see the lavender taffeta bustle sash?"

Again, Debbie caressed the material.

"Go on," the clerk insisted. "Put it on."

Scooping the dress from the woman's arm, Debbie draped the burgundy brocade across a group of hat boxes. She removed the pink outfit and wiggled into the second gown. With a smile she returned to Jenny. "Could you help me?" she asked fumbling with the buttons up the front. "Also, would you please tie the bow?"

Jenny nodded.

Moments later, standing before the mirror, she smiled. "Yes…this one…I love this one."

"Magnificent," Jenny chirped, clapping her hands. She helped Debbie secure the skirt; a fluffing here and there, then stepped back. "I think that'll do fine. The pleats will allow you room and the jacket will help conceal your… blessing."

My blessing? Debbie nearly sobbed beneath the rush of emotions.

The clerk draped the overskirt atop the bustle and helped her into the jacket, then Jenny slowly turned Debbie around. "You look stunning."

A sideways glance in the dusty mirror and Debbie's breath caught. "I do love it." The giddiness blossomed. She traced the velvet trim. "It's so elegant." *Yes, I feel like a lady, again.*

"Now…for a pair of my best soft-soled slippers, then we'll fix your hair. And let's add a lovely lace cap with matching ribbons that will accent your beautiful face."

"Oh, yes," Debbie said on a giggle. She stopped just short of a gleeful hoot.

"I've a pearl-embellished comb with an attached hair piece to give you more volume. 'Twill be a perfect match for your tresses, too. Why, you'll look gorgeous. Well, more gorgeous than you already are," she snickered.

"Wonderful," Debbie said. Warmth spread across her cheeks. *Tonight I'm going to forget the past and enjoy myself. I deserve at least one evening of happiness.*

* * *

Jason stifled a cough as the coal-burning locomotive belched smoke from the engine. Side-stepping the crush of new arrivals, he darted to the opposite side of the platform. With a frown, he glanced down the tracks toward the boxcar where he'd stored Infinity. A scan further and still no sign of Butterfield.

Where the hell is he?

A hard tug and he pulled his watch from his pocket. "Damnit, John, come on," he grumbled.

The conductor stepped into view and announced the final boarding.

Jason skimmed the crowd a final time, then huffed. On a hard pivot, he climbed aboard the train and made his way down the aisle. With a sigh, he dropped onto the first empty bench.

A stream of passengers boarded and Jason scraped his gaze across each traveler. *Wasted time. Wasted energy.*

He tapped his boot heel against the metal floor board, peering outside. The seconds crept past like hours.

A rustling brought his attention to Liz as she lowered onto the bench beside him.

He tightened his shoulders and scooted across the seat to give her more room. *What in the hell is John thinking? Bringing his granddaughter along only slows us down?*

"Could you raise the window," she asked, fluttering her hand before her cheeks.

Her squeaky voice rippled along raw nerves.

"The air in here is stifling," she added. "I cannot imagine anyone wanting to inhale that nasty cigar smoke."

Jason pushed up the window pane. Anything to keep her quiet. Bracing his shoulder against the wall, he turned toward her and chinked out a half-smile. Short, snappish huffs answered as she fidgeted in the seat. Her lace-gloved hands struggled to press down the puffiness of her bustled dress. He suppressed a snicker and narrowed his gaze. Curls dangled from the inside of an aqua blue bonnet and her coiled, copper tresses bobbed with her every twist.

She glanced up and smiled. "Sorry, I don't mean to take up all the room."

"You're fine," he said, shifting his gaze back out to the platform. "Where's your grandfather?"

"Oh, he's tending to our trunks." She placed her hand atop his forearm to recapture his attention. "You men are so lucky. You can travel for two weeks with one case, while I need at least three or four. I'd take five, if I could. A lady needs her personal items, you know."

Jason snorted. "I'm sure you do."

Butterfield loomed into view at the end of the aisle. "Over here," Jason yelped, waving a hand.

John nodded, shuffled to his seat and tossed his expensive derby onto the worn leather.

"Damned porters," he grumbled, flopping onto the bench across from Jason. "They don't know their asses from a wishing well."

"Now, Grandfather," Liz quipped, "don't get all riled up. You know those boys work for mere pennies."

His face flushed. "I don't give a damn if they work for chicken scratch, they should do their jobs."

Jason chuckled. "He just misses growling at my father."

"How's that old bastard, anyway?" Butterfield lit a fresh cigar and Liz swept her hand past her nostrils to ward off the smoke.

A frown tugged at Jason's brow. "Mother admitted him into St. John's. Some days are fair, others we think we'll lose him. She hardly leaves his side."

"She loves the man," Butterfield mumbled.

Jason nodded. "Yes, she does." The train jerked forward, iron wheels squealing. He grabbed the armrest to steady himself from the jostling. *That was damn near as shrill as Liz's voice.* He grimaced as his gaze shifted back out the window. A quick skim over the countryside brought him a momentary escape from his sadness.

The landscape changed from pastureland to rolling hills. Lulled by the rhythmic clack of metal against metal he closed his eyes and he conjured up the image of his lover. Wisps of lavender wafted from Debbie's long flowing hair to heighten his recall. The possibility of seeing her again thundered through his veins with as much velocity as the train wheels gripping the steel. The warmth of her body, the anticipation of tasting her again, of drawing her into his embrace. The hours that still separated them tore a hole in his heart.

Punkin', every mile of this track brings me closer to you.

* * *

A day later and New Orleans rolled into view. The train came to a hissing stop. Passengers clambered about the railcar gathering their belongings. Jason stretched and peered at the hustle and bustle that surged past the window. Sunlight glistened off the metal rooftop of a nearby building. His gaze shot sideways. Trees draped with Spanish moss swayed above the congested city. The chatter of departing passengers brought his attention back inside.

Butterfield grabbed his derby, then pushed his way into the crowd and disappeared from view.

Once the aisle had cleared Jason stood. His muscles tightened and a tingle swept through his legs. Grimacing, he rubbed each calf to ease the stiffness. The five scheduled stops on this journey south had given him little time to stretch, but allowed ungodly hours of thinking… about Debbie, about hope of a reunion, and about their happy-ever-after consumed his time.

Straightening, he stepped aside to permit Liz to exit.

Jason glared at the back of her bonnet as he followed her onto the platform. Annoyance nipped at him, blamed fully upon his lack of sleep. He wasn't her guardian, nor would he ever be. A suppressed grumble hovered in the back of his throat.

Turning to face him, she inquired, "Where's Grandfather?"

Her razor-sharp tone dug deep and he scanned the area. Spotting Butterfield, he pointed. "Over there. I assume he's making arrangements for the horses to be delivered to the fairgrounds."

"Oh, yes, I see him." A handful of pamphlets fluttered by on the scent of an incoming rain and she placed her hand atop her bonnet. "My, it's windy."

Perhaps a swift gust would blow her back to Kentucky. Pivoting, he hustled to the baggage car and gathered their belongings, then stacked the trunks on the platform.

Minutes later, John returned with a rented carriage.

"Over here," Jason called.

His friend reined the team of horses to a stop near the platform and then jumped down and helped Liz up into the buggy.

With a grunt, Jason tossed the cases onto the backseat as John came shuffling around.

"I'll take her to the hotel, then meet up with you at the stables." He pulled Jason to the side of the rig. "She takes all day to unpack," he grumbled.

"Women do love their trappings." Jason said with a wink. Turning, he headed for the fairgrounds.

First Debbie's kidnapping, then Infinity's injuries and father's health. God help me handle all this.

Three-quarters-of-an-hour later, he stepped into the stable. Infinity's stall waited at the far end of the building.

"Glad to see you made it here in one piece, big boy," he said as he stroked the animal's slick coat. He raised the troubled hock to check for swelling.

"Looks good," he said, patting Infinity's muscular rump. "Get some rest. You'll need to be in top form come race day."

Jason exited the stall and scanned the stables for an office. No sign of a registration booth. He lowered his brows as he spotted a man wearing a wide-brimmed hat.

"Sir," Jason hollered.

The man pivoted and pointed to himself. "Me?"

"Yes." He scuffed through the sawdust toward the well-dressed stranger. "I need to register an entry. Can you help me? I don't see any signs to direct me."

The newcomer pointed across the track. "Below the grandstand. On the west end."

"Thank you," Jason said, squinting an eye as the sun broke through a passing cloud. "By the way, name's Jason Jackson. My horse is in the third stall from the end."

Infinity poked his head over the gate just as the man glanced backward. "Nice looking animal. Saw them bring him in." He lifted his hat, scratched a balding head, then resettled the wide-brimmed straw into place. "Frank

Grant's the name. I have a couple of horses here myself. My place got burned out a few years back. Been tryin' to rebuild my herd. I'm in need of a young stud for my mares. Wouldn't be interested in selling yours, would ya?"

"No." Jason said. "Plan on studding him out myself next year."

Their gazes locked. "I'll get the name of your stable before the meets over. Maybe I can breed a mare or two with him. But I'll need to check his bloodlines first. "

"No problem. I'm sure you'll be pleased."

Jason stepped aside as a stable-hand rushed past. "How's the hired help around here? I could use someone for a few days to feed my horse and muck the stall."

"Not sure. Brought my own workers. Hard to get good help these days. Why, I had to go back to the bayou just to find a fella that worked for me before the fire. I've known Ed and his wife Cotton for years. Dependable folks." Grant lowered his gaze for a moment, then reconnected with Jason. "Might ask someone in the office when you sign-up."

"Sounds good," Jason said, extending his hand.

The man's palm slid against his, their hands shook. "See you around." He smiled, then meandered away.

* * *

Evening shadows draped across the city as Butterfield's carriage bumped and jerked along New Orleans' narrow streets. Jason skimmed his gaze over the folks on the walkway in hopes of catching a glimpse of Debbie.

"Nice place, New Orleans," John said. "Those red bougainvillea hanging from the balconies sure are purty."

Jason fidgeted in the seat. "The city is different all right," he mumbled, forcing his gaze away from the shoppers. Admiring the place was the last damned thing he wanted to do.

"The Mrs. and I came here several times," John added, rambling on and on…. 'We love the city. And what about that swamp land? Good God, it goes for miles. Just like Crystal Falls."

"Easy, John, you're not talkin' to my father." Jason glared at his friend through squinted eyes, wishing the horse would pick up the pace. "I'd like to get to the hotel before they run out of rooms. 'Sides, I want to start lookin' for Debbie."

"Can't blame you," John chuckled. "If they're outta rooms, you can come bunk with me."

Jason frowned. *I'd rather sleep with the horses.*

The carriage stopped in front of the Plaza Hotel. "Here we are," John announced. "Finally," Jason mumbled/

"Gonna put the carriage up for the night, unless you need it."

"Naw. I'll walk," Jason said, jumping from the rig. After I stow my gear in my room, I'm headin' out." He climbed the front steps and glanced over his shoulder.

"Hope you find Debbie," Butterfield's reply following him in.

A quick wave was his only response.

A doorman wearing a gold and purple uniform greeted him and swung the huge oak panel wide.

Jason headed toward the registration desk. As he stepped closer, his attention was drawn to a group entering the ballroom. Curiosity beckoned and he weaved past the crowd and peered inside.

Gasoliers lit the room and sparkled against the silverware. An overpowering aroma of flowers filled his nostrils and he forced back a cough. A wave of music entwined with chattering voices and echoed about the room.

His gaze shot sideways to locate the band tuning their instruments. Memories of Debbie's rehearsals flooded into recall. He smiled, wishing he could hear her beautiful voice in concert once more.

An ear splitting crash severed his thoughts. He rocked back on his heels.

His glare settled on a waiter piling shattered cups onto a tray. *Broken...just like my hopes of finding Debbie among the guests.*

With a heavy sigh, he headed for registration. Nearing the staircase, a white-haired man with a cane nodded. He offered the stranger a cordial smile. Passing, the man teetered and grabbed for the railing. The black lacquer walking stick slammed against the marble floor with a resounding clang. Jason pivoted.

The man fumbled to lift the stick.

Two steps forward and Jason scooped up the silver-knobbed cane and handed the expensive piece back to the gentleman.

Their gaze collided. A wicked chill streaked through Jason when their gaze met.

Slate-blue eyes sent his heart slamming into his throat.

"Thank you," the stranger replied on an icy grin.

Jason forced an answering smile, then pushed past. He signed the registry, then swept up the room key and stuffed the piece into his pocket.

He glanced back, a frown tugging at his brow.

It was as if I looked at Satan himself.

He shoved out the door.

* * *

The court house clock chimed seven as Debbie dashed through the side entrance to the Plaza Hotel.

William smiled as she slipped her hand into his open palm. He leaned forward and brushed his lips against her trembling fingertips.

Debbie glanced to the doorway of the banquet room. A ribbon of awareness wrapped around her with silken threads. The sensation tugging her forward...a chalky dryness clogging her throat.

Her gaze skimmed the area for an answer to her anxious anticipation.

What... Who... Jason?

"You look lovely, my dear," William said, splitting apart the mesmeric hold that had seized her heart. He settled his hand upon the wooden crutch. "I'm sorry I can't escort you properly to your seat. These are such a nuisance."

She forced a smile and slid a palm across his coat-sleeve. Once more, her gaze swept the area. What ignited the longing that ramped through her?

"Shall we?" he whispered.

She nodded and his strong grip propelled her to the banquet hall.

They traversed the room to their assigned seats.

Large floral arrangements towered above the patrons gathered around linen-covered tables. Debbie's gaze drifted upward to the huge gasoliers overhead. Teardrop prisms dangled from them, sparkling like icicles on a winter's day.

Another rush of awareness washed over her. A gasp lodged in her throat. She shifted on the chair, glancing sideways. The hair on the back of her neck prickled. Who...or what tugged at her soul, demanding her attention? She bit her lip and lowered her chin.

"Is something wrong?" William whispered, leaning closer. "Has someone offended you?"

"N-No... I was just... thinking," she stammered.

His brow arched. "But you're upset."

Avoiding his words, she brushed aside her fan dangling from a ribbon on her wrist, then spread the linen napkin across her lap. *Upset? Yes, I'm upset. I need answers, not more questions.* She squared her shoulders, regaining her composure, then turned to face him. "I was thinking of home."

"And that would be Kentucky?" He leaned closer. "You've mentioned the state once before. Where exactly is home?"

She struggled to breathe through the tightness in her throat. Voices chanted in her ears as a landslide of memories tumbled into her mind. Her words toppled over her lips like water cascading down Crystal Falls. "Jackson

Estates, near Lexington."

He chinked a grin. "Ah-ha, an estate. I knew you came from quality folks."

With a heavy sigh, she said, "I rarely speak of this to anyone...well, except Cotton." Her gaze met his. "There isn't really much to tell." She glanced away. "We raise thoroughbreds and I lived there with my chosen family."

"Chosen?"

"Yes, my birth parents are dead."

He offered a quizzical frown. "I'm sorry. My questions have upset you."

Their gaze reconnected. Her twisted nerves ramped up her emotions and her words spilled out at a wicked pace. "If you must know, I never had a chance to know them. My father died before I was born and I lost mother when I was just a child. I lived with my aunt Mary until I moved to Kentucky."

"If not family, then what brought you here to this fair city?"

She tightened her lips against the horror of the truth. "Not by choice. What I've lived through, no human should ever endure."

His brow arched at the harshness in her voice.

Clapping shattered their conversation. A gentleman stepped to the podium and introduced the guest speaker. Debbie's frayed nerves eased as the conversations around her melted away. She bit back her torment while the man rambled on about the good work done by the local churches, providing for the needy. Ten minutes later and unable to recall any of his words, she joined the other guest in polite applause.

William leaned sideways, his elbow bumping hers and snickered. "I think he gives the same speech every year."

The chairman exited the stage and the waiter slipped a dish of fresh shrimp before her. She seamed shut her lips as the fish odor fused with a scent of the cut flowers that adorned the center of the table. Swallowing down the churn of nausea, she glanced around for the nearest exit. "Please excuse me. I need to step away for a moment."

"Certainly," William said, rising in a gentlemanly fashion.

She brushed past the waiter and weaved between the tables to a glass-paneled door. Entering the courtyard, she slumped against a wrought-iron chair. Gulps of fresh air expanded her lungs and suppressed the queasiness. She lifted her fan and waved the sandalwood before her cheeks. With a jerk, she loosened the bow around her waist. Trembling fingers tugged at the top button of her gown. Straightening, she inhaled a full breath, then slowly released her discomfort on a sigh.

The pace of her breath slowed and she straightened. Just as she finished putting every piece back into place, a rustle from behind captured her attention. She whipped around. A gasp tumbled from her lips as an elderly woman stepped before her.

"Excuse me," the patron said. "I believe we're seated at the same table. Have you known William long?"

"No." Debbie said, brows tightening. "We're just friends." *I have no time for this meddling woman.* "If you'll excuse me, I must return inside." She strode toward the door.

"Are you aware," the stranger chastised. "He prefers the companionship of... men?"

The coarse statement cut Debbie like a saber, freezing her steps. Blood boiled through her veins. How dare she make a mockery of William. *He's good to me and you are nothing but a Laffoone in a corset.*

With lifted chin, she snapped, "His preferences are none of my concern."

Debbie narrowed her eyes and her cheeks exploded with heat. She stepped closer and drove her closed fan into the woman's chest. "And he doesn't need a busybody like you talking behind his back. He's a kind and gentle person. Give him the same respect you would if he were your brother. He has a right to choose his way of life, the same as you."

The woman scrunched her face. "Well!" she scoffed, then pushed past and vanished through the doorway.

Chapter Thirty-Three

Alive with music and entertainment, New Orleans bustled with activity. Indeed, the largest city in the United States never slept. Evening shadows covered rows of brick-and-stone-faced buildings. And the *Vieux Carre*, the inner beat of the city, flourished beneath its night life. Taverns and outdoor cafes overflowed with patrons, all listening to bands parading up and down each narrow street

Stepping out of the hotel, Jason pushed his way past a group of dancing party-goers and stopped at the base of the steps.

His nerves sizzled in anticipation of finding Debbie. *Which way should I go first?* A mellow glow from the street lanterns drew his attention and his gaze centered on a lamplighter.

The man steadied a long black rod on his shoulder as lady revelers zipped past. His withered features brightened beneath a half-grin as he tipped his hat to the folks that colored the streets of New Orleans.

Jason bit back a snort. *Just like Tom.* All that was missing was a stern reminder of not rushing through life. He'd say slow down and right your ship, boy. Rocking the boat won't get ya there any sooner

The lamplighter glanced up and winked at Jason as he settled his hat back on his head.

Jason eased aside his nerves and focused on the direction of the hospital. He pulled the investigator's card from his pocket and turned to the doorman. Flickering light glistened against the gold buttons on the man's uniform.

Their gazes met. "Could you give me directions to the Royal Hospital run by the Ursulines?"

"Of course." The man pointed eastward. "Take Chartres Street south and you'll run into the convent. Their hospital lies just across the street."

Jason nodded, dropped a coin into the man's outstretched palm and then hustled down Canal St.

Quarter-of-an-hour later, he arrived at the hospital.

His heart beat so hard his ribs ached. Excitement tightened in his throat as an arousal set his groin ablaze.

The taste of Debbie's lips beckoned him.

Soft…Moist. ..Desirable.

Visitors pushed past him as he thumped through the crowd. Perspiration dampening his palms, he prayed she'd materialize before his very eyes.

He scanned the corridor.

Grey walls and high ceilings reminded him of the covered bridges up north that his beloved appreciated so well. He settled his gaze on a middle-aged nun seated behind a desk. Three footfalls took him to the woman and he leaned forward, flattening his palms against the cool wood.

Her head rose and her sharp glare met his. "Can I help you, sir?" She stuffed her pen into the ink well near her elbow.

The lump in his throat expanded. "I-I'm looking for a woman named Debra Jackson. I was told she works here."

The woman removed her glasses, her glare deepening. Jason straightened, then leveled his hand to just below his shoulder. "She stands about this tall; has greenish-brown eyes and long brown hair."

"Yes…Mrs. Jackson left an hour ago"

Mrs. Jackson? He tightened his jaw as a nagging disappointment thickened his voice. "She's my step-sister. I'm here to take her home."

The woman paused. "If she hasn't already had her baby she should be here tomorrow afternoon."

Jason rocked on his heels. *Baby?* Surely they were speaking of two different women. He fumbled in his pocket and retrieved a tin-type, then thrust the likeness of Debbie before the stern-faced sister. "Is this her?"

The nun peered at the image and nodded. "Yes."

He struggled to cage his escaping hope. "I-I can't wait until tomorrow," he said, calming his voice. "I must see her now." He leaned closer. "Where does she live?"

The woman narrowed her eyes. "I'm not allowed to give out personal information. Come back tomorrow, instead. Mrs. Jackson reports in at 1:00." The black hood of her habit pulled taunt as she lifted her shoulder. "Now get out of here before I have you thrown out."

On an audible gulp, he stepped back. Disbelief melded with confusion to tug at his impatience.

With a razor sharp glare the woman snapped, "Move."

Jason clinched his teeth and turned around, heading for the entrance.

* * *

Debbie returned to the banquet room, sidestepping the wooden crutches that stretched across the chair. Lowering onto her seat, she scanned the room and spotted William in the entryway speaking with a white-haired man.

Her heart lurched against her chest.

She narrowed her eyes, hoping to pierce the heavy shadows that concealed the features of the other man.

A spurt of fear bubbled through her veins and her stomach churned.

Surely this isn't...Laffoone. He's out of the country.

The lump in her throat expanded.

The stranger patted her friend's shoulder and then disappeared into the darkness.

William hobbled back into the room and limped toward her. With a wave of his hand, he motioned for her to join him. "Bring my crutches?" he called out.

Her frown deepened, but she obeyed. "How'd you get over here?" she asked, handing him the wooden supports.

"I hopped. Thought I could put my weight on that foot, but I can't stand the pain." Clearing a path for William, they made their way back to the table. He dropped into his chair and sighed. "I'm not use to being confined."

She brushed her skirt under her and slipped onto the satin-covered seat. On a sigh, she snaked her arm beneath William's elbow and inquired, "Who were you talking to just now?"

"An acquaintance. Laffoone's been in England. He stopped by to ask if I'd seen Seth and to say that he sets sail for France in the morning."

Debbie choked back a gasp as she squeezed her eyes shut, holding away the image of the bastard on the boat. She swore never to allow the monster in her life again, yet he was a mere stone's throw away. *What possible connection could Laffoone have with William and Seth?*

The waiter brushed against her arm, eager to refill her wine glass.

"No...no thank you," she stammered, placing her gloved hand across the rim of the crystal. "I've had enough."

The servant bowed and backed away.

She glanced at William. "I'm not feeling well." On a whimper she clutched his wrist. "I-I must leave, now."

"I'll see you home," William said, rising beside her.

She opened her eyes, her heart pounding. "I-I think it would be best if I walked the few blocks. The fresh air will do me good."

"Debra, you must allow me to escort you. The streets are far too dangerous for a lady such as you to walk alone." He turned to the servant and snapped his fingers.

"Yes, suh?" The waiter inquired.

"Have my carriage brought to the front door. The lady isn't feeling well."

"Yes, suh," he said. "Right away, suh."

William stood, extending his hand. "Shall we? I don't move very fast, you know."

Debbie balanced her shoulder against his. Her gut wrenched as she glanced back at the archway where Laffoone had stood. A chill crept beneath her skin. Could the devil be lurking nearby? As they passed through the lobby and out to the street her nerves grew tight.

Entering the carriage, the scent of bougainvilleas filled the night. The sickening sweet smell only added to her nausea. She slid onto the plush seat and tucked in the fullness of her evening gown.

With a grunt, William lifted the crutches and settled onto the bench across from her. Royal blue tapestry surrounded them, reminding her of the luxury that once embraced her back home.

She pushed aside the oppressive velvet curtains to allow the evening breeze to cool her burning cheeks. If only she could stop the torment, the biting emotions that swirled through her mind.

The clattering of horse's hooves intensified the hammering of her heart as the carriage turned onto Canal St. Her gaze swept across the crowd as they traveled along the boulevard. Her nerves coiled. What was she searching for? Laffoone? Or was it an answer to the strange presence in the banquet room?

Shimmering light from the streetlamps danced across the crowded strollers. And then, she spotted a tall man wearing a western hat.

Her breath caught.

Jason?

Frantic, she pushed closer

"Jason," she shouted, grabbing for the door handle.

"Debra." William clutched her arm. "Debra," he hollered, hauling her back inside. "You can't jump out."

Frantically she fought against him. "But… that's Jason. Let me go. Don't you see? He's come for me." Her stare burned into his widened eyes. "Stop this carriage," she snapped. "I must get out before I lose him."

She swirled back and a frown pinched her brow. The man…her Jason… had disappeared into the twilight. Tears streaming down her cheeks as she swept her gaze across the crowd. "I-I need to go back. He's looking for me."

William ordered the driver to turn around and for the next half-hour the horses plodded along Canal Street with Debbie raking her gaze over every man that came into her view.

Finally, on a frantic sob, she slumped backward in the carriage. How foolish could she be?

No Jason. No hope. No nothing.

William touched her hand. "I've asked too much of you tonight. If that was your true love… he will find you," he whispered. "Right now, you need to think of yourself and the baby. Let's get you home."

* * *

The following morning, several trainers gathered at the fairground to watch the morning workouts. A brisk wind scattered dust and sand across the turf as the horses thundered past. A bank of dark clouds loomed on the horizon threatening a barrage of local showers.

Jason lowered his field glasses as Infinity galloped past. The animal showed no signs of fatigue from the long journey and appeared ready to race.

Impatience tugged at him as he pulled out his watch. *Damnit, I need to get to the hospital.*

His rider reined the horse to a halt before him. "Good job," Jason said. "Cool him down and return him to his stall."

Nodding, Billy led Infinity toward the stable and Jason fell in beside him, matching the rider stride-for-stride. "You're doing a nice job of holding him tight on the curves," Jason said, setting a fast pace toward the stable. "Just don't get boxed in. No bumping. Sure as hell don't need to be disqualified."

Billy nodded, then led the horse to the cooling area, where Jason heard Butterfield barking out instructions to his rider.

"What the hell's wrong with you," Jason broke in, directing his words to the young man. "Listen to John. He was training horses before you knew how to walk."

Butterfield's brows lifted. "Go do as I say, Johnson, or you'll be working as a stable hand."

On a huff, the rider swung around, swearing beneath his breath as he stomped off.

"Damn help," John grumbled, turning toward him. "And what the hell's wrong with you this morning? Never seen you so riled. Yellin' at the help is my job."

"Went to the hospital yesterday. Debbie does work there, but they won't tell me where she lives, so I gotta get back there."

"Then what ya doin' standing here, boy. Go find her."

"She won't be in 'til this afternoon."

"Well, glad you came to the track, 'cause I was about to come looking for you." He leaned back and pulled the unlit cigar from his lips. "Have you heard about the storm?"

Jason stepped aside to allow a horse and rider pass. "No, I've been right here." He arched his brow. "Storm? What storm?"

"Even heard they're gonna cancel the races."

"Cancel...what the hell are you talking about?"

John dug his fingers into Jason's upper arm and led him away from the bridle path. "I was having breakfast at the hotel this morning and overheard two ship captains talking. They said they came through a terrible storm just south of here. Horrible winds and a lot of rain."

"Sonofabitch," Jason sneered, glancing around the stable area. "This land is much too low. That much rain will flood the entire fairground."

Butterfield wiped his forehead on his shirt sleeve. "What should we do?"

"Do? Jeezus, John…I've got enough problems right now. Can't waste time worrying about a storm."

Just then, Liz strolled up. "Why the grim faces?" she asked, smiling.

Their gaze's met hers. "There's a storm on the way."

Her features washed pale.

"This city is surrounded by water," Jason snapped. "For the safety of our horses, as well as ourselves, we need to get out of here before this thing hits."

"I agree," John said, slipping the cigar butt back between his teeth. "But it's too late to catch a train home."

He thumped his friend on the chest. "I'm not going anywhere without Debbie. After that, we'll go to higher ground. You see about getting the horses loaded and ready to go." He turned to Liz. "And you stay at the hotel. No shopping. You got that?"

Wide-eyed, Liz nodded.

"Mr. Jackson," a voice rang out. "Jason Jackson!"

A lad raced toward them from the bridle path.

"Here," Jason called, raising his hand.

You Jason Jackson?"

"Yes."

"I have a telegram for you." The boy stuffed his hand into his jacket, pulled out a yellow paper and slapped the folded message into Jason's hand.

"Here, kid," Butterfield said, flipping the boy a silver coin.

Jason tightened his jaw as he ripped open the telegram. A heartbeat later, he closed the note and his gaze met John's. "It's from Mother. Father has died in his sleep."

"Aw…hell," John muttered. "He can't do that."

Liz hugged her grandfather and Jason turned away, his eyes sliding shut. He could hear Butterfield snuffling behind him. *I knew this would happen.* He sucked in a ragged breath.

Looking back through a blur of tears, he spotted Liz helping her grandfather to a nearby bench.

Jason tossed away the crumpled paper just as Liz turned back, facing him. He set out across the lawn toward the stable. The crunching footfalls of Liz followed after him and he picked up his pace.

Infinity greeted him at the stall door. Jason wrapped his arms about the stallion's neck.

"Well, big boy, father's gone." He ran his fingers through Infinity's silky mane. "I need Debbie and you've gotta win tomorrow. He's countin' on both of us, but his final wishes ride with you."

Chapter Thirty-Four

An earth-shaking clap of thunder cleared the streets of downtown New Orleans. Ragged black clouds raced across the heavens and strong gusts of wind stripped baskets of bougainvillea from the balconies and sent them swirling down the streets. Shoppers ducked into local cafes, while others scurried back to their hotel to wait out the storm. Trash from last night's party-goers whipped along the walkways.

Debbie weaved past merchants boarding up their shops and covering their glass windows.

Her wet shoes squeaked with each step as she shoved through the hospital entrance. An image of the tall cowboy weighed heavy on her mind as she scurried down the corridor to her assigned station.

Had she dreamed up Jason? *Probably.*

The head nurse looked up and smiled. "So glad you could come in early."

Debbie nodded. "The doctor asked me to come help prepare for injuries from the possible tropical storm."

With a snap of her wrist, the nun peeled a paper from her clipboard. "Here's your assignment for today."

"Thank you," Debbie said, accepting the paper. Just then a breathtaking pain lanced her stomach. Her hand splayed wide and the paper fluttered onto the floor. A deep groan rolled from her throat. Dizziness swept in. She gasped, then leaned forward and grabbed her side.

"Are you all right?" the nurse asked swirling upward.

On a deep breath, the pain faded. Debbie straightened and then forced a smile. "Yes, I believe so."

The woman's voice softened and the worry in her eyes dissipated. "Should you be working so near your birth time?"

`"I'll be fine." Debbie drew in another deep breath. "What better place could I be than in a hospital?"

The woman settled back into her chair.

Just as Debbie bent to retrieve the fallen paper a commotion from behind grabbed her attention. She pivoted.

Her eyes widened as two men trudged up the hallway, puffing as they transported a blood-soaked patient.

Audible groans escaped their lips as the weight of the person shifted on the stretcher.

Debbie glanced sideways as the head nurse rose and ordered them into a nearby room. They hoisted the woman onto the bed. With a frown, the nurse motioned for Debbie to join them.

Quick steps brought her to the patient's bedside and she peered into the woman's face. "Cotton," she shrieked. "What happened?"

Her friend stared at her from beneath swollen eyelids.

"A m-man shoved me down," Cotton whispered, tears rolled down her temples and soaked hair. "I-I didn't do nothin'. He yelled awful things, den run a knife in ta my belly."

With trembling hands, Debbie cut away the crimson material, revealing a profuse gash. Her thoughts immediately flashed back to Pearl and the horror of that hellish day. On a hard swallow, she stifled her tears. Cotton needed her now and she'd do everything she could to save her friend.

The nurse spread a clean cloth over the wound, then covered Cotton's stomach with a sheet. "I need to get Dr. Kingston. He's just down the hall."

Debbie nodded. Once the nurse left the room she clasped Cotton's hand. "I know you're in pain. I'm so sorry this happened to you."

The woman closed her eyes and agony creased her features.

"I'll have them give you something."

"Please get Pappy. I-I needs him," Cotton mumbled.

"Yes, yes. Right away." Debbie squeezed her friend's hand. "Is he at home?"

"No, he's at da fairgrounds workin' fer Mr. Grant. Dey's 'spose to have some kind o' big race tomorrow."

Debbie dabbed at the tears that slipped down Cotton's cheeks. Fresh blood darkened the sheet. "You lay still. The doctor will be here in a minute and we'll get you all fixed up." Debbie struggled to keep her voice calm even though panic surge through her. Time was of the essence and she must find Ed. A shudder vibrated across her skin. *Cotton may be dead before I can get him here.*

A heartbeat later, the doctor and nurse rushed through the doorway.

Debbie stepped aside.

After a quick examination, he looked up, a scowl creasing his face. "This wound is mortal," the man said.

"Surely there's something you can do," Debbie pleaded.

He shook his head.

"I'm going to find her husband. I know where he is."

The nurse turned and dug her fingers into Debbie's arm. "You can't leave work. The storm's building in intensity."

"If anyone asks, tell them I'm having pains and needed to go home. I'll be back as quick as I can."

The nurse narrowed her eyes. "You'll be dismissed if you go."

Debbie jerked her arm free. "Then, so be it," she hissed. "I won't let her die without Ed." She swung around and dashed from the room. With heart pounding, she scuffed down the hallway and shoved through the front door.

Strong arms gripped her and pulled her to a stop. She glanced up. "William," she shrieked, struggling to break free.

"Oh William. I-I'm so glad you're here." Her words spilled through quivering lips. "I-I need your help." Short gasps captured snippets of air. "You must help me. I need to go to the fairgrounds. Cotton's been stabbed. I need to find Ed." She grasped his arm. "Please, I beg you."

"My carriage is parked near the corner." He pointed the tip of his crutch toward the rig. "I'm on my way to the doctor, but my driver will take you."

"Perfect," she said. "I won't be long." She patted his hand and scurried off.

Arriving at the fairgrounds, Debbie asked for directions then hurried toward the stables. A brisk wind tugged at her dress. She lowered her hand to suppress the uplifting draft.

In the distance, she spotted the stables.

With skirt-tail fluttering in the wind, she scurried down the bridle path. Her work shoes scuffed along the hoof-beaten trail. Gasping in stamina, her lungs burned while she fought for each breath.

Several strides later, her legs cramped. She struggled to maintain the rigorous pace, but the pain forced her to stop. She grasped her knees, then inhaled and straightened once more. *Cotton needs me to find Ed.* Determination lifted her shoulders and she forged on.

Arriving at the stable, she bumped into a lad carrying a bucket of grain.

Stepping sideways, she hollered above the wind. "Where can I find Mr. Grant?"

"He's gone in to town," the slender urchin replied, tugging at his tattered denims."You better get outta this storm, ma'am."

Debbie gripped the lad's shoulder. "Do you know a Negro that works for him named Ed?"

The lad waved his hand behind him as he braced his knee against the swaying bucket. "He's outback coolin' down one of our horses."

"Thank you," she said, releasing her grip.

Cornering the building, she saw the old man near the water trough.

"Ed," she screamed, her hands waving in frantic movements.

Ed looked over the animal's back. "Lord-a-mercy, Debbie. What brings ya out here during dis storm?"

"You must come with me. Now. Cotton's in the hospital. She's hurt. Stabbed. She needs you."

He dropped the sponge, snagged the horse by the collar and ran the mare to her stall. With a jerk, he pulled his hat from a hook, then rejoined Debbie. "Let me tell da boss I's leavin'. I'll be right back."

A commotion at the opposite end of the corridor drew her attention. A well-dressed lady and a tall man wearing a cowboy hat stood in a tight embrace.

Debbie sucked in a deep breath.

She wanted to turn away but something compelled her to keep staring.

The young woman's hands cupped his chin and she tiptoed, kissing his cheek. He shifted and his face came into full view.

Oh, *my God... Jason.*

Her heart skipped a beat. "Jason," his name tumbled from her lips.

She lifted her hand, but her words froze in her throat.

Tears filled her eyes.

She locked her knees to prevent them from buckling.

Her mind whirled.

Darkness beckoned. She wanted to charge into his arms, but restrained her desire. Devastated, she slumped against a nearby post.

"No, no," she whimpered, smothering the words behind clinched lips. *This can't be... he's found someone new.*

Her heart sank. She fought to support her weight and raked the sleeve of her dress across her cheek. A brutal chill raced through her. All her hopes and dreams shattered as the bitter truth stung like a thousand bees. He was no longer hers. She lowered her chin.

He mustn't see me...I won't destroy his life again.

"I's ready, Miss Debbie," Ed said, adjusting his hat as he rushed toward her.

She straightened, then grasped his arm. "Let's go," she said, fighting back her misery. "We must hurry."

She glanced over her shoulder for one last look at her beloved. His eyes were closed as the woman tightened her arms around him.

Rounding the stable, Debbie brushed past an elderly man seated on a wooden bench. He glanced up and their gazes met.

John Butterfield.!

As if in a daze, Debbie followed, struggling to keep pace with Ed's long strides. They moved by the grandstand and soon arrived at the waiting coach.

The horses galloped at a feverish pace toward the hospital. Visions of Jason holding another woman in his arms nearly stole away her breath. Pain crashed over her. Her eyes squeezed shut to block the image, but the ache in her heart refused to dissipate.

She inhaled and then slowly exhaled an audible whimper.

So many questions riddled her mind.

Who was this woman?

How long had Jason been seeing her?

And most important, did he love her?

A sob broke free from Debbie's lips. Their embrace told her everything she needed to know. She'd prayed every day he would find her, and now she had nothing to hope for. Her life suddenly crumbled away like the sandy banks below Crystal Falls.

Chapter Thirty-Five

The whistle of a departing train cut through the air. Travelers scurried on board before the darkening sky released the horror within.

Jason flipped open the face cover of his watch. Three hours before Debbie returned to work. He had plenty of time to purchase his tickets. After all, she would be coming home with him.

He snorted.

God, I can't wait.

After a ten-minute wait in line, Jason shoved up to the ticket window.

"Heading to Lexington, Kentucky. I need to book a reservation for two and a space for my horse in the stock car."

"Na…naw. Ain't no ca..car fer the ha…ha… horse."

Jason frowned. The chatter from passing travelers pounded in his ears distracting him from the clerk's stuttering words. He leaned closer to the ticket window. "Is there a later train heading north?"

"Na, na…no sir. The, the…that's the only one 'cause of the storm."

"Then when can I get the animal out of here?"

"Thur…Thursday." The man adjusted his visor, then rested his weight on bent elbows.

Jason lowered his brow. "That's four days from now."

The timid man offered a crooked smile and then nodded.

With a grumbling curse, he ordered, "Book it. I don't want to stand here and argue with you."

Grabbing a pen the clerk filled out the paperwork and shoved the boarding pass across the pitted wood.

Jason stuffed the ticket voucher into his pant pocket. Growling beneath his breath, he stomped along the platform. A dozen steps later, he spotted Butterfield tracking toward him.

"Just heard they cancelled the race," John said, dousing his cigar butt in a rusty pan of rain water. "Did you get a seat?"

"Yes, two of them. Debbie and I will be leaving on the five-fifteen, tomorrow. But I can't get Infinity out 'til Thursday. I'm hoping to get someone to bring him to the station and load him for me."

With a grunt, Butterfield pulled out a fresh cigar. Striking a match to the expensive Cuban tobacco, he inhaled a full drag. As he exhaled, the grey plume of vapor vanished into a strong draft overhead. "I'll ask Grant to bring the horses Thursday. He won't mind." He flipped ashes from the tip of his stogie and then continued. "We need to get home, too. Gotta be there for the funeral. Damn, it's hard to believe the old man's gone."

"Father was a lucky man. You're a good friend, John," Jason stated. "Come on, let's see if we can get you a seat on tomorrow's train."

Taking a few steps, John grabbed Jason by the arm and jerked him to a stop.

Jason's eyes widened. His brow lifted as he stared into Butterfield's somber face.

"Speaking of Grant, I saw his groomsman with a young lady today," John said. "She looked like Debbie."

"What?" Jason yipped, then glanced around. He pressed near the old man face, "Where?"

"At the fairgrounds. Not long after you got that telegram. They crossed right in front of me."

Jason pushed nose-to-nose with Butterfield. "Are you sure it was her?"

"Easy boy," John said, rocking back. "I said it looked like her. I'm not sure of anything. Besides, this woman was expecting. But this gal was wearing a work dress, something like they wear in a hospital."

"Did she say anything?"

"No. She looked right at me and kept on going."

"Where did they go?"

Butterfield's features washed pale. "Hell, I don't know. They were headed toward the front gate, I think."

"I need to go," Jason said, glancing over his friends shoulder. "You get your tickets and I'll meet you back at the stable."

Pivoting, he maneuvered through the crowd, his heart thundering as he leaped from the platform and headed for town.

* * *

Jason smacked his palm against the hospital door and shoved his way through the entrance. Leg muscles burned as he sprinted down the corridor. Fumbling into his shirt pocket, he jerked out the tattered photo. By damned, he wasn't leaving without her this time. His blood pounded his temples as he glanced into each room. *Where the hell is she?* Finally, he bumped into a doctor exiting a ward.

"Sir," Jason said, gulping for air. He grasped the man's upper arm, then jammed the tintype to the light. "Does this woman work here?"

The man took the picture and studied it for a long moment.

"Looks like Mrs. Jackson."

Jason swallowed hard. "Debbie, I mean Debra Jackson?"

"She's up on the second floor today."

Jason turned and dashed down the hallway and took the stairs two steps at a time. He glanced around, then a nurse pushing an invalid chair caught his attention.

"Miss," he called. She turned to face him. "I'm looking for Debra Jackson."

"Oh, she left about a half- hour ago."

His chin lowered. Disappointment smacked him full in the face. "Do you have any idea where she went?"

"Probably home. Never seen her so upset over losing a patient."

He pushed closer. "Where's home?"

The woman's features tightened. "I can't tell you that."

"She's family. We've been trying to find her." His glare burrowed into the woman's eyes. "Don't you understand? I need to find her before the storm hits. It's important."

"How do I know that?"

"Please lady. Her father died yesterday."

The woman drew a shallow breath, her features laced with doubt.

He felt the weight of her evaluation as her eyes narrowed.

"Well, all right then," she finally said, releasing an extended sigh. "She's staying at the Sutton House."

"Where's that?"

She gave him directions and he raced from the building.

Several heart-pounding minutes later, he rounded the corner of the two story brick structure. He glanced up checking the address. Sutton House was etched in stone above a weathered set of double-doors.

He shivered as a rush of excitement prickled his skin. The lump in his throat expanded as he swung open the carved wooden panels. A narrow staircase loomed at the end of the dark hallway.

His knees grew weak as he stepped across the polished floor. The aged wood creaked as his footfalls traversed the landing and up the worn steps. A wall covered with aging paper separated the two apartments. He paused, then selected the one on his left. With a brisk knock, a moment later, an elderly woman eased open the door. A frown deepened her wrinkled brow as she peered at him.

"What do you want?" she asked, her gravelly voice nipping at his nerves.

"I'm looking for Miss Jackson," he said, offering a smile.

The woman drew up a boney finger and pointed across the hall, then slammed the door shut.

Jason turned and raked his fingers through his hair. Perspiration moistened his palms as he curled his fingers and rapped hard on the door.

No answer.

He knocked again.

Then, the latch clicked. The door eased open. Debbie filled his view.

"Oh, my God." The words tumbled from his lips as he pushed open the panel. Wide-eyed, her gaze met his and tears spilled down her cheeks.

He stepped forward and pulled her into his arms.

She whispered his name. Her arms folded about his neck.

He embraced her and nipped kisses across her cheek and down her neck, burying his face against her shoulder.

He pushed aside her chestnut locks and tasted the tender white flesh he had so longed for. "Oh, Debbie, I've missed you so much."

"J-Jason… I thought I'd never see you again," she whispered, her arms tightened, then her lips sought his once more. Each kiss deepened. He lifted her aside and shoved the door shut.

Catching his breath he asked, "Why didn't you come home? I was so afraid they'd killed you."

She pushed back. "There were days I wished I were dead." She pivoted, then lowered her hands onto her stomach. "Jason, I couldn't come back to you like this. I would never do anything to hurt you."

He peered at the swell beneath her wrapper. "Don't you know it hurt me more not knowing what happened to you? It was a living hell."

"But you have a new life now," she said.

"What?" He reached for her once more, placing his hand on hers. "You're my life. There is no one else."

"But I saw you in the stable with that woman."

"What woman?" His mind swirled to make sense of things. "You mean Liz? She's nobody to me. That's John Butterfields granddaughter."

. "What about you? Are you married?"

"No," she whispered, stepping away from his reach. She lowered her gaze. "The men that kidnapped me...they...they raped me...and .."

Those beasts. The morons. The bastards. I should've killed them all. "Oh, Punkin, I'm so sorry." He pulled her to him and wrapped his arms around her trembling body. "It's my fault. I should've protected you."

She began to sob. "Jason, you did everything possible. They just outnumbered us."

"I'd rather they'd killed me than hurt you."

"Don't say that," she muttered as tears cascaded down her cheeks.

`He kissed her forehead, then tightened his muscles, engulfing her with his love. As her belly pressed against his, her stomach moved. His breath caught in his throat, then he released her and stepped back. "Am I hurting you?"

"No," she said, adjusting the belt on her robe. "The baby is moving a lot."

"Are you all right?'

"Yes, I've been having pains for the past two days. I keep thinking it's time, but nothing has happened so far."

"Can you travel? I've got two tickets home on the five-fifteen train, tomorrow."

She shook her head. "I don't think that's a good idea. I could get half way there and have the baby."

"Then we won't go. We'll wait for you." He pulled her back into his arms. "I'm not leaving you...ever again. Wherever you are, that's where I'll be."

"There's something I must tell you." He slipped his hand into hers and led her to the bed. "Please sit down."

Her brows lowered as she brushed her hand beneath her and dropped onto the coverlet.

Kneeling, he tightened his grip on her hand. "I got a telegram from Mother." His gaze locked with hers. "Father passed in his sleep yesterday."

She gasped, pulling from his grip. With trembling shoulders, she slammed her palm across her mouth. Her eyes squeezed tight as tears flowed down her cheeks.

Jason pulled her up into his arms and drew her near him. Her heartbeat thundered against his chest. "He's been very ill. I'm just thankful he went peacefully." He pressed his chin to her shoulder and his lips brushed the delicate fold of her neck. Her body quivered in his embrace. "I'd just received the message about father and Liz was only consoling me. That's what you saw in the stable. I've no interest in her. I love you, Punkin. I'll always love you."

Her arms slipped between his and she pulled him closer, resting her cheek on his chest. His breath rushed across her ear as he nestled into her chestnut locks.

He inhaled. His eyes slid shut as the mellow scent of lavender filled his lungs. How he'd longed for this moment. To touch her. To taste her lips and drink in all that was Debbie.

Their bodies melted together in a lingering embrace.

Moments later, she straightened and her gaze met his. "I'm so sorry I couldn't be with father in his final days. I loved him so much." She hesitated. "Your mother has to be devastated. I can only imagine how alone she must feel without either of us there to comfort her."

He brushed wisps of hair from Debbie's forehead. "Maybe that was God's plan for them to be alone in his last moments."

She reached for her handkerchief and dashed away her tears. "Perhaps," she whispered, slipping her hand onto his. "He was a wonderful father even though his blood doesn't flow through my veins. I couldn't love him more."

"Don't you see? His coming back to my mother brought you to me. That proves our love was meant to be." He drew her in his arms once more. "I'll never let you out of my sight again," he said. "I adore you. I want you with me forever."

"Oh, God, Jason, I've missed you so much," she whimpered.

"Let's get married right now," he said, pushing back. "I can't wait another minute. Please be my wife." He lowered to his knee and grasped her hand in his. "Marry me, Punkin. Now...tonight."

Chapter Thirty-Six

Five hours later

The shutters slammed against the window frame. Debbie flinched as flashes of lightening danced along the walls. Rising, she traversed the room, secured the lock on the wooden panels, then drew closed the curtains.

Turning, she met Jason's gaze.

A mellow glow from the flickering oil lamp prompted the memory of their long-ago *rendezvous* in the kitchen.

He smiled, then opened his arms, beckoning her to return to their bed.

On a satisfied sigh, she slipped into his embrace.

"You haven't really answered my earlier question," he teased. "So, what do you say, Punkin? Shall we get married?"

His heartbeat radiated against her breasts. She inhaled his scent…musky, masculine, *mine*. Warmth rushed through her veins. She wanted to remain locked in his arms for all eternity.

"I want to be your wife more than life itself." Her gaze lowered, then returned to his. "But what about the baby? I can't burden you with this child."

"Burden," he said, stepping back, allowing his hands to grip her upper arms. "What do you mean burden? This is my child. I know it…Yes, you may have been raped, but that child that grows inside you is mine."

"B-But… we can't be sure. Don't you see, that's why I never came home. There will be name calling and mocking behind our backs. I can't do that to you."

"Stop it." His voice shook as the words tumbled from his lips. "I love you. We can deal with whatever life throws our way. Look at mother. I'm her bastard child and she lied to protect me."

Debbie turned to him. "She knew Taylor was your father."

"True, she did. But...I know in my heart that I'm this baby's father. That's all that matters to me."

He stepped behind her and brushed his lips against the crease of her ear. The warmth of his breath flowed around her. "I love you," he whispered sending tingles across her shoulders. "As long as we are together, everything will be all right."

Tolerable...maybe. But...the kidnapping, the rape, the fear I endured will never go away. And Laffoone...that miserable beast scarred my life forever. Perhaps, over time, the misery will ease, but my life will never be the same.

The tingles traced her spine and she pivoted to cup his chin. His lips met hers once more. As a pounding rain dashed against the shutters, their passion deepened. Amidst that magical moment, a muffled pop within her body took her breath.

Fluid swept down her leg.

Flinching she pushed back and peered up at him. Heat filled her cheeks. "T-The baby's coming," she murmured.

Jason's eyes widened. "Right now?"

She nodded as a tentative smile lifted her lips.

"Shouldn't we go to the hospital?"

"N-No." She shook her head, wisps of hair catching his evening beard. "Ida, the lady I work with, said she'd help delivery my ba..." She gasped as her lower stomach pulled tight.

He stepped back and peered down at her. "What can I do?"

"Fetch Ida. She lives downstairs, first room on the right. And hurry, Jason, I don't want to be alone."

Debbie slipped into a clean gown, then stretched across the bed. Thunder cracked outside, vibrating the shutters. She stared at the ceiling, biting back her fear as again her stomach pulled tight.

Heart pounding, she raked in a ragged breath and counted the seconds between each pull across her abdomen.

Several minutes later, she heard heavy footsteps on the stairs. The door opened and Jason stepped inside.

"She wasn't there," he announced, "Her son said she went to visit her sister and wouldn't be back until tomorrow."

Debbie frowned. "Oh, no..." Another pain ricocheted across her belly. "Then we must go to the hospital."

"I'll get a carriage," he snapped, worry darkening his features. He turned and dashed toward the door. As his hand slipped against the knob he glanced back. "And don't move, I'll be right back."

"Please hurry," she pleaded.

Once again, the door clicked shut.

Another tightness and she bit back a scream. Time crawled by at an unbearable pace.

The door swung wide and Jason hurried to her side. "I have a carriage downstairs." He scooped her into his arms, cradling her against his chest. "Hold on, Punkin, I'll get you there as quick as I can."

She locked her arms around his neck and nestled her head on his shoulder.

* * *

The driver steadied the carriage door against the force of the howling wind. Jason slipped Debbie onto the tufted seat and stepped inside. Once settled, the coachman swung the panel closed behind them.

The team of Belgium horses jerked the buggy forward.

Jason cradled Debbie in his arms as they jostled about the seat.

Another contraction rippled through her body as her baby fought hard to be born. Torrents of rain dashed against the coach and the wind whipped at the velvet curtains soaking their clothing.

With a mighty crack, a jagged fireball of lightening divided a nearby tree. Huge branches burst into flames and scattered onto the street beside them.

Debbie burrowed deeper into the comfort of Jason's embrace. The carriage jerked forward and frantic shouts from the driver echoed from beyond. The shrieks of horses and pounding hooves entwined with the whistling wind.

The coach lurched, propelling the carriage sideways.

Jason braced his foot against the opposite seat. A jolting crash exploded beneath them. Cracking wood ripped into the rig, stopping inches from his thigh. He grabbed for leverage as Debbie screamed, tumbling to the floor.

The violent motion of the carriage ceased and Jason leaped sideways out of the window. "Sonofabitch," he hissed. "The axle broke from the coach and the horses are pulling the driver away."

Jason sank back against the seat and took a deep breath. "You all right, Punkin?"

She nodded, forcing her weight forward.

"Just lay still. We gotta get outta here." He sucked another breath. "I'll go first…then I'll help you."

Snuffling, she eased back against the cushioned seat.

Jason shoved to his feet, then thrust the broken door aside. He rose through the opening and the wind tore at his clothing. He balanced against the wrecked carriage.

Moments later, he reached for her. She slid forward and then wiggled through the opening. Whimpering, she hurled into his arms. He drew her close, shielding her shivering body. "Can you walk?" he shouted as the rain pelted his face.

"I-I'll try," she stammered, "but we must hurry." She unlocked her arms from around his neck, then gasped as another pain drove through her. "I c-can't make it. The wind is too strong."

Jason glanced over his shoulder. "I'm taking you back to the apartment. The hospital's too far."

She regained her grip, then twisted as her body tightened once more. "Hurry, Jason. Please hurry." The heat of her breath puffed against his neck. Her fingernails dug deep into his shoulder. With a grimace, he forced his stride longer.

The driving rain blurred her vision as her lover maneuvered down the empty street. Blowing debris whirled around them as she bit back her misery. "I'm afraid," she whimpered, her words stolen by the wind.

Another pain lanced through her, seizing her breath.

The power of the storm tore at their fortitude.

* * *

Jason's heartbeat drummed in his ears as he fought to remain afoot. Several strides later, he stopped to catch his breath and hovered against the brick wall of a building.

The Sutton House waited across the street, yet between them and safety surged a corridor of raging water.

With a sustaining gulp of air, he strengthened his hold on his beloved and forged ahead into the churning current. Unseen debris crashed against his ankles as he forced his steps forward.

An earth-shaking clap of thunder boomed overhead, and two strides later, he climbed the steps to the boarding house.

With a jagged breath, he kicked open the front door and surged up the stair to the flat. Three steps later, he eased her onto the bed.

Jason glanced toward the wardrobe. "Let's get you into something dry."

"There's a clean gown in the top drawer of the dresser." She pointed at a maple chest. With trembling fingers, she unbuttoned the wet garment and tossed the piece to the floor. Modesty forced her beneath the covers.

With a sheepish grin, he handed her a towel.

Moments later, another pain cut through her belly and she drew up into a knot.

"Oh, God," she yelled. "It hurts."

"Sounds like you're getting close," Jason said, stripping off his soaked shirt. "I need to take a look and see."

She lowered her brows. "Y-You haven't delivered a baby before," she panted, biting back another scream.

"I've delivered foals. It's basically the same procedure.

"Jason," she shrieked, pushing higher onto the mattress. "I-I'm afraid."

"Everything will be all right, Punkin," he said, flipping up her gown. "Just do as I say."

She panted, then gritted her teeth. "Ahhh!" she yelled, lurching forward. .

Jason tightened his shoulders and repositioned her on the bed. "Take a deep breath…now push."

She strained forward, bearing down.

"Good," he yelled. "Keep pushing."

As the storm rattled the outside world, Jason at last guided his child into their lives. "It's a girl," he announced, lifting the baby.

Debbie spiked onto her elbows, getting the first glimpse of her daughter. She smiled, then dropped back onto the pillow. "S-She's beautiful," she whispered, tears streaming down her face.

Jason washed the baby and wrapped her in a blanket. His smile widened as he lowered the child into her arms.

She cradled the baby, then kissed her head. With a gentle tug, she pulled aside the coverlet to get a closer look. Little pink cheeks and a head full of sable hair filled her gaze.

The infant wiggled, her face flushed red and she began to cry.

Debbie rocked the little one in her arms until she settled. "Look, darling," Debbie whispered. "She has a dimple just like your mother's."

He leaned closer. "Yes…and on the same side, too." He pressed his lips to Debbie's forehead. "I knew she would be ours." With a smile, he slipped between the covers and drew them nearer. "She's beautiful," he stated. "Just like her mother." He swept aside her damp hair and rested his mouth against her ear. "I love you."

"I'm so glad you were here." Her hand slid behind his neck. "And now we are a family."

Chapter Thirty-Seven

Nearly midnight and the storm's fury offered no hint of releasing its grip on the city. Debbie's soft breath touched Jason's ears. He eased the baby from Debbie's arms and lowered her into the cradle.

Rain pounded the closed shutters, demanding his attention. He drew a breath as a strong gust of wind murmured between the locked slats.

Quick steps carried him to the window and he brushed his fingertips along the frame.

Tiny droplets gathered on the cool sill, but no water seeped inside.

Damn weather. Lightning flashed through the shutters' seams, followed by the rolling sound of thunder. *I hope Infinity is all right.*

He ambled back to bed and slipped between the covers.

The warmth of Debbie's body touched his and he nestled his face onto the pillow beside her tresses.

Memories were reborn of them together, in bed, the night he'd asked her to marry him. The taste of her body and the passion they'd enjoyed surged to his groin.

For the moment, he harnessed his desire, for she would be there for his taking for the rest of his life. He pressed closer and listened to the sound of her heartbeat. With a sigh, he drifted into a gratifying sleep.

* * *

The scream of a hungry baby brought Jason straight up in bed. He glanced at his daughter, then his gaze swept Debbie.

She smiled at him.

"Guess I better get up," he chuckled, then slipped from the bed and drew the infant into his arms. "I think she's ready for a change, too."

Jason dressed while Debbie took care of their daughter's needs, then brought the infant to her breast to suckle. Buttoning his shirt, he eased down on the bed beside her.

"Thank you so much for helping me last night," she said. "I don't know what I would have done if I had been here alone."

"I'm glad I could help." He glanced down at the baby. "Have you considered her name?"

"Yes." she said. "I think I'll call her Kate. "

"Kate?" he asked.

"Yes, that's what Packey always called your mother."

He folded her hand in his. "She'll be pleased."

Stuffing his feet into his boots, he tracked to the window. With a shallow grunt, he shoved aside the curtains and opened the shutters. "The storm is slowing down," he said. "I'll need to get to the fairgrounds and check on Infinity soon. Hard telling what that place looks like. With all that rain, those horses may all be dead."

"Darling, would you stop by the hospital on your way. I need to let them know I've had the baby and won't be able to work for a few days."

"I'll do better than that," he said, returning to her side. "I'll tell them you won't ever be back. I'm taking you home as soon as you can travel."

She scooted up in the bed and placed the now-sleeping baby beside her hip. "That sounds wonderful. I can't wait to get home." Her face grew somber. "Are you sure I can...?"

"Of course you can. Everyone will be happy to see you. Everything'll be fine."

She lowered her gaze to Kate. "I hope they'll accept her."

"Stop worrying. They'll love her as we do."

The morning air drifted in, filling the room with the delightful aroma of baking bread. "Mmmm," she said. "That smells delicious. I'm famished."

He shoved his hand into his pocket and drew out a handful of silver, then quickly counted the coins. "I'll be right back," he said, then hustled out the door.

Several minutes later, he returned with an assortment of pastries and a container of fresh coffee. "Here, take your pick while I fix your coffee. Two cubes of sugar, right?"

She nodded and reached for her favorite Danish. Closing her eyes, she savored the sweetness as the sugar melted against her tongue.

"Here," he said, lowering the coffee mug onto the side-table.

She glanced up. "Something wrong?'

"No," he confessed. "I just love watching you."

Her cheeks ignited. Restraining a giggle, she glanced toward the window. "How are things outside?"

"Terrible," he said. "The shopkeeper said he had trouble getting to work this morning. There's flooding all across town. One place the water was waist deep."

Jason pulled out his pocket watch. "I need to get going. Gotta check on Infinity. The whole damn place may be under water."

"Please be careful."

"Sure thing, Punkin," he said. Rising, he pressed his lips to her forehead. "You just worry about you and little Kate." A smile widened his lips as he drank in her beauty. "Will you be all right or should I ask someone to stay with you?"

"I'll be fine," she said, grinning. "Just hurry back."

He touched her cheek. "You can be sure I'll be back. I'll never let you get away from me again."

The baby whimpered. Debbie lifted Kate to her breast.

With one last glance, Jason exited the room.

* * *

Upon arrival at the fairground, Jason scanned the area. He glanced up at the grandstand. An empty reminder of what once was filled with happy patrons. The overwhelming silence sent a chill up the back of his neck. He narrowed his eyes and he forced his gaze on the raceway. Only a wooden railing outlined the oval track. Debris continued to slosh in the filthy water that had settled across the entire area.

The stables were submerged in several feet of water. Many horses had broken from their stalls. Jason shifted his gaze to the animals gathered on a small hill. Infinity was nowhere to be found. He turned and skimmed other horses aimlessly wondering in chest deep water.

He sloshed into the murk and pushed against the weight of the water, heading to the stables. With each stride, his denim pants grew heavier. He skimmed the area, checking each horse in hopes of finding Infinity, but his stallion was not in sight. Heartbroken, he groaned and headed back to the entrance.

I need to find Butterfield.

An hour later, he found John in the hotel dining room.

He scanned Jason from head to toe. His bushy brows pushed together as he wiped his chin with the napkin. "What the hell happened to you?"

"Long story. I found Debbie, delivered her baby and went to the fairground in search of Infinity. Have you seen him?"

"Hell, no. I've been here at the hotel," John mumbled.

Jason flopped into the chair next to his friend. "I need a drink. Half of the Mississippi river is in there."

"I was afraid that was gonna happen…" John paused, then narrowed his eyes. "What do you mean you delivered a baby?"

"Debbie's and mine. Kate. Anyway, we've gotta find our horses," Jason grumbled, leaning closer.

"Don't have too," John said, poking his finger through the cup's handle. "When things started getting rough, Grant and I loaded up all our horses and they're over at his place. He's been through storms like this before." The old man chuckled. "Tropical storms are like women. Unpredictable as hell." He frowned and pushed closer. "Debbie had a baby? Then I was right. That *was* her at the stables."

Jason held back a smile. "Yes, and we are getting married." He rested his elbows on the edge of the table.

"Well, I'm glad to hear this," Butterfield said as he wiped his lips, then dropped his napkin next to his plate. "I'll have Grant bring the horses in Thursday to the train station."

"I'll meet him at the station and see the horses get loaded, if you'll pick 'em up when they get home."

John shoved his plate aside, then reared back in his chair. "A baby, huh? Well, aren't you the lucky one." His chuckle filled the area. "Aren't you comin' with us?"

Jason's gaze deepened. "No…" He hesitated to allow the waiter to pour more brew in Butterfield's cup, then continued, "I'm staying here until Debbie can travel. But, we'll be home in a week or two. Now, I need to go up to my room and get my clothes." He rose to his feet. "Then I've gotta send Mother a telegram. I hope she understands why I can't be home for the funeral."

"She's an exceptional woman. I don't think you have to worry. Besides, you're bringing home her granddaughter."

Jason took a deep breath. "I know, but I should be there for her."

"We'll be there. You just take care of Debbie and that new baby of yours."

Jason gave his friend a cordial smile and left the dining room.

Chapter Thirty-Eight

Debbie released a sigh. Cradling a sleeping Kate against her breast, she reveled in the warmth that tingled her skin.

She closed her eyes.

How wonderful to have Jason in her life once more. She smiled. Visions of him standing by the well at Crystal Falls flooded her mind. Bronzed skin. Broad shoulders. Narrow waist. His handsome image fluttered into recall and her heartbeat quickened. A remembrance of him drinking from a metal cup with the water dripping into the thick dark hair on his chest...

A knock on the door fractured the image. She blinked and pushed up onto her elbow. "Yes, who's there?"

"Seth." His voice muffled through the cracks around the frame.

"Come in," she said.

"Good morning," he said, stepping inside. A quick shove pushed the panel closed behind him. The rug muffled his footfalls toward her. "I stopped by the hospital. They said you no longer worked there."

"That's right." She smiled, nodding toward Kate. "We're going home."

He pulled a chair beside the bed and lowered onto the seat.

A smile crossed his face as he peered at the infant. "And who do we have here?"

"My baby girl...Kate meet Seth," she said, pushing the blanket aside.

"May I?" he asked, reaching forward.

Debbie eased her daughter into his arms. "Careful. She just went to sleep."

He cradled the child. "She's beautiful, just like her mother."

Warmth billowed across Debbie's cheeks as pride pulsated through her. "I love her already."

"She's perfect," he whispered. Their gazes locked. "How long before you leave?"

Debbie angled back against the bed pillows. "Jason says I must recuperate a few more days. I do hope you and William will come to visit."

He glanced up and smiled.

Just then the door creaked open and her gaze shot up to meet Jason. With a shove, he pushed closed the panel.

"Darling," she said, "I'd like you to meet my friend, Seth. He and William have been so helpful to me."

Jason nodded.

Seth lowered the child into Debbie's arms and then stood, pulled a gold watch from his pocket. He flipped open the cover. "I really must be going. I'll try to see you again before you leave. You have a beautiful baby."

She smiled. "Thank you for stopping by."

A cold glare swept toward Jason before he glanced back at Debbie. With a nod, he disappeared through the doorway.

Turning, worry creased Jason's face. "I've got a bad feeling about that man."

"You needn't worry. He isn't interested in me. He has someone he loves very much." She resettled Kate and a fleeting concern pulled at her brow. "Besides, you know you're the only man I'll ever love."

She reached out her fingers, wiggling toward him. "Come. Tell me about your day."

Jason slipped his palm against hers and then stretched out on the bed beside her. An easy tug pulled her in his arms. He pressed his cheek against hers. "I went to the fairground. It's completely beneath water."

"Oh, no," she gasped. "What about Infinity?"

"He's safe. Butterfield took all the horses to a friend's stable." His lips nibbled along her neck. "And now, here I am." He chuckled. "Told you I'd be back."

She touched his cheek with her fingertips, then curved her body against his. "I'm so thankful you never gave up looking for me."

He brushed aside her hair and his lips tracked across her cheek to her ear. The rush of his breath rippled through her.

"Nothing bad will ever happen to you again, my love…I promise."

She snuggled against his huge frame as he caressed her. Her desire radiated like a raging wildfire. If only she could give him her complete love. Her craving ripped at her, but she pushed back and rolled away. "I can't be with you, just yet," she said on a sigh. "But, soon. I promise."

He slid his hand across her shoulder and squeezed. "I understand. I'll wait forever, if I must."

* * *

Thursday morning Debbie stirred from a sound sleep and opened her eyes. Jason sat in the rocking chair with his daughter tucked in the crock of his arms. The smile that graced his handsome face nearly took away her breath.

As she pushed onto one elbow, he glanced up. "Good morning, my love. Kate and I thought we'd let you sleep in." He adjusted their child and stood.. "How 'bout a cup of coffee?"

"Mmmm, I'd love that."

"She's probably hungry, anyway," he said. "Here, you take her while I get us some breakfast."

"Coffee will be fine for now," she said, accepting the child. "Let me feed her, then I'll eat."

He slipped into his denims and began buttoning his shirt when a knock rattled the door. Their gazes met briefly before Jason pivoted and opened the door.

A frail woman stared up at him. "Is Mrs. Jackson here?" she quipped.

Jason stepped aside and the woman's taffeta dress rustled as she swept past him into the room.

"Mrs. Butler, what are you doing here?" Debbie laid Kate upon the coverlet. "I-I left the rent with your son last Tuesday."

"I'm not here for my rent," she snapped. "I was told you have a man living with you. And yet, as I recall, you stated you were a widow." She tightened her lips and turned back to face Jason. "It appears rumors were right."

Debbie glanced at Jason, then back at her landlord.

The woman frowned, then leaned closer. "I won't have any shenanigans going on here. I run a respectable establishment and I plan to keep it that way."

Tears welled in Debbie's eyes as she searched for words to explain. "But… Mrs. Butler, Jason is…"

He interrupted, "Ma'am, Debbie's my sister and I've come to take her home. We're leaving as soon as she can travel."

Debbie forced a smile.

The woman locked her gaze on Kate's tiny form. "So you're movin' out?"

"Yes. We'll be gone soon."

"Well, if you're family… then I guess it's fine." Her gaze shot back to Jason. "But, ya gotta be gone by next Saturday."

"I promise," Jason said, with a reassuring smile.

The woman turned to Debbie. "Pretty baby. What is it?"

"A girl. I named her Kate, after our mother."

"Nice name." She made her way to the door. "My son will bring you the overpayment on your rent."

"Just keep it," Jason said. "We appreciate your understanding."

With an expressionless stare, she nodded and then exited.

"That was unexpected," Debbie said, with a sigh. "I didn't know what to say. Sometimes I forget we are family."

"I could tell she had you backed into a corner. I figured that would be the easy way out."

Kate whimpered and Debbie began nursing her, then glanced up.

"It's all right," he chuckled. "I'm going to be your husband. Besides, I've already seen every inch of you."

"I know. I guess modesty just has a way of taking over."

He walked to the door. "I'll be back with your coffee, then I'll need to get going."

"You're leaving again?"

"I'm off to meet Mr. Grant at the railway station, remember?"

Her thoughts returned to the bayou and the day Ed introduced her to Mr. Grant. She smiled. Ed and Cotton...such beautiful souls. They guided her through the most horrific days of her life and helped change her from a frightened girl into a woman unafraid of the shadows. And now, without Cotton, Ed had to draw on his own strength to raise his children. *Such a dear, dear family.*

With a sigh she tucked away the memories. "That's right, you're shipping Infinity home today."

"He nodded; I'll need to be there by noon. Shouldn't be gone but a few of hours." His gaze met hers. "You'll be all right, won't you?"

"Of course. Do whatever you need to do. I'm going to try to get up some today."

"Wait until I get back? I don't want you to fall."

She smiled. "You're wonderful. I love you so much."

He kissed her forehead. "I won't be long."

* * *

In less than an hour Jason bid her goodbye and headed out. Debbie decided to take a nap while he was away and rolled onto her side. Kate lay in her cradle, wrapped in a colorful quilt, sucking on her fist.

You're so precious. How could I ever have considered giving you up?

Her thoughts were interrupted by a knock on the door.

"Who's there?" she called.

"Seth."

She sat up and slipped into her robe. *Again?* "Just a moment." She rushed across the room and opened the door. "What brings you back this way?"

"I've changed jobs. Meeting my new boss shortly. Thought I'd drop in and see you before I leave."

She lowered to the rocker. "I'm so happy for you. Tell me more."

He stepped closer. "I'll be working on a ship. Be gone for months at a time."

She arched a brow. "But, what about William? Is he going with you?"

"No, he'll stay here and look after the mill." Seth sauntered to the window. Brushing the curtain aside, he peered to the street below. "He doesn't want me to go. But, this is my chance to see the world. Sure gonna miss him."

He turned back, his features drawn. A strange light filled his eyes.

"What's wrong," she asked. "You seem troubled."

"I... left something in my carriage," he muttered. "Excuse me, I'll be right back."

He rushed past her and slammed the door on his exit.

* * *

Seth stepped onto the sidewalk that fronted the building just as Laffoone eased from the shadows.

Half dozen footfalls later, Seth met the white-haired man.

"What are you doing down here?" Laffoone grumbled. "Where's the baby?"

Seth dropped his gaze. "I don't have her. I-I can't do this."

"Why not? You've done this before."

"I know, but I like this girl. Besides, Will is going to be furious when he finds out."

Laffoone shoved Seth against the brick wall. "What the hell's wrong with you? This is business."

"But this time it's different. I-I know her."

"Damn it, man. You do this, or I'll tell William about your involvement in selling these babies."

Seth jerked free. "It's different when we steal the prostitute's babies. They don't want them, anyway. But this…"

"You moron. This is a clean child. Do you know how hard it is to find one that doesn't have a disease? Half the time we end up throwing dead babies into the sea. This one is worth a fortune."

"Can't we wait for another? I mean--"

"No. I just paid her landlord twenty dollars to get the details on when they're moving out. We need to snatch that baby now."

"I j-just can't. Not this one."

"You're in too deep to back out now, my friend. Get your ass back up there and get me that child before anyone suspects foul play."

Seth lowered his chin. "I don't like seeing nice people get hurt."

"You won't say that when you get paid." Laffoone smirked.

A heavy heart thumped inside Seth's chest as he made his way back up the stairs toward Debbie's apartment. He paused at the door and inhaled, then eased open the panel.

She glanced up from her rocking chair as he traversed the room.

"Is everything all right?" she asked, pulling the knitted throw across her lap.

"Yes," he said, stepping up to her. He bumped his foot against the mahogany side table and her half-filled cup of coffee flipped onto the floor. "Oh, Debbie...I-I'm so sorry."

She forced a smile. "That's fine." She wiggled a finger toward the washbowl. "Just hand me that towel over there."

Moving behind her, he withdrew a small vial from his pocket. A few shakes emptied the contents into the handkerchief he'd pulled from his vest. As she turned to glance at him, he slapped the cloth over her nose and mouth.

"Akkk..." she gasped, grabbing for his arm.

Seconds later, she slumped over the chair.

Seth rolled her limp body onto the bed, then draped the coverlet across her shoulders.

In one quick motion, he turned and scooped up the newborn. Wrapping the baby in the patchwork quilt, he hurried out the door.

On a burst of speed he descended the stairs, then surged from the building.

A quick glance spotted Laffoone pacing near the street corner. Three strides later, Seth shoved the baby into the old man's arms. "Here, take her."

"Be at the dock by sundown tonight, or we'll sail without you," Laffoone grumbled as he tucked the infant under his arm like a sack of flour. "You'll get your money then." On a sharp curse, he disappeared into an enclosed carriage.

The driver cracked his whip, the team of horses surged forward, and the black-lacquered rig disappeared from view.

Chapter Thirty-Nine

The door to Debbie's apartment stood ajar and Jason's heart slammed against his ribs.

What the…?

Fear ripped through him. He lunged forward, shoving the panel wide and bolted into the room. His breath caught. Debbie lay motionless on the bed, her back facing him.

"Debbie," he shouted, falling to his knees beside her. A quick tug and he rolled her over. With a groan she fell limp into his arms. "My God, what happened?"

He cut his gaze toward the cradle. *Where's Kate?*

A hard swallow lodged in his throat. He lifted the covers and peered beneath; hoping to find their child nestled there.

Truth rammed him in the gut.

Gone.

He grasped Debbie by the shoulders. "Wake up," he urged, shaking her softly. "Where's Kate?" He lowered her to the mattress, then straightened and spotted a rag on the side-table. The cloth smelled sickening sweet. Horror choked his worry. *Chloroform.*

Once more, he jostled her limp body in his arms. "Debbie, you've gotta wake up."

"Mmmmm," she murmured.

Fear spiked every nerve in his body. He propped her against the pillow.

Perspiration rolled down his temples as he fought to rouse her.

He reached for a clean cloth and wiped her face.

Minutes later, she blinked and her eyes fluttered open.

He cupped her chin in his hand. "What happened? Where's Kate? She's not in her cradle."

Debbie shook her head as her eyes slid shut. "Seth," she muttered. "Where's Seth?"

Jason arched his eyebrow. "Was Seth here?" He clinched his jaw, then shouted, "Debbie…listen to me. The baby's gone. Did he take her?"

She raised and the corner of her mouth twitched.

If he took Kate, I'll kill that sonofabitch.

Her eyes rolled beneath her lids and then she lowered her cheek against his shoulder.

He dug his fingers into her shoulders. "Debbie, look at me. Did Seth take the baby?"

She peeped at him through narrowed eyes. "Don't know," she mumbled.

Jason tightened his muscles and again doused her face with the clean wet rag.

She pulled back and wedged her hand up between them. "Don't," she scorned. Her torso wobbled as she leaned forward and stared at him through glassy eyes. "Don't do that."

"You must wake up," he demanded. "You've been over-powered by medicine."

She pushed back long strands of hair from her face, then rocked to the side and glared into the cradle.

"S-She's g-gone?" Her gaze shifted to meet Jason's. "Seth… took my baby?" She whimpered and fell back against the pillow. "W-Why would he take Kate?"

"Try to remember," Jason prodded. "Did he say anything? Anything at all?"

"Think, darling. Did he say where he was going?"

She frowned. "A trip…He said something about a trip. I can't remember. Across the ocean, I think."

"Did he say when?"

"No…s-soon, I believe."

Jason paced the floor, then kneeled before her. "Is there anything else? Something that might help me?"

"H-He forgot some papers and went back to his carriage." She pointed to the empty cup. "And when he returned, he knocked over the coffee."

"He did that to distract you," Jason grumbled.

"But, w-why would he take my baby? He's kind and thoughtful. He w-wanted to help me."

"He was gaining your confidence, Punkin. The bastard knew exactly what he was doing."

Tears spilled from beneath her lashes as she lowered her chin. "Kate's gone. Oh, my God, Jason."

Her tears multiplied.

Jason pulled his gun from the top drawer of the dresser. He opened the chamber and spun the compartment, counting the bullets. On a sharp curse, he snapped the piece back into place. "I'll find him."

Debbie stumbled to her feet as the door slammed shut. Staggering, she crossed the floor and twisted the key, securing the latch. Slumping against the wooden panel, her shoulders quaked beneath her tears.

Her legs buckled.

Darkness swept over her and she collapsed onto the braided rug.

* * *

An orange glow crossed the horizon as the setting sun faded from view.

Jason lengthened his stride as he crossed the shipyard. He weaved past huge cargo boxes, stacked and ready for loading onto the vessels before him.

He drew to a stop.

Night shadows hampered his view as he scanned the pier.

If Seth is part of a kidnapping plot, they're probably heading for Europe.

His gaze lifted to the sails. A frown creased his brow. *Damn, I hardly know one flag from another.*

His focus shifted.

He strained to separate the sounds surrounding him.

Grinding machines, dock workers and passing wagons all melted together. But no sounds of a baby could be heard.

He eased away from cover and headed toward the ramp.

Disappointment nipped at his hopes.

He pivoted and began the long journey back. Nearing the final ship, his gaze settled on an elderly Negro man sitting beside the gangplank, fishing.

The man glanced up.

Jason stopped.

Squinting one eye shut, the old timer said, "I've been watchin' ya, young man. What's ya lookin' fer?"

Jason pulled up short and described Seth. "A slight built man with dark hair…probably in his mid-thirties. Carrying a bundle. A baby, wrapped in a patchwork quilt."

The man placed his cane pole to his side and lifted his lantern. "What ya want with him?"

"He's taken my daughter. A newborn, only days old."

Jason lowered onto one knee as the man set down the lantern and pulled in his line. He picked up a long bladed knife, cut a slice of fish and held it up to the light. "I comes here every day and I sees a lot goin' on." He baited his hook and dropped the line back into the water. "They think 'cause I'm old I can't see and don't know what's happenin'. I may be old, but I ain't dead, yet."

Jason's throat tightened. Impatience spreading through him. "What do you see, old man?"

"I see's regular freight bein' loaded, but I see's folk comin' with an arm load of blankets. Dem covers is hidin' babies, cause I hears 'em cryin'." His gaze met Jason's. "Nothin' more precious than a youngin'."

"You're a wise man," Jason said. He reached into his pants pocket and drew out a gold coin and dropped it next to the lantern. "Is this the ship they go on?" he asked, pointing beyond the man's shoulder.

The Negro nodded and wiped his fingers on the bib of his overalls. "Here comes one of 'em, now."

Jason rose, turning on his heels. Out of the darkness, Seth stepped into view carrying a large carpet bag. As he drew closer he stopped and dropped the baggage.

Jason started toward him.

Seth turned and ran.

Heart pounding, Jason surged forward. A dozen or so footfalls later and he reached out grabbing the back of Seth's jacket.

With a swift tug, Jason pulled the son of a bitch to the ground.

Lunging forward, he fell atop Seth, then straddled him.

Grabbing the man's wrists, Jason penned him to the ground. "Where's my baby," he snarled.

"I-I don't know what you're talking about," Seth muttered through gritted teeth.

"You took her. Where is she?"

Seth struggled to pull away.

Jason withdrew his gun and ground the barrel beneath Seth's chin, wrenching the man's head further back. "You've got three seconds to tell me where Kate is, or I'll blow your damned head off," he hissed, leaning lower.

Seth lurched sideways, knocking the firearm from Jason's hand.

With a growl, he dove for the pistol.

The bastard rammed his elbow into Jason's ribs and stumbled to his feet.

With a grunt, Jason grabbed Seth's ankle, pitching him onto a pile of wooden flats.

Cracking boards muted Seth's whimpering yelp as he collapsed atop the wood. For a moment, he lay dazed and motionless.

Jason retrieved his pistol and again placed the cool steel barrel beneath the man's chin.

"Now, I'm gonna ask you one more time. Where's my baby?"

Seth lifted his forearms across his brow. "S-She's behind me... on the *Mary Ann.*"

Jason glanced at the three masted ship, lurking in the faded light. "Why did you take her?" he growled, pressing the barrel deeper into his throat.

"Because I owed Laffoone money. He was gonna kill William and take the business to settle my debt."

Jason cocked the hammer on the gun. "What does that have to do with Debbie and my daughter?"

"When Laffoone first brought her to town he wanted her for himself. She wouldn't have anything to do with him." The man gulped a breath. "When he found out she was having a baby... w-we struck a deal. I'd get the baby... and he'd forgive my debt."

"So you gained her trust?"

"I tried to back out," he pleaded.

"You sonofabitch," he growled, his lips tightening. He lowered the pistol, holstered his weapon and then slammed his fist into Seth's chin, whipping the man's head backward onto the pallet. Jason stared down at the motionless figure. "I never want to see you again."

* * *

The *Mary Ann* had legacy upon the sea, but the years had stolen away her glory. Her rails were now heavy with rust, yet she proved adequate to face the perils of the salty sea.

Jason glanced up at the flag masts.

What terrible secrets she carried within her hull. Kidnapping was rampant in most international ports and he wondered how many other ships carried such illegal treasures.

First Debbie...and now Kate.

He glanced at the fisherman. The old man sat, legs folded, transfixed on his line in the murky water lapping at the pilings below.

Jason drew his pistol, skirted the shadows and then he boarded the vessel. His heartbeat drummed in his ears as hatred raked his veins.

He eased up the bridge and onto the *Mary Ann*. Beneath his boots, chips of paint from the masts crackled with each of his steps.

Jason widened his eyes and advanced toward a dimly-lit entrance. He pressed his shoulders against the cold metal frame and then glanced into the hallway.

A few feet away, a stairs descended to a lower level.

Inching forward, one by one, he eased down the narrow rungs into the bowels of the ship.

A weathered door fronted him at the bottom of the stairwell. He pressed his ear against the wood.

Muffled voices vibrated from within.

Easing his hand forward, he pressed the latch. The door squeaked open. He bit back a grimace. With a jerk, he turned to face a white-haired man leaning upon a cane.

"And who might you be?" the elderly man asked, as amusement brightened his eyes.

"I might ask the same of you."

Laffoone chuckled. "Get out. Now! Or I'll have you arrested for trespassing."

"I hear this is a ship filled with infants." Jason raised his chin along with his revolver. "But more importantly…mine."

"You don't know what you're talking about. Get out of here."

Jason cocked his pistol. "I'm not leavin' until I have my child."

The man laughed. "I'm not afraid of you, boy. I own this ship and half the property in New Orleans. Now get the hell off my boat."

"I'm not going anywhere and you've got zero seconds left." Jason raised his boot and kicked the old man sideways. Laffoone tumbled to the weathered deck, his cane rattled off into the shadows.

A moment later, Jason stepped forward and planted his boot on the bastard's chest.

The cabin door swung open and a heavy-set woman peered out. Her face washed pale at the sight of Laffoone on the floor. She gasped and rocked backward.

Jason pushed his pistol into his holster, then leaned over and grabbed the fallen man by his shoulders and jerked him to his feet.

"Shut the door," Laffoone yelled.

Before she could respond, Jason kicked open the door, knocking the woman backward. In one swift motion, he hurled Laffoone into the room, throwing him onto the floor.

Jason glanced around.

Two Negro women huddled against wooden boxes filled with sleeping infants. *Make-shift cribs?*

The woman in charge began wiping the blood from the cut on her busted lip.

At a glance, Jason recognized the colorful patchwork quilt in the closest crib.

He took a breath, then pulled his gun once more. "Everyone stand back and you won't get hurt," he said, waving the heavy-set lady aside.

She stepped into the corner beside her companions as she dabbed at her swollen lip.

Laffoone shifted, scooting toward the door.

Jason swung around and cocked his weapon. The click of the hammer reverberated through the enclosure. "You move one more muscle and you're a dead man."

Pressing against a crate, Laffoone clutched his knee.

Jason glanced at Kate, then scooped the baby up with one hand. As he turned, the glint of a weapon caught his eye. Laffoone had reached into his boot and withdrew an ivory-handled derringer. The weapon discharged just as Jason lunged sideways, shielding the infant. A burning pain burrowed into Jason's shoulder.

Laffoone lurched forward, firing again.

Another shot rang out behind Jason and his gaze swerved to see Laffoone crumple over into a dead heap.

The women screamed.

Splatters of blood surrounded the man's fallen body.

Wide-eyed, Jason spotted a silhouette in the doorway. "Seth," he whispered

"Yes," he mumbled, clutching his stomach. "I couldn't let him take Debbie's baby." The man slumped to his knees in the doorway. "P-Please tell her and William I'm sorry."

He fell forward onto the floor.

Jason nodded, then glanced down at both lifeless body.

"This evil business stops right here, right now." His gaze scraped over the frightened women. "May God have mercy on your hard-hearted souls."

A moment later, the sheriff barged into the room, the smiling fisherman from the dock lurking in the shadows behind the officer.

Chapter Forty

Heavy footfalls in the hallway brought Debbie forward. Fright swept through her as she surged to her feet. "W-Who's there?"

"It's me, Punkin. Let me in."

On a sob, she stumbled across the room, released the lock and swung wide the wooden panel.

A blood-soaked shirt hugged his broad shoulders, yet he held a sleeping Kate tucked in the curve of one arm. Tears streamed down Debbie's cheeks. "Oh, my God, Jason, come in."

He stepped across the threshold. "Here, take her," he mumbled.

Debbie separated the blanket and a rush of warmth healed her aching heart. A quick kiss on the infants forehead and she placed the baby in the cradle. Straightening, she faced Jason. "What happened?"

He shucked off his shirt as she pulled him toward the washbowl to tend to his wound.

"I found that friend of yours. Seth. We fought."

A gasp caught in her throat. "S-Seth?"

"And they had Kate on a ship."

"Who's they?"

"He and Laffoone."

"Laffoone? H-He's a vile heathen." She bit back a sob.

"After a scuffle, he shot me. Then Seth showed up and killed him, but not before taking a bullet himself. They're both dead now."

He pressed his finger against the wound. "Bullet's still there."

"It'll need to come out," she insisted, pushing aside his hand. Confusion stretched tight across her chest, the ache piercing and violation of her trust in Seth, her hatred of Laffoone, all pulling at her joy of the reunion with Kate. Instead, she shrugged away the confliction and focused on her beloved. "I'd remove the bullet, but I don't have the proper instruments to do so. We need to go to the hospital, Jason."

He nodded.

"I'll clean it and bandage this before we leave."

With a lingering sigh, she cleaned the swollen area with carbolic acid, then covered the wound with gauze. "I hate to wish ill of anyone, but the world is better off without those devils.

He nodded. "I'll get the baby and we'll leave."

* * *

The next morning Debbie sat up in bed and yawned. Her gaze cut to Kate and a smile tugged at her lips at the infant fast asleep in the cradle. A quick search for Jason, however, came up empty.

Moments later, fully dressed now, she stared out the window, searching for his broad-shouldered frame. Early shoppers filled the sidewalks below, diners sipped their coffee at the outside café and a shopkeeper swept his front walk.

She frowned.

No sign of Jason.

She glanced at the clock on the chest behind her. The intricately scrolled hands of the piece pointed east-west. *Nine fifteen.* Would their lives always be in this constant state of worry?

Where are you?

Worry continued to grow inside her. An hour later, Jason pushed through the apartment door, his arm still in a sling.

"Where were you?" she asked, accepting his kiss on her forehead.

"I went to make sure Infinity got on the correct train north." He smiled, then added, "Both of you were asleep. I didn't want to wake my girls. I also did a few other things. Hold out your hand."

She obeyed and he settled a beautifully-wrapped blue box onto her palm, it's ribbon the exact color of Crystal Falls.

"W-What's this?" she asked, her gaze meeting his.

"Well...go ahead, open it."

Careful not to awaken Kate, she ripped away the colorful paper, Her throat tightened as she bit her lip. Easing open the lid she squinted as a gold chain glinted in the morning light.

The rays of the sun shimmered across the piece with a welcoming home enthusiasm. A gasp escaped her throat. *The elk's tooth.* "Oh, Jason. Where did you find this?" she whispered. "It's just like the one you gave me."

"It's the very same," he announced, a smile wreathing his face.

"But... I-I had to sell the tooth so I could afford this place."

"Saw this hanging around the neck of Butterfield's sister-in-law. Her husband bought this for her while on a trip to New Orleans. He rewarded me with the piece for saving his life. Long story, but this led me to you."

Tight lips restrained his smile.

"Incredible," she exhaled. "I wanted to buy it back. When I returned, the shop owner said he'd just sold it." She released a heavy sigh.

"My wedding gift to you," he whispered, pulling her against him. "Truly a symbol of our love."

"I shall always wear this." Tears welled in her eyes. "But...I-I've nothing to give you."

"You and Kate are all I'll ever want. Be my wife and give me your love."

She nestled her head against his shoulder. "I will always love you."

The warmth of his body enclosed around her in an everlasting hold.

And she released a lingering sigh as his head dipped and he glided his tongue along her neck

"I love you, too," he whispered. "I can't wait until we're married. I want you more than anything in this world."

His warm breath caressed her ear, his teeth nipping her lobe. A tingle rippled down her spine.

"Let's get married tomorrow," he groaned.

"Yes," she answered on a throaty sigh. "And then, take me back home."

* * *

They were married that afternoon in a simple ceremony before a preacher. A few hours later and with a slumbering Kate in Jason's arms, they boarded the five-thirty train bound for Lexington.

As the train clattered northward, the swampland of the bayou slowly changed into the cotton-fields of the Mississippi plateau. Moss-covered cypress trees gave way to tall pines as the great southern states of America swept past.

Debbie rewound her thoughts like a clock.

Dear Cotton. What an influence she'd been. And Ed. Although he now grieved the loss of his wife, healing would be found in the waters of the bayou he loved. Her heart swelled with pride for the couple who'd forced her to find her self-confidence and true identity as a woman.

She would never forget these astonishing people.

And the bandits, wicked Laffoone and all the horrors of the Adams House…forevermore behind her.

Two days later, they arrived in Lexington. A smiling Jeremiah waited for them at the train station. Little had change in those long months she'd been away. Debbie's eyes widened as the carriage rolled past the fieldstone gate posts onto Crystal Falls. Thoughts of Packey and Pearl and the horrible dogs' attack reappeared.

What a dreadful experience.

Her eyes welled with tears when she caught sight of the comforting outline of the Jackson mansion.

So many times she thought she would never see this place again.

Jeremiah pulled the team to a halt at the front entrance, then clamored down and helped her from the buggy.

"Thank you," she whispered.. "It's so very good to be home."

"Yes'm," he replied, stepping aside."We's glad to have you back, too."

Millie greeted them at the door and assisted them upstairs to their room.

"Where's mother?" Jason asked, scooting their luggage near the bed.

"She's at the cemetery. Goes up there near every day, rain or shine."

Jason walked to the window and peered out in search for his mother. He turned to Debbie. "I must let her know we've arrived. Will you be all right here for awhile?"

"Yes," she said, pushing him toward the door. " You go be with her. She needs you. I'll come later, after I've fed the baby."

After a quick kiss, Jason headed to the stable.

A moment later, James entered, just as he finished saddling Blue.

"Welcome home," the lad shouted with a wide grin. "How was the trip?"

"Good. I found Debbie. She's up at the house." Gathering the reins, he noticed the lad staring at his injured arm. "I tripped over a rake at the fairground and hurt my shoulder. It'll be good as new in a few days."

James nodded, then straightened, his chin lifting. "I took care of things just like you asked me to do. And Infinity got back all right. We're havin' a lot of folks stoppin' by to ask 'bout breedin' him."

"Soon," Jason replied, swinging up into the saddle.

"Glad we're getting back to business, again," the lad said beaming. "And Coal's doin' great, too. He's gonna be a fast runner one day, just like Infinity."

"I'm sure he will." Jason nudged his horse toward the open door, then paused and glanced back. "I knew I could count on you, son. And now you take good care of Coal, 'cause he's your horse now."

A blush crossed the stable boy's face. "Mine?"

"Yep, yours," Jason chuckled as he nudged Blue into a gallop from the stable.

At the cemetery, he reined to a halt, dismounted, then tied his horse to the post beside his mother's mare.

In the distance, he spotted his mother. She glanced up, her gaze meeting his. A heartbeat later, with arms open wide, she ran to greet him.

After a long embrace, she reared back. "Oh, Jason, I'm so glad you're home." Her breath caught as her gaze dropped to the sling on his arm. "But... you're hurt,"

"A minor accident," he declared. "I'll be fine. And I'm sorry I couldn't get back in time for father's funeral."

A shadow crossed her tired face. "So many people came. And all asked about you and Debbie. And Kate...my granddaughter." She glanced around. "Where are they?"

"Up at the house. They're eager to see you."

Jason strolled with her to his father's gravesite.

"Oh, Jason, I miss him so much," she whispered, leaning against him.

"We're all gonna miss him."

"He was my life. I just don't know what I'm gonna do without him."

He patted her hand. "You're a strong woman and your whole life's ahead of you. Sides, you have Mason to think of, now... and me and Debbie. And your granddaughter, too."

"But, you'll eventually go to law school. I'll be left alone, again."

" I've decided not to go to New York."

"But you've always dreamed of becoming a lawyer."

He laughed. "That's all it was, mother... a dream. My place is here now.

With you. Crystal Falls needs us all. We're a family. Life changes."

Her gaze met his and she whispered, "I'm so thankful Taylor gave me you."

"I'll take care of you, Mother. Don't spend your life grieving. It's time to start a new journey. He would want us all to be happy."

She nodded, then crumpled her handkerchief and dabbed her tears away. "Let's go home, darling," she said, raising her chin. "I want to see Debbie and to meet the newest member of our family."

Epilogue

Six weeks later,

A breeze rustled the leaves on the nearby trees. The full moon cast silver-blue shadows across the waters of Crystal Falls. Waves lapped the shoreline as the current raced downstream to a final destination. Just like Debbie's journey…these waters, too, would end up in New Orleans.

Jason slid the empty picnic basket onto the buggy's back seat, and then rejoined Debbie on the blanket near the campfire. He smiled. *The same red-checked blanket I covered her with on the night of our first courtship.*

"I'm so glad your mother asked to watch Kate tonight," Debbie said as he settled beside her. "We finally have that picnic we missed last year."

"Yes." He brushed aside a wisp of hair from her forehead. "But, I'm glad you chose to come to the falls, instead." He pressed his lips to her ear. "It's so beautiful here…just like you."

She giggled, then turned to face him. An instant later, her smile disappeared. "We've missed so much." She stretched onto her back, staring heavenward. "I shall never forget the places I've been, or the people I've met. But even through all the horror, I learned how precious life can be." She rolled sideways to meet his gaze.

He leaned toward her and captured her lips with his.

An hour passed as they made love, the healing breeze shifted toward them both. "Do you know how many times I've dreamt of this," he whispered. His hand slid across her naked curves. "I want you more than you can imagine."

She arched her brow. "Again. Yes, again. He chuckled as he nibbled his way across her shoulder and onto her bare breast. "Don't make me wait, Jason. I-I need you now."

"Again?" They laughed. He pushed aside the elk's tooth necklace dangling between their naked bodies. A smile tugged at his lips.

The symbol of our love.

And together as the moonlight spilled across the land, they reclaimed one another.

The spirits danced and chanted their approval, lifting the evil that taunted their family these past months. Once again, allowing love and harmony to bless Debbie and Jason as they began life anew alongside the glistening waters of Crystal Falls.

THE END

About the Author...

I hope you've enjoyed reading CRYSTAL FALLS, book one in the three-book series "The Jackson Family Saga"...This epic novel took readers on an adventure of love and loss, sweeping them from Kentucky's lush pasturelands to the murky bayous of New Orleans. Book Two, A BRIDGE OF DREAMS, debuts the winter of 2018. And book three, AWAKEN MY HEART, follows the next summer. History, romance, and a fast-paced adventure pull you into the aura that is Christine Wissner's world. Fasten your seatbelts, dearest readers; it's quite a lovely ride.

Christine loves connecting with her avid readers! Website: www.christinewissner.com

Come follow her on Facebook & Twitter, too: www.facebook.com/christine.wissner.5 - www.twitter.com/cwissner8

9 780998 967318